PENGUIN BOOKS

Tell Me a Secret

Tell Me a Secret

JANE FALLON

PENGUIN BOOKS

PENGUIN BOOKS

UK | USA | Canada | Ireland | Australia
India | New Zealand | South Africa

Penguin Books is part of the Penguin Random House group of companies
whose addresses can be found at global.penguinrandomhouse.com.

First published 2019
001

Copyright © Jane Fallon, 2019

The moral right of the author has been asserted

Set in 12.5/14.75 pt Garamond MT Std
Typeset by Jouve (UK), Milton Keynes
Printed and bound in Great Britain by Clays Ltd, Elcograf S.p.A.

A CIP catalogue record for this book is available from the British Library

ISBN: 978-1-405-93312-4

www.greenpenguin.co.uk

Dedicated to Paws2Rescue for their
amazing work with street dogs in Romania.

www.paws2rescue.com

Prologue

Everyone is staring at me.

This is my worst nightmare. And I don't just mean I'm uncomfortable with the focus all coming my way. Although there is that too. But this is an actual nightmare that I have regularly: I'm fucking up and everyone is watching. Except that this time I'm awake and it's really happening.

I am fucking up and everyone is watching.

I have no idea what went wrong. I had everything planned right down to the last second. It was my first real chance to make a big impression in my new position. My first opportunity to prove to Glen that he was right to promote me. To prove to myself that I'm up to the task.

Except that it seems I'm not.

All my old insecurities come flooding back. I'm not good enough, skilled enough, confident enough. But this time I know this isn't down to me. I know I did everything right.

And I also know exactly who must have undone it all.

PART ONE

I

I hear a pop and then a cheer. Seconds later a glass of Prosecco – more fizz than drink – is thrust into my hand and Glen is leading everyone in a toast. To me. I still can't quite take in what's happening.

'To Holly,' they all chorus and I hate myself for blushing. And then of course I blush some more because I'm feeling self-conscious about it. Hardly a move designed to instil confidence in my new-found authority. I take a swig far too quickly and cough as the foam hits the back of my throat.

'Thank you,' I manage to say.

I look round at them all, glasses raised, big grins on their faces. Juliet, of course, is nowhere to be seen. She claimed a sudden doctor's appointment and headed for the door as soon as it became apparent she might be expected to congratulate me. But the other members of my department are all there: assistant Emma brandishing a glass of water because bubbles make her sneeze; short, stocky Lorraine almost as wide as she's high; Joe leaning back in his chair beaming his open smile; Glen holding his glass aloft, but with one eye on his phone, knowing he should be here but wondering how soon he can politely get away; and finally Roz, my desk mate for the past three years, my ally, my campaign manager in my fight for promotion.

I hold my glass higher in her direction, ready for her excitement to mirror my own.

I would never have got this promotion without Roz. There's no one I want to celebrate with more. She's standing there in between Emma and Lorraine, six inches taller than both of them. Glass raised. Grinning from ear to ear. Peroxide-blonde hair spiked up. White teeth held hostage by vivid magenta lips. Canary-yellow top. Red skinny trousers. Heels. She looks like someone turned the lights on.

'I always knew you'd get it,' she says. She knocks back her fizz, leaving a lipstick mark on the glass.

The others are filling up their flutes again, happy to be having a sanctioned skive. Happy for me. I think. In a contest between me, Juliet or a random outsider I'm pretty sure they were all in my corner.

Glen taps his glass to get everyone's attention. Ready to make a speech. Roz rolls her eyes at me and I stifle a laugh. Glen loves the sound of his own voice.

He coughs. 'So, I'd like to formally congratulate Holly . . .'

'I dare you to interrupt and ask him if he's been working out,' Roz whispers in my ear and I snort. I try to turn it into a cough. Glen and his vanity is one of our favourite topics.

'Let's have a quick one after work,' I mutter to Roz as he drones on. 'Just me and you.'

'I can't.' She pulls a face. 'We've got a dinner.' Roz and her husband Hugh have a social life – mainly courtesy of his job – that leaves me exhausted just thinking about it. It sounds fabulous, don't get me wrong, but I find myself worrying about when she gets to have a night at home slobbing around in her PJs. Of course, I'm the opposite. Pyjama-clad nights in beat glamorous nights out by about 364 to 1. The one being the work Christmas party. And trust me, that's not up to much. The last one was held in the studio where the series we all work on is filmed, in amongst all the regular standing sets, although I don't imagine they'll do that again this year, because someone peed in a prop vase that has been in our central family's living room for years and is supposed to contain the ashes of their fictional dead grandfather.

Listening to Roz's tales sometimes makes me glad that ours is a typical work friendship. Our socializing is always tacked on to the end of a working day. A drink or two in one of the local pubs. A debrief. But outside of that we have very different ideas of what constitutes a good time. Of course, I lap up all her stories. I just would rather have an early night than feature in them.

Glen seems to have reached the point where everyone is about to raise their glasses again in another toast. I have no idea what he's said about me but I assume it's all good. People are smiling anyway. Everyone clinks my glass.

'Well deserved,' Glen says when it's his turn.

'Thanks,' I say. 'I really do appreciate it.'

Roz reaches to the back of her chair for her jacket. Picks up her bag. Pulls her fingers through her short blonde hair.

I see Glen look over. It's only twenty to six and it's pretty much frowned on for anyone to leave before the hour.

7

'What?' she says, flashing everyone a smile. 'You're all only going to be boozing anyway. I couldn't get any work done if I wanted to.'

She drops a kiss on my head as she passes. 'See you tomorrow.'

By ten past I'm on my way too, teetering gingerly on the icy pavements, slightly tipsy after three glasses of Prosecco. I wrap my scarf over my nose and mouth, pull my coat tight round me and head for the station. I'm still glowing from the news. Or maybe it's the drink. I didn't expect to get the job. I thought I was the outsider. That Juliet had the experience, the more impressive CV. I wonder if she'll resign now that her ambitions have been thwarted.

Lorraine and Joe were all for us moving on to the pub but I managed to convince both myself and them that starting my first day as script executive with a raging hangover wouldn't give the best impression. So it's home to a microwave M&S lasagne and an early night. I know how to let my hair down.

On paper I am the sad middle-aged lady living alone with only a cat for company. That's me. The butt of a million jokes. I realize that makes me sound like I'm tragic. I'm not. I love my basement flat. And the being alone bit is only temporary till I find a lodger. Plus we all know fifty is the new thirty, and I'm only forty-three so that makes me positively youthful. And I didn't always live on my own. I have a daughter, Ashley, who's twenty-two.

Father unknown. Or, at least, I know who he is; I just never kept in touch. She's living with her boyfriend in Bristol where they were both at uni until last June.

She's just found out she's pregnant.

I'm not going to lie: I cried when I found out. And not through joy either. She's too young. She barely even knows who she is yet. I know what it's like. I've been there. And, even though I can't imagine my life without my daughter, I don't think I would choose to go there again. The one – big – difference is that she's not on her own. I know that she and Ryan thought long and hard before they decided to keep the baby and I'm proud of them that they dealt with it head on. They're in it together. But do I wish it hadn't happened? Is it terrible to admit that I do?

It was Ashley's pregnancy that persuaded me to let her room – the spare room as we're now trying to get used to calling it – out for some extra cash. Once I heard about the baby – Ashley and Ryan both came to stay and they tearfully broke the news – I knew that I couldn't let them struggle like I had. Having to choose between buying teabags or baby wipes. (Teabags won out every time. Sorry, Ashley.) Between paying for a haircut or a school trip (I don't think a pair of scissors even touched my hair for fifteen years). If nothing else I can offer to help out financially. Just till they get on their feet. Although God only knows how much I'm dreading sharing my kitchen with a stranger. Possibly a psychopath. Or, even worse, someone who wants to be friends. Since Ashley moved to Bristol three and a half years ago I've got used to my own company. I like it.

After years of single mumdom I finally put myself – and my career – first when Ashley left for uni. Before that work was a means to an end. A way to keep us afloat but still leave me enough time to cook dinner every evening and attend every parents' meeting, netball match, play or concert. Oh, and take a day off at a moment's notice whenever my daughter was sick, along with every single holiday and inset day. Climbing a corporate ladder was out of the question. I know people do it. Of course they do, millions of them. But it was a choice I made. It was the way I wanted to do things. Suddenly, though, I was on my own, a mother without a child to look after. I wanted to carve out a new identity for myself. I'd made a lot of connections through the part-time script-reading work I'd been doing for years for various theatres and TV companies to make a bit of extra cash. So I always got to hear when jobs cropped up. With *Churchill Road* I think I was just in the right place at the right time. And, let's face it, they were probably desperate.

Anyway, that's why this promotion means so much to me. It's a milestone. I want to shout it from my rooftop but instead I settle for calling Ashley, who insists that she always knew I was going to get it, and my best mate Dee, who squeals so loudly her boyfriend (or partner as she always refers to him, insisting 'boyfriend' makes her sound as if she thinks she's sixteen, whereas I think 'partner' gives the impression they run a law firm together) comes running in from the next room to see what's wrong.

'Shall we come over? Are you celebrating?' Dee always wants an excuse to party. I imagine 'partner' Gavin rolling his eyes at her, the prospect of a night vegging on the sofa ebbing away.

'No. I have work tomorrow and I'm already a bit pissed. Let's do it at the weekend.'

'Definitely,' she says. 'Don't think you're getting away with it.'

I potter round the kitchen getting myself something to eat. Fighting the anti-climax. Wishing I was in the pub with Roz celebrating my good fortune, making it feel real.

'Holly Cooper, Script Executive,' I say out loud, trying out my new title for size. Smokey slinks in through the cat flap. Looks round as if he wonders who I'm talking to.

'I got the job,' I say to him as I spoon food into his bowl. 'Really, though, I got the fucking job.'

2

There are a lot of hangovers kicking about in the office next morning, none of them mine. Lorraine and Joe flop about like a pair of beached fish occasionally gasping for water. Roz is also looking a bit green around the gills.

'Are you OK?' I say as soon as I've hung my coat up. She's in before me, which is an occasion in itself.

'Too much to drink,' she mouths.

'Tell me all about it. Let me live vicariously through you.'

Roz never needs much encouragement. We spend far more time gossiping than working, although somehow everything always gets done. Maybe that'll have to stop now. Maybe I'll have to assume a new, serious work persona and start tutting when I think people are shirking.

'Just Le Gavroche,' she says, leaning over her desk. We sit opposite each other, a thin line of pen holders, Post-it notes and other bits and pieces – scripts, face wipes, boxes of paper clips, lip gloss – marking the boundary. Juliet and Joe sit in a similar arrangement across the room, although her side is devoid of all personal touches. Pens lined up in perfect rows. Scripts in neat piles, corners lining up. Mine and Roz's look like two matching Leaning Towers of Pisa. Emma has a small desk near the door with room for just her desktop and a phone. Lorraine is at a makeshift table up against the wall.

'Just' and 'Le Gavroche' are words that should never be in the same sentence if you ask me. It's a bit like saying 'Oh, this? It's only platinum'.

'Wow,' I say. 'Who with?'

She names an actual film star, a client of Hugh's. 'And her husband.'

'Oh my God!' I say. 'What was she like?'

Roz shrugs. 'Nice. Bit up herself. And she basically pushed a lettuce leaf round her plate all evening. I thought she was going to start crying when the waiter offered her bread.'

I snort a laugh. One of the things I love most about Roz is that for all her name-dropping she's fundamentally unimpressed by stardom.

'Was the food amazing?' I ask. I really should get on with some work.

'Incredible,' she says. 'I've been there before though. I always have the turbot. It's to die for.'

'Your life is ridiculous,' I say.

'Anyway.' She leans down and digs in her bag, pulls out a Paperchase carrier. I actually gasp. No one understands my stationery obsession like Roz. 'I got you a little thing. To say well done. It's only tiny . . .'

I practically grab it out of her hand. Inside are two of the most fabulous fat notebooks I've ever seen. A big one and a little one. Both hardback and decorated with identical Siamese cats.

'Oh my God, I love them . . .'

'I thought now you're going to be the boss you'd actually have a reason to write lists. Although obviously most normal human beings would do them on their phone . . .'

'Not *the* boss. *A* boss. I'm still pretty low down on the pecking order.'

'If you say so, ma'am,' she says in her best Victorian street urchin voice.

'Well, I couldn't have done it without you. And I love my notebooks. In fact I'm going to make a list now. What can I make a list about?'

'You –' she turns her attention to her computer and, presumably, work '– are very weird.'

I'm in a strange kind of no man's land where my new position won't officially start for a couple of weeks, until my contract is finalized (like I'm going to argue about anything. I would happily sign on the dotted line now for the title and ten pounds a week less) but everyone knows about it thanks to Glen's announcement last night. Not to mention the fact that I'm on three months' probation. I'm management but I'm not. So the dynamic in my little department has shifted. Just a fraction. When Lorraine starts relating a story about how she has just sent an email to the wrong person because the three double vodkas on top of three glasses of fizz last night have clouded her brain, I notice Joe give her a subtle head shake and she swiftly changes the subject. Even Emma, always diligent, seems more deferential than usual. Mid-morning when Glen comes over and tells me I might as well move into the small glass office vacated by my predecessor sooner rather than later I'm tempted to say no. I'm so used to being one of 'us' I'm not sure I'm ready to become one of 'them'. But I remind myself this is what I've been working towards.

'I'd be in there like a shot,' Roz says once he's gone. 'Pictures on the wall, feet up. Shouting at one of the underlings to make me a coffee.'

I laugh. She's right. I should be enjoying this. 'Will you help me?'

'Of course,' she says, standing up. 'Anything to get out of doing actual work.'

'Did Juliet say well done yet?' Roz asks once we're inside my little cube, door shut. I look through the glass. It's like watching my co-workers in a zoo. I suddenly feel really nervous about being singled out from the pack. I'm making it seem as if I've been picked for an elite mission or that I'm going to be making life-and-death decisions. The truth is I'm going to have a new title, my tiny see-through office and a bit of responsibility for other peoples' fuck-ups, not just my own. That's all.

Glen is the big boss. The series producer. He reports to the channel, takes all the flak, and generally steers the whole ship. He took over two years ago and he swept through the place like a whirlwind, killing off characters he thought were dull (or the actors playing them too demanding), reshuffling departments and shaving off any dead wood. Some people can't stand him, but I think he's just what the show needs. Fay and Jeremy are the producers who oversee every aspect of each batch of episodes from the scheduling to the editing; Roz, Joe and Juliet are script editors (as was I till yesterday), responsible for coming up with storylines, guiding the writers through the scripts, and making sure the plot flows seamlessly from one episode to another. Lorraine is the trainee editor who helps us all out by checking for inconsistencies and timing the scripts as well as doing any research necessary (such as for the ongoing story of one of the main characters' battles with Parkinson's), and Emma is the department assistant. I am now the bridge between the two worlds: the producers and the script editors. Basically, if one of the papers runs a story about how the quality of storylines has taken a turn for the worse, that'll be my fault.

The show we all work on is a three-times-weekly early-evening soap. Or 'continuing series' as the channel would prefer it to be known. *Churchill Road*. Set around a fictional school on a fictional estate in west London, it appeals mainly to teenagers and students. It's a machine cranking out episodes week in, week out, with an insatiable appetite for new stories. However outlandish.

Juliet is sitting at her desk opposite Joe, fair straw-like hair hanging over a script, pen tapping against her teeth in a way that once had Roz shout 'Will you fucking stop doing that?' so loudly that someone from the accounts department down the hall came running in to see if a fight had broken out. Juliet had looked up and said, 'Just Roz being her usual melodramatic self,' and turned back to the document she was reading, pen poised. Tap tap tap. We decided she does it to annoy us.

I scoff. 'Of course not. Because that would involve her trying to look pleased for me. And we all know she'd never pull that off.'

'Glen must have told her she hadn't got it, just before he gathered everyone round. Did you see how quickly she got out of there?'

'Fuck. She must properly hate me now.' I watch her, focused on her reading.

Roz laughs. 'She hated you already. I wouldn't worry about it.' She flops into the little armchair in front of the desk. 'I might just sit here all day. I could do my work from here, right?'

I raise a cynical eyebrow at her and she laughs. 'It's gone to your head already.'

She helps me stack my piles of scripts and notebooks on the shelves and then leaves me to it. I finish putting my few bits and pieces in the desk drawers and sit down behind my desk. Now what?

I try to remember what Marcus, my predecessor, used to do all day. Basically a lot of nosying into what the rest of us were up to in so far as I can remember. Along with mapping out the storylines for the months ahead. I decide that the best use of my time is to get up to speed with everyone else's episodes. So I send a (what I hope is jovial and not too dictatorial) email to Roz, Joe and Juliet asking them to send me copies of any drafts they're currently working on.

I get a thumbs up through the glass from Joe and a few

minutes later he drops a freshly printed script on my desk with the promise that the rest will follow shortly. I start to work my way through it, glad to have something to do. By the time I get to the end I realize I haven't taken anything in. I take a few deep breaths to calm myself down and start again, making notes as I go along. I don't know why I'm feeling so stupidly nervous. I got this promotion because I deserve it. I say that to myself over and over in my head like a mantra.

By the time I've worked my way through Joe's episodes there's still nothing from either of the other two so I occupy myself making towers of out-of-date paperwork to shred. At three minutes to six there's a ping to say I have a new email and there's a message from Roz: no note, just twelve attachments. That's something, at least. I look up at her and wave my thanks. I send them off to print. I can look at them first thing Monday. Even I'm not keen enough to lug them home with me.

By five past most people have started to drift off. I pull my coat on wondering if I should be making an effort to stay later. Or would that make everyone else think I was judging them if they left on time? Would they all feel they had to stay later too, and then so would I, and we'd end up all being here till midnight? It's a minefield.

Roz is still at her desk when I walk past.

'Fancy a drink?' I say. It's usually the other way round. Roz loves a quick one at the end of a working day, the chance to analyse our co-workers. Usually that just involves us both moaning about what a bitch Juliet is or Roz complaining that Emma (who I think is quite sweet, but Roz thinks is wet) does her head in with her mimsiness.

'Can't tonight either,' she says, pulling a disappointed face. 'I promised Hugh a takeaway on the sofa. How was your first day?'

'Weird.' I dig through my bag for my Oyster card. I call across the room, 'Juliet, you'll send me all your episodes, won't you? I need to get up to speed.'

She peers up at me, reading glasses perched precariously on the end of her nose. 'When I get a moment to sort them out. Is there a rush?'

'Not really. Thanks.' I turn back to Roz. 'At least I have yours to keep me going.'

When I applied for the script executive job I told Roz and Joe because I wanted to be sure they'd support me if I got it. Joe had only recently joined us, having decided to make the move from theatre to TV, so I knew he wouldn't be applying himself, and Roz has always made it very clear she has zero interest in trying to move up the ladder. She has a problem with authority even if that authority is her.

'I'd have to hate myself, how would that work?' she'd said when I asked her and I'd nearly choked on the Snickers bar I was eating, laughing. We knew that Juliet was hoping she might be the lucky one. She'd been there the longest of the two of us, since the show's beginning five years ago. It wasn't a stretch to imagine she might think the job was hers for the taking.

I sought Roz's advice constantly while I was filling in the application, trying out my responses on her.

'Fucking hell, you sound as if you're applying to become a hooker,' she'd said when I'd read her my answer to the question 'How do you feel you could bring out the best in others?', which was something along the lines of 'I believe I am skilled in making people feel relaxed and easing tension in stressful situations.'

Part of the form was to pitch an original storyline that could stretch for ten episodes or more, which seemed a bit ridiculous seeing as Glen had heard most of my ideas many times, but I suppose was there to give him a clearer picture of any external candidates' skills. Because the job had to be advertised in the big wide world, obviously, it was never going to be as straightforward as a choice between me and Juliet. Roz critiqued all my ideas for me, pushing me to think about them harder, guiding me to choose the one that would best stand out. I was drawn towards an idea I'd had bubbling around in my head for a while about our over-achiever sixth-former character Morgan failing her exams and having a breakdown. It was barely more than a few beats strung together, but I thought at least it was something different, and Morgan's character has become quite boring and predictable. Roz persuaded me that a more conventional – but more fully developed – strand about a teacher/student relationship might come across better.

'It's sexier,' she said. 'And that's all they care about, after all. It'd get ratings.'

'Do you think?' I said, pushing my baked potato lunch round with my fork. We were in the greasy spoon just along the road from the office. 'It's just a bit . . . obvious.'

'Who cares?' She speared a bit of tomato. 'When did that ever matter on this show?'

'You might be right,' I said. The show has been on for five years and pretty much everyone has slept with everyone else by this point. Everyone is everyone else's father/mother/long-lost sibling. The audiences lap it up.

Roz had smiled. 'I'm always right.'

And in retrospect she was. Like I said, I couldn't have done it without her.

3

My celebration with Dee turns into a 'let's clear out Ashley's room' intervention. But with added alcohol. Dee is an organizer. She can't stand to watch people faffing around, unable to make a decision. I've seen her march up to someone at a shop counter before and tell them the blue suits them much better, the grey would make their eyes look washed out, now if they could just pay and move on we'll all be happy. It usually works too. It's amazing how many people just want someone else to take control.

She has called my daughter and got her permission to box up the last of her stuff in an effort to galvanize me into action. She knows I've been being avoiding the whole lodger thing. It fills me with horror; I'm not going to lie. But even with whatever raise my new position brings I still need the money if I'm going to help Ashley and Ryan stay afloat once they've only got his salary to rely on. I'm not complaining: TV pays well compared to most other things. But a lifetime of being a single mum takes its toll financially. Apparently the average cost of bringing up a child is over two hundred thousand pounds. It's mind-boggling. That's an awful lot of packets of fish fingers (the only food Ashley would eat from the age of five to nine. I used to sneakily substitute them for the vegetable versions sometimes in an effort to get some greens into her. She always knew) but it all adds up.

Hence Roger the lodger. Or preferably Loretta the subletter.

We open a bottle of red first. Dutch courage. I know Ashley's not moving back home any time soon but clearing out her stuff feels so final. Which is ridiculous given that she's never really lived in this flat, except in the holidays. Still, her room is her room, and it contains all the things we've been carting around from place to place since she was tiny.

'This room is a goldmine,' Dee says, chucking a pile of CDs into a box that she's conjured up from somewhere (she actually arrived with ten, flat-packed, complete with tape and a marker pen). 'Have you decided what you're going to charge?'

'No idea,' I say sulkily as I put Ashley's *Famous Five* books in a box. She's hung on to all her childhood favourites and I can't stop myself browsing through each of them.

'"Zone two. Close to the Thameslink . . ."'

'"Shared kitchen, shared bathroom." Oh God, I don't know if I can share my bathroom. Maybe I should put "women only"?'

'I don't know if you're allowed,' she says, emptying the contents of a drawer out on to the bed. Pens, hair scrunchies, old lip glosses spill everywhere.

I sit down next to them. 'I don't know if I can do this.'

Dee looks at me with what I always describe as her 'explaining things to a toddler' face. 'How much is their rent?'

'I know.'

I bought this flat when I first started working on *Churchill Road* with the help of a decent deposit, courtesy of the sale of my mum's house after she died, and a huge mortgage. It was all my mum ever wanted – for us to move out of our endless string of rented flats, always at the mercy of unscrupulous landlords and exorbitant rent hikes – if, that is, we wouldn't move up to Milton Keynes and in with her (we wouldn't). Ashley and I had lived in six different places in her short life. The fact my flat was a basement, and so dark you had to put all the lights on even in the summer, helped. But it's still a stretch to make ends meet every month.

'Do you think I need to decorate?' I say, looking round at the tired paint with little patches missing where years-old Blu-tack has been ripped off, and knowing the answer.

'I'll help you.'

'Thanks. That's enough for tonight though.' I pile the four boxes we've filled so far in a corner to emphasize my point.

'OK, Gran,' she says. This is her hilarious new joke. She finds the idea that I'm about to be a grandmother in my early(ish) forties both gobsmacking (as do I) and comedy gold. In the couple of weeks since I broke the news to her she has called me Gran – or Grandma, or Nan, or Granny – approximately forty-eight thousand times. She never tires of it. I, on the other hand, am struggling to come to terms with seeing myself in a role that conjures up visions of blue-white curls and shiny ill-fitting false teeth. Most women are having babies at my age, not grandchildren. My way to deal with it is to ignore Dee, starve her of the laugh she's craving. It's not working, but it's all I've got.

'So,' Dee says once we've settled down in the living room with the real-flame gas fire turned up high and our glasses topped up. Smokey stretches out luxuriously on the sofa between us. 'How's Juliet taking it?'

Dee has never met any of my work colleagues but she's heard enough stories about Juliet over the years to have a good idea what the answer will be.

'With her usual good grace. I'm secretly hoping she might decide it's too humiliating to have me as her boss and leave.'

'Do you think she'll make things difficult for you?'

I lean back into the cushions. Do I? 'I don't think she'll make things difficult but I don't think she'll make them easy either, if you know what I mean. I just have to be grown up about it.'

Dee flicks her too-long fringe out of her eyes, something she does approximately every two minutes. I once timed her when we were drunk and talking about what irritated us about the other one (I'm an earring twiddler apparently. I twirl the two tiny gold hoops in my left ear round and round while I talk. I have no idea I'm even doing it. 'Sometimes it's fifty times. I've counted,' Dee had said and I'd spent the rest of the evening alternating between trying not to touch them and shouting 'And again!' every time her hand strayed up to her hair). 'What's the worst she can do?'

'Exactly,' I say.

She raises her glass. 'Well, I'm proud of you. Just so you know.'

'I'm proud of me too,' I say. And I am. Terrified, but proud. I just hope I'm up to it.

4

On Monday morning I'm the first in our department to arrive at work. I bought myself a new bag in Stables Market on Saturday – cute but not expensive – and last night before I went to bed I packed it carefully like I used to the night before the first day of the new school year.

I spent a lot of the weekend finishing boxing up Ashley's things, although now I have no idea where to put them all. Mine is not a flat with impressive amounts of concealed storage. Dee's parting shot on Friday was that I probably needed to 'freshen up the communal parts' before I advertise the room.

'The kitchen, the bathroom, the living room . . .'

'They're not using the living room!' I'd almost shouted. 'The living room's my haven. They can put a TV in Ashley's room.'

'You'll need to make that very clear when they come to view it,' she said. 'And the hall could probably do with a lick of paint.'

I groaned. 'Why am I doing this again?'

'Because you need extra money. And the company probably won't do you any harm either.'

Dee is one of those people who hate being on their own. Her idea of hell – a whole day stretching before you with nothing to do except to please yourself reading a book or going for a solitary walk – is my idea of heaven. She's always trying to get me to join things or go out with her to 'meet new people' because she thinks the amount of time I spend alone is unhealthy.

I fobbed her off with a promise to meet her and Gavin for lunch at the Roebuck on Sunday.

'See?' I said as she left, cramming a woolly hat down over her dark head, which only made her fringe cover her eyes even more. 'I have a social life. I have a lunch date in my diary.'

'Me and Gav are not a social life,' she said, hugging me.

I make myself a coffee in the little kitchen that we share with the accounts department and the general office. The milk smells like it is achieving its goal of becoming yoghurt by Wednesday so I leave it black. And then I remember that I hate black coffee, but at this moment the caffeine seems more important than the taste. I detour via the print room to collect the mountain of Roz's scripts and outlines that I left printing when I went home on Friday evening. My plan is to get in a good hour of quiet reading before anyone else arrives. I need to be on top of things.

There's a small pile of papers beside the printer but a quick scan of them shows them to be a schedule. Maybe someone moved my stack out of the way. I have a quick scout round the general office thinking either Emma or Lorraine might have decided to organize them for me. Nothing. So I check on my desk. Again nothing.

I know three-hundred-odd pages would be hard to miss so I walk round again, check the big drawers under Lorraine's and Emma's desks, take another look round the print room, even looking in the recycling bin in case they've been mistakenly thrown in there. The cleaners have been known to do stranger things. Empty.

Frustrated, I send Emma and Lorraine a quick text – *Did you pick up a load of scripts from the printer on Friday night?* – and then I remember that Lorraine had left before me anyway, so it could only be Emma. They both respond within minutes. *No.*

Rather than waste time I decide I can read one of the scripts on my desktop and send the others to print again. I know we're all supposed to do it and save paper, but I hate reading scripts on my computer. I find it hard to get a sense of how long things are or the pacing. But it's better than doing nothing.

I pull up my emails, searching for the one from Roz. It's not there. Or if it is it's not making itself obvious. I enter her name into search. I have hundreds of emails from her but nothing from Friday that contains any attachments. I go back to my inbox, scroll down again. I can't find it.

I stomp over to her desk, turn on her computer. I can check in her sent mail. Roz and I know each other's passwords. Have often asked the other one to check something, or print something off if we're busy. I find it easily enough. Forward it to myself. Then I find the shortest one of the attachments and send it to print.

I go straight to the print room to wait for it. It's suspiciously quiet. I check the printer for lights but it's as if it's oversleeping from the weekend. I bend down to find the plug. The socket is switched off. Relieved, I turn it back on and hear the satisfying roar as the machine wakes up. I wait for it to chug and rumble and do whatever it is that it has to do that takes so long, but then there's nothing. I notice a flashing message. Out of ink. I reach for the cupboard where the cartridges are kept. Locked.

I feel disproportionally annoyed. I know I'm being ridiculous. I have plenty of other work I could be getting on with. Instead I sit at my desk fuming, drinking my bitter black coffee, unable to concentrate on anything until Emma rolls in, bundled up like a snowman and clutching a two-litre bottle of milk in a gloved hand, at twenty past nine.

She appears at the door to my office. Nose red from the cold. 'Did you find that stuff?' she says, unravelling a scarf from round her neck for what seems like way too long a time.

'No. I don't fucking understand it. It was printing when I left on Friday. Do you have the key to the cupboard where the ink cartridges are?'

'It's in the drawer of the filing cabinet in there, where it always is. We're not really supposed to print everything out anyway. Waste of paper.'

I ignore her.

Five minutes later she pops her head round my door. 'Done,' she says. 'Someone had taken out the old cartridge and not bothered putting a new one in. Unbelievable.'

'Probably because they're locked away in a cupboard as if we're a bunch of kleptomaniacs who can't be trusted,' I snap.

'And the key wasn't where it's supposed to be ... I found it on my desk.'

I send everything to print again. Ask Emma to grab whatever she can as soon as it appears. And then I wrap myself back up in my coat and head downstairs for a walk round the block to calm myself down.

Roz and I are having a drink in our go-to pub round the corner. A guidebook might describe it as 'a slightly rancid-smelling haunt for local ne'er-do-wells' but it's the closest one to the studio and we're both inclined to be lazy. Or rather we're having a drink outside our go-to pub, because Roz wants to vape. Despite it being two degrees above freezing. I don't want to vape. I want to sit in a warm room, steamy with after-work crowds.

I'm having a coffee. Not because I felt like coffee but because I thought it might be the one thing that would stop me from turning into an icicle. I circle both (gloved) hands round the cup and hold it up near my face for maximum heat-to-bare-skin transference.

'"Quiet, non-annoying, clean, mostly absent tenant wanted . . ."' Roz says, taking a theatrical drag. She's helping me decide what to put in my ad. When I get round to it.

'I like the "mostly absent" bit. "Would suit someone who works in London during the week but fucks off somewhere else every weekend."'

Roz laughs. '"Hopefuls will be required to take a vow of silence and promise to clean the bathroom after every visit."'

I put my coffee cup down on the table. 'Oh God, don't . . .'

She's still on a roll. '"Ideal for the person who really lives with their partner but just needs somewhere to dump their stuff in case it all goes wrong."'

'I've got it!' I say triumphantly. '"Just give me your money and live somewhere else."'

'Well, that's that sorted.'

We sit there in silence for a moment. Roz pulls her fingers through her hair to make it stand higher on top.

'God, Emma's annoying,' she says. I wait, knowing she'll enlighten me. 'She's got a rat up her arse about whose responsibility it is to wash the coffee mugs.'

I shrug. 'I suppose it's not in her job description to do everyone's.'

'Who cares. Leave them then. The cleaners come in every night.'

'I think her point was that we run out if no one ever washes them.'

She rolls her eyes. 'Oh my God, really though. She's put it on the agenda for the next department meeting.'

I can't help it, I shriek with laughter. 'No!'

'Yes! I saw her typing it up.'

I sip my coffee. 'Well, that's going to be fun.'

'You might have to deal with it,' she says, smirking. 'Now you're head of the department and all.'

I pull a face that I hope says 'fuck you'. Change the subject. 'How's Hugh?'

'Lovely,' she sighs. Roz is not someone you would describe as a romantic. She once told me she'd dumped a bloke because he bought her flowers on Valentine's Day.

'It was the lack of imagination,' she said when I protested. 'That was the best thing he could come up with when he thought about how he could show me how much he loved me. The same thing twenty million other women were being given.'

'Chocolates are worse,' I said, and she'd scoffed.

'At least you can eat chocolates.'

But where Hugh is concerned it's as if she forgets she's Ms Cynical 2018. They've been together for years – married for nearly three. It's sweet how much she adores him. I, on the other hand, have been single for almost as long. In fact I can count the serious relationships I've had in the past twenty years on one hand. Actually, that's an exaggeration, I could count them on three fingers. The Holy Trinity: Boring, Cheater and Wet.

She tells me about a party they went to on Saturday in an old church in Mayfair, thrown by a record company Hugh looks after. The guest list sounds like the line-up for Glastonbury. She was chatted up by the lead singer from a band I've never heard of but who, apparently, are the new big thing. He'd been so persistent asking for her number, despite her protestations that she was married, that in the end she'd made one up and written it on his arm. Roz is a great anecdote teller, and I can see the whole scene unfolding.

'I put a love heart next to it, and wrote "I'm all yours" with a kiss. He was practically salivating.'

I laugh. 'I wonder how many times he's tried calling it.'

'I'm hoping it's some other girl's number,' she says. 'It could be the start of something beautiful, like a bad romcom.'

'It's so weird about your scripts,' I say when we reach a lull in the conversation. I've spent the day working my way through them – Emma adding a new one to the pile as soon as she had rescued it from the printer and bound it together. 'I mean, I left them printing out. I checked before I went home, and the printer was working. There was a pile of pages already. I saw them.'

She looks at me. Draws on her e-cigarette. 'Juliet was still there when I left . . . You don't think . . .?'

I pick up my drink, put it down again. 'Shit. No . . . she wouldn't . . .'

Roz shrugs. 'Why would the cleaners throw away papers that had clearly just been printed out? Why would someone take the printer cartridge out and not replace it?'

'Fuck.'

She throws her e-cigarette back in her bag. 'I mean, who knows? But it feels a bit odd to me.'

I think about it. Can I really imagine Juliet bothering to sabotage me? Doing something as petty as this? To what end? So that I don't perform as well as I could? It's a stretch.

'I don't know. It seems unlikely.'

She stands up. 'Well, those scripts didn't lose themselves. Let's go inside. I'm freezing.'

Inside I head for the bar because it's my round while Roz hunts down a table. I get myself a gin and tonic and another Chardonnay for her. It takes me a while to find her but, when

I do, she's sitting with a couple of women from accounts who I barely know. They look like twins with their pumped-up cleavages and matching lips. They've clearly had a couple already because they're both talking way too loudly and at the same time. I sit down on the spare chair, hoping that they might be heading home soon. I want to pick over the Juliet question some more, but I can't in front of these two.

'Holly, you know Lucinda and Janet, don't you?'

I smile at the two women, making non-committal noises. They barely pause for breath long enough to say hello.

'He didn't even bat an eyelid,' the one called Lucinda says. 'Not even when I told him I'd bought them as an early anniversary present for him. Like I'm going to waste good money at Agent Provocateur for his benefit.'

Janet cackles. 'So Ray is still none the wiser?'

'No, thank God,' Lucinda says, swigging from a long and probably very alcoholic drink.

I loathe the pair of them instantly.

'Luce has a gentleman friend,' Roz says to me in a stage whisper. 'Ray is her husband.'

'Nice,' I say in a way that I hope comes out sounding as sarcastic as I mean it to.

They all prattle on. A couple of times the people at the next table look round as if to say 'Can you keep the noise down?' and I look away because I don't know what else to do.

I sip my drink, letting their inane chatter waft over me. When Janet offers to get another round in I turn to Roz and say, 'Or, do you want to move on somewhere quieter?' hoping she'll get the hint, but she just turns to the other two and says, 'What do you reckon, ladies? Shall we stay here or go somewhere else?'

'We'll never get a table anywhere else,' Lucinda says. I wait to see if Roz will suggest we go our separate ways and, when she doesn't, I decide to cut my losses. I might as well at least get an early night.

'I won't have a drink, actually, thanks,' I say to Janet. 'I think I'll make a move. I'm knackered.'

'Lightweight,' Lucinda says, guffawing. I pretend I haven't heard.

Roz pulls a disappointed face. 'You're abandoning me.'

I smile at her, even though I'm a bit pissed off. 'I think you'll survive.'

Back home I feed Smokey, then heat up the remains of last night's pizza. I think about making a salad to go with it but I can't be bothered. I flop on the sofa, fork in one hand, plate in the other. Try to imagine what it'll be like coming home and finding a stranger making a mess in my kitchen. How I'll be able to curb the urge to shout 'Clean that up' every time they spill a drop. Will I have to designate them space in my fridge? Or provide them with their own? Are we going to have to negotiate about buying milk and loo rolls? It's making my head hurt thinking about it.

I should put a lock on my bedroom door, I think. In case they're a kleptomaniac. Or even just nosy. It always seems so clear-cut in films. Someone advertises a room and one of two things happens: the new person fits in seamlessly and within days they and the home owner are best friends (or lovers) and spend all day drinking coffee together at the kitchen table, or they're a psychopath and within weeks have driven the landlord insane or skinned them alive and started wearing them as a coat.

I get a pad and pen out of the little drawer in the coffee table and make notes. 'Lock on bedroom door!!' 'References.' Then I add 'Fridge?' And 'Cat lover only.'

I decide to have an early night but my brain is buzzing. I potter around, loading the dishwasher, sorting through laundry, trying to calm myself down. I think about what Roz said. That Juliet was still there when she left the office. That maybe she was the one who took the scripts, removed the ink cartridge from the printer. I know that she must be disappointed she didn't get the job. To be honest, I expected her to get it, so I'm sure she did too. I hate to think that someone's got it in for me, but maybe she has. Maybe I need to watch my back.

5

Let me explain why we dislike Juliet so much.

I can't even remember when it began. When I joined the company she and Roz were already here, having started on the same day, and already at loggerheads. Juliet was pleasant enough to begin with but she made no real effort to get to know me. Roz, on the other hand, invited me out to lunch on day one and we clicked immediately. Same sense of humour, similar likes and dislikes. On a dating website we would have matched. From the get-go Roz made no secret of the fact she and Juliet didn't get on. She would tell me stories about how uptight she was, how humourless. I had gone there intending to make my own judgements about everyone as I always try to do but I suppose it did make me look at her in a slightly different way. A bit wary, if you like.

Maybe Juliet wrote me off the minute she saw me and Roz getting on, but I always felt as if she wasn't giving me a chance. Whenever I expressed an opinion in meetings she would pick it apart. She has a default sneering tone, not helped by her accent, which is all privilege and entitlement, gymkhanas and skiing holidays. She went to private school, then Cambridge where she got a first in English. None of this equips her to do the job we're doing any better than me or Roz in my opinion – just the opposite in fact, because how can she possibly understand the world of the show when it's so alien to anything she's ever known? – but it does make her intimidating as hell in arguments. I've always had a kind of cap-doffing obsequiousness in the face of confident posh people (and don't get me started on doctors) that generally speaks far more about my insecurities than their assumption of superiority. I hate myself for it but I seem powerless to stop it. They make me feel inadequate.

As for Roz, who grew up on a council estate in what sounds like one of the roughest parts of Brighton (when I mentioned the name of it to Dee who hails from nearby Burgess Hill she shuddered), well, let's just say 'unashamedly posh' is in the front of the window of her own personal Shop of Horrors.

There was no defining moment when I decided I didn't like her. No big showdown. It was just a fact of life. She takes everything so seriously; there's no joy in her. Disapproval oozes out of her like sweat. We have nothing in common.

Juliet has the kind of blonde ruddy looks that wouldn't seem out of place in a Barbour and riding boots, with a cocked rifle under her arm. Roz used to mutter 'Tally ho!' at me whenever she walked past. Which was childish and a bit mean, but also cracked me up every time. And so the lines were drawn pretty quickly. We tolerate each other, don't get me wrong. She's good at what she does, and our paths have never had to cross too much before. Only now I'm her boss and I'm expected to have an opinion on everything she does.

The following morning there's a pile of scripts on my

desk. Juliet's. I spend most of the day reading through them, keeping my head down. They're in good shape and I'm relieved that I'm not going to have to discuss anything in them with her. She's made her point, hopefully. A petty attempt at sabotage that was about as effective as a petulant child stomping their feet. The worst that could happen happened. Which was that I wasted an hour of my life. Big deal. Pathetic. With any luck she's got it out of her system.

It's peaceful in the office. Joe is down in the studio, watching a batch of his episodes being filmed, and will be all week. Fighting off attempts by the cast to change the lines to things they think sound better but which make no sense or directly contradict something that's been said before. Roz, Juliet, Lorraine and Emma are all engrossed in their work. It's one of those periods where it's almost as if everyone has agreed on the need for silence.

My phone rings.

I pick it up. It's one of those big desk things, and the display shows an internal extension, but one I don't immediately recognize.

'Hello.' It's a familiar woman's voice. She carries on before I can respond. 'Holly? It's Amanda. I just wanted to say thank you . . . Gosh, how lovely of you to send me those beautiful flowers. And such a huge bouquet! I'm having to go round borrowing vases left right and centre . . .'

I have no idea what she's talking about. Amanda is one of the stars of the show. Locked in a rivalry both on and off screen with Caz, the actress playing her sister, their characters, along with their parents and their teenage children, are the backbone of the series. The episode that transmitted last night was a two-hander, the pair of them trawling through the mess of their relationship. It's no secret we were thinking of the BAFTAs when we planned it. I have never sent Amanda flowers. I've never sent any of the cast flowers. That would be weird.

'Um . . .' I say, when she leaves a long enough gap for me to butt in. 'I wish I could say it was me, Amanda . . .' Little self-conscious laugh. '. . . but I think it must be someone else . . .'

'No.' I hear a rustling. 'It says on the card: "Bravo! What a tour de force! Congratulations, you did us proud. Holly." And then, in brackets, "script department". That's you, right?'

I gloss over the fact that I have never in my life used the terms 'bravo' or 'tour de force'. Someone has sent flowers and put my name on the card. For a moment I struggle to think in what way this might be an attempt to stitch me up, and then it hits me. Last night's episode was a two-hander. Two actresses acting their socks off, giving it their all. I, the new head of the script department, appear to have sent one of them flowers. Unless Caz is trying to get through as we speak to thank me for hers I assume she hasn't received a bouquet of her own. But she'll soon hear about Amanda's and all hell will break loose.

'What's the name of the florist?' I say, trying to sound casual. She tells me and I write it down. 'I think Emma must have sent them on my behalf because I was saying this morning how brilliant you both were, and that we should do something . . .'

41

'Well, it's very kind, however it happened.'

'You're welcome,' I say. I just want to get off the phone now. 'And congratulations again — both of you were amazing.'

She goes off happy and I get straight back on the phone to the florist's, after googling the number. I almost get bogged down in trying to establish who sent the first bunch, but the woman on the other end tells me she has no record, they must have paid cash. I ask for an identical bunch to be sent to Caz, but she can't remember what they looked like. So I ask for something that costs the same, gasp at the price, then have to pay five pounds extra for an emergency delivery. Hopefully I've averted an incident but I'm furious. Not just about the money I can't afford to spend — I consider for a second if I could get away with trying to claim it back on expenses but we're really not that kind of show — but that this is someone's — Juliet's — idea of a joke. No, scratch that. Juliet doesn't do jokes. I don't think I've ever seen her laugh. She lives a joyless existence. If she's done this then she's done it to make me look bad, pure and simple.

I look out into the office. Juliet is no longer there. I grab my coat and steam over to Roz's desk. 'Come for a walk with me.'

Roz takes one look at me and, I assume, realizes now is not the time to plead busyness. I keep walking out into the corridor. Lorraine and Emma both look up as I go, but I ignore them.

'That fucking bitch,' I say when Roz catches me up.

'I take it we're talking about Camilla Parker Bowles?' She stumbles on her heels trying to keep pace. I slow down.

I tell her what's just happened and she listens with her mouth open, reaching the conclusion that the whole point was to cause friction between me and Caz way more quickly than I did.

'You've got to give her credit, it's original,' she says.

'What if Amanda hadn't called to say thank you? I mean, for fuck's sake. Caz probably would have started a hate campaign against me. As it is I'm fifty-five quid down and I look like a desperate saddo who sucks up to the cast by sending them flowers.'

I slam out of the door into the car park. The freezing air hits me like a slap and I pull my coat close round my neck.

'Where are we going?' Roz asks in a slightly desperate voice.

I keep moving. 'I have no idea. I just had to get out of there. Let's walk round the block.'

'Can we go to the café instead?'

I look back at her. Her nose is already pink. Cheeks flushed. Roz and extreme temperatures do not go well together. 'Shit, sorry. Yes, let's.'

We walk on for a moment and then I come to a sudden stop. 'What if that's where Juliet's gone?'

'I can scout it out before we go in. Are you going to say anything to her?'

'I don't know. I mean, the stupid woman in the shop couldn't even tell me who put the order in . . .'

'Think about it carefully first. You don't want her to

lure you into losing your rag. Then she'll go bleating off to Glen and you'll look like the bad guy.'

I consider this. It's true that Juliet and Glen have a good relationship or, as Roz would prefer it, she sucks up to him and he likes it. But he and I do too. And he had a big say in me getting the job over her, after all. Maybe I should open his eyes as to what she's really like.

'I mean, what's she actually done so far?' Roz is saying. 'Nothing that can harm you. If that's the best she's got then who cares?'

'What if there's something else? Something worse?'

Roz shrugs. 'I don't think she's that clever.'

We walk on in silence for a moment. I tell myself not to overreact. She's doing this to provoke a reaction. Above all else I shouldn't give her what she wants. By the time we reach the café, and Roz has checked that the coast is clear, I feel calmer. We get takeaway coffees, start the walk back.

'Think zen,' Roz says, and I laugh. The previous boss of the show, Catherine, once decided that lunchtime yoga would be a good bonding exercise. Probably because her husband was a yoga teacher and needed a bit of extra cash. Roz and I went along one time, but even though we managed to get past the sight of our co-workers' Lycra-clad bums in the air neither of us could survive the meditation session at the end. The omming made us howl with laughter and the frustrated teacher shouting 'Think zen' at us, in a voice that was anything but, finished us off. We've said it to each other ever since in times of stress.

We're walking along the long corridor, back to the office,

44

when I spot Juliet up ahead, coming out of the Ladies. My heart starts to pound. I feel myself go red in the face. Roz puts a hand out and touches my arm, a gesture designed to remind me to keep calm. I know she's right. I know there's nothing to be gained from calling Juliet out. I know I should keep my dignity.

'What the fuck do you think you're doing?' I've said it before I can stop myself. I shrug Roz's hand away.

Juliet looks round as if I might be talking to someone behind her. Realizes there is no one behind her. Looks back at me. 'What are you talking about?'

'You know exactly what I'm talking about.' It hits me as I'm saying this that it sounds as if we're rehearsing a scene from the show: 'You slaaag'; 'Who do you think you're talking to, you're the effing slaaaaaag.'

'Why would I ask the question if I did?' she says in that sneery way she has.

'Just know that I know it was you. If you do anything else I'm going straight to Glen.'

'Good,' she says. 'You do that. Maybe he'll have a clue as to what the hell you're referring to.'

I can't bear her condescending tone. I open my mouth to say more but just at that moment the door to Glen's office opens and he steps out into the corridor. He looks at the three of us standing there, Juliet and me glaring at each other. 'Everything OK?'

'All good,' Roz says cheerily, and then she takes my arm and steers me towards the office.

6

As I'm thinking about packing up for the day Glen puts his head round my door.

'Got two minutes?'

'Sure.' I follow him out of my office, through the open-plan area and into his larger space at the end of the corridor. For some reason it doesn't occur to either of us that we could close the door to my room and chat in there. Roz and Joe have already left for the day, Emma is winding her overlong scarf round her face again and Juliet has her head in a script. She looks up as we pass. I've managed to avoid her all afternoon. Mostly by looking the other way whenever she appears in my field of vision.

Glen reaches into the small fridge by his desk and produces a screwtop bottle of white wine. 'Drink?' he says, opening it without waiting for an answer.

'Love one.' I pull two plastic cups from the water dispenser and put them down in front of him and then sit at one end of his grey sofa.

'How are you getting on?' he says as he pours.

'Oh. OK, I think. It's going to take me a while to get completely up to speed with what everyone else is doing. . .'

'Of course,' he says. He hands me a cup and I sip, resisting the urge to chuck it all back in one go.

'So . . .' he says, and then he leaves such a long gap I start thinking maybe I'm meant to fill it. Luckily I can't think of anything to say because he finally speaks again.

'I appreciate it must be difficult trying to redefine relationships with people you've worked with for a long time.'

I wonder if Juliet has been to see him. To complain about me before I can complain about her. Of course it may just be that he overheard us talking in the corridor. The atmosphere was so thick when he opened his office door he must have been able to feel it. I think about telling him what's happened but what would I really be saying? Juliet may have moved some scripts I came in early to read, and she sent some flowers on my behalf. Put like that it hardly sounds damning. And I don't want him to start thinking I'm not going to be able to manage the people I'm meant to be working with. 'What? No. I mean . . . I think things just need to settle down a bit.'

'Well,' he says in a measured tone. He sits on the armchair opposite me and leans back. I've never really thought about it before but he's actually not bad-looking in an 'it took a lot of hard work to look this laid-back' kind of way. He certainly thinks he is. He has a beard, the kind that he probably oils and combs every day and has neatened up at the barber's once a week, his eyebrows have not a hair out of place. His clothes are impeccable, as if he spends way too long worrying about them. He lives in Shoreditch, need I say more? I prefer my men clean-shaven and sweaty from the gym. What men? I hear you say, and you'd be right. The imaginary men in my head.

'. . . it's always difficult when someone else gets the job you'd set your heart on . . .'

I'm hopeful that I detect an acknowledgement in there that Juliet is the one who is behaving badly, not me.

'Well, I think Juliet probably feels a bit hard done by because she's been here the longest . . .'

'I imagine they both have issues with that.'

I wonder if I've misheard. 'Both?'

'Juliet and Roz.'

'Oh no,' I say, realizing he's got the wrong end of the stick. 'Not Roz. She's totally behind me.'

·He nods. 'I suppose that makes sense. If she didn't get it herself she'd rather it was you than Juliet. That's the impression I get.'

'She didn't even want it, though.' I'm confused by the turn this conversation has taken. Why are we talking about Roz here?

Glen raises an eyebrow. 'Oh, but she did. She didn't tell you she applied? I thought you were mates.'

'We are. What? Roz went for the job?'

He nods.

'My job?'

'Yes. Is that such a surprise?'

'Really?' I'm at a loss for what to say. I think about all the evenings in the pub when we pored over my application form. Me saying to Roz 'Are you sure you don't want to go for it?' because if she'd said yes I would have supported her. Happily. And her pulling that face. As if.

'I'm really confused,' is all I can come up with eventually.

'Anyway, my point is that you were the one we all felt was the best candidate. There's a reason for that. You need to rise above whatever was going on out there in the corridor.'

'Of course,' I say, trying to seem professional. Glen doesn't need to see how much this has rattled me.

'Don't you think that's weird?' I say to Dee. We're in the chintzy bar at the end of my road, which Dee conveniently passes on her way home from work as a receptionist at the Royal Free, half a glass of Merlot down. Because we arranged to meet at seven and I arrived at approximately two minutes past she was already in a bit of a huff when I walked in, making a point of checking the time on her Fitbit.

'You're late,' she said. 'I've been sat here for ten minutes, like a saddo.'

'Because you were eight minutes early.'

'That's not the point.'

'No, it really is,' I said, leaning down and giving her a hug.

Now she screws up her face. 'Maybe she was just embarrassed to tell you? She probably knew you had a much bigger chance of getting it.'

'Not on paper. She's got years more experience than me.'

Dee shrugs. 'It's insecurity, that's all.'

'It's just strange,' I say, finishing the glass. 'I told her all my story ideas and she helped me pick out the best one. And she never said anything . . .'

She holds up her own glass as if to say 'Do you want

another' and I shake my head. 'Are you going to mention it to her?' Dee asks.

I think for a moment. 'I have no idea. No, I don't think so. I mean . . . if she was so determined not to tell me . . .'

She pulls her coat from the back of her chair. 'It'll blow over. Just keep your head down and do a good job.'

Outside it's started to snow. Not in a picture-book Santa in Lapland kind of way, but that horizontal frozen slush that gets into your eyes and never settles except in treacherous icy patches. Even though I only have to walk two hundred metres I jam my woolly hat down and pull my scarf up, leaving just a tiny viewing window. Dee and I hug like two snow-suited babies, arms out straight, and we go our separate ways.

'Don't worry about the Juliet thing either,' she calls after me. I know I must have bored her to death with my work woes.

'I won't,' I shout back. 'Hopefully she's got it out of her system.'

Inside my flat it's bitterly cold. Smokey greets me like someone who's been lost on the frozen wastes of Siberia and thought they might never experience warmth or food again. I reach out a hand to feel the nearest radiator. Nothing.

'Fuck's sake,' I say aloud. Without even taking my coat off I head for the cupboard in the kitchen that houses the boiler and turn the knob to top up the pressure. Then I press reset and, thankfully, it bursts back into life. I turn on the gas fire in the living room, open a tin of food for

Smokey and put his bowl within whisker-singeing distance. I had been planning on thawing out and mulling over my day in a deep hot bath with a glass of wine on the side, but by the time the water heats up now I'll probably be asleep, so I just change into my PJs as quickly as I can without exposing too much flesh to the elements at any one time, microwave a bean chilli with rice and eat it huddled next to my cat on the living-room floor.

I'm living the dream.

7

I've decided that I have to go all out to impress Glen to assuage any worries he has about whether or not I'm the woman for the job. So, a week into my new position, I'm pitching him my idea for the Morgan character. I know it's taking her in a very different direction, and it's a bit more serious than our usual 'who's shagging who?' fluff, but I've been mulling it over, and I think it's just what we need at the moment. Our ratings have been on a long slow decline for some time, even with all of Glen's changes and although it's tempting to just bury our heads in the sand and keep churning out the same old stuff, that seems foolish in the long term. We could all end up out of a job. And I've decided I need to stick my neck out. Show him I'm up to it.

'Oh yes, Roz's story?' he says when I mention it. 'It's not a bad idea.'

His comment throws me completely off course. 'Um . . . no, it's mine. But anyway . . .'

Glen looks momentarily confused. I decide to let it go even though all I really want to say is 'What do you mean Roz's story?' I need to focus on what's important here. I talk him through the whole story arc and he nods along.

'Yes, and then she goes off the rails. Ends up waking up in hospital with no idea where she's been,' he says, when I reach a certain point. 'Have we talked about this before? It's so familiar.'

'I don't think so.' I tell myself to concentrate. We talk for a bit about whether or not the viewers might enjoy seeing a completely different side to our Miss Perfect character, or if it might alienate them. About whether Sammy, the actress playing Morgan, could pull it off, and how she might feel about the challenge. But my mind is racing.

'Plot it through and let's see how it would work alongside everything else,' he says, turning to some paperwork on his desk. 'And then we'll see.'

'I thought maybe the hospital ep could be the first week in September, and work back from there.' We always look for a big story to give us a boost the first week the kids are back at school, once everyone has returned from their summer holidays and they're sitting back down in front of the TV in the evenings.

'Good idea,' he says, and I take that as my cue to leave.

Back in my own office I shut the door and try to fathom what that was all about. The only person I've talked to about that idea before was Roz. Glen clearly has already heard it and he thinks it's Roz's. Roz wanted my job. It hardly takes Hercule Poirot to put the pieces together. It's what I do about it that's the issue. Confronting Roz head-on is pointless. She'll just deny any knowledge, declare Glen senile and it'll make things too awkward between us. I'm still festering about it when she knocks on my door and then comes in without waiting for an answer.

'God, I'm bored,' she says, flopping down in the arm-chair. She's wearing a chunky fuchsia polo neck over tight red tartan skinny leg trousers, and red DMs. Usually she's in vertiginous heels but the ice has defeated even her.

'I'm snowed under,' I say, hoping she'll take the hint. She doesn't.

'Look at her,' she says, staring at Juliet through the glass. 'Do you think she reads *Horse & Hound*? Or *The Lady*? "Twenty ways to get the best out of your manservant".'

Usually I'd laugh. I don't feel like it today though. 'I don't think she's that posh.'

'She's like Zara Phillips's posher, horsier sister. Is it home time yet?'

I force a smile. 'No. And I need to get this finished before it is,' I say, indicating a script on my desk.

Roz heaves herself out of the chair. 'OK, OK, I can take a hint. Drink tonight?'

'Zumba,' I say apologetically. It's a lie. Dee and I gave up zumba weeks ago in favour of a shared bottle of wine. The après-ski without the ski. Life's too short.

'Later,' she says, waving a casual hand as she leaves.

Because I've cried zumba I have to leave dead on six, as my fictional class starts at seven near my West Hampstead home. On the way to the station I call Dee, establish that she's on an afternoon shift but that she'll pop into mine on her way home at about half seven. Dee always walks to and from work, even though it takes her a good forty minutes each way to and from the hospital and her

Kilburn flat. She's obsessed with her step count. I get regular updates in text form (*12,000 today!!!!*) to which I usually reply something like *What? Drinks?* or *Deaths in the hospital due to your incompetence?* Dee has threatened to get me a Fitbit for my birthday in August, and I've told her that if she does I'll just attach it to Smokey and send him out mouse hunting while I sit on my backside eating cakes.

Not that I'm completely unfit. No, scrub that, I am. But I get away with it most of the time because I'm also quite slim. Some kind of freak genetics that I'm sure will catch up with me one of these days. Dee, of course, is a world health expert just by working on the reception of a busy hospital, so she knows better. She's full of stories about people who looked skinny but keeled over dead out of nowhere, and when the doctors opened them up they found their organs were 99 per cent flab. Or something. I never really listen.

She once told me a man had been brought into A and E with stomach pains only for the doctors to find, when they opened him up, that he'd eaten a whole Lego castle. When I'd spluttered in disbelief she had looked indignant.

'One of the surgical techs told me.'

'Well, then it must be true,' I said. We were walking to West End Lane to have a coffee. 'Just out of interest, how did they know it was a whole Lego castle? Did they reassemble it?'

She huffed. 'Don't be stupid.'

'And why did they only find out once they'd cut him open? Seems a bit drastic. Didn't they ask him what he'd eaten? Or X-ray him before they stuck the knife in?'

'Obviously they X-rayed him . . .'

'So they didn't just find it when they cut him open?'

Dee stopped walking. Gave me a sideways look. 'No . . . I don't know . . .'

I flung an arm round her, pulled her in for a hug. 'I love you,' I said, laughing.

'Why do you never believe anything I tell you?' she said, mock hurt.

'Why do you always believe literally anything anyone tells you?'

'That is so not true,' she'd said. But it was. Still is.

At home I have a quick shower, rustle together a basic tomatoey sauce that I can reheat later with pasta when Dee gets here – Gavin is away for work, as he often is (he's a pharmaceutical rep) and we often eat together when she's on her own. Then I settle on the sofa and call Ashley. She'll probably be in the middle of cooking dinner. She and Ryan seem to have gone from hedonisitic, carousing students to settled homebodies the minute they graduated, which should probably be every mother's dream especially now there's a baby on the way, but it worries me a bit. Ashley was always so ambitious – she has dreamt of being a costume designer ever since I can remember – but lately she's been full of talk about how her stopgap job at a large chain of pub/restaurants has a graduate scheme for would-be assistant managers. Which, again, should be a good thing. She's being responsible. She's doing the sensible thing. It just seems a shame to see her give up her dreams so easily.

'I'm at work,' she says when she answers. I can hear the bustle of the pub in the background.

'Oh, OK. Just checking in. Everything all right?'

'Great. Well, except we have a stag party booked in for twenty-five people tonight.'

'How lovely,' I say. 'Hopefully they'll move on somewhere else when they've eaten.'

'Hopefully,' she says, and I can tell she's distracted. I've been to the pub and I can picture her there in the all-wood surroundings. People always remark on how much she looks like me – long wavy chestnut hair, brown eyes that I've always thought were one size too small (mine, not hers. Hers are perfect), heart-shaped faces. There's almost no trace of her father in there. Like her body knew he was never going to be in the picture so why bother representing him? Like me she usually wears her hair off her face. But unlike me she has full dark eyebrows – mine have always been straggly and in need of filling in – and that's him. That's her father's legacy.

'How are you feeling?' She's been being sick in the mornings fairly regularly. Another thing she's inherited from me.

'Oh, you know, fat, hormonal, nauseous. So pretty much the same as before I was pregnant.'

I laugh. 'Are you eating?'

'Oh my God, Mum, why do you always ask me that? Of course I'm eating. If I wasn't I'd be dead.'

'Eating enough, I mean. Or eating healthily. Both. Either.'

'Yes, and sometimes. I need to go; we have customers.'

'Ring me when you can,' I say.

'Will do. Love you,' she says, and I know she's already straight back in work mode.

It's not that Ashley's father didn't want anything to do with her. Well, it is, but it wasn't her he rejected, it was an anonymous sexless baby. I tell myself that if he'd ever met her he would have fallen in love with her; it was impossible not to. And I let him off. Because he was so young. We barely knew each other. I didn't want to – as they used to say at the time – ruin his life. Of course, I was young too but, somehow, that didn't seem to be so important.

By the time I found out I was pregnant I had finished uni and I was back at home wondering what to do with the rest of my life. I knew who the father was because he was the only person it could be. I'd split up with my last boyfriend six months before, I'd had one one-night stand since (I never was a partier) with a boy called Lawrence – Lol – who I'd met a couple of times at the Central Union club night. That had been three months before and I was three months pregnant, give or take. You go figure. I thought about trying to track him down as soon as I found out, but I had no number for him, not even an idea where he might be spending the summer. I thought I was probably doing him a favour, because what twenty-year-old boy wants to be saddled with a baby by a girl he's met maybe five times in his life?

I did go back one afternoon the following September – hugely pregnant by that point. I wanted to make sure I was doing the right thing, and I thought, if I saw him, my gut would let me know. He was the year below me, so I knew he would still be studying, and I knew his subject – Anthropology. I wandered around the campus, my rounded belly bringing sideways glances from everyone I passed. I went back and forth between his department and the Union a couple of times, circled the library. On the second trip I finally spotted him heading towards one of the cafeterias with a group of friends. It was like seeing a vague acquaintance. Not that I ever thought I might have any kind of feelings for him, beyond he seemed like a nice bloke and a fun way to pass a night, but I couldn't fathom telling this virtual stranger that he now had some responsibility for my unborn child. I didn't want this random lad in my baby's life, or in mine.

Of course, my mum had lectured me about the practicalities. How hard it was going to be trying to get by as a single parent. How even if all that happened was that Lol (or Lol's mum and dad more likely) offered some kind of ongoing small financial contribution it would make my life and the baby's so much less of a struggle. It's funny that neither of us ever really considered that he had a right to know. That by not telling him maybe I was depriving him.

As I watched him messing about with his mates I knew that I couldn't do it. Apart from the fact that I had no clue how to break it to someone I hardly knew that they were about to be the father of my child (Hi, Lol, remember me? . . . No, not Polly, Holly. We shagged once. About six months ago . . . Yeah, yeah, I'm fine, thanks. You? Good. Anyway . . .), it just felt too cruel to throw such a huge grenade into someone's life out of nowhere. Why should two of us have our lives blown apart? Of course, if Ashley's pregnancy had happened in the same way I would have been down there myself, lecturing the boy that it takes two people to make a baby, that if you're old enough to father one you're old enough to deal with the consequences, no squirming out of your responsibilities, sonny. But I was twenty-one, my hormones were haywire, my back ached and I just wanted to go home.

So I turned away, wandered back the way I'd come. I felt at peace with my decision. Suddenly famished, I stopped at a café on the main road and bought a sandwich and a bottle of water for the journey home, faffing about between a cheese and onion bap and a chicken salad. In the end I bought both. I couldn't really afford to but I decided it was a celebration. I was treating myself. I had done the right thing. Sort of. I had, at least, confronted the idea of telling him and made the conscious decision not to. I wasn't burying my head in the sand.

As I came out, stuffing them into my bag, I almost bumped into someone coming in. I muttered an apology, and so did he, and then I looked up and saw that it was him. Lol. I was so confused that I probably did a double take. He must have said goodbye to his friends and come back through the campus while I was fannying about with sandwich choices.

'Oh. Hi,' I said casually, intending to move on past without stopping.

He gave me a flirty grin. I had a sudden flash of how sexy I'd found that look all those months ago. An evening spent in anticipation of what would come later. He was a good-looking boy. All angles and limbs and floppy hair, but comfortable with it.

'All right?'

'Good, yeah,' I said, angling round him to get to the door. As I edged past him I saw him clock it. My bump. He actually pointed at it.

'Shit. Are you . . .?'

I don't think he had any thought that it might be anything to do with him. Not at that moment.

'Yep,' I said, looking anywhere but at him. 'Six and a half months.'

'Right. Wow . . . I mean . . .'

I don't know why I said it. Whether I was annoyed that he was being so obtuse – being let off the hook was a gift I could give him, not something he should assume for himself by being so dense as not to put the pieces together in the first place – or I suddenly felt I owed him the truth, I couldn't say now. But I looked him straight in the eye and said, 'So it must have been early March . . .'

I left it hanging there for him to pick up. It only took a moment and then I saw his face drain of colour.

'No fucking way.'

'It's true,' I said. And now I was annoyed. 'There wasn't anyone else around that time. No one anywhere near.'

He looked around as if he was hoping a film crew might jump out and save him by telling him I was really Sacha Baron Cohen in disguise.

'You can't prove it's mine,' he said, all trace of the flirty

61

smile gone. He wasn't being aggressive. He looked as if the bottom had just dropped out of his world. Much like my face when I found out I was pregnant, I imagine.

'Well, I think you'll find I could once it's born if I wanted to . . .' I said coldly.

'Why didn't you get rid of it?' he said, sounding desperate. It was a question I didn't really know the answer to myself, if I was being honest. I said the only thing that made sense to me.

'Because I didn't want to.'

'Your decision,' he said. 'You should have told me then. Let me have a say.'

'How?' I said. 'What's my surname? Where do I live?'

He looked at me, the penny dropping. We barely knew each other. How would I have found him over the summer?

'Is it too late now?' he said.

'Yes, Lol,' I said, as if I were talking to a child. 'It's too late now. Six and a half months is too late. Even if I wanted to. Which I don't.'

'This is fucking mental,' he said.

'Listen.' I wanted this conversation to be over. I wanted to get out of there. 'I haven't come here to demand you get involved. I came to see if I thought I should let you know . . . just in case . . . and for the record I'd decided I shouldn't. I was on my way home . . .'

I expected him to say something like 'What, you were just never going to tell me?' but actually he looked at me with such hope in his eyes it was palpable. He might be about to get away with it after all.

'I don't want anything from you,' I said, swinging my bag over my shoulder. I wondered if I should ask his surname, just in case one day my baby's life was completely fucked up by the fact they didn't have any clue how to trace their father, but I knew if I asked him he'd panic that I was going to put him on the birth certificate, or that in thirty years' time a stranger would knock on his door shouting 'Daddy!', and I figured on balance it wasn't worth it. He'd probably make up a fake one. If my child had a burning passion to find their dad in years to come it would be easy enough to check the records of who was studying Anthropology, graduating in 1996. How many Lawrences could there be? I'd help them.

I pushed my way out through the door without saying goodbye. I wondered if he might call me back, ask more questions. But he didn't.

When I think about him now I think about how young we both were, about how I'd had months to get used to the idea. I wonder if I should at least have forced my details on to him in case he ever had a change of heart. It's hard to judge him. We were kids. We both handled it badly.

My mum – who must have been shocked and disappointed beyond belief although she never showed it – offered to help me bring the baby up. Her first – and only – grandchild. But I knew if I stayed at home I'd end up there for ever. Working in the dry cleaner's where she worked too, if I was lucky. So I moved back to London, into a shared house with three of my ex-uni friends who didn't seem too freaked out by the prospect of having a baby about the place. When Ashley arrived I stayed at home and cooked and cleaned for them all in lieu of rent, like a nineteenth-century housekeeper. I found part-time work reading scripts for a couple of local theatres, which was terribly paid but it was cash in hand and I could fit the hours in whenever I got a chance. I watched my flatmates all step on to the first rungs of their chosen ladders and, even though I was envious of the fact they were making progress in their careers, I never once regretted my decision.

Dee arrives bearing gifts. That is, a bottle of wine and a French stick because the last time I made pasta for us both I didn't have any bread in and she's never let me forget it. It's actually snowing when I open the door to her.

'You're not going to walk home in this?' I say as soon as I see her.

'I've only just got here.' She gives me a hug.

'I'll call you a cab when you leave.'

'No cabs are going to be coming up here tonight. I'll be fine.'

'Jesus. Well, don't stay too late. Or you could sleep in Ashley's room.' I follow her through to the kitchen. Watch as she unswathes. Then I hang her coat, scarf, hat and two jumpers over various radiators.

'I can't really. I need clothes.'

'I can lend you something.' We're not far off from each other in size.

She looks at me. 'Holly, I love you, but I'm not wearing your knickers.'

I throw the pasta into boiling water, heat the sauce through while Dee randomly starts poking through my kitchen cupboards.

'You'll have to designate them storage space,' she says, pulling out the spiralizer I've used, maybe, twice in the three years I've had it. I take it from her.

'I know. I'll get round to it. I want that, though; put it back.' She rolls her eyes but does as I ask.

'You're in denial,' she says. I know she's joking, but I also know she's right.

I fill her in on the latest at work. 'Do you think I'm being paranoid?' I say when I get to the bit about Glen thinking my idea was Roz's. 'I mean, why would he say that?'

Dee tops up our wine glasses while I dish up the food. Smokey hops up on to one of the chairs next to us and neither of us bothers to shoo him away.

'Well . . .' She looks off into space as if she's considering. 'It could have been a genuine misunderstanding, I suppose. Bit of a coincidence, though.'

'Maybe she mentioned my story to him once and he just forgot that she said it was mine?'

I wait for her to say 'Of course' but she doesn't. 'Is that what you think happened?'

'You don't . . .' I tail off. I'm not sure I want to even give my theory a fair hearing. That I'm ready to believe it might be true. Sod it. 'You don't think – given we now know that she wanted the job – that she quizzed me about my idea so she could put it on her application form?'

I sit back and watch Dee's reaction. Of course she buys it. She's Dee. She loves a conspiracy theory.

'Oh my God,' she says. She flicks her fringe out of her eyes. 'That's it.'

'She wouldn't.' I try to remember Roz's and my conversations about which storyline I should put forward on my application. I clearly remember her saying the Morgan strand was too risky.

'The audience don't want the characters to develop too much, you know that.' We'd been walking through Acton near the studios, after picking up a sandwich. I can even remember what she was wearing – her bright green coat and orange tights. She looked like Orville's tall skinny sister. 'They think they want to watch new stories, but actually they just want a variant of the same thing over and over again. They love Morgan because she's Little Miss Perfect. They know where they stand with her.'

'She's so dull though.'

She'd sidestepped a kid on a scooter. 'I know that and you know that but the Great British Public don't care.'

I wasn't sure. I'd had a couple of conversations with Glen about pushing the boundaries and moving the show onwards rather than stagnating. But Roz was so sure of her own opinion it made me nervous. In the end I'd come down on the side of better to be a bit safe than very sorry.

I push my food around my plate. 'Oh God,' is all I can come up with.

'Only one way to find out,' Dee says with relish.

8

Which explains why I'm hanging back at work waiting for everyone to leave the next day. Actually most people have made the break early because a heavy snowstorm is predicted and so we all have to behave as if the second Ice Age has arrived, and we need to stock up on water and ready meals for the coming decade. Only Emma, always conscientious, and Juliet, who only lives round the corner and so has no fear of cancelled public transport, remain. (I remember how scathing Roz and I were when we found out she had moved close to the studios. As if she'd decided she was in it for life. No ambition beyond working on *Churchill Road*. Fucking saddo, Roz had said, laughing.)

Today has not been a good day. When I got back from a long script meeting with one of the writers – which we decided to hold in the café as it was close to lunchtime and we were both famished – there was a pink Post-it on my desk that said 'Could I speak to you this afternoon? Patricia'. Patricia is one of our original cast members. She plays the matriarch of one of the estate's biggest families and is formidable both on and off screen. Having trained at RADA (unlike anyone else in the cast) she believes herself to be a cut above the rest, and that none of us have any idea how to properly make a good drama. She regularly likes to present herself in the script department and give the most senior person she can find the benefit of her accumulated wisdom. Before, she used to hunt out Marcus. Now, word must have got through that I'm her new target. I'll be honest, she intimidates the shit out of me.

'Did you see Patricia when she came up?' I said to Emma, hoping she'd be able to give me a heads up about what her latest issue was.

Emma looked up from her computer. Pulled a sympathetic face. 'No. I've been out.'

I flicked my eyes at the silent TV screen on the wall, where the feed from the studio plays all day, to see if Patricia was involved in the scene currently being shot. Grabbed the remote and turned the sound up. There was no sign of her.

'I'll go and hunt her down, get it over with.'

'Good luck,' Emma said. 'I'll make up an excuse to come and find you if you're not back in half an hour.'

'Twenty minutes,' I said, grimacing. I made my way down the stairs and across the car park to the building that housed both the studio and the cast dressing rooms. Patricia has the biggest, a nod to her seniority. She hates being disturbed unless it's because she has to go to set that second, but I figured she had asked to see me so she must be expecting me to show up.

I checked the name on the door. Twice. And then I knocked. There was silence, so I knocked again more loudly.

There was a shout. 'Who is that?'

'It's . . . um . . . it's Holly. You wanted to see me . . .'

I waited. I could hear movement in the room and then the door was flung open, Patricia standing there in a dressing gown with an eye mask parked on top of her head. Her make-up was slightly askew. Most of the cast try and sleep on their backs if they nap, to minimize the time taken to reapply later, but clearly not Patricia. She filled the doorway. She's a big woman. Even though she must be nearly sixty she could definitely take me in a fight.

'I told Chris no disturbances,' she said, naming the runner who escorts the cast back and forth to the studio and generally scrabbles around getting them whatever they want, whenever they want it.

'Oh God. Sorry. Were you asleep? It's just you said you wanted to see me and I thought it might be urgent . . .'

'What are you talking about?' she boomed. She has a voice to match her stature. Out of the corner of my eye I could see Chris the runner hovering at the end of the corridor like a frightened rabbit.

'You left me a note . . .'

'I have no idea what you're talking about,' she said and I had the feeling she wanted to add 'you stupid girl'. 'What note?'

And then it hit me. A sickening, sinking feeling in my stomach. Juliet. I breathed in slowly.

'There was a note on my desk . . . it said you wanted to talk to me. I take it it didn't come from you?'

'Clearly not.'

'I'm sorry. I think someone must have got their wires crossed. Really sorry to have disturbed you.'

'What would I want to speak to you about?' she said accusingly, as if she wasn't the one who always initiated the conversations about the ways in which the storylines were lacking. Still, I was duty bound to be polite. Mustn't upset the talent.

'Well, I don't know . . . something in one of the scripts, I suppose . . .'

She rolled her eyes as though that was the most ridiculous idea she'd ever heard. 'And you're the new script executive, are you?'

I stammered out a yes.

'God help us,' she said, and she shut the door in my face.

I stormed past Chris without saying anything. I knew she'd probably give him a bollocking later but my mind was on other things. Back up in the department I went straight into my office and slammed the door, then got up again and stomped back into the main office.

'Did someone put a note from Patricia on my desk?' I said, glaring at Juliet.

She looked right back at me with that level gaze she has that I always find disconcerting, as if she was challenging me to accuse her. I looked away.

Roz, Lorraine and Emma all looked at me blankly. Joe was in the studio but I couldn't imagine it being his idea of a joke. Roz was the first to speak.

'What note?'

I turned back to my desk. The Post-it wasn't where I'd left it, on top of my notebook. I hunted around a little. Realized that whoever had done it had now destroyed the evidence.

'It's not there now,' I said, coming back out. 'But there was a note saying Patricia wanted to speak to me.'

'Didn't she?' Emma said, confused.

'No. She didn't know what I was on about. I looked like an absolute idiot. Not funny.'

'We were all out at lunchtime, anyone could have put it there,' Lorraine said haughtily.

'Did she lecture you about the nature of drama?' Roz said, trying to make light of it. One of Patricia's favourite sentences starts with 'When you've been in this business as long as I have you'll start to understand the nature of drama . . .' I was having none of it though.

'I've just made a total tit of myself.' I turned and walked back into my office, slamming the door behind me. I slouched down behind my desk, fuming. When I looked up everyone had their heads down working. Or at least, pretending to.

Even though I'm starting to get a bit worried about my own journey home, I'm determined to try and get a look at Roz's application. I need to see it for myself. If she wanted the job so much that she was willing to nick my ideas to try and get it. I don't want to believe it's true but it's starting to look that way. Still, I'm not sure it's worth being snowed into the office overnight for.

My commute is on the Overground direct from Acton to West Hampstead, which is usually amazingly convenient, but the whole capital comes to a standstill if there's so much as a leaf on the line. I'm just wondering if I should

71

call off my mission when Emma and Juliet start packing up at the same time. I nod at Emma's suggestion that I shouldn't stay too late, offer up a curt ''Night' to Juliet, who blanks me, and they're gone. I wander out into the main office and watch as they amble along the corridor to the stairs. We're only on the first floor so there's no lift. Downstairs is the art department, the prop store and a scenery storage area. I watch Emma and Juliet emerge side by side and pick their way gingerly along the icy path.

I have a quick check that no one else on my floor is around. There's no sign of life in either Fay's or Glen's offices. Jeremy's coat is still there but he'll be in the studio till seven, as will Joe. The other offices are deserted. I run back to the script department, click on Roz's computer and enter her password. I have no idea what she will have called her application or where she will have saved it. I scan through her downloads, keeping my eye on the door. Almost immediately I find a document labelled 'Script Exec Application', and a load of numbers. I open it, my hands shaking, but the responses to the questions are blank.

I hear a shout from downstairs: someone calling goodnight. I flick the home screen back up and jump away from the computer, trying to look casual. Through the window I can see someone – I can't tell who, they are so swaddled – walking towards the gate and home. I take a deep breath, tiptoe back to Roz's desk. I need to think of another way to find it. And then it occurs to me: she will have emailed it in. We were asked to submit to the HR department in an effort to make it look as if it was a fair fight between us and any outsiders. I bring up email, try to remember some part of the address and then, bingo, there it is. Without stopping to read any part of it I print both the accompanying letter and the form. I panic about whether I should run and grab the documents as they come off the printer, or take the time to remove the traces of my search from the desktop first. In the end I do that, taking the risk that if anyone does suddenly show up, the chances of them needing something from the print room are small. Once I've double-checked that I've closed both the email and the attachment I run and grab the printout and then I return to the computer and click on a series of Roz's favourite websites – Twitter, Facebook, Instagram, Digital Spy, a couple of holiday sites I'd seen her looking at earlier, just to bury what I've done deeper in her search history. Roz has a tendency to flick constantly between social media sites, barely pausing on one before she's on to the next, so she would never question that they would show up in her most recents.

And then I stuff the evidence deep in my bag and get out of there.

The station is almost deserted. It feels more like three in the morning than quarter to seven in the evening. As (bad) luck would have it one of the only other people there is Janet, one of the ghastly accounts duo. I keep my head down and hope she doesn't spot me, but, of course, she does. She waves an arm and then slip-slides her way over to where I'm sitting on a bench.

'It is you! I thought it was,' she booms.

She crashes down beside me. 'This is bloody unbelievable, isn't it? I had no idea it would get this bad this quickly.'

Roz's email is burning a hole in my bag. I'm thankful I haven't yet taken it out but all I want to do is get somewhere I can be on my own and study it.

'Where do you have to get to?' I ask, hoping she won't hear how loaded my question is.

'Kentish Town. How about you? I didn't know you came this way.'

Great, so now I have her for the whole journey. And I don't even want to think about the fact that I'm going to have to start trying to time my commute to avoid hers from here on in. 'West Hampstead.'

'Ooh, nice,' she says, in a way that makes me feel defensive.

'It's nearly Kilburn, really. And it's a tiny basement so . . .' I look along the track, willing the train to come, even though I know it's hopeless because the board says seven minutes. Remember that teenage game, seven minutes in heaven? Imagine the opposite of that.

I struggle to think what polite conversation we can make but all I can come up with is 'How's Lucinda's bit on the side?' and then I hate myself for asking, because I really don't want to know. Janet's round face lights up; she's delighted to fill me in.

'Hot as hell,' she says excitedly. I smile weakly. She prattles on, and I only half listen but at least it beats

74

having to think of something to say myself. From what I can gather, Hot Scott is 'ripped', 'buff' and fifteen years younger than Lucinda, a fact that seems to make Janet salivate. I'm tempted to ask her how she would feel if it was the other way round, if Lucinda was the man, drooling over a much younger woman, but I can't really be bothered to engage. Every now and then I steal a glance at the board, willing the minutes to count down until I notice that the train we are waiting for seems to have disappeared from the screen altogether, and now the next one says twenty-three minutes.

'I might try the Tube,' I say, standing up. I'm hoping she won't say she'll come with me, and thankfully she doesn't.

'I think I'll wait,' she says. 'By the time you've walked to the Tube station this one'll practically be here. And who's to say the Underground's even running?'

'I'll chance it,' I say, knowing she's right. I won't get home any quicker this way, but I might get home without strangling someone. And, besides, once I'm on my own I can kill any waiting time by reading Roz's application.

I trudge through the snow, barely able to see two feet in front of my face. When I get to the Underground station there's a man outside writing on a whiteboard, announcing that they'll be closing at half past seven – in fifteen minutes – due to the weather. I'm lucky though. There's a train about to close its doors, so I throw myself inside without even checking how far it's going. Anywhere in the right direction will do at this point.

There are only two other people in the carriage, and I can just about tell, even though they're both wrapped in scarves and hats, that I don't know either of them. I pull my gloves off and reach into my bag for the printout.

I remember that the section asking for a storyline idea was towards the back, along with the request that applicants continue on a separate sheet if they didn't have enough space. I find it easily. And there it is . . . my story about good girl Morgan going off the rails because of exam pressure. It's beat by beat how I explained it to Roz, even with some things in there that she advised me to take out if I were going to submit it myself.

To be honest, the main emotion I feel is confusion. Is that an emotion? I'm not sure, but anyway. Why would she need to do this? In so far as I have always been able to tell, Roz is good at her job. She's a natural at storytelling, and even though she can sometimes err on the side of being lazy I've always thought that was because she knows she'll always pull something out of the bag when it counts, rather than because she doesn't care. For all her cynicism I think she loves what she does.

I flick idly through the rest of the form. A couple of the answers bear a strong resemblance to the responses I mulled over with her. But then those questions are so generic that's almost bound to be the case whoever is responding. I lean back in my seat. Tell myself she didn't get the job anyway, so what does it matter? But the idea that she would blatantly fish for information about what I was putting on the form – even persuade me to change what I was intending to write – so she could use my ideas on hers make me furious. It's just so . . . sneaky. Why didn't she tell me she was going for the job too and then we could have helped each other? Or decided not to? Either way would have been fine.

I call Dee on my walk from the station. Tell her what I've discovered.

'Shit,' she says. 'You don't think . . .?'

I will her not to say it. I don't want to even acknowledge that it could be true. That the person who is really smarting that they didn't get my job isn't Juliet. It's Roz.

9

'So,' I say. 'This is weird . . .'

Roz fills the kettle, turns to me. 'What is?'

It's the next morning and I have basically followed her to the office kitchen because this is the grown-up way in which I have decided to handle the Great Storyline Robbery. Avoid full-on confrontation at all costs. I know Roz well enough by now to guess that my telling her what I've seen on her application form would lead to a screaming match, followed by a campaign of all-out hostility and a phone call to HR accusing me of accessing her private documents. I've seen her go on the defensive before. She's like a wounded animal, lashing out in every direction. I remember she used to be quite friendly with one of the make-up artists until they asked her not to keep helping herself to bits of their kit when she was down visiting. Roz went crazy, accused her of being jealous, bad-mouthed her to anyone who would listen. People who have been her friend become public enemy number one overnight. I don't have it in me to deal with it.

'I mentioned that Morgan story to Glen and it was like he already knew it. He thought it was yours.'

I'm not imagining it: there's a split second where she

looks caught out. But she covers it up pretty quickly as she rifles through the teabags and selects a peppermint.

'Why is that weird? He barely knows what day it is half the time.' Roz is not one of Glen's biggest fans. She thinks the fault for the declining ratings lies squarely with him and his decision making. There's no way I can push the issue without giving myself away, but her expression is enough to let me know that she hasn't had some kind of memory-erasing mind meltdown that left her believing that my storyline was actually hers. Not that I ever thought she had, obviously. But it's good to have it confirmed.

I force a laugh and try to cover my tracks. 'True. I must've mentioned it to him at some point. I just can't remember. I'm getting old.'

I wait while she dunks the teabag and takes it out.

'How's life?' I ask in an effort to change the subject.

'Hugh's taken on a big high-profile client and he's fighting a huge shitstorm in the press about something . . . He's been working twenty-four hours a day.'

'Not David Summers?' David Summers is a much loved actor, famed for his family values and clean-cut living. Rumours abound that he's also the issuer of a super-injunction after news reports of a lurid cocktail of illicit sex, drugs and all-round bad behaviour by an anonymous star hit the papers last week.

Roz raises her eyebrows. 'It's meant to be top secret.'

'I knew it was him!' I can't help it, I'm impressed. Not just by her proximity to superstardom, but because Hugh really must be at the top of the PR game to have attracted a client like him. 'Have you met him?'

'I haven't said that's who it is,' she says, but she's beaming a conspiratorial smile at me. 'And no, I haven't. Not yet.'

'Blimey, though.'

'Don't tell anyone.'

'I won't. Of course not.'

We walk back towards the department. I bite my tongue to stop me from asking all the questions her revelation has made me want to ask. Like 'Did he really do all those things he's supposed to have done?' Obviously we rub shoulders with minor celebrities all the time but where David Summers is a regular at the Oscars, our cast are more likely to show up at the opening of a nail salon.

'We are OK, aren't we?' I say eventually. I want her to reassure me. To tell me something that makes me think my suspicions were wrong. 'I mean, you're really all right with me getting the job?'

She looks at me and if I didn't know better I'd say she was genuinely confused about why I would ask that. 'Of course I am.'

'OK, good. If you had a problem you'd tell me . . .?'

'What are you trying to say?' she says.

'Nothing. I just . . . So long as we're all right.'

'Stop being so cryptic, Holly,' she says with a smile, but it doesn't reach her eyes.

Roz and I usually have lunch together any day we're both free. So, when it gets to ten to one and we're both still working at our desks, despite my burgeoning misgivings about her, I send her an email: 'Food?'

From where I now sit I can see her at her desk opposite my former, now empty, one, her back to me. She's looking at her screen but at what I can't tell. Then I watch as she stands up and reaches for her coat. Smiling, I do the same. I'm shoving an arm into a sleeve, tugging my hand past the ripped bit of lining that snares me every time, when I see her walk over to Lorraine who is also in the process of swathing up for the cold.

I stuff my phone into my pocket and head for the door, tugging my gloves on just as I see the two of them walk out together without acknowledging me. Roz laughs an exaggerated laugh and I think I see her give the tiniest glance back in my direction to check I've clocked it. I turn left and head for the toilets. Shut myself in a cubicle and sit on the lid.

I still have scripts of my own to manage, at least until my probation period is up, so when I head back to the office I ask Emma to pick me up a sandwich when she goes out, so that I can get on with making notes on a pair that have come in. She looks at me a bit strangely, as if she's wondering why I've put my coat on just to take it off again but, being Emma, she doesn't say anything.

'It's cold,' I say stupidly, indicating my layers, and then I sit back down at my desk, coat still on, until she leaves.

I'm finding it hard to concentrate. Usually I love getting a first draft. That feeling that you might be about to read something amazing (often evaporated by page seven, when you realize nothing makes any sense and you don't believe a word that comes out of anyone's mouth), but not today. My mind keeps wandering.

Maybe Roz didn't get my email. Maybe she thought I was busy and she didn't want to disturb me. I get up, walk over to her desk and click on her desktop mouse. Her inbox is up on the screen. The message from me no longer in bold, because it's been read.

I take a deep breath to steady myself. I suddenly feel like the unpopular girl at school. The one everyone decided to pick on that term. I remind myself that this comes with the territory. But Roz was the last person I expected it from.

Here's the thing about Roz. She can be quite mean. But she gets away with it because she's always funny. I often laugh first and then think perhaps I shouldn't have. To be honest I'm in awe of the way she doesn't give a fuck what people think of her. It's so unlike me. But I've always believed she has a good heart underneath. That – barbs in the name of humour aside – she would never really want to hurt anyone.

I force myself to concentrate on one of the first drafts, scrawling notes in the margins as I go. It's not just criticism. For every comment that something isn't working in the script I need to come up with a suggestion of how to put it right. It's a lot of work, but it's the bit of my job I really love. The bit I'll really miss, I realize, once my promotion is made permanent. If it is. Which it will be. I can't even let myself think it might not be.

By two o'clock, when Roz and Lorraine come bouncing back into the office, I've finished the first one and am on to the second and I'm feeling much better just by being in control of work.

Five minutes later Roz appears in the doorway. 'I only just saw your email,' she says, pulling a sad face. 'Sorry. You looked as if you were working hard, so I didn't want to bother you.'

'No problem,' I say with a smile, knowing what she's saying is a lie. 'I was.'

10

'West Hampstead near Tube/Overground/Thameslink. Lovely furnished room available for single quiet professional. Share kitchen/bathroom with owner. £700 pcm.'

Dee stops me from adding 'no one under 30' or 'no psychos', telling me I can use those filters but only secretly after I've met them and judged for myself. It's the blandest possible ad but I tell myself bland is good. I want my tenant to be bland. I want her to be a little mouse who is too scared to ever come out of her room and who goes to bed at ten. I want my space. I want my privacy. As Dee points out, I want to have my cake and eat it too.

The room is ready. Painted a calming but neutral sandy shade. Furnished with Ashley's old divan bed, bedside table, chest of drawers and a small table with two chairs that I hope will encourage them to eat in their room. The curtains have been washed and pressed. The window is on the street side, with a not-so-lovely view of the basement well, the stairs and the bins. But I'm going to sweep out there (first time in . . . well, the first time) and maybe put some geraniums in pots along the sill. God knows how long they'll last because the sun never reaches that spot, but I'll tell whoever takes the room that they're their responsibility so they won't blame me when they die.

Dee and I are halfway through painting the hallway. I've already finished the bathroom and cleared some space in the mirrored cupboard. The flat is starting to look like a different, much lighter space and I've begun to wonder why I didn't do this years ago. Not the lodger bit. The painting and decluttering. I don't think I've redecorated anywhere since we moved in three years ago. After this I'm going to tackle the kitchen and the living room and then I'm thinking I might as well do my own room because I imagine I'm going to be spending a lot more time in there soon. Ashley's boxes are still piled up waiting for her to come and collect them. And then, once that's done, I'll take a photo of the space looking as big as I can make it look, and the ad will go on SpareRoom.

Dee looks up from where she is cutting in round a doorway, brush in hand. 'Have you still got Roz's application? Let me just see how close it really is to your story.'

'No, Dee. It's bad enough that I've looked at it . . .'

She flicks at her fringe. 'No, it's so bad that you've looked at it that it wouldn't even register if I did too. Besides, she'll never know.'

Reluctantly I head into the kitchen and find the form under a pile of junk mail, where I'd hidden it to make myself feel better. I hand it over. Dee wipes a paint smear from her hand on to the old T-shirt she's wearing before she takes it.

'Blah blah,' she says as she reads down the first page. '"Age forty", lives in Holland Park . . . nice.'

'Hugh is some kind of mega-successful PR.'

She carries on scanning through. Looks up at me.

'Didn't you say she's from Whitehawk?'

'Yes. Why?'

She waves the form at me. 'It's just that it says here she went to Brighton College. That's like a super-posh private school. Maybe she got a scholarship.'

I snatch it back. 'No, she went to the local comprehensive. She's always banging on about how much she hates private schools.'

'That doesn't mean she didn't go to one.'

'We've actually talked about it though. How similar our schools were . . . Are you sure Brighton College isn't, like, some crappy tech where she might have done her A Levels or something?' I know I'm clutching at straws.

Dee takes the form back, points at the dates. 'Nineteen eighty-nine to ninety-six. That's a long time to be taking her A Levels. And she started them at, what, eleven? I know people who went there. It's posh with a capital P. And a capital O, S and H.'

'Why would she lie about that?'

Dee shrugs. 'Chip on her shoulder?'

I sit down on the floor, lean against the radiator. 'I mean, wouldn't you just say "I got a scholarship" or even just avoid talking about school altogether? Not make up a whole load of stuff about going to a comprehensive? She's always made it sound like a really rough one too. She brings it up all the time in story conferences. Do you remember that story we did about the sisters who kept sneaking back into the school at night to sleep there, because their mum was a prostitute and she used to bring her clients home? She said that happened to a girl in her class.'

'Maybe she thinks it gives her more credibility with the writers?' At the centre of *Churchill Road* is the failing school that most of our characters either attend or work at. And it's true that when we're arguing about storylines there's always an element of 'I know that world better than you do, so I'm right' from some of the writers. Even though most of them now live in multi-million-pound houses and their kids are privately educated.

'God knows.'

Dee picks up her brush and carries on painting. 'It's sad,' she says. 'I wonder what else she's lied about.'

'Do you think she hid those scripts I couldn't find?' I say a few moments later. 'And sent the flowers . . . the note from Patricia?' The more I think about it the more it makes sense. 'Oh God, I basically accused Juliet outright.'

'Stranger things have happened,' Dee says. 'I mean, if she wants your job it's in her interest that you don't look too impressive during your probation period.'

It's too awful to contemplate. Roz is my friend, my ally. 'Shit. It's her, isn't it?'

Dee pulls a sympathetic face. 'It's looking very likely.'

Roz is holding court at the weekly department meeting. She's dyed the tips of her white-blonde hair pink over the weekend and spiked it up with what looks like a whole tube of hairspray. She's telling a story about a restaurant opening she and Hugh went to last night in Mayfair. It sounds fabulous; I just don't know why she's chosen this moment to tell everyone about it. I find myself listening to her intently, trying to spot any trace of a more rarefied accent under her street-cred tones, but it's impossible to tell. And then I remember that I'm supposed to be running this meeting.

'OK,' I say as loudly as I can bring myself to. Once again Glen is watching me.

Roz carries on. 'And while we were having dessert Tom himself came over to see if we'd enjoyed the meal,' she says, name-dropping the celebrity chef whose new venture this is.

Lorraine gasps. 'Oh my God! What was he –?'

'Lorraine!' I bark and she stops dead mid-sentence. 'That's enough chatting. Let's get on with it.'

I catch, out of the corner of my vision, her rolling her eyes in Roz's direction. I choose to ignore it.

On the way out afterwards I hang back when I see Juliet is the last to leave.

'I owe you an apology,' I say, looking at the floor. 'I thought . . . well, it doesn't matter but the point is I jumped to a wrong conclusion. And I should never have spoken to you like I did, even if I'd been right. Which I wasn't. I don't think.'

She waits for me to finish. I half expect her to give me a hard time, but instead she just says: 'OK. Is that all?'

And walks out before I can say yes.

I'm staring at my computer. At my email to be precise. A couple of minutes ago a message from Glen popped up.

'Sorry, is this a serious question?' I haven't emailed Glen today. I haven't had any dealings with him except for the department meeting. Except that apparently I have. Because scrolling up from his sparse six words I find that they're a response to something sent by me. By my email account, at least. Timed at seven minutes past one – when I was on my way to the café to get a sandwich.

'Just had to say how hot you're looking today. New beard oil? X'.

I break out in a cold sweat. Check through my sent emails to make sure this is the only one. Then I compose a response to Glen: 'Sorry, that email was meant for some-one else!' I consider adding 'LOL' or even 'Ha!' but I worry that'll make me sound even more vacuous than I must already do. Then I wonder if I should say something like 'It was a joke, obviously' so that he doesn't think I send emails like that to people seriously, but that might make the whole thing feel like a bigger deal, as if I'm pro-testing too much. In the end I keep it short and to the point. Press send before I can overthink it any more. I make a note to ask Emma to show me how to change my password. It's on my list of 'things a woman my age really ought to know how to do, but has never bothered to get around to'.

I look out into the general office. Everyone bar Joe is there, ostensibly getting on with work. The harsh fluores-cent lights that Juliet always insists we have on to enable her to read without straining her eyes give everyone a ghostly pallor. Whenever she goes out one of the others always turns them off, leaving just the individual desk lamps casting moody pools. Roz is typing, the picture of innocence. I think about stomping over there and accusing her but she'd just deny it and make a scene that Glen would probably hear from his office down the hall. She'd find a way to make me look worse than I already do. I stare at my screen for a while, seething, waiting for a response from Glen but there's nothing.

I spend the rest of the afternoon furiously collating everything that I have so far for the twice-yearly story conference that is fast approaching. An email went out last week inviting all the current writers, and asking them to submit story ideas in advance. I've already prepared a document highlighting any looming gaps we have coming up, and identifying any characters that are light on material. The story conferences often end up being the place where we identify the ones who are falling off the radar, and – obviously with Glen having the last word – earmark them for possible death or a sudden decision to move away.

I'm halfway through updating the list of all the cast contract dates, along with the details of those actors who have already asked for time off in December to do panto, even though it's only March. Panto pays far better than we do. They all want to do it, but it means writing a character out for nearly three months, so we only allow one actor per year the opportunity. Ever wondered why a character randomly announced a trip to see a long-lost relative in Australia, out of nowhere, in January? That'll be because we'd had to release the actor to be Widow Twanky from the end of the previous November. In all honesty it's a massive pain, and it always causes rows. I think about suggesting to Glen that we just say no to all requests, but I know there would be a mutiny.

A few stories have started to trickle in – on first look nothing very interesting, but we're duty bound to discuss them all so as not to bruise any writer's ego. I write an email to all the editors reminding them that the date is looming, that any ideas they want to contribute will be welcome.

And then I write up a version of my Morgan breakdown story and file it with the others. I want to make the point that it's mine.

Roz, Lorraine and Joe are sitting outside the local café that we all patronize because it's the only one with decent food within walking distance. There's either that, the pub or the greasy spoon and you need to be a serious gambler to risk the odds of food poisoning by eating in there too often. Even though the snow has melted it's still freezing and they're huddled in their coats and scarves while Roz vapes. On second glance I notice that Lorraine is vaping too. This is new. I've never even seen her smoke. She's also wearing big garish turquoise earrings. Roz's own mini-me. I'm tempted to walk straight past but I'm hungry, and it's cold and I don't see why I should have to go somewhere else just because I feel uncomfortable.

'Hey,' Roz says, waving at me. 'Come and join us.' I notice Lorraine shoot her a look.

'Bit cold,' I say, forcing a smile and heading inside. I pay for my sandwich, and when I go back outside the conversation suddenly halts, which clearly means they've been talking about me. I feel the traitorous prick of tears behind my eyes, tell myself this comes with the territory: I knew when I applied for the job that things would change if I got it. Maybe not this much but still . . . I hold my head up high, keep walking.

'See you later,' I say as I pass.

'Bye,' they chorus and then, when I'm a few steps down the road, I hear Lorraine say 'Whoops' and then laughter.

11

Ashley has a couple of days off work so she drives up from Bristol, and on Thursday, when I get home from work, there she is unpacking all the boxes Dee and I packed up for her and spreading the contents over the floor of her room. As always when I see my daughter I'm filled with a rush of love so strong it almost knocks me over.

'What time did you get here?' I say, grabbing her into a big hug. Her tiny rounded stomach is just about showing on her still slim body if you know what you're looking for.

She plants a kiss on my cheek. 'About an hour ago.'

'More to the point, what are you doing? Dee and I spent ages sorting all that stuff out.'

'Mum, I don't want half this crap, honestly. You've put my school report cards in here. And that medal I won for gymnastics when I was eight.'

I pick the offending items up from the floor. 'Well, we can't throw them away. One day you'll wish you had them.'

She looks round at the mess. 'Maybe I should get one of those storage-unit things.'

'Don't be silly. I don't want you to have that expense. Just take what you can and I'll worry about the rest.'

She picks up one of the now empty boxes and throws a few things in. 'That's about it. Honestly, anything else you can chuck unless you think it's a family heirloom. It looks amazing in here, by the way.'

'Well, it did,' I say, laughing. I've been painting the rest of the flat like a demon in the evenings and early mornings in an effort not to have time to dwell on how things are going at work. Consequently I've finished everything bar the kitchen and my own bedroom. 'Come on, let me feed you up.' She looks tired and a bit run-down, but I'm her mother, I would think that.

'I was hoping you'd say that. I'm starving.'

I am pathetically grateful to have someone to cook for other than myself so I fuss around with salmon fillets while Ashley makes a salad.

'How's Ryan?' I'm very fond of Ashley's boyfriend, even if I sometimes wish he had loftier aspirations than working his way up the ranks of a supermarket management scheme. Who am I to judge? He's a nice boy. He's definitely one of the good guys.

'He's OK,' she says. Like all parents, above everything I want my child to be happy. I tick that worry off my mental checklist.

'Do you want me to come back up when you're interviewing possible tenants?' she says later when we're eating. Smokey – who is not allowed on the kitchen table – is on the kitchen table. I don't have the heart to push him off. He's Ashley's cat really. She chose him from the Mayhew when he was the tiniest runt in a litter of tiny runts that had been found in a box in a car park. They used to sleep together every night until she left home, and I'm pretty sure I know where he'll bed down tonight.

'Well, I'd never say no to the idea of you coming home but Dee's offered to sit in on the interviews with me. You know what she's like. She'll assume they're all serial killers, which is probably a good thing on this occasion.'

'Good, because you'd end up picking someone because they complimented your decor or what you were wearing.'

'I'm glad you have such faith in me. Since when was I such a pushover?'

She pretends to think. 'Well, let me see. There was that time when I was six and I wanted to get out of going to Brownies so I told you you were the world's best cook just before I asked you, or when I wanted a rescue kitten for my seventh birthday but I knew you'd say we couldn't have one, so I told Charlie's mum you were the kindest person to animals ever, in front of you . . .'

'. . . and then we got Smokey. Oh my God, you've been playing me my whole life.'

'Of course,' she says, grinning. 'It's my job.'

She asks me how work is since I got promoted and I tell her the edited version. The version where everything is going smoothly and the people who work for me all respect me and support me. I don't want her to worry.

'See,' she says, beaming. 'I knew you'd be brilliant.'

After we've eaten we change into our PJs. Ashley emerges with her hair in a high ponytail, face scrubbed of make-up, looking about fourteen again. Well, fourteen and pregnant. We snuggle up on the sofa, me with a glass of wine and her with a fizzy fruit drink, the cat between us, and watch *While You Were Sleeping,* her favourite film. It's about as perfect an evening as I can imagine.

In the morning I take her in a cup of tea before I leave for work. She'll be gone by the time I get home. She's curled up on her side with Smokey tucked into the bend of her knees. I'm tempted to leave them to it, even though I promised her I'd wake her. I tap her shoulder half-heartedly and she unfurls like she's the sleepy cat.

'What time is it?'

'Quarter past eight,' I say. 'I'm just leaving. Drive carefully.'

'Mmmm,' she says, and I have no doubt she's going to go straight back to sleep when I go. I'm glad. 'Love you.'

'You too.' I pull her into a hug. 'Text me when you get back home.'

'So . . .' Glen says. We're sitting in his office. I still have my coat on. He nabbed me as I walked past on my way in. My first thought was that he was going to ask me about another email I'd sent him. Maybe this time asking him where he gets his eyebrows shaped (I'm sure he does), so I'm struggling to look at him. Thankfully he has other things on his mind.

'We should start thinking about whether Lorraine is up to the job once your probation is up.'

I try to ignore the fact that he says 'once' and not 'if'. I know he's probably just being diplomatic. 'To being made editor?' I say, which is a stupid question because what else would he mean?

He nods. 'We'll need to replace you and the whole idea of the trainee scheme is to give them a break if they're up to it.'

All of my instincts are screaming no. I have no idea really at this point whether Lorraine would make a competent editor or not, but from what I've seen of her lately the idea of promoting her fills me with horror.

'Wouldn't we have to advertise?'

'Not if we're just removing trainee from her job description I don't think.'

I make a mental note to check with HR if this is the case. 'Right . . .' I say slowly.

Glen leans forward in his chair, picks up his flat white from the table. Takes a long sip. 'You have doubts?'

I have to consider carefully before I reply. The last thing I would ever want him to think is that this is personal. 'No. Not doubts. I just don't know what I think yet. I haven't crossed over with her much. It's Roz she's been shadowing.'

'OK, well, there's no mad rush. Keep an eye on her over the next couple of weeks and let me know your thoughts. Your call.'

I smile and stand up. I need to get out of there and process this. 'Great. Will do.'

Lorraine has moved her things to my old desk opposite Roz, and the two of them are sitting there cackling away about something when I walk in. Joe is bent over a script, reading; Emma is typing furiously. Juliet, I assume, is in

97

the studio. We've been doing a good job of avoiding one another since my apology. Or, at least, I've been avoiding her. I can't face her condescending tone, her look of righteous indignation.

I feel a ridiculous need to let them all know I'm not just swanning in late, so as I hang up my coat and scarf I turn to Emma with an exaggerated eye roll and say, 'Glen nobbled me.'

'I saw you in there,' she says sympathetically. 'Do you want a coffee?'

'Definitely. Thanks.'

'Ooh, me too,' Roz says loudly.

'And me, if you're making,' Lorraine echoes. I have to stop myself from saying that I don't think the trainee should be asking the department assistant to make their coffee.

'Sure,' Emma says. 'Milk and sugar?'

'Yes, and two,' Lorraine says. Not even a please or thank you. I shut the door to my glass cube so I don't have to listen to her and Roz chatter.

I need to show Glen that he can rely on my judgement. That I'm not a flake who sends him weird, inappropriate email messages out of nowhere. I stick my head out into the main office. Wait for a break in Roz and Lorraine's incessant gossiping.

'Roz, have you got a sec?'

She looks round. 'Sure.'

She pulls down her purple jumper as she stands. She's carefully mismatched it with a bright green skirt, purple tights and green ankle boots. Garish green plastic ear-rings dangle from her lobes. She pushes a hand through the pink-tipped spikes of her hair.

We've barely spoken since I found out she'd applied for my job. I don't know how to be around her at the moment so I've avoided her as much as I can, claiming busyness in the run-up to the conference. She flops into the chair opposite my desk.

'You OK?'

'Good,' I say. I want to try, as much as possible, to keep the conversation to work. 'I just wanted to have a chat about Lorraine. See how you thought she was doing –'

She interrupts before I can even finish. 'Oh, she's great. Really picking it up fast, I think.'

Well, I knew she wasn't about to say anything critical. 'Has she done any eps on her own yet?'

'Are you thinking she might get your old job? Because I think she'd be fab—'

Now it's my turn to interrupt. I don't want Roz rushing straight to Glen to sing Lorraine's praises. 'We haven't even thought about that yet. I just wanted to get myself up to speed.'

'Right. Well, I was going to let her take the lead on the batch that are just about to come in. I'll keep an eye on her, obviously.'

I feel as if I'll never get a true picture of Lorraine's abil-ities if I just take Roz's word for it. She has a hidden agenda, a vested interest in making sure her acolyte comes across well. 'Actually I was thinking I'd get her to give notes on my latest lot of first drafts.' My intention is to give her the scripts one morning and ask her to give me her thoughts that afternoon. That way Roz won't be able to help her out so easily. It'll be all her own work. And I truly want to be fair. If it looks as if Lorraine has the makings of being a great editor then I don't want my personal feelings to render me blind to that.

Roz looks a bit put out. 'Oh. We're in a bit of a rhythm.'

'She can still stay shadowing you. I just wanted to let you know I'm going to be asking her to do something extra, that's all.'

Roz shrugs. 'Fine by me.'

'Great. Thanks.'

It must be obvious that the conversation is over but she stays put, legs flopped over the arm of the chair, green boots swinging.

'Thank fuck it's nearly the weekend. Do you have any plans?' Roz and I used to while away hours like this, idly chit-chatting. I don't really feel like it now if I'm being honest, but I'm not sure how to get rid of her without looking like I'm being offish. More than anything I find it hard to deal with her pretending everything is still fine between us. That we're still friends. That she's not trying to trip me up.

'Painting my kitchen and bedroom,' I say. 'That's the last big thing I need to do before someone can move in.'

'Fab. So did you decide on what to put in the ad in the end?'

I find the website on my phone and read it out to her.

'Do you think that hints at "quiet female with no desire to socialize with me" enough?'

She laughs. 'No. But that's what the interviews are for. What's it on? Gumtree?'

'SpareRoom initially. I'll widen it out if I don't find anyone.'

She yawns loudly, lifting her arms above her head. 'God, I'm bored. Don't you think Emma looks like Velma from *Scooby-Doo* today?'

I look across. She's spot on. Emma has a shapeless brown fringed bob and is wearing an equally shapeless mustard-coloured roll-neck jumper today. She just needs the glasses. I'm not in the mood for encouraging Roz's snipey comments though, however accurate or funny. So I just ignore it. 'What are you up to at the weekend?'

'Not much. Dinner tomorrow night at Scott's.' She gives me a big smile. 'Otherwise I have to pin Hugh down to plan our trip. Ooh, that reminds me I must book some time off. We're thinking of going to Italy. Portofino maybe, or Taormina in Sicily. Hugh knows a great hotel there with a suite that has its own pool on the roof. Oh, am I supposed to check with you now?'

'I suppose so. Any time's fine. Just not in the run-up to the story conference.'

'Well, that's, like, two weeks away so I don't think that'll be a problem. Even I can't organize the holiday of a lifetime that quick. I'll check with him and let you know.'

'Sure. I should probably . . .' I indicate a pile of scripts on my desk. Hope she takes the hint. Thankfully she does. She flicks her legs off the arm of the chair. Stands.

'Later.'

I'm eating my sandwich lunch at my desk. Emma is hovering in my doorway, looking anxious.

'Shall I tell him to go away?'

'No. Just . . . I don't understand why it wasn't in my diary . . .'

She colours red as she always does when she's put on the spot. 'Me neither. I remember putting it in . . .'

Apparently there's a man waiting in reception who has an appointment to see me. His name – Mark Walters – rings a bell. I'm pretty sure he's a would-be writer who sent me a sample script. About a month ago, before I got my promotion even, I gave Emma a list of five or six potentially interesting new people and asked her to set up meetings with them, spread out over the next couple of months. We all do it periodically. The show eats up writers and there's always kudos to be had if you discover a new talent.

'I know. It was definitely in there at one point.'

'Well, I didn't delete it,' she says defensively. Emma isn't usually defensive so she must feel as if I'm accusing her.

'I didn't say you did. Neither did I.' Someone did though. My diary can be accessed either via Emma's or my computer, and we all know who has the password to mine. I remind myself I need to change it.

'I'll ring down and get them to tell him you're running another fifteen minutes late. And then I'll dig out his stuff and you can have a quick look.'

Luckily at this point Mark needs me more than I need him, so he's unlikely to kick up a fuss or stomp out saying he has another appointment elsewhere, and even if he did it would be his loss, not mine. That's hardly the point though.

'Thanks.'

She goes off and a few minutes later there's a ping as an email comes in from her. 'He's fine. Here's his CV and script report.'

I start reading through. We get so many scripts submitted that it's impossible to remember who wrote what without detailed notes. I take deep slow breaths, trying to calm myself down.

'Can I speak to you for a minute?' Lorraine is at my door. She didn't even knock.

'Not now. In about an hour.'

'It won't take a second.' She doesn't move, just hovers there.

'I said not now. I have to read this through,' I snap.

'Fine,' she says sulkily. 'I only asked.'

'Come back after my meeting,' I say, trying to moderate my irritation. 'And shut the door please.'

In the end, of course, Mark is none the wiser. I avoid talking specifics about his script and he's just happy to be there, to have got a foot in the door. He's knowledgeable about the show and insightful about the characters and he seems as if he would be easy to work with. According to my notes I had a reservation about some of his dialogue being a bit wooden but I decide to add his name to the list of possibles for our yearly mentor scheme anyway. He'll be able to prove himself or not.

As soon as he's left I ring through to Emma asking her to pop in. She clearly thinks I'm going to tell her off, because she looks even paler than usual (Emma is one of those people who always looks as if she's just been found after living under a rock her whole life, as if she's never even seen the sun).

'How did it go?' she says with a quiver in her voice.

'What? Oh. Yes. Fine. I need you to help me change the password on my computer.'

'Oh. Of course.' She comes round to my side of the desk. 'You just need to do this, look.' She fiddles about a bit and I don't really concentrate. 'What do you want to change it to?'

I need to come up with something Roz won't guess but not so random that I'll never remember it myself. I decide on Margaret – Ashley's middle name, after my mum – and twenty-four, the number of the house I grew up in. Let's see her work that out.

'You mustn't give this to anyone. I mean it – anyone.'

'As if I would,' she says. 'Do you think someone's been accessing your diary? Is that what this is about?'

'I don't know. A few odd things have happened.' I don't want to tell her my suspicions. Not that I don't trust her, but it feels a bit unprofessional to involve her in whatever is going on. And she doesn't ask, which I'm grateful for. I'm sure if I were in her shoes I'd want to know the gossip.

'I'll check through all your emails and make sure there's nothing else that's gone astray.'

'Thanks.'

'Do you want a coffee first?'

'Please,' I say gratefully.

She's no sooner out of the door than Lorraine is in. I stifle my irritation. Fake a smile.

'Is now a better time?'

She sits down opposite me before I can say yes or no.

'Apparently,' I say. I can't help myself.

'I just wanted to say I'm interested in the position. If you're going to replace your old job.'

'Right.' Of course Roz has mentioned it to her. 'Well, we haven't decided what to do yet —'

She interrupts. 'You'll need another editor though, won't you?'

'Probably,' I say. 'But we're talking about restructuring the whole department so who knows at this stage?' We're not, but she's not to know that.

She looks a bit taken aback. 'Oh. I don't see how we could manage with only three editors.'

'Like I said. Nothing's been decided yet.' I get a tiny stab of satisfaction from the fact I've taken the wind out of her sails. Even if it's only temporarily. 'But it's good that you've registered your interest. Thanks.'

I look down at my desk as if I'm getting back to work,

effectively saying 'Chat's over'. Thankfully she takes the hint.

'OK. See you later.'

'Yep,' I say, not looking up.

I get a text from Ashley at lunchtime: *Not left yet, don't panic* and one at half five saying *Just got home xxx*. When I get back to the flat I find that she has painted my bedroom walls. It's a bit patchy and her edges leave a lot to be desired, and she's used the pale yellow that was meant for the kitchen instead of the relaxing sagey green I'd chosen, but the gesture absolutely floors me. I burst into tears standing there in my coat and scarf.

12

Later in the evening I finally get up the courage to click on SpareRoom to see what the responses to my advert are. I log into the site and see that there are two. Actually, there are five but three of them have messaged already to say they've found somewhere else. The first of the hopefuls is a man, well, a boy, of twenty-two. He looks perfectly nice but I just can't imagine sharing my space with a lad whose mum probably still makes his packed lunch. I know it's unfair, and a massive assumption, but I can't help thinking I'll end up cleaning up after him. I decide there's no point meeting him for now.

The second is much more hopeful. A thirty-four-year-old divorcee called Susanna looking for a new start. She works in a radio station as the receptionist so, who knows, we could even have things in common. I stare at her photo – smiling, pleasant, relaxed against a backdrop of what looks like a pub garden – and try to imagine if we might get on. It's worth a try. I send her a message asking if she would like to come and view the property one evening next week. That way I have a couple more days to see who else pops up.

I spend a while browsing through the profiles of people who are looking for rooms to rent but it just seems too odd to contact a stranger out of the blue and ask them if they want to come and live with me, so I close the page down.

I'm meeting an old school-gate mum friend, Clare, later at the Vue in Finchley Road, but not until eight because the film – some dystopian future nightmare Oscar contender – doesn't start till twenty past.

I have a quick shower and put on a happy face. I'm really fond of Clare; I've known her for seventeen years and we regularly have a drink or an evening at the cinema or theatre – she's another single mum, and we bonded on our first day of dropping our little ones off at primary school. Ashley and Clare's son Charlie have been friends on and off ever since (the off being after they decided to take their relationship to a whole other level when they were fifteen. Clare and I were already choosing hats when it all went wrong because Ashley decided she liked another boy better. They didn't speak for a year after that) but we don't confide. It's not that sort of friendship. It's light and easy and she's probably exactly who I need to see this evening.

On Saturday morning I lie in for a while because Clare and I went for a pizza and a few glasses of wine after the film (which was dire, by the way. I almost fell asleep. Or maybe I actually did. I remember her nudging me at one point so I may have been snoring). I snuggle under the covers with a coffee and the cat and look to see if I have any new SpareRoom responses. This morning there are three more: Carolyn 27, Lenny 36 and Pete 52. I don't know why I'm being so ageist but there's just something too sad to contemplate about a fifty-two-year-old man wanting to rent my tiny basement bedroom. Where has he been up till now? I assume in the throes of a traumatic divorce that has seen him have to leave the marital home and his beloved children. Or, worse, with his old mum till she keeled over and died in the middle of doing his ironing. I know I shouldn't be so judgemental but it's my room so I figure I'm allowed. Pete is off the list.

Carolyn lists her likes as *TOWIE* and tanning. Her picture shows her pouting through huge – I assume fake – lips, under an avalanche of huge – I assume fake – blonde tresses. I know I'm being a snob but I can't. I just can't. I don't dismiss her completely, but I put her down as a last resort.

Lenny is a branch manager for a large chain of soup and sandwich takeaway shops. He's into Scandi noir and fitness. He also looks very smiley in his picture – I imagine everyone does, however much it pains them – so despite my nervousness about sharing with a man I message him. Then I take screen shots of his and Susanna the divorcee's profiles and email them to Dee with the header 'Either of these look like psychos??'

Susanna has replied to my message to say she would love to come and see the room and would Tuesday evening work? I send Dee another email asking if it suits her – even though Susanna doesn't look the type to cosh me over the head and steal all my money. She replies within minutes: 'I have two words: Ted and Bundy. And yes, Tuesday is fine.' By which I assume she means that Ted Bundy didn't look like a serial killer. Except that, as he was one, maybe he is exactly what a serial killer looks like. Actually, I think that's her point. Anyway, Susanna, or Lenny, would have to take on me and Dee at the same time and she's pretty feisty when she's cornered, let me tell you.

I get up to make myself more coffee, head back to bed. My bedroom faces the back of the house, towards the tiny peaceful patio garden. I open the curtains and let in the watery morning sunlight, listening to the birds ramp it up now the bad weather is over. I think about sitting out there once the spring warms up but I now can't picture it without seeing Susanna or Lenny sat out there next to me, chatting loudly to one of their friends on the phone or even just drumming on the arm of their seat. I feel irrationally cross with them both. Who do they think they are, ruining my quiet idyll? And then it hits me: what if this is the last weekend I have the flat to myself?

I feel restless. Dee and Gavin have gone up to see his mum in Birmingham for the weekend. I could ring another friend, suggest doing something, but I can't really face the veil of pretence that everything is fine that I feel compelled to wear with everyone other than my bestie. I don't know why. It's not that I'm trying to hide anything; it's more that the idea of explaining the whole story to anyone new feels too exhausting. And what would I be telling them anyway? That a colleague who used to be my closest work friend might be trying to sabotage me? That she's used a story that she knew was mine to try to get my job, a job she insisted she didn't want? That she doesn't invite me for lunch any more? It sounds paranoid at best.

Dee and I are perched on my sofa like two nervous debutantes hoping to be asked to dance. The flat is the tidiest it has ever been or ever will be again. There are fresh flowers in a vase on the coffee table and some in the kitchen, a cover for the diffusers that are hidden behind the sofa and in the hall cupboard to mask the faint smell of damp. Smokey is wearing a cravat, much to his disgust. Don't ask. Dee thought it would be cute.

It's five to seven. Divorcee Susanna – to my mind the most suitable candidate on paper – is due on the hour. I left work half an hour early to get back in good time and do the last-minute titivating and achieved almost nothing, then Dee arrived ten minutes ago and has gone through the flat like a benevolent hurricane, straightening cushions and placing ornaments just so.

Work has been strange the last two days. I've been distracted, watching Roz, trying to work out what she's up to. Trying to watch my back. I'm second-guessing everything. I have no doubt now that the Patricia note was from her, the message to Glen, the meeting removed from my diary, that she got rid of the pile of scripts I'd left printing and removed the cartridge from the printer. She's not the person I thought she was. She's after my job and I have to protect myself.

Dee looks at her phone. 'She's three minutes late.'

Being three minutes late is enough of a reason to tell someone the room has already gone in Dee's book.

'Do you think she'll look like her photo?' I say. I'm feeling anxious. I always talk rubbish when I'm feeling anxious.

'This isn't a date, Holly,' Dee says, laughing. 'Just relax.'

I hear the clatter of shoes on the steps down from the street. 'She's here. Oh God.'

I'm at the door before she even rings the bell, anxious to get it over with. Susanna is smiling. She looks normal. She is not brandishing an axe. I breathe a sigh of relief.

'Ooh, you made me jump,' she says. She does indeed look like her photo. Long blonde hair, parted on the side. An open expression. Laughter lines. She looks . . . well . . . nice. Easy-going. Like someone I could be friends with.

'Come on in. I'm Holly.' I stand aside to let her pass. Dee is waiting in the doorway of the living room and I raise my eyebrows at her and smile in a way I hope says 'I like her'. 'This is my friend, Dee.'

Dee leans forward and shakes her hand. 'Nice to meet you.'

I don't know what the etiquette is. Do I take her coat? Offer her a drink? But then we only have half an hour. It's not a social visit. In the end I leave it.

'Let me show you the room first and then we can have a chat if you're still interested.' I lead the way, trying to imagine what it would be like to be seeing the flat for the first time. It still smells of paint, which I think is a good thing. It shows I've made an effort.

'The bathroom is there,' I say, waving my hand. 'But this would be your room . . .'

I stand back to allow her to go in first. I once read that that was an estate agent trick to make a room seem larger, not to crowd it with people.

'Hello!' she says. 'Who are you?'

I peer in behind her to see Smokey lounging on what would be her bed.

'Smokes!' I say, shooing him off. 'Sorry, he knows he's not supposed to be on there.'

'He's adorable,' Susanna says, bending down to stroke him, and she gains another gold star.

'He's a diva, is what he is.'

'Aren't they all?' She looks around. 'It's a lovely room.'

I'm practically ready to sign her up on the spot. She has a decent job, and she's good for the rent. I'm just thinking that I should probably wait till I check her references just to be on the safe side when she starts talking and then she just doesn't stop. It's as if someone has turned on a hose.

'I've been staying with a friend in Angel, which is convenient but you know what it's like, you feel as if you're imposing after a while, even though I offered to pay her rent, but she wouldn't have it, she says I can stay as long as I want, I think she feels sorry for me because the only reason I met Gary in the first place was through her and then, of course, he turned out to be an absolute bastard, went off with his secretary, I mean, can you imagine anything more clichéd, I said to him you're just a walking mid-life crisis but he didn't even care, anyway, Kim, that's my friend I told you about, she likes having me there but I think it's time I got my own place, ooh what a lovely colour on the walls, and this is just as convenient for work, I hate commuting, don't you, what is it you said you did again, oh yes, you work in TV, I thought about doing that but I ended up in radio somehow and there I stayed, not that I do anything creative, not like you, are bills included by the way . . .'

It's one looong unformed sentence and it never ends. Never. I accidentally catch Dee's eye – she's hovering in the corridor – and I almost laugh. I have to turn away. I zone back in. Susanna is now saying something about her mother and the fact she never liked Gary.

'. . . she actually cried as I walked down the aisle but not from happiness if you know what I mean, anyway she has never once said I told you so, so I suppose that's a blessing, can I look at the kitchen, I don't really cook much but I suppose I ought to make sure there's space if I ever want to, are there nice restaurants round here, I tend to eat a lot of takeaways if I'm being honest . . .'

I can't get a word in so I just turn and walk towards the kitchen in the hope she'll follow. She does and it's like being stalked by an agitated goose.

'Let me just look in the bathroom as we go past, oh that's nice, I'm very tidy by the way, my friend Kim says she sometimes forgets that I'm around because I'm so tidy . . .'

I find that hard to believe, unless Kim has a large store of earplugs. My head is starting to hurt and I'm having to stop myself from shouting 'Will you shut up for a second!' at her. I look at Dee pleadingly. Help me.

'. . . seven different kinds of granola, I mean, can you even imagine . . .'

'Susanna!' Dee's voice booms out. Susanna stops dead in her tracks. Dee smiles at her. 'Holly just needs to fill you in with a few things because we only have half an hour.'

I open my mouth to speak, grateful for the momentary silence. But before I can get a word out she's off again.

'Sorry, was I rambling, I have a tendency to ramble, my boss is always telling me I should go on air because I always know how to fill a silence, I hate silence, it's weird isn't it when people don't want to chat . . .'

'Bills included, one month's deposit, one month in advance and you would need to provide two references,' Dee booms over the top of her.

Susanna doesn't even draw breath. 'That all sounds good and the rent is seven hundred a month isn't it, that should be manageable, eventually I'll probably be looking to buy a place of my own once my divorce is finalized but I'm definitely looking for somewhere for at least six months, does that sound all right, with an option to renew for another six, I think that's what you said, I wonder if I should look round here when the time comes, it's a lovely area . . .'

Somehow Dee steers her towards the front door.

'. . . anyway, I'm very interested, I know you have other people to see but it's the nicest place I've seen and . . .'

'We'll be in touch,' Dee says, practically pushing her out.

'Lovely to meet you,' I call as she heads up the stairs.

Dee shuts the door. Turns and leans on it dramatically. 'Jesus Christ.'

'Oh my God, Dee,' I say, sinking down on to my haunches. 'Actually, can we just not talk for a minute?'

'I'm having a glass of wine.' She walks through to the kitchen.

'Get me a big one,' I call after her. 'I don't care if Lenny thinks I'm a lush.'

We have five minutes before Lenny is due. I follow Dee into the kitchen and slump on to one of the chairs. 'I almost offered it to her! I was thinking I could cancel him even if he was on his way.'

'Well, there's a lesson to be learned there. Don't rush into anything before you've met them both. And remember, nothing says you have to take one of these two. The ad's still up, isn't it?'

I nod. I feel as if I've had a very lucky escape. I take a big swig of my wine and brace myself as I hear footsteps on the stairs outside. 'Here goes.'

This time I wait for the buzz of the doorbell before opening the door. Thirty-six-year-old soup and sandwich shop manager Lenny hovers nervously. He's more attractive than his photo, probably due to the designer stubble that's appeared since it was taken. I don't know why that was the first thing I noticed; the last thing I want is the complication of a flatmate I'm attracted to.

He holds out a hand for me to shake, and I notice his eyes are a very deep brown, almost black. 'Hi. Lenny. Here about –'

'Of course. Come on in.' I stand back to let him pass. Go through the same process as with Susanna ('Let me show you the room first . . .'). Dee is nowhere to be seen.

'Great,' he says, looking round appraisingly. 'Is there a washing machine?'

'In the kitchen. Here, I'll show you.'

He sneezes. 'Sorry. Hay fever.'

'In March?'

''Fraid so.'

He follows me back out. I open the door to the bathroom as we pass to let him look in there. Dee is still in the kitchen.

'Hi,' she says, raising her wine glass.

'This is Dee, my friend. This is Lenny.'

'Nice to meet you,' he says. 'And you're OK with me cooking? Not that I do it very often. I tend to eat my stock.'

'Oh yes,' I say, laughing. He seems nice. 'Soup and sandwiches on tap.'

He rolls his eyes. 'It's not the world's greatest job but I'm doing it for the experience. I want to open my own sandwich bar. All organic. Vegan options. Juices. You know the sort of thing. But I thought I ought to get some idea of the business side of things first.'

'Can you open it round here?' Dee pipes up. 'We could be your taste testers.'

'Do you need to see anything else?' I say. 'You do know the living room is off limits?'

He nods. 'That's fine. I've got a TV I can stick in the room.' He sneezes again. 'Sorry.'

'Do you want a Piriton?'

'Had one. I'm fine. Really.'

'It'll be Dee's perfume,' I say, and I'm gratified to see he laughs.

'Do you want a drink?'

'Just some water. I'd love to say yes to a wine but I'm going to the gym after.'

I find a bottle in the fridge. 'Oh yes, you're into fitness.' You can tell. I'm just saying.

'That's my vice. I'm pretty boring.'

'Boring is good,' Dee says.

'Boring is very good,' I add. I hand him his water and wander through to the living room. Something about Lenny feels very relaxed. Despite my insistence that I only wanted to share with another female I can imagine that living with him would be relatively painless.

'Have a seat.' I indicate the armchair. 'Oh, this is Smokey . . .'

I don't say any more because Lenny sneezes three times in quick succession and then starts to gasp for air. His lovely brown-black eyes are streaming.

I look from him to Smokey and back again. 'I'll put him in the other room.'

'No,' he says, backing out himself. 'I'm fine. I just need fresh air. Sorry.'

I'm a bit confused. 'I said in the advert. Cat.'

'No,' he says between wheezes. 'You said "Must love cats". You didn't say there was one living here.'

'I thought that was implied . . .' I mean, really. Why else would I have asked? 'You could keep the door to the room shut so he didn't go in there . . .'

'It won't work.' He's on his way to the front door. 'Sorry, Holly. It was lovely to meet you and the room's really nice but . . . achoo!'

'No problem,' I say. 'Good to meet you too.'

He goes off into the night, sneezing away. I feel bad. Maybe I should have made myself clearer in the ad? I turn away from the door to find Dee creasing up.

'Fuck's sake,' she snorts. 'You couldn't make it up.'

'I liked him, too.'

She raises her eyebrows.

'Not like that. He just seemed like a nice bloke. Maybe I should tweak the ad tomorrow. Put in "Warning: there is a cat living at the property" or something.'

'No incessant talkers.'

'No incessant sneezers more like.'

Dee squawks. Sometimes when she laughs I think she sounds like a parrot. 'Poor bloke.'

'I mean, for God's sake, what a waste of time.' I sink down into the armchair.

'More wine,' is all Dee says.

'Wine isn't the answer to everything,' I say sulkily, but by the time she comes back from the kitchen I'm holding my glass out for her to fill like a toddler with a juice cup.

I tap on the open door. 'Emma said you wanted to see me?' It's Thursday afternoon, two days after the disastrous interviews.

Glen looks up. Frowns. 'Did I?'

'Um . . . apparently.'

'Did she say what it was about?'

'No.' I feel my cheeks colour. All Emma's email said was 'Glen wants an urgent word when you've got a moment'. I didn't see her after I came back from a meeting with the design department and found it, because she's got the afternoon off for a hospital appointment.

'I don't think I've even spoken to Emma today. Maybe it's an old message?'

'Maybe,' I say. It isn't. It wasn't there first thing and now it is. 'Sorry to have disturbed you.'

'No problem,' he says, looking back at his computer screen. I take that as my cue to leave.

Only Juliet and Joe are at their desks. 'What time did Emma leave?' I say, looking between the two of them.

'About quarter to two,' Joe says. 'Everything OK?'

'Yep,' is all I can manage. I go into my office, shut the door and check my email. The one about Glen was sent from Emma's computer at five to two.

'Fuck's sake,' I say to no one.

'I swear I didn't send it.'

Emma is tearful. It's Friday morning and I've been fuming all night about the situation at work. I'm talking to her in the print room, away from prying, gloating eyes.

'I know you didn't. I just needed to check in case Glen had had some kind of bang on the head or something.'

She sniffs. Pulls a tissue out of her sleeve and blows her nose. 'What is going on?'

'It's nothing for you to worry about. I think someone's

got it in for me, that's all, and they think it's funny to make me look stupid. Just change your password and make sure no one sees you entering the new one.'

'Who's got it in for you?' she says, wide-eyed. 'And why? I thought you got on with everyone. Well, not Juliet so much. Oh, is it her?'

I don't want to tell her who it is. I don't want to risk Roz finding out I'm bad-mouthing her. That I've put all the pieces together. She'll go into denial mode. Start hurling counter-punches. I need to catch her in the act. Not that I think Emma is indiscreet, not in the slightest, but things have a habit of leaking out once they're said aloud. But, equally, it's not fair on Juliet to allow Emma to think it's her. 'No. I don't think she would be that mean. Listen, I can't really talk about it, OK? But from now on could you let everyone know that any messages have to go through you? And then you can check they're legit before I make a twat of myself again.'

'Of course. I'm really sorry, Holly, that this is happening to you . . .'

'And I know you won't but don't talk about it to anyone.'

'I won't. I swear.'

Dee and I are back on the sofa, waiting for Hattie, 34, a dental hygienist who's into fiction and hygge crafts. Of the five new hopefuls that have offered themselves up as potential tenants she's the only one I can bear to meet (the others having been rejected on the basis of being too smug, too religious, too eager to please and downright scary).

I sigh loudly. 'We'll just let her have a quick whizz round and then we can forget about it for this evening.'

'Who knows?' Dee says. 'Maybe Hattie will be your dream lodger.' I don't know why she's suddenly turned into Pollyanna.

I untie my hair, run my fingers through it and tie it up again. 'Don't let me offer it to her just because I'm desperate.'

'I promise I'll wrestle you to the ground if you try.'

I fill Dee in on today's work trauma, and she's incensed on my behalf.

'You need to fight back,' she says. 'I think she's trying to make sure you don't get through your probation.'

Shit. 'I can't believe she'd be that vile,' I say, although I'm not sure I really mean it. Who knows? 'And besides, I have no proof she's done anything. It really could all be Juliet. Or Lorraine. Or someone in a different department.'

'Yeah, right. What would Lorraine have to gain from it?'

'Fuck knows.'

'At the very least we now know Roz is a liar. And a convincing one at that.'

The doorbell rings before I can answer. I stand up reluctantly. 'Here goes.'

I open the front door, an old hand at this now. On the step is a tiny woman swaddled in a big black puffa coat.

'Hattie?'

I half expect her to say 'No, I'm collecting for my

sponsored swim at school' but instead she smiles and says yes, she is.

She makes nice noises at the room and then I take her to the kitchen via the bathroom. My heart's not quite in it, if I'm being honest.

'I don't really cook much,' she says. 'If it was OK with you I have a little fridge and a microwave and I'd just put them in my room. I'd only really need to come in here to fill the kettle and wash up.'

Now my ears perk up. This sounds good. 'That would be fine. Do you have a TV too? Because the living room's, you know . . .'

'Just my computer,' she says. She has a quiet voice. Not so quiet that it's hard to hear, but it's quite soothing. 'I watch everything on there anyway. Netflix.'

'So, you're a dental hygienist?' I feel as if I should start making an effort.

She nods. 'Private practice in Marylebone. I work ten till six, Monday to Friday, and then most weekends I go and stay with my mum in Eastbourne, to give the carers a break. She has MS.'

'Wow,' I say. 'That's rough.'

She smiles, showing little white even teeth. I imagine her spending all her tea breaks at work flossing with the practice's state-of-the-art equipment. 'Not really. I just need to get her meals and make sure she takes her meds. And it's lovely down there. I like getting out of London.'

'Would you like a drink?' I say. 'And then come and say hi to my friend in the other room, and we can chat through anything you want to know. If you think you might be interested, that is.'

'Oh, I definitely am. Water would be lovely.'

'Or a glass of wine?'

She accepts my offer and I pour one for each of us and take her through to meet Dee. Hattie takes off the giant coat and perches on the edge of the chair, hands folded in her lap. She looks like a kid dressed in her mum's clothes but I like her style. DMs and skinny jeans with a big baggy jumper that hangs down over her hands. Dee raises her eyebrows at the wine and I raise mine back to indicate – hopefully – that she's a possible.

'So, Hattie was just saying that she goes away at the weekends to look after her mum,' I say, once they've introduced themselves.

'Oh,' Dee says. 'Great. I mean, not great but, you know . . .'

Hattie laughs. 'It's OK. I know people like their own space. I do too, to be honest. And it's not every single weekend. Just . . . I mean, I don't want to get your hopes up.'

She's funny. I like her.

'Where do you live now?' Dee again.

'I rent a room in Maida Vale. I've been there for three years. I love it but my landlady's selling. Well, sold actually. It's about to go through. Oh, she said she'd be happy to give a reference.'

'Excellent,' I say. 'So, how soon could you move in?'

She jumps as Smokey appears from nowhere and leaps

on to her lap. 'Hello, gorgeous,' she says, ruffling his ears. Tick. Another item off the list. 'Sooner rather than later if that was OK. I want to be out of Mary's – that's my landlady's – hair before she has to start packing up. But if you needed a few weeks that'd be OK too. She wouldn't mind . . .'

I look at Dee. I want to offer Hattie the room before someone else snaps her up but, of course, I've promised to be cautious. 'OK, well, obviously I have to have a think and I'm sure you do too . . .'

Dee is scowling at me. She gives me a hard stare as if to say 'What are you doing?' I realize that for all her scepticism she's thinking the same as me.

'Oh, sod it,' I say. 'If you want the room, it's yours. You can move in whenever you like.'

'Really?' Her face lights up. 'That's fantastic. I'd love to.'

We talk about the practicalities and then she leaves after we agree she can move her stuff in on Sunday. I need to get some kind of contract for her to sign before then. Shit, I should have been more organized instead of hoping it'd all go away.

'What is she, like twelve?' Dee says as soon as Hattie is out of sight.

'Thirty-four. She reminds me of Winona Ryder.'

'Cool Winona or crazy shoplifting Winona?'

'Cool Winona. Did I do the right thing? You liked her, right?'

'Definitely. She's perfect. The weekends away were the clincher.'

'I know. I mean, poor woman, with her mum being ill and all that . . . and it feels as if she'll spend most of her time in her room when she's here.'

Dee holds her glass aloft. 'Cheers to that.'

And just like that I have a lodger.

13

Sunday is a beautiful Spring day. The kind that makes you feel as if everything is going to be OK. Dee and I have decided to walk into town for lunch so that she can get her steps up and I can keep out of the way while Hattie moves herself in.

Yesterday I phoned the number she gave me for her current landlady Mary and I left a message when it went to voicemail. Later, when I came back from Waitrose, there was a return message. Yes, Mary could confirm that Hattie was a good tenant. Always paid her rent on time, no problems to report.

I downloaded a generic contract and she popped round last night to sign it, and to pick up the keys. I was a bit anxious about her coming over without Dee being there. What if it was awkward? What if I got cold feet? Decided she was actually really annoying, or she suddenly announced she liked to dissect animals in her spare time, or listen to 'Galway Girl' by Ed Sheeran on repeat. Or even once a week.

I could see her looking around, appraising the place, probably wondering if she'd done the right thing. It struck me then that this must be as awkward for her as it was for me. Moving in somewhere where you'll always feel like a somewhat unwelcome guest. So I offered her a drink, and we sat at the kitchen table for a while, nursing cups of tea and chatting. I like her. I think we'll get on.

'It'll be about thirteen thousand by the time we get there and back,' Dee says in the same excited tone a six-year-old uses to tell you it's their birthday tomorrow.

'Who said anything about walking back? It's all uphill.'

'That's the best bit,' she says, swigging back the last of her coffee.

'You really are a fucking freak.' I take her mug from her, rinse it out in the sink. I don't want to send out the message that leaving dirty dishes in the kitchen is acceptable. I'm hit with a wave of panic. Am I ever going to be feel as if I can be myself in my own home again? Wallow in my own chaos if I feel like it? I bat it away. 'Come on, let's go.'

Dee likes to move at a pace that can only be described as 'training for the Olympic power-walking event'. We've only just set off when I start thinking this is a bad idea. She's barely breaking a sweat while I can hardly talk without wheezing.

'When's your story conference thing?' She knows I've been angsting about making sure it runs smoothly. Emma organizes all the practicalities like booking the room and food and drink but I have to produce a document that contains all the stories – submitted by both the writers and the editors – in some kind of sensible order and provide everyone with an up-to-date timeline of what is happening to each of the characters, and the actors' contract dates. I want everything to be perfect. We always hold it in a local hotel, over two days so there are no interruptions, but that also means there's no fallback if you forget anything.

'Monday and Tuesday week. It's come round so quickly.'

'You're all prepared though, right?'

I nod. 'Pretty much. There're still a few stories trickling in, but everything else is done.'

'Thank God. I feel as if I'm as nervous as you.'

'That's why I love you,' I say. 'Although I'd love you a whole lot more if you'd walk at a pace where I could breathe at the same time.'

'See,' she says, looking at her wrist. 'We've done a thousand steps already.'

'Great. Do keep me posted every thousand, won't you? Because I'd hate not to know.'

'You can scoff but you'd be amazed by how many people barely even do that some days.'

I laugh. 'I wouldn't though. I don't have an opinion.'

We keep on motoring down the hill towards Regent's Park. 'What's Gavin doing today?'

Dee rolls her eyes. 'Sulking.'

'What about?'

'He wanted us to go to Homebase.'

'Oh shit, sorry.' I sometimes get the impression that Gavin finds Dee's friendship with me a bit irritating. Not that he doesn't like me. He does, or I think he does. But I think he feels he'd see a lot more of her if I wasn't around. Which is pretty unfair considering how often he goes away for work. I've sometimes worried about being the needy time-rich friend but I also get the feeling that Dee often likes an excuse to come and hang out at mine. They're happy in so far as I can tell, although lately I've felt as if they've been drifting apart. Not quite the unit they once were. I first met Dee when I was doing some temping years ago and I ended up covering mornings for someone who was off for four weeks at the doctor's surgery where she was then a receptionist. She and Gavin had only been married a year at that point. It's nearly twelve now.

'God, no, don't be. It's the last thing I want to be doing with my weekend. He's got some idea in his head about retiling the bathroom and he'd only want me to help.'

'OK, well, I'll consider it as a favour then. You owe me.'

'He's doing my head in, if I'm being honest,' she says, suddenly serious. 'Ever since . . . you know . . . he's got really irritable. I feel as if I can't do anything right.'

She doesn't need to say any more. The 'you know' refers to the fact that Dee and Gavin decided to draw a line under their years-long attempt to get pregnant a few months ago. They had no idea what the problem was; there didn't seem to be anything fundamentally wrong with either of them. But the three attempts at IVF that the NHS allowed them had failed. She was about to turn forty and was exhausted by the whole thing, the disappointments and, even worse, the false hopes. Dee had wanted to try for adoption, but Gavin had said enough was enough. He just wanted them to get on with their lives with each other. She never really talks about it but I know she's devastated.

'Oh, Dee.' I know she can't bear sympathy so I have to tread carefully. 'You can come round and make me walk stupidly long distances any time you feel like getting out of the house. And if you want to talk about it, you know . . .'

I leave it hanging out there. She doesn't say anything, just reaches out an arm and drapes it round my shoulders for a second, pulling me towards her.

I get back to mine at about half past three. Dee and I had lunch in Selfridges and then perused each floor from top to bottom like a pair of forensic scientists. She bought a Ted Baker cardigan and I found a peacock-blue notebook and some Benefit goodies, and then I persuaded her to share a taxi home. So, all in all, it was a good day.

'Still nearly eight thousand,' she said, waving her wrist at me in the cab, and I smiled indulgently.

'Do I get a gold star?'

'No, but your heart will thank you.'

She offers to come in with me, but I feel as if that's a bit unfair on Hattie on her first day. And besides, I need to be a grown-up.

'Come over tomorrow night if you feel like it, though.'

She grimaces. 'I might. I'll call you.'

Inside the flat is quiet and I wonder if Hattie has gone out exploring her new area. Or if she's even moved in at all. In the kitchen I open the cupboard I allocated her and there is a neat pile of plates, and a couple of pans. I'm tempted to peek in her room, but I know that's a line I shouldn't cross. And a couple of minutes later when I hear the door open and her tiptoe out to the bathroom I'm glad I didn't.

'Hi,' I say. I know I have to make an effort. I draw the line at offering her a cup of tea, though, despite the fact I've just put the kettle on. I don't want to set a precedent I'll regret.

'Oh, hi.' She smiles.

'Are you getting settled in?'

'Yes. Lovely, thanks. Have you been doing anything fun?'

'Dee and I walked to Selfridges,' I say.

She looks at me as if I've announced I've just done Land's End to John o'Groats. 'Can you do that from here?'

'You can but it's more about the walk than the destination. I was knackered by the time I got there.'

'I might try that one day. You'll have to give me the best route.'

'Sure.'

She pushes open the bathroom door. 'Well . . . see you later.'

I fill my mug quickly. By the time I hear her come out and go back to her room I'm ensconced in the living room with my tea and a book. That wasn't so bad.

14

Emma has proofread all the documents for the story conference. There are still tweaks to be made, so I hold her off printing them for now but at least I know they're in pretty good shape.

'Don't show them to anyone else. Apart from Glen, obviously, if he asks.'

'Of course not. And I'm going to change my password once a week.' I've made her suspicious of everyone, and I feel a bit guilty, but it's probably not a bad thing at the moment. She actually asked Joe what he was up to when she saw him in the print room the other day. He said 'printing something' and, funnily enough, she had no answer to that.

'Thanks.' I smile at her to, hopefully, put her at ease, but it probably looks more like a crocodile is coming to get her. 'I really appreciate your help.'

I'm head down in a script when there's a tap on my door and Roz is standing there. Hot-pink jumper, red skirt, orange tights and red shoes. Orange seahorses dangling from her ears.

'Am I allowed to come and talk to you any more? Emma told us all we have to go through her now.'

She obviously has no idea I'm on to her. I'm tempted to

tell her I'm busy but keeping my enemy close feels like a sound self-preservation strategy so I force a smile. And besides, if I'm being honest I could do with a distraction. Now I no longer have someone to exchange a bit of mindless chatter with the days feel very long.

'Of course. What's up?'

'Nothing. I'm bored. It's not the same now you're shut away in here all the time. I have no one to play with.' She flops into the chair. Looks out at Glen and Emma talking in the main office. 'Do you think Mrs Glen trims the beard for him? Or do you think he does it himself?'

Roz and I used to speculate for hours about Glen's wife, having never seen her. I thought she was probably cool and arty with a severe black bob. Roz has always had her down as wet and adoring.

'It doesn't bear thinking about.'

'How's the lodger hunt going?' She swings her legs over the arm.

At least she wants to keep the conversation on fairly neutral ground. 'I found someone.'

'Already? That's crazy. Tell me everything.'

So I tell her about Hattie, realizing as I do how much I seem to have lucked out with my quiet, unassuming tenant.

'Result,' she says. 'Maybe she'll do your cleaning while you're out.'

'She's very tidy.' It's true that the bathroom is still spotless and, apart from a couple of times finding it occupied when I want to use it, I wouldn't even know I was now sharing it if it weren't for the small collection of unfamiliar toiletries and the hot pink wash-bag on the side of the bath. Last night, knowing we were both going to be getting ready for work this morning we had a quick conversation about timings. Hattie doesn't need to leave till a full hour after me – I like to be at work for nine, when the filming day starts, in case of any script issues – so she doesn't need to even start getting ready until after I've left. Knowing I wasn't going to have to stress about getting up extra early to claim my spot had made me feel much better about the whole thing.

'Cool.' She sits there, legs swinging. 'Oh, I forgot to ask you – how did Lorraine get on with the script notes?'

I had finally given Lorraine the scripts to read a few days after my conversation with Roz. I'd waited until it was Roz's turn to cover the studio, when I figured I could keep an eye on Lorraine to check she didn't get help and, to be fair, she'd stayed at her desk all day and read them through. When she came back to share her thoughts with me – barely able to look me in the eye because I had obviously been declared the enemy – her notes had been surprisingly comprehensive. And she'd suggested some quite radical, but effective, changes. But I struggle to imagine her dealing with the writers, her manner is so blunt. It's not something I particularly want to discuss with Roz, though.

'Oh. Yeah. Pretty good, I suppose.'

'So, are you going to give her the job?'

'I haven't talked to Glen about it yet.'

Roz huffs. 'Surely it's your decision now. You're the head of department.'

'Not officially, yet. It's a grey area.' I'm not sure if this is true. I'm pretty certain that if I went to Glen and said 'I want to hire Lorraine as the new editor' he'd say 'Fine', but it's as good a way as any to shut Roz up.

'When's your probation up anyway?' she asks casually.

'Not for ages. What's it been? Four weeks?'

She gazes out of the window into the main office. Joe and Emma sit at their desks, heads down. I assume Juliet and Lorraine have both gone out to get lunch. Separately, obviously.

Roz yawns expansively. It's so obviously one of those attention-seeking gestures that demands you ask what's causing it that I stay quiet. I'm in no mood to hear about her latest glamorous escapades.

'I'm knackered,' she says after a moment, clearly frustrated by my lack of interest. 'We went to the Fat Duck last night. Heston invited Hugh personally.'

She waits for a reaction and I feel obliged to give one. 'Wow. How was it?'

She stretches her arms high above her head. 'Incredible. You know you have to wait weeks for a table usually.'

'Right. So, does Hugh represent him then?'

'He handles the PR for the restaurant.'

'Nice,' I say. 'I should get back to the studio.'

It's my week to monitor filming, while they shoot a batch of episodes that I have nurtured since the first draft. What that essentially means is that I have to sit in a small room off to one side of the studio with a monitor and a two-way communication system to the gallery from where the director watches a bank of screens that show the feed from the different cameras. Most of the time you can get on with your work, but every now and then a line is missed or changed in some subtle way that will have a knock-on effect later or even delivered in a way that misses the meaning altogether, and then you're expected to contact the gallery over the intercom. The thing about soaps is that they're cheap. There's no money for editing time beyond a day to cut in any exterior footage and to sling the whole thing together. So what you see in the studio is pretty much what ends up going on TV. It's important to get it right.

I stand up to make my point. It's making me nervous leaving my office all day after everything that's been going on, but Emma is standing guard on my instructions (she's taking it very seriously. When I came up this lunchtime she practically knocked me over, running for the door muttering 'Thank God, I've been bursting for the loo') and I've locked any important documents in my desk drawers.

Paranoid? Who said that?

I'm flicking through some notes between scenes when there's a tap on the door. I always leave it open because there are no windows, just a sofa, a low table, the monitor and the intercom. It can feel a bit like sitting in a vault. I look up, and standing in the doorway is Robbie, one of our teenage cast members, eyebrows raised as if to ask if it's OK to disturb me.

'Hi! Come on in.'

He slouches in and I shuffle some papers off the other end of the sofa to make room for him.

Most of the more experienced actors will come and seek one of us out if they have a problem with a line, or there's something they don't understand. The younger ones tend to wing it and change the words to whatever they think they should be on the day, only to get into a strop when they're told to change them back. Robbie is one of the worst, so I'm heartened that he's decided to come and discuss whatever issue he has first this time.

'Is everything OK? Have a seat.'

He stays where he is. 'I'll only be a second,' he mutters, face crimson. I'm reminded of how young he is to be dealing with this weird overnight flash of fame. He wasn't even an actor before. He worked in a garage on the weekends and one of the casting directors asked him to try out after he cleaned her car and she thought he'd be perfect for the teenage tearaway role we were currently casting. He's not a natural. He's basically playing himself. He's been in the show for six months. I can't imagine what he'll do after this is all over.

He doesn't say anything, just turns redder. I try to draw on my experience of dealing with an adolescent Ashley. Basically ask the most obvious question you can think of. 'Did you need to ask me about something?'

It all comes out in a rush. 'Someone said you have your story thing next week and I just want to know if you're going to write me out because I'll have to start looking for another job.'

It's obviously completely forbidden to discuss our future plans with the cast until anything is set in stone. Imagine the panic it would cause. Still, as far as I know we're all on the same page that Robbie's character, Jono, is a success. The audience have warmed to him. I can't 100 per cent put him out of his misery, though, just in case.

'You've still got six months on your contract, haven't you?'

'Does that mean you can't get rid of me?'

I can't help it. I laugh. And then I feel bad. He's considerably younger than my daughter and he's having to handle being thrust into the spotlight with no safety net.

'Sorry. No. I mean, it has happened occasionally but . . . you know I'm not allowed to talk about any of this stuff, and we don't make any firm decisions about anything until after the conference anyway, but – between you and me – I can say that it's never even been discussed . . .'

'So, no?'

'I can't say. Not because I'm being a jobsworth but because, like I said, nothing is actually decided yet. I will say this – I can't imagine it happening. Jono's really popular at the moment.'

His whole face lights up. 'Is he? OK. Cool. I know I can't hold you to it, but thanks.'

I remember someone mentioning to me that he was supporting his single mum and three younger sisters. 'Try and enjoy it while it's happening.'

'I am. I will.'

As soon as he's gone I open my laptop. Check the document that contains all the stories up for discussion. There are a couple that centre around Jono but they're not very inspiring. I decide to try and add one or two of my own.

Dee and I are sitting in my kitchen sharing a bottle of wine. She's telling me her theory that her next-door neighbour is a people trafficker, which seems to be based solely on the fact that he has to go to Eastern Europe for work occasionally.

'Didn't you tell me he had a business importing stationery?'

She looks at me over the top of her glass. 'Well, they all have to have a cover story. And there's a young woman living in his house now. But she only ever goes out with him. Never on her own. I reckon he keeps her locked in.'

'Right.' I suppress a laugh, try to retain a serious face. One of my favourite things to do is to allow Dee to dig herself in deeper and deeper when she tries to defend her crazy theories. 'And what about the rest of them?'

She shrugs. 'He's probably sold them on. Or he has them holed up somewhere working for him for free.'

'Boxing up stationery?'

'The stationery is a smokescreen,' she says indignantly. 'Obviously.'

'You really should report him to the police if you're so sure.'

She huffs. 'I'm not sure, am I? Not yet. Stop taking the piss. How's Whatsherface?'

I'm assuming Hattie is out. There has been no noise from her room – although there never is, to be fair, apart from the occasional ping of the microwave or the low rumble of voices when she watches something on her computer. But I've been caught out several times already, thinking I'm alone in the flat when it turns out I'm not. Although now she's seen me dancing round the kitchen, holding Smokey high in the air and singing 'Circle of Life' to him, it probably couldn't get much worse.

'Sssh. She might be in there,' I say in a hoarse whisper.

'No way,' Dee says. 'I've been here for an hour. She'd have coughed or something.'

'She's very quiet. It's like living with a ghost.'

Dee lifts her fringe off her forehead, flattens it down again. 'That's good. That's exactly what you wanted.'

I pour more wine into both our glasses. 'I know. I like her actually. And not just because I hardly ever see her, although that definitely helps.'

Right at that moment there's a loud noise as someone puts the key in the lock and both Dee and I jump then dissolve into giggles. Hattie goes straight to her room but a couple of minutes later she appears in the doorway, minus her coat but brandishing her kettle.

'Hi. Do you mind if I just . . .' She indicates the tap. Then she recognizes Dee. 'Oh, hello. How are you?'

'Of course,' I say. I feel bad that it must be a bit intimidating to have to face the pair of us, laughing like a couple of hyenas, when all she wants is some water.

'How are you settling in?' Dee says.

Hattie gives her a big smile. 'Great. I really like it.'

'Do you want a glass of wine?' I say, feeling suddenly as if I should make more of an effort. 'Come and join us.'

'Oh. Well, I'd love to, but I don't want to intrude . . .'

'Don't be stupid,' Dee says.

Hattie puts the kettle down decisively. 'OK, I will.'

'The glasses are in there,' I say, waving at one of the top cupboards. She helps herself and then comes to sit down. It's the first time I've really had the chance to get a good look at her since she moved in. She has delicate features that remind me of a bird and big dark brown eyes that make her look like a Manga cartoon. Apart from the eyes everything about her is tiny. She makes me feel like a giant.

She pours herself a small glass of red, sits down at the table.

'Been anywhere nice?' I ask. It feels a bit awkward now.

'Just a quick after-work drink. It was one of my colleagues' birthdays.'

'Ah, the dreaded work celebration,' Dee says. 'At least you managed to escape fairly early.'

Hattie laughs. 'I'm a lightweight. I'm always the first to leave.'

They bond a bit about working in healthcare, although their work environments couldn't sound more different – Hattie's rarefied private practice and Dee's overstretched, underfunded hospital. I'm just happy that they're getting on. Relieved, like I used to be when Ashley had a successful playdate with a classmate. One less thing to worry about.

Hattie asks about my work and I find myself telling her way too much detail about everything that's been going on. It's the wine talking, but it feels good to get it off my chest to a virtual stranger, if only to get a sense of how implausible it all sounds said out loud. To give her credit she doesn't look bemused, or tell me it's probably all a figment of my overactive imagination. She opens her big eyes wide and says, 'God, how awful. That must be a nightmare for you. Can you talk to your boss about it?'

I shake my head, feeling tears prick my eyes – again, courtesy of the wine. 'Not without any definite proof of anything. He'll just think I'm not capable of running a department. Which maybe I'm not.'

Dee looks at me sharply. 'Don't be stupid. No one deserves that job more than you.'

That only makes me cry for real. And then thinking about how much I'm embarrassing myself by blubbing in front of my new tenant makes it impossible to stop. 'Shit. Sorry.'

Dee hands me a tissue and I blow my nose noisily. 'Honestly,' Dee is saying to Hattie. 'I could kill that fucking bitch.'

'You know who it is, then?' Hattie says.

'I think so,' I say. 'Yes. Someone in my department.'

Hattie screws up her face sympathetically. 'You just need to get through your probation period, and then they'll stop. Because, what'll be the point . . .?'

'Exactly,' Dee says, answering for me. 'My guess is once

you're confirmed in the job she'll hand in her notice. And good riddance.'

I wipe my eyes, give my nose another sharp blow. I need to pull myself together. 'You're right. I just have to get through these next two months unscathed.'

15

Everyone is staring at me.

This is my worst nightmare. And I don't just mean I'm uncomfortable with the focus all coming my way. Although there is that too. But this is an actual nightmare that I have regularly: I'm fucking up and everyone is watching. Except that this time I'm awake and it's really happening.

I am fucking up and everyone is watching.

I have no idea what went wrong. I had everything planned right down to the last second. It was my first real chance to make a big impression in my new position. My first opportunity to prove to Glen that he was right to promote me. To prove to myself that I'm up to the task.

Except that it seems I'm not.

All my old insecurities come flooding back. I'm not good enough, skilled enough, confident enough. But this time I know this isn't down to me. I know I did everything right.

And I also know exactly who must have undone it all.

I look around at the sea of expectant faces. I have literally no idea what to say.

*

The morning started out well. The hotel had laid out coffee and Danish pastries on the long conference table, as I'd requested. I'd got there an hour early. Needlessly. I just wanted to make sure everything was as it should be. I'd already spoken to Emma who told me she'd been at the office since seven thirty in case of any unforeseen problems with the printer, but that all was going to plan and she had a taxi waiting to bring her and all the documents to meet me. She would be on her way any minute.

I'd emailed the final version to her last night, having waited until the last minute in case I thought of any more changes I wanted to make. In the end I hadn't looked at it at all, all weekend, beyond checking the page counts as I lined them up to send. I was satisfied that I'd done as good a job as I could. I even put a note on the email to Emma – 'No need to check again, I haven't changed anything.' That may have been my undoing.

The first two writers – Sue and Pete – arrived together just before ten to ten, having found themselves on the same train. Two minutes later Emma burst in and started to distribute the documents round the table before she even took her coat off.

'Oh. Congratulations, by the way,' Sue said, giving me a hug. 'I knew you'd get the job.'

'Thanks. I'm thrilled.'

Pete chimed in with his good wishes too, and I felt the warm glow that comes from being valued. I'd always got on well with the writers and I was happy they seemed to have confidence in me.

The rest of the writing team – eight more – arrived in quick succession along with Glen, Roz, Juliet, Joe and Lorraine and, after the usual hellos and brief catch-ups, we all took our seats. Emma left to go back to the office with instructions to call Lorraine if there was an urgent message for any of us, particularly Juliet, whose episodes were currently shooting. I reminded everyone else to turn their phones off until lunchtime.

Glen leaned back in his chair. 'You all know Holly is the new Marcus, so she's going to steer the ship today.'

I was greeted with a few 'Yays' and one round of applause. I cleared my throat. Reminded myself that I could do this standing on my head.

'OK, let's go,' I said. 'I'm just going to run through the "State of Play" document so we all know where we are.'

I opened it to the first page. 'Right. The Challenors,' I said, naming our central family, around whose four generations everything else revolves. I didn't need to consult the notes; I knew everything that was happening or about to happen to all our characters. 'So, Mary and Ronnie are about to celebrate their thirtieth wedding anniversary and that's where she's going to find out he has a twenty-six-year-old daughter, Catriona, who has tracked him down . . .'

I heard a stifled giggle. Looked up briefly to see Pete pointing something out on my document to Leanne, the fellow writer sitting next to him. I struggled to regain my train of thought.

'. . . Catriona's mum, as you all know, will turn up in episode seven forty and will be a woman Ronnie met at the hospital when Mary was kept in for complications during her second pregnancy . . .'

Try as I might I couldn't ignore the fact that the one isolated laugh had now turned into a rumble. I glanced round, confused. I caught Juliet's eye and she flicked the document in her hand and gave me a hard stare as if to say 'Look at this'. I picked up my own copy, skim-read the first paragraph. Nothing strange there. Then my brain registered something further down.

'Catriona will be played by' – here I had inserted the name of the actress who had already been cast. I distinctly remembered typing it. Mel Carmichael. But now the rest of the sentence read 'some has-been who used to be in a girl band but can't act to save her life'.

I looked up, looked round the room again. I could see some of the writers flicking through the rest of the document, pointing things out to each other, laughing. And there in the midst of the chaos Roz, innocent-faced. I pushed the papers to one side. Fought off the urge to cry.

'OK,' I said as loudly as I could. 'I've got no idea what's going on there but let's keep going without referring to the document. Could you all pass them up here please?' I didn't want them carrying on, looking for whatever other horrors might be in there. Luckily I knew I could get through this without referring to the notes. I could feel myself glowing red as I waited for the rustling of paper to stop. I couldn't bring myself to try and make a joke about it. I couldn't even let myself try to work out how it had happened yet. I just had to get through it.

'So . . .' I said without waiting for the chatter to subside. 'Catriona . . .'

Somehow I managed to regain order and plough my way on through the characters. Then I reminded everyone that two cast members were coming to the end of their contracts and that we needed to make a decision on whether or not to renew them and it was time to start discussing the submitted stories. Right on cue the door opened and a hotel employee in a black uniform carried in fresh pots of tea and coffee.

The story document stretched to nearly a hundred pages, a potential new storyline on each one. It would take us the best part of two days to go through them all, discuss them (apart from the ones that were obvious no-goers from the off), and then vote on whether or not to proceed with them. The latter part of the afternoon of the second day would be given over to brainstorming new ideas for any characters who still didn't have enough going on.

I turned to the first page. Breathed a sigh of relief when I saw that all seemed to be as it should be. They'd had their little bit of fun at my expense and now I could salvage the rest of the day by brushing it off and moving forward as if nothing untoward had happened. I just needed to be professional.

'So. Challenor family first up.' I read the title of the story. '"Mary's Revenge". We have five ideas in along similar lines for how to deal with the aftermath of Mary finding out about Catriona, so I suggest we look at them all and then discuss . . .'

It took us more than half an hour to reach a consensus, which turned out to be an amalgamation of three of the submitted stories. I checked that Lorraine was keeping comprehensive notes, but I'd also sneakily turned my phone on to record the discussions because I no longer trusted her.

Once we were all agreed I suggested we move on to the next story. I turned the page. Title 'Ronnie's Mum Moves In'. But I'd hardly got the words out before I realized that the text underneath read: 'Blah blah blah. Who cares? Some trite load of old shit written by a washed-up hack who couldn't get a writing gig anywhere else. Blah blah.' A ripple of chatter rose up as everyone else caught up with me. I flicked through the pages. All the rest of the stories were the same. 'Blah blah.' The occasional 'Tired unoriginal bollocks' or 'Clichéd crap'. I swallowed down the impulse to be sick.

'What on earth is going on?' Glen said, turning to me. 'Is this a joke?'

'Hardly,' I said, my voice barely a whisper. 'It was all fine on Friday morning. Emma'll vouch for that.'

'Well, sort it out,' he snarled. It's not often Glen loses his temper, which makes it all the more terrifying when he does.

I looked round at the sea of faces. All of them looking back at me. I opened my mouth but nothing came out.

'I need to phone Emma,' I say now. I stand up and leave the room on shaky legs. I hear a wave of laughter as I close the door and, even though I know they're laughing at the situation, not at my misfortune – well, most of them are – it stings. I walk to the end of the corridor and tuck myself into a fire escape doorway.

'Emma, what the fuck . . .' I say before she even manages a hello. I blurt out what's happened and wait while she checks the document I'd sent through to her last night. Of course it contains the same alterations, why wouldn't it?

'It was all OK when I read it through on Friday,' I say, pointlessly. 'Do you have an earlier version saved?'

It goes quiet for a moment. 'I've got one from a week ago. It's not completely up to date and it probably has loads of typos but –'

'OK,' I interrupt. 'Can you print off sixteen copies and get it here ASAP? I'll have to improvise till then.'

'I'm on it,' she says, and I'm grateful she doesn't try to start a conversation about what might have happened. That will have to wait. I have a room full of people to think about. I put the phone down. Take three long deep breaths and force myself to march back in there, head held high. Everyone looks at me expectantly.

'Right. I have absolutely no idea what's going on but I can only apologize. I'd just like to make it clear that I was completely unaware the document had been tampered with. Those comments were unforgiveable. Emma is bringing over an earlier version ASAP, but until then I think we should try and continue as best we can.'

I look at the page headed 'Ronnie's Mum Moves In', try to avoid seeing the offending text. Check the name of the person who submitted it. 'Davina, this first one is yours so I wonder if you can talk us through it in broad strokes.'

It's a shame it's Davina because of all the writers she can be the trickiest. And I imagine she's feeling slighted by the – all-too-accurate – barb about her being washed-up. She pulls a bit of a face.

'I can't remember all the ins and outs.'

'Just give us the broad strokes. We can always revisit it once Emma gets here. Please,' I say and I think she must catch the desperation in my voice because she actually gives me a sympathetic smile.

'OK,' she says. 'Bear with me, everyone . . .'

Somehow I get through the rest of the day. Emma turns up about forty minutes after I call her, red-faced and sweating. The replacement document is missing about thirty stories but we muddle through. At lunchtime I pull Glen aside.

'I can't apologize enough.'

He gives me a steely look. 'Care to explain?'

'I'm not sure I can. I think someone's trying to sabotage me but I don't know how they managed to access the story document.' In actual fact I assume that Emma hasn't been as cautious as she might have been entering her new password, but I don't want to drop her in it.

'Who? Not one of ours, surely?'

I also don't want to voice my suspicions out loud, even though I have no doubt that I'm right. There's no way Glen would believe that Roz was capable of this. I need proof.

'I don't know. But a few strange things have happened. I just . . . I don't want you to think I'm rubbish at my job,' I say with a catch in my throat.

'Holly, I have no idea what's actually going on, but I appreciate you wouldn't have made those changes yourself.'

I almost burst into tears with gratitude. Or relief. Or both. Of course no one would think I'd sabotaged myself like that. Unless I were insane.

Glen is still talking. 'It's probably just a practical joke gone wrong.'

It isn't. I'm sure of that. It's an attempt to make me look incompetent at best.

'Probably,' I say, trying to smile.

'Let's just hope it's a one-off.'

'I think it's going OK otherwise, isn't it? We have a few good ideas.' I want to get the focus back on the positive.

'Always hard to tell at this stage. But yes, so far so good.'

I don't want to go back into the conference room where everyone is milling about eating the hotel-provided sandwiches. I can't trust myself not to pin Roz against the wall, ask her what the hell she thinks she's doing. I can hear her holding court, making everyone laugh with a story about what some celebrity – I can't catch who – had said to her at a swanky A-list birthday party she and Hugh had attended at the weekend. The gist seems to be that they'd assumed she must be the latest fabulous new star he was representing – there's always a thinly disguised boast in Roz's stories – and that she had thought it funny to string them along and talk in detail about the movie she had just

starred in having been plucked from obscurity after a gruel-
ling open casting call.

'I told them it had been selected for Sundance and
Cannes,' she says to much hilarity. 'And that there was
Oscar buzz.'

'And did they buy it?' someone says.

'Totally. I think Hugh was a bit pissed off with me.'

I stand there, not knowing what to do with myself. I'm
ravenous, despite everything, and I wonder about finding
the hotel bar and getting a sandwich there, but I've left
my bag in the conference room and I'm not sure I'd be
able to persuade whoever served me to put it on the pro-
duction's bill. I'll just have to hope there's something left
when we all convene again in twenty minutes' time and I
can have the odd bite while other people are talking.

My stomach growls. I decide I should at least go and
hide somewhere else, before someone catches me lurking
out here and wonders what I'm up to. My mind is made
up for me when Juliet exits the conference room, presumably en route to the Ladies. I turn away and start to walk
towards the reception area.

'Are you OK?' I almost jump when she speaks to me.

'Fine. Yes, thanks.' I make to move off again. The last
thing I need is her gloating.

'What was all that about in there?'

I try to shrug it off. 'Just someone playing a joke on me,
I think.'

'Right,' she says. 'Not a very funny one.'

'No.'

She hovers there for a moment as if she wants to say something else but I don't want to hear it. I want to be on my own.

'I'm going for a quick walk,' I say, waving an arm in the direction of the nearest exit. 'I just need some fresh air.'

Outside I find a bench where I think no one will be able to see me, shivering in the cold because I'm not wearing my coat. I put my face in my hands and don't even try to stop the tears when they come.

16

'That fucking bitch.'

I'm on the phone to Dee, sitting on the train having first checked there was no one I know in my carriage.

'I hope you fucking punched her fucking face in.' Dee doesn't swear very often but, when she does it's as if all the bad words she's been saving up come gushing out at once. It also means she puts them in slightly odd places. I remember once she was furious with someone for cutting in line when we were waiting to get on a bus, and she'd snapped, 'Get the fuck back to where you fucking well are meant to fucking be,' at them. They'd looked at her and said, 'Sorry, can you repeat that? I didn't quite understand.'

'How can I say anything? I've got no proof it's her.'

'Of course it's fucking her.'

'I know that. Jesus,' I say, too loudly. The woman across the aisle from me looks up sharply, and I mouth a sorry at her. I adjust down to a hoarse whisper. 'I just can't prove it yet.'

'OK, well, it's time for the gloves to come off.'

'Oh, the gloves are most definitely off. Fuck her. I'm done.'

'That's my girl. I'll help you,' Dee says. 'We just need to find something that we can use to bring her down.'

'Shit,' I say. 'Are we really going to do this?'

The second day of the conference passes off without incident. We all agree on a higher than usual number of storylines including – I am heartened to say – my own about Morgan. I flick my eyes at Glen when it comes up to see if he looks confused when I claim it as mine, but he registers nothing.

I am as open and friendly towards Roz as I am towards everyone else. Dee and I decided that I need to avoid giving her any clues that I'm on to her. In fact I sent her a text message last night once I got home, fuelled by rage and something else: an almost evangelical drive to wipe the smile off her face.

OMG. What the fuck was all that about today? Juliet??? x.

I actually laughed out loud when I read her response. *It must be! What a fucking bitch. She's just jealous. And you handled it brilliantly xx.*

Yes, I'm sure no one noticed haha x.

Thankfully there was no sign of Hattie when I got in last night, although I could hear the low murmur of something she was watching coming from her room. I microwaved a frozen macaroni and cheese without even bothering to make a salad to go with it, topped up Smokey's bowl, poured myself a large glass of white and shut myself in the living room.

*

I decided that the best thing I could do was concentrate on making day two run as smoothly as it could, so I checked through my emails and saved files for any of the missing stories and printed them off. Just one copy. Then I sneaked out to the kitchen and got myself another drink, dug out my copy of Roz's application form and started going through it line by line.

I realized that I was skimming over the parts that I'd looked at already, so I made myself go back to the beginning, examine every word. Name: Roz Huntingdon. Age: 40. Marital Status: Single.

I almost did a double take. Checked again that the box that was ticked corresponded to the word I thought it did. Then I picked up the phone to call Dee back.

'Roz put that she's single on the form,' I said without even bothering to say hello.

'Can they still ask you that?' Dee said. 'Isn't it a violation of your human rights or something?'

'Who cares. They did, and she put single.'

'That's weird,' Dee said. 'Maybe she thought HR would think she'd be more dedicated if she wasn't married?' She was in her element, trying to spot a conspiracy. 'Like, I don't know, she wouldn't be rushing home on the dot every night to cook him his tea?'

I snorted. 'Can you imagine Roz being that sort of nineteen fifties housewife?'

'Well, no,' Dee said, despite never having met Roz. 'But who knows what she thought might help get her the job?'

I wasn't buying it. 'Maybe she didn't even notice.'

'Come on. How many times did you check and recheck your form?'

I switched the phone to my other ear. 'That's me though. I'm paranoid.'

'No one puts anything on an application that they don't mean to be there. If they make a mistake they just start again. Maybe they've separated and she couldn't face telling anyone yet?'

'I wondered about that, but there's no way. We were talking about him yesterday. She's all over-excited about something he's got going on at work.' I was tempted to tell her about David Summers but I was sworn to secrecy. And that's a thing I have. If I promise someone I won't tell something I never do. I'm carrying a lifetime of other people's secrets. Affairs, plastic surgeries, drinking problems. You name it, someone has confided in me about it, and I've kept it to myself. I have a whole secret soap opera going on inside my head.

'I've got it!' She shouted so loudly that I jumped. Smokey shot across the room. 'Maybe she's having an affair with someone in HR and she doesn't want him to find out she's married.'

I pondered this for a second. It wasn't the most outrageous Dee theory ever (that would be the one about Alexa listening to all our conversations and reporting back to the authorities if she heard key words. I tried shouting about where I could buy a gun and whether you could find all the components to make a bomb in B&Q in front of mine to try and prove a point, and the police didn't batter down my door, but she was still insistent) but I doubt Roz has ever even met anyone in the HR department outside of a job interview. We're in our own little world at the studios and we rarely have any reason to interact with the channel. That's not to say she couldn't have met them somewhere else but the coincidence just seems too extreme. Let alone the fact that I couldn't imagine Roz having an affair and never having given away any clues. 'Too many variables. She's having an affair. She's lied to the man about being married. He just happens to be the person who's going to be dealing with the applications for a job she wants. No, it can't be that.'

'Maybe they're just not actually married. They call each other husband and wife but they never got round to the legal bit?'

I didn't even have to think about that one. 'I remember it. It was a couple of months after I started on the show. They went off to the Caribbean somewhere and did it there. We had a collection and everything.'

'That could be it, like those people who pretend they've got cancer to fleece all their friends.'

'No. We got them a little painting by that artist she loves. I forget his name. Two hundred quid. And, besides, Hugh's loaded so that doesn't make any sense.'

'It does if they've got enough rich friends . . .'

'No . . .'

'Well, then there are only two explanations. She ticked the wrong box by mistake and didn't notice, which is frankly unlikely, or she deliberately lied about it.'

'I think I'm over-thinking it.' I was used to Dee always jumping to the most outlandish conclusion. And I knew this was nothing, I knew I should dismiss it, but for some reason I couldn't. I still can't. It's niggling away at the corner of my brain two days later.

There's a tap at my door and I look up to see Juliet standing there. I wave her in while trying to look as if I'm busy and I don't have much time.

'Sorry to disturb you,' she says in a way that makes me think she's not sorry in the least. Behind her I can see Roz and Lorraine getting ready to go to lunch. Roz looks over, raises her eyebrows as if to ask if I want to join them. Lorraine is standing behind her, gurning in her fuchsia sweater, turquoise skirt and dangly salmon-coloured earrings in the shape of flamingos. Something that Roz pulls off effortlessly looks contrived on her. Trying way too hard. The last thing I want to do is to spend any time with the two of them but it's important that I act as if nothing is amiss, so I mouth, 'See you there.' Then I turn back to Juliet.

'It's fine. I thought you were in the studio today.'

'They're moving sets. I just came up to let you know we have a problem with Simon's next batch,' she says. Simon is one of our most experienced writers and usually a safe pair of hands. 'He's taken on a commission from ITV and it's turned out to be much more work than he expected. He thinks he needs to concentrate on that.'

'What?' I say. 'He can't do that. What draft are they in?'

'First. And they're a mess. He clearly knocked them off in a couple of days, and when I told him he pretty much had to start again he said he didn't have time.'

This isn't an unheard-of event. Some of our long-standing writers have a tendency to treat the show with a bit of contempt, as if they're just killing time until something better comes along.

'It's not that big a deal,' she says. 'There are a couple of the others free I can ask to take over. I just thought I should let you know.'

'Fine,' I say. I should be grateful that she's got it in hand, but I just feel irritated that it's happened at all. 'Did you know about the ITV job when you commissioned him?'

'Well, yes, but I thought he'd make it work. Obviously.' She sounds defensive, as if she thinks I'm questioning her judgement, which I suppose I am.

'Well, let's not give him any more eps without checking if he's going to put the work in in the future,' I say. It comes out sounding more critical than I intend.

Juliet looks at me, and I can tell she's pissed off, even though she keeps it well hidden under the unemotional veneer she always wears. 'It's just an unfortunate clash. He wasn't to know the other bunch would keep changing their minds about what they want.'

I bite my tongue. She's right. It's not a big deal; I'm just programmed to find anything she says to me irritating. And at least she's handling it like a pro. 'Of course. Thanks for letting me know. Keep me up to date with whoever ends up taking over.'

'Will do,' she says and she heads for the door. The one thing I would say about Juliet is she's always professional. She never seems to take anything too personally. Including me having basically accused her of being a jealous maniac.

'Juliet,' I say as she's about to leave. Because something has just occurred to me. The uneasy niggle that I've had since my conversation with Dee last night has resolved into a fully formed memory. Or, at least, I think it has. Juliet stops. 'Do you remember when Roz got married?'

She pulls a face. 'How could I forget the Vivienne Westwood dress and the Jimmy Choos?'

It's true that Roz went into great detail at every opportunity about the crazily expensive dress and shoes that Hugh had insisted she splash out on. For quite some months.

God knows what Juliet is going to make of my next question. 'Did you ever see the photos?'

She scoffs. 'No. Actually, didn't the photographer lose them all or something? Or just run off with the money and never deliver?'

That's it. That's what I remembered. Roz had returned from the Caribbean tanned and refreshed-looking, full of stories about how fabulous everything had been, but distraught that there was no photographic record of the day.

I remember asking 'Didn't you take any on your phones?' and her saying that they had both decided to leave their phones in England. That they'd wanted a complete break so they could devote time to each other and not be constantly fretting about work. They had taken photos of the rest of the holiday on disposable cameras they'd picked up, she said. She would bring them in as soon as they were developed. But, of course, she never did. And I'd never given it another thought.

'Why do you ask?' Juliet says now, puzzled, and why wouldn't she be? And I have to smile and say, Oh, it's nothing, I just suddenly couldn't remember if I'd ever seen them or not, and I knew there was a reason but I couldn't think what it was. Luckily she buys it. Or, at least, she's so uninterested she doesn't question it.

When she's gone I send Dee a text. *Roz and Hugh's wedding pix got 'lost'. No one's ever seen them!!!*

Almost instantly I get a reply. *Oh my God!!! I knew it!!!*

And then, thirty seconds later, before I even have the chance to ask her what she thinks she knew, I get another. *Have you ever met Hugh???*

I haven't. Even though Roz and I are – were – best work friends we've never socialized outside beyond an end-of-day drink. It's never really occurred to me to suggest we meet up on a weekend, or spend time at each other's homes. Like lots of people, I imagine, we compartmentalize our social lives. I have, however, seen several photos of Hugh and his Greek god looks over the years. Including one on Facebook, with Roz standing next to him.

No, I reply. *But that doesn't mean anything. Have seen pix of the two of them.*

My mobile beeps. *What's her surname again?*

I send back *Huntingdon* and then I do what I imagine

Dee is also doing right now – while she's sitting at her reception desk, fending off the general public – I go on to Roz's Facebook page. There's the picture of her and Hugh together as her cover photo. I'm friends with her on there so I can see more than Dee will be able to but then I remember that Roz has always made a big deal about not putting anything personal on social media, so there's precious little to see.

Hugh is listed as one of her friends. Hugh Whitehall. I click through to his page. His profile picture is of him, tanned on a sunset beach, Greek god abs on show. His relationship status says 'Wouldn't you like to know?' I click back to Roz. Hers is blank. Back to Hugh. His place of work is listed as 'Fitzrovia PR'. And that's it. That's all I can see.

There's a ping to say I have another message. *Is this him?* Dee asks, attaching a copy of the photo of Roz and Hugh together. I reply that it is.

Nice, comes the response.

I'm about to google Fitzrovia PR when there's a tap at my door and Emma is there, back from the sandwich shop, asking if I want a cup of tea. I remember I said I'd meet Roz and Lorraine. I close my browser down.

'I'm going to pop out. I need the fresh air. Thanks though.'

'So . . .' Lorraine says once we've nabbed a table inside the café. They were sitting outside when I got there, but I insisted it was too cold. Whatever else, I'm determined not to be a pushover any more. '. . . I can't believe Juliet is that much of a bitch. Well, I can, but . . .'

'I know,' I say, wide-eyed.

Roz shrugs. 'I can. She wanted your job . . .'

'But to stoop to something that low,' I say, trying to suppress a laugh I feel coming on. 'It's sad. I mean, pathetic. Really pathetic.'

They both nod sagely as if this is indeed true. I can't believe how stupid they are that they think they've got away with it so completely. Assuming Lorraine knows what's been going on, but I feel as if Roz must have needed help at times. A lookout if nothing else.

'You'd have to be some kind of tragic loser . . .' I say, warming to my theme. I need to be careful not to overdo it '. . . to get pleasure out of trying to ruin someone else's life.'

'That's exactly what she is,' Roz says without batting an eyelid.

'Billy no mates,' Lorraine says and guffaws. I laugh politely.

'What was she doing in your office just now?' Roz says. There's a slightly anxious edge to her voice.

'Fucking Simon has blown us out for ITV,' I say. 'She was just letting me know.'

'Oh, right, so you weren't confronting her about it?' I realize that this is why she wanted to spend her lunch break with me. If I accuse Juliet and she can somehow prove that it couldn't have been her then things might get tricky for Roz.

'No. Not yet anyway. I don't know what to do, to be honest.'

She nods. 'I mean, you can't prove anything, right? You don't want to steam in there and end up looking like an idiot.'

'Exactly,' I say, as if I'm taking her sage advice under consideration. 'I don't think there's anything I can do beyond try and make sure she doesn't get the chance to make things any worse. Do you see why I insisted all my calls and appointments go through Emma now?'

'God. Of course. Good idea. So, obviously you think she was behind that fake message from Patricia?' Lorraine is loving the gossip. Her eyes are owl-like, made even bigger by the garish eye shadow she's wearing.

I nod. 'And a few other things.'

'None of which you can prove,' Roz says, nodding sympathetically.

'It did occur to me that I could look on Emma's computer and see the last time the story document was modified. Because Juliet was out somewhere for a big chunk of Friday, do you remember? At the dentist or somewhere. So if it happened then it couldn't have been her.'

Do I imagine it or does the tiniest look of fear pass over Roz's face? Just for a split second. 'Of course! So, did you?'

'I did. Sadly Emma put the words "Story Document" into bold when she opened it just before she printed it off on Monday morning. So that's the date and time it gives me.'

Roz suppresses a smile. She thinks I don't notice but I do. 'Shit. What're the chances?'

'Shame she didn't check the rest of the document while she was at it,' Lorraine chips in.

'She just scanned the first couple of pages apparently,' I say. 'And, as we know, they were fine. There was no time to go through the whole thing. It wasn't her fault.'

'What does Glen think about it?' Roz might not rate Glen, but even she wouldn't want to earn the wrath of the big boss.

I shrug. 'That it was a practical joke. I didn't want him worrying it was anything bigger. It doesn't look good on your appraisal: "Someone has a vendetta against me."'

'You're right. Hopefully that's it now, anyway. She's done her worst.'

I bet Roz can't believe how easily she's got away with it. I'm almost more insulted about that than what she's been doing in the first place. Do I think it's over? No chance. Not so long as I'm still on probation. Not so long as there's still a chance I might fuck up completely.

Satisfied for the moment, Roz launches into a story about meeting David Summers at the Dorchester last night. Apparently Hugh had a meeting with him and she went along at the end to pick him up and head out for something to eat. She was waiting in the lobby lounge, enjoying a G and T, with no idea of what time Hugh would be finished but not really minding because she was people watching, when he appeared in front of her with David Summers in tow.

'Do you mind if David joins us for dinner?' he'd said. 'I've reserved a table in China Tang.'

Lorraine's eyes almost pop out of her head. Clearly Roz has confided in her about David Summers being Hugh's client, and the instigator of the super-injunction, but Roz getting to spend time with him herself is a whole other level of awesomeness. A few weeks ago I would have been hanging on every detail myself. Now I couldn't care less.

'What was he like?' She takes a big bite of her ham salad roll and wipes a smear of mayonnaise from her chin.

Roz affects an air of nonchalance. 'Do you know, he actually seems really nice. Normal. It's hard to imagine all that . . . you know . . .'

'Was he friendly?'

'Very. But not at all letchy. I liked him, in all honesty.'

'Wow,' Lorraine says, looking at her starry-eyed. 'You're so lucky.' I make non-specific noises of agreement, concentrate on my sandwich. Roz starts on a story about how David Summers told her he loved her style 'but not in a creepy way', and I zone out.

I watch her mouth move, not listening to the words, and indulge myself in thinking about all the ways in which I could repay her.

17

Emma knocks on my door.

'Hi.' She hovers nervously in the doorway. 'Have you got a sec?'

'Of course.'

She comes in and closes the door. Emma always enters a room as if she's about to get a telling-off. As if she'd rather be anywhere else.

'Sit down,' I say. She has a sheaf of papers in her hand and my first thought is that she's uncovered another piece in the plot against me.

'Um . . .' she mumbles. I clear my throat and she starts nervously. Then she takes in a sharp breath and it all comes tumbling out.

'So, now the story conference is over I wanted to show you these . . .' She thrusts the papers at me. 'They're probably rubbish but I thought, well, if I don't show you then what's the point . . . So I wondered if you could have a look and tell me if they're any good or if I'm completely barking up the wrong tree, because the thing is I've decided I'd like to become a script editor one day, so, you know, I want to put myself up for the trainee position if it becomes vacant soon . . .'

It's probably the longest speech I've ever heard her

make. I look down at the papers she's handed me and see that they're storylines, six in all.

'Why didn't you give them to me before the conference? We could have included them.'

'Oh no. You had enough to worry about without me boring you with my ambitions and, anyway, they're for your eyes only because they're probably crap . . .'

I want to tell her that half the battle of being an editor is having confidence but instead I just tell her I'll have a read-through when I get a minute.

'When did you decide this?' I say as she edges back towards the door, desperate to get away.

'Oh, I've wanted it forever. But I've never told anyone before. I just . . . I'm not putting Lorraine down at all, but I've been watching what she does and I know I could do it. Don't mention it to anyone, will you?'

'Of course not, but if you're serious you're going to have to at some point . . .'

'I know. I wanted to see what you thought first.'

'OK,' I say, wanting to put her out of her misery. 'Let's have a chat when I've read them.'

'Yes. Thanks. And you can tell me straight if you think they're terrible . . .'

I smile at her. 'I will.' And then, because I can see how anxious she is, I add, 'Good for you.'

'Oh,' I say as she's about to leave. 'That last load of first drafts that came in for me? Have a look and let me know what your notes would be. When you have a chance. No rush.'

*

171

On Saturday I wake up with a mission. Hattie has left to visit her mum for the weekend and, despite the fact that I hardly ever see her, the flat feels different knowing no one is home but me. I'm tempted to play loud music and sing along at the top of my voice, have a shower with the bathroom door open or mess up the kitchen just for the hell of it. In the end I settle for tea in bed.

Hattie and I shared a glass of wine on Thursday evening. She showed up with a cold bottle from the off licence round the corner and I accepted a glass, even though I didn't really feel like one because I got the feeling she'd bought it with the specific hope of us sharing, a way of paying me back for the drinks she'd had with me and Dee the other night. Not that I expected to be paid back in the slightest. But it was a sweet thought. Inevitably the talk turned to my work and I told her an edited version of what happened at the conference. I played it down. Made it sound more like a practical joke than a genuine attempt to discredit me. I don't want to come home and talk about it every night. I don't want Roz to take over my life here as well as in the office. My flat is my sanctuary and I want to keep it that way.

Hattie's mum had taken a bit of a turn for the worse, she told me when I asked, anxious to take the focus off me and my problems. Compared to what she was going through they were trivial, let's face it. Ego versus life and death. She talked about it in a matter-of-fact way, and I got the feeling it happened often. That it was a cycle of her mother fading and then rallying.

'It's the nature of the disease,' she said, delicate fingers stroking the stem of her wine glass. 'It comes in waves. Unpredictable waves.'

'I'm so sorry,' I said, unable to think of anything more original to say. I felt terrible that I couldn't remember exactly what was wrong with Hattie's mum. She did tell me at her interview and it felt too late to ask again now, as if I didn't care enough to hold the fact in my head. I knew it was a progressive illness, but which one eluded me. Still, I remembered from when my own mum was sick that sometimes it's enough just to know that people know. You don't need them to understand all the specifics, you don't want them to keep on asking you about it, you just want to know that if you behave a bit oddly or you suddenly break down and cry they know why.

'It's shit, in all honesty,' she said. 'But it's how it is.'

Anyway, it occurred to me late last night – once I was tucked up in my room with a final glass of wine – that I have Roz's address for the first time. I've always known she lives in swanky Holland Park, home to music moguls and old rock stars. Not in one of the enormous white stucco mansions, I remember her telling me – those cost many many millions, and as well as Hugh is doing he's not there yet – but in a pretty cobbled mews. I remember being blown away that she lived in an actual house in one of the smartest areas of London. Something the rest of us could only ever dream about. Something not even our on-screen talent could afford to do. (To be fair, they don't earn half as much as the general public assume they do, hence the willingness of so many of them to appear waving in front of baying crowds at iffy nightclubs or to sell every detail of their most personal moments to the tabloids any chance they get.) But now, courtesy of her application form, I have the actual details.

I decide to take a stroll round the area. I'm curious to see her home. To see if I get a glimpse of the famous Hugh. And it's a beautiful day so I might as well enjoy it while it lasts. I'm up and out before I can change my mind. It's only a five-minute walk to the Tube. I haven't even had breakfast but I decide to wait till I'm down there. I'm sure Holland Park has many chi-chi cafés. Or, at least, a Starbucks.

I spend an age waiting at Bond Street for the connecting Central Line train, wondering what I'm doing here. I think about turning back, but I have no other plans for my Saturday so I figure I might as well spend it looking at nice houses as doing anything. It's only when I emerge at the other end and think to look at Maps on my phone that I realize it might have been better to stay on till Shepherd's Bush. That's the thing about London – which surely I should know by now having spent my whole adult life here – the Tube station that has the name of the area you're going to isn't necessarily the closest to your destination. Still, Roz's road doesn't seem to be too far. I cross over and turn off the main road and weave my way through the smart streets, past houses that people probably pay tens of millions of pounds for, even though they're hardly ever there because they also have homes in Cap d'Antibes and

Aspen. Their live-in staff almost certainly spend more time here than they do. I'd quite like a job with a perk like that. I pass a nanny in a uniform, walking with a red-faced, grizzling toddler tottering on reins beside her. He's probably the heir to a multi-national corporation. I look up, half expecting Mary Poppins to fly past.

My stomach is growling but I haven't spotted any cafés since I left the main road. I pass a pretty mews. I can picture the one where Roz and Hugh live from all the times she's talked about it – the cobbles, the pastel houses, the row of hanging baskets, overflowing in summer, that the owners all agreed on together. I check the address. This isn't it. It strikes me that most mews are called Something Mews. Devonshire Mews, Kynance Mews, Colville Mews with the crazy Union Jack-covered Temperley building. Roz's isn't. Is that odd? I assume there are exceptions to the rule.

As I keep walking, veering to the right all the time, as the map demands, I notice that the area is definitely starting to get a bit shabbier. The buildings are still magnificent but a bit more run-down. No more shiny Mercedes parked outside. Fewer perfectly trimmed box balls flanking the front doors or gleaming brass numbers. One is a B and B. More and more seem to have several doorbells where they have been divided into flats. Then, as I get closer to Holland Road, the style of the houses changes. The stuccoed mansions make way for Victorian terraces. Still lovely architecturally but would they have been grand enough to have mews built behind?

More B and Bs and budget hotels. I cross the main road. I would definitely now say I was in Shepherd's Bush if asked. Not even the 'Holland Park borders' – if there is such a thing. I don't really know this area well so I wonder if I might stumble on a hidden gem somewhere behind these run-down buildings. London is like that. Mansions sit shoulder to shoulder with council estates. I strap my bag across both shoulders, fold my arm over it protectively and hate myself for doing so but, like everyone else, I'm conditioned to go into self-preservation mode when my surroundings start looking less salubrious. I'm guilty of judging a book by its cover. Or, in this case, an area by its chipped paintwork.

Roz's street is the next on the left. I can tell before I even get there that it's not a mews. There are no cobbles. No hanging baskets. It's just a road of very ordinary Victorian or Edwardian houses. Three storeys and a basement. Perfectly nice if a bit shabby. Let me put this in context. This may not be the breathtaking environs of Holland Park but I still couldn't afford one of these houses if I worked every day till I was a hundred. Roz and Hugh live at number five, which, annoyingly, seems to be at the opposite end. I know that if she spots me there's no way she'll believe any excuse I make about it being a coincidence. Could I make up a friend who lives in the area? Brazen it out? Claim I got lost on the way to Westfield? Feign surprise that she lives here? (Things not to say: 'Oh my God, I thought you lived in a cobbled mews that's so pretty tourists go out of their way to photograph it!!' She once told me this, I kid you not.) But I haven't come all this way just to turn round and go home without seeing where she lives for myself.

It's still early for a Saturday, and I know Roz is a late riser at the weekends – or so she tells me; it's anyone's guess. I decide to put my head down and risk it. I walk briskly from one end of the street to the other, watching the numbers count down. Out of the corner of my eye I see number nine, number seven. Number five looks as shabby as the rest. The railings along the front of the steps leading down to the basement are rusty. The paint is flaking in huge chunks from the bay window of the raised ground floor. Blue curtains are pulled across but sagging where they've come away from the rail. As I approach the front door I risk a look. There are four bells. Four flats. Wherever Roz and Hugh live they don't live in a house.

There's nothing else to see short of hiding behind one of the neighbours' bins hoping to catch Roz and Hugh entering or leaving later. It's not worth the risk. I'm so confused I know that it must read on my face. I'm a walking emoji. For all Roz's talk of Hugh's success, clearly he's not earning the money she likes to hint that he is . . . What do I mean, hint? She all out says it. It's something that always made me feel a bit uncomfortable, the way she would be so boastful about how wealthy they were. Or maybe he is, he just hasn't got round to buying a decent place to live yet. Maybe he's one of those people with a chip on his shoulder who tries to stay 'real' and close to his roots despite the fact he could buy his neighbours out ten times over. Maybe they're living here temporarily while their mews house gets refurbished by one of London's top interior designers and she's just never mentioned it.

Or maybe their whole fabulous life is a big fat lie.

18

'Did you take a photo?' Dee sits there open-mouthed. We're having Sunday lunch at the Spaniards, out in the garden under a heater because the inside is all booked up. Dee vetoed any closer pubs because otherwise she'd never get her steps in. Gavin declined to join us, as he has to travel up to Leeds later for a meeting first thing tomorrow. I get the impression that suits Dee fine.

'What? No. I was terrified she was going to look out of the window and see me.'

She flicks at her fringe with her fingers. 'So, no flash house. No Caribbean wedding. No rough school. What about her is real?'

'I've got no idea any more.' I pick at my oversized Yorkshire pudding.

'Interesting. You should pay Fitzrovia PR a visit.'

'And say what? Is your wife a compulsive liar? Where's all your money because you clearly haven't put it into your home?'

'I don't know. Just to get a sense of him. Don't you think it's odd you've never met him all these years?'

'I've never met Juliet's boyfriend. I don't even know if she has one.'

'Because you hate her,' Dee says, taking a long swig from her lime and soda. 'But Roz was your friend.'

I steel myself to ask Roz if she wants to have lunch. I want to start paying attention to her stories. See if I can identify any cracks. It's too much to hope that she won't invite Lorraine along as well but then I figure maybe that's good, maybe Roz will be even more expansive with two people to impress, especially when one of them hangs on her every word like a starving dog begging for scraps. She also shouts over to Joe, asking if he wants to join us, pointedly leaving Juliet and Emma the only ones not included, but he declines, claiming too much work. I've noticed that Joe seems to have been putting a bit of distance between himself and Roz lately. He's gone up in my estimation.

We walk to the café in the spring sunshine, Roz holding court about David Summers yet again. How Hugh has an idea to have him do some kind of humanitarian work to help rebuild his reputation.

It was reported in the paper this morning that David has been made ambassador for an international children's charity. Someone is obviously trying to do an Angelina Jolie on his image. Hugh, apparently.

Because the weather has suddenly turned warm both outdoor tables are taken. I recognize four people I half know from the design department at one of them, and I nod a hello. We join the short queue of people waiting to order their sandwiches.

Lorraine pipes up: 'Was that Hugh's idea?'

Roz looks around as if she thinks everyone in the vicinity might be hanging on her every word and she needs to make sure she doesn't give away any secrets. 'Of course,' she says in a loud whisper. 'Brilliant, isn't it?'

'So, what . . .? It's to make people think he's a nice person?' Lorraine, I fear, is not the sharpest needle in the haystack sometimes.

'Exactly. Which he is. But the idea is that people see that and forget the rumours about all the other stuff.' She picks out a tuna mayo sandwich and I do the same. I lean over and take a fruit-flavoured fizzy water out of the fridge.

Lorraine helps herself to a cheese salad baguette. 'Can't Hugh just prove that the rumours aren't true?'

Roz looks at her as if she's just asked the most stupid question ever. 'He's working on discrediting those stories. Obviously. But it's hard when you don't want the general public to even know it's David the stories are supposed to be about. You know what people are like. No smoke without fire and all that.'

Lorraine takes a big bite before she's even handed over her money. 'Everyone knows though, right?' she says through a mouthful. I'm glad she came along now because I can see her questions are rattling Roz without me having to say a thing.

'No!' Roz says too loudly. The people at the indoor tables all look over. She adjusts her voice down. 'Not everyone's obsessed with googling the shit out of every piece of gossip they hear. Most people have no clue, and Hugh is doing a brilliant job of trying to keep it that way.'

Lorraine looks stricken. 'No. I mean, of course. You're right.'

Roz flaps her card at the machine. 'He just needs to make sure David is seen in as positive a light as possible until someone else huge takes out another super-injunction and everyone starts trying to work out who *that* one is. It's criminal really that the papers can talk about it at all, and even drop hints.'

Out of the corner of my eye I see the design department guys getting ready to leave so I slam some money down and dart outside, leaving Roz and Lorraine at the counter, just beating a couple of old boys to the table. I feel a bit guilty, but not so bad that I give it up.

'Nice work,' Roz says when they come out, having thankfully picked up my change.

'Hugh must really be at the top of his game,' I say with a smile. I don't want her getting all defensive and clamming up about her personal business. I'm convinced that now I'm looking for it I'll spot a useful piece of ammunition at some point.

'Exactly,' she says, fiddling with one of her dangly feather earrings. 'Most of what he does is making sure people stay in the spotlight, that what they're doing gets as much attention as it can. But something like this, where he's trying to save someone's whole reputation, well, let's just say if he succeeds all of David's friends will be beating his door down next time they need help.'

'Awesome,' Lorraine says.

'How did you and Hugh meet?' I take a bite of my sandwich so I don't have to look at her. I'm scared I'll give away my ulterior motive. The bread is soggy, turned to mush by the tuna and mayonnaise. A large chunk slaps on to the table and I busy myself mopping it up.

'At a party.' Roz pushes her cat's eye sunglasses up her nose. 'He was a friend of a friend of a friend. He came up to me in the kitchen and said he'd noticed me as soon as he walked in because I stood out from the crowd.'

'Aww,' Lorraine coos. 'Did you fancy him right away?'

'Definitely. Not that I let him know that obviously. I was very standoffish. He told me later it drove him crazy.'

Lorraine laughs. 'Have you got a photo of him? I've never even seen him.'

Do I imagine it or does Roz hesitate for just a second? She starts scrolling through her pictures. 'I've hardly got any on this phone. I had to delete everything because my storage was so low and I'm terrified of putting everything on iCloud in case I forget the password. Oh, wait, here's one.'

She holds the phone out to Lorraine, who makes appreciative noises. 'Oh my God, he's a total hottie. Show Holly.'

Roz swings the phone round to me and I see it's the same picture of the two of them that she has as her Facebook cover photo. Is that strange? I can't decide. I try to think if Dee has reams of pictures of Gavin clogging up her mobile – it's so long since I had a long-term relationship of my own that trying to recall my own history is pointless – and I conclude that, while she doesn't spend

183

her time taking portraits of him he inevitably shows up in quite a few shots just because he's there. And Ashley's phone is like a catalogue of everything she and Ryan have ever done.

'He's definitely a looker,' I say, because I can tell she's waiting for a response.

'Oh God,' Lorraine suddenly says in a whisper that's as loud as her normal voice. 'It's Emma.'

I look up and Emma is approaching the café. I smile at her and she smiles nervously back. I wonder if she heard. She walks past us and inside.

'She looks as if she got dressed in the dark today.' Lorraine cackles. 'Did you see those shoes? They're like something my granny would put on. And she's nearly eighty. And she has corns.'

Roz laughs loudly. Lorraine beams. Gold star from the teacher. I concentrate on my sandwich, head down. Say nothing.

Back in the office I text Dee: *Roz only has one pic of Hugh on her phone. Is that odd??*

A few minutes later I get a response: *I just counted up and I have 37 of Gav on mine. And I don't remember taking any of them. It just happens. I would say VERY SUSPECT!!*

I look through the glass and across to where Roz sits, pink-tipped blonde head down, making notes.

I have no idea what to do next.

19

Luckily for me Dee has a plan. Also luckily for me when it all goes wrong – as it inevitably will – there's no way either Roz or Hugh will realize it's got anything to do with me.

It's Hugh's fortieth birthday this week. I know this from hearing ad nauseam about the big plans for his party. Roz has hired a room in a smart pub in Holland Park – 'They're going to decorate it for free for us, because they love Hugh' – and Dee has decided she and Gavin are going to gatecrash and she is going to, as she puts it, 'observe them in their natural habitat'. The very idea of it gives me cold sweats.

'It'll do us good to have a night out,' she said when she announced her intention. Roz had made a show of saying how sad she was not to be able to invite me and Lorraine ('I'm already way over the number the room's supposed to hold'), but she promised us a full blow-by-blow account on the Monday morning, no doubt listing all the famous faces who show up for the birthday boy.

'Aren't they going to realize they have no idea who you are?' I asked Dee. We were in our usual bar at the end of my road, having a quick after-work catch-up.

She shrugged. 'I'll make something up.'

'What if they have a bouncer on the door? With a guest list?'

'Then we'll have a drink at the bar and go home.'

'And Gavin's up for it?'

She flicked her fringe. Raised an eyebrow. 'He has no idea. He thinks we're going out for dinner.'

I laughed nervously. 'Just talk me through again how stalking them is going to help me?'

'I don't know. But don't you want to find how much of what she says is true? What else she's lying about? It's not as if we've got anything else to go on. Or do you want to just sit around while she tries to lose you your job?'

I couldn't deny I was curious.

'OK. Oh my God. I don't know about this.'

Dee rolled her eyes. 'What's the worst that can happen?'

First, though, I have to get through the rest of the week at work. Things seem to have quietened down, at least for now. The calm before the storm, I'm sure. I can't believe Roz has given up her quest to have me discredited. Meanwhile I'm racking my brains for ways in which I can fight fire with fire. Out of inspiration, I decide to start with the basics. Roz, like most of us, prefers to make notes on each draft of a script as she reads them and, because of the sheer volume, the speed with which we have to turn them round and the fact that all the writers come into the office to talk through them (as opposed to being sent them), at least on the first draft, she rarely types them into her computer. There's no point.

I know that she had first drafts arriving this week, so I watch to see her, head down, scrawling in the margins. I want to ask Emma if she knows when the writer is booked to come in, but that would be giving myself away. I have to time this right. Too soon and – even though it would be an inconvenience – Roz would have time to go through the whole process again. I try to access her diary when I find myself the last person in the office, but she's changed her password and by the time I've put in three rejected guesses I'm sweating like a first-time shoplifter and too scared to try again. I could never be a career criminal.

I'm about to give up. The idea of being caught is too humiliating to contemplate. It's already Wednesday; the scripts came in on Monday. I absolutely know Roz will have scheduled something in with the writer before the weekend, such is our punishing schedule. Twice I have to stop myself from asking her outright. The whole point is that – even though she will almost certainly guess it was me – she will have nothing concrete to go on, no trail of breadcrumbs I've dropped to follow.

I suffer another lunch with her and Lorraine, listening to more details of the party (celebrity guest DJ – 'I'll leave you to guess who it is but let's just say if you named three DJs you'd heard of he'd be in there'; cake made by Dominique Ansel – 'Hugh handled the opening of the flagship UK store'), but I'm still none the wiser. Finally, in the afternoon, I'm in the main office talking to Joe when Emma shouts over at Roz that Michael – the writer – has called to ask if they could make the meeting ten thirty tomorrow instead of ten because he has to take his daughter to school first.

Roz sighs. She is not a fan of professional people who put their children first. I learned early on not to bang on about Ashley too much in front of her because she would glaze over. If Ashley had been younger I certainly would never have let her know if a childcare issue had got in the way of work.

'OK. If we have to. Tell him to get here as early as he can. Tell him we need to be done by twelve because I've got something else after.'

This probably isn't true. She just wants to make a point. We pretty much all know this but no one says anything.

'No problem,' Emma says, picking up the phone. 'I'll call him back.'

Now I just have to find a way to lose the scripts without anyone knowing.

I'm lucky that, for once, everyone leaves promptly at six, apart from Juliet who will be in the studio until seven. I have a minor panic when I think Roz might be about to take the scripts home with her to look them over one last time, but then I see her put them in the bottom drawer of her desk. She doesn't turn the key in the lock. Why would she? I just have to wait until the coast is clear, grab them and run.

I wait way longer than is necessary, terrified that someone might remember something they've forgotten and come back for it. And then I start thinking what if the filming wraps early and Juliet walks in, so I check the TV screen on the wall to make sure they are in the middle of a scene, steel myself, put my coat on, stride over to Roz's desk, open the drawer and stuff the three scripts in my bag before I can change my mind. I don't have time to shred them. I have no option but to take them home with me. I just want to get out of there.

On the train platform I consider throwing them in the bin but I have visions of all the TV shows I've seen where the police go back over the CCTV to catch the criminal in the act. OK, yes, I admit, I may be overreacting a tiny bit. But besides, it would be just my luck that a member of the public would pull them out and go running to the press with one of our closely guarded storylines. I sit there with them burning a hole in my bag. Once home I stuff them under my bed in one of those big plastic boxes where I keep jumpers I never wear. My heart pounds. I'm not cut out for this.

Thursday goes exactly as I imagined it would. I'm in my little glass office when Roz arrives at about ten to ten. She takes her coat off and hangs it up. Waves a hello. I try to act naturally, wave back and smile. She goes off to the kitchen and returns with a coffee. Joe, Lorraine and Emma are already at their desks. Juliet's coat is slung over the back of her chair. I made sure I was a couple of minutes later than usual in the hope I wouldn't be first in and therefore prime suspect, and Emma and Joe will be able to vouch for the fact that they, at least, were here before me. Roz perches on the side of Lorraine's desk. I can't hear what they're saying but they're laughing about something, oblivious – or more likely indifferent – to the fact that the others are trying to work.

It's five past ten. Roz goes round and sits at her own desk. She opens the top drawer, reaches in and pulls out her make-up bag. Gets out a lipstick and a little mirror and touches up her magenta gloss, something she does at least five times a day. Runs her tongue over her teeth. I can hear my pulse in my ears. I try to keep my head down, concentrate on working – or at least, looking as if I am – but my eyes keep drifting over, like a motorway rubbernecker. Lorraine leans over and shows her something on her phone. Roz cackles.

Ten past. Roz calls over to Emma to ask if she'll go to the café and pick up decent coffees when Michael arrives.

'Of course,' Emma says. 'No problem.'

Roz reaches down towards the bottom drawer of the desk. Slides it open. It's as if everything is playing out in slow motion. Her hand reaches in. Feels around. She leans over. Opens the drawer wider. Stands up and crouches next to it, peering in.

I force my head down towards my desk, even though I'm now staring at nothing. I allow just my eyes to drift back up.

Roz opens all the other drawers in her desk in turn and rifles through them, getting more frantic.

She looks over at Lorraine. 'I can't find my scripts.'

Lorraine jumps up to help her and they start going

through the desk drawers again. I can hear Roz saying, 'I put them in here last night. For fuck's sake. Emma, do you . . .'

Emma's phone rings. She answers. Looks over apologetically at Roz. 'Michael's here.'

Roz slams down a pile of papers on her desk.

'I can print you off another set,' Emma says and Roz snaps back at her, 'That's no use. They have my notes on.'

She glares around the office accusingly. I make myself look up, look confused and sympathetic. Her eyes alight on me.

'What's happened?' I say.

She turns away. She knows it's me; of course she does. But there's nothing she can do to prove it. Welcome to the club, I think. Welcome to my world.

'You'll have to tell him we need to postpone till tomorrow,' she barks at Emma. 'He'll have to come back in.'

I know that Michael lives way down in Sussex somewhere. It's not a question of him just hopping back on the Tube and popping in.

'OK,' Emma says, picking up the phone. 'What time shall I say?'

Roz ignores the question. 'And then print me off a new set and I'm going home to work on them there.'

Emma gets on the phone. I can't hear what she's saying but then she covers the mouthpiece with her hand and calls over to Roz. 'He says tomorrow is difficult. He could do Monday.'

'Fuck's sake,' Roz says again too loudly. 'Just tell him to rearrange things. He needs to come in tomorrow.'

'Do you want to speak to him?' Emma pleads, understandably not wanting to be the one to have to deliver Roz's unreasonable demand.

'No,' Roz barks. 'Just tell him.'

Ten minutes later she has her coat back on, a new batch of scripts in her bag and she's stomping out of the office. Michael held his ground and said that he had family commitments and he wasn't going to ruin everyone else's plans just because Roz had had to cancel at the last minute. He's booked to come in on Monday. Good for him. I briefly wonder if I should try hiding Roz's scripts again but I think I'd be pushing my luck. And besides, there's no way she will leave her notes somewhere I can find them after this.

At lunchtime Juliet walks into my office without knocking. I look up, irritated.

'Yes?'

She looks down at me, sitting behind my desk, and I immediately feel at a disadvantage. 'I just wondered what was going on. Emma told me about Roz's scripts going missing, and I know similar things have been happening to you. If there's a problem shouldn't Glen be told about it?'

'Everything's under control,' I say snappily. The last thing I need is her questioning my judgement.

'Let's hope so,' she says, turning and walking out.

Later I shut my office door and pick up the phone to call Michael in my capacity as head of department.

'Listen,' I say once we've got the niceties out of the way. 'I heard what happened this morning. I just wanted to check you were OK about coming back in on Monday.'

'I've got no choice, have I?' He's still in a bad mood. I wonder if I can steer him towards complaining to Glen about Roz, but it's a risky move. 'I'll be honest, Holly, I was a bit pissed off by Roz's attitude. I mean, she's the one who fucks up and then she tries to insist I cancel my plans and come back up tomorrow.'

I think about how I would handle this if I were just doing my job properly, without any of the politics. I would try to smooth things over. 'I know. It was out of order, but I think she was just in a panic. She probably feels like an idiot for overreacting.'

He sighs, unconvinced. 'Let's hope so.'

'Go off and have a nice weekend. Look on the bright side, you don't have any work to do now.'

Thankfully he laughs. 'You should be a politician.'

'Like I don't have enough problems,' I say.

'I appreciate you calling. You didn't have to.'

'I'll probably see you on Monday,' I say, putting the phone down. I'm glad I made the call. I remind myself that I mustn't lose sight of the fact that the most important thing is doing my job well. If I can do that then I can keep it, I can keep on helping my daughter out, I'll be bulletproof.

20

Dee is on the phone. It's Saturday evening and I'm home alone. I have no plans this weekend. None. With everything that's going on at work I just need some time to veg out on my own, to process what's happening. I'm thankful that Hattie, although she hasn't gone to her mum's, has gone out for a drink with friends in south London, and will be staying over afterwards. We did have a coffee together this morning because she came in to fill her kettle when I had just boiled mine and it would have felt churlish not to offer. She's easy to talk to. I was tempted to tell her the latest – the party, my retaliation – but I held back because I don't know her well enough yet. I don't want her thinking I'm some kind of vengeful psycho. I'll fill her in next time she, Dee and I share a glass of wine. That way I can make it sound more like a funny anecdote and less like a bad B movie.

Anyway, this evening, far from relaxing, I've been pacing the floor waiting for news from Dee's mission. She called me just before they left home, to tell me that Gavin, far from being annoyed once he'd found out where they were actually going, thought it was completely hilarious. He had offered to be the one to strike up a conversation with Hugh. I could hear him laughing in the background, and it made me happy that they were having fun, that they sounded more like the Dee and Gav of old.

'Just be careful,' I said. 'Don't say anything that'll give the game away, either of you.'

'You don't say,' she said sarcastically.

I ignored her. 'I love that you're doing this. Take photos.'

That was an hour and a half ago. Anxious though I've been I didn't expect to hear anything from her until late in the evening. Until, probably, they were on their way home at the earliest. Maybe even until tomorrow. That hadn't stopped me checking the time every five minutes, or motoring my way through the lion's share of a bottle of Pinot Gris.

My mobile rings. Even though I've been staring at it most of the evening I still jump and spill my wine.

'Are you there?' I say by way of greeting. I mop ineffectually at the spillage with a cushion.

'We are.' I can't hear any background noise. 'The weird thing is that Hugh isn't.'

'Maybe he's making a big entrance later. Guest of honour and all that.'

'I don't think so,' she says. 'Because it's not just him that's not here. No one's here. There's no party. I asked one of the bar staff in case you got the night wrong and they had no idea what I was on about. They said they never let the upstairs room out for parties any more because they had too many complaints from the neighbours.'

'Are you in the right place?'

'We're where you told us to be.' She quotes the name of

the pub and the road at me. It's definitely the place where Roz claimed the party was going to be. At least I think it was. Shit, what if I've got it wrong?

'I'm sure that was it. Damn.'

'Hold on,' Dee says. I can hear Gavin saying something in the background but I can't work out what. I feel terrible that I've made them traipse halfway across London for nothing. Ruined their fun night out. 'Ooh, good idea,' I hear her say.

Then she's back on the phone. 'Gav says what's their address? It's near here, isn't it?'

'What? No, you can't go round there . . .'

'We'll drive past it and have a look. Just out of interest. See if they're having it there and she made up the stuff about the pub to make it sound like a bigger deal.'

I have to admit I'm curious. I want to know the extent of Roz's lies, how much anything she says is based on the truth. 'OK.'

I give her the address, double-checking the number of the house. 'I don't know which flat they're in, but I guess it'll be obvious if there's a party in one of them. You can't gatecrash it if it's there, though. It'd be way too obvious.'

'We're just going to have a look. Stop panicking.'

I make her promise to call me again once they've established anything. And then I pour myself another glass of wine.

Twenty minutes later my mobile finally rings. I answer so quickly she must realize I've practically had my finger

196

hovering over the key for that whole time, because she says, 'Sorry, sorry. It took longer than it should to find it and then we parked up outside for a while . . .'

'And?' I say impatiently.

'She's got short blonde hair, right? With pink bits?'

'Exactly. So it is there? The party?'

'No. No sign of a party. Nothing. But we did see a woman with hair like that in the ground-floor flat. It looked as if she was cooking. She was in her PJs so I don't think she was expecting fifty people to descend any second.'

'So she made the whole party thing up? Unbelievable. I wonder if it's even his birthday. Did you see him?'

'No. But then we could only see into the kitchen. It's a bit of a shithole, to be honest.'

'This whole thing is so fucking weird. So what are you going to do now you're all dressed up and nowhere to go?'

'Best night we've had for ages,' Dee says, laughing. 'Now we're going to drive home via the chippy and fall asleep on the sofa.'

'Sounds perfect,' I say. We make a plan to see each other on Tuesday evening, but not before I promise to ring her and report back on whatever Roz says about the party on Monday.

'Not that she's likely to be chatting to me about it. She one hundred per cent knows I was the one who took her scripts.'

'Good,' Dee says. 'That means she knows you're on to her. She won't dare try and fuck things up for you again.'

'Let's hope so,' I say. More than anything I just want things to be back to normal.

'I guarantee it.'

Roz is holding court in the weekly meeting. We're all there but, in truth, her audience numbers are dwindling. The only person lapping up her stories now is Lorraine. Well, and me today, because Roz is describing the fabulous birthday party that she threw for Hugh at the weekend, in colourful detail.

I want someone to ask her where it was, just so I can check I had my details right, and thankfully Glen – who is for the most part oblivious to the tensions swirling around just under the slick surface of the department – does just that.

'The Admiral,' she says, clearly pleased that someone is showing an interest. 'In Holland Park. We took over their upstairs on Saturday night.'

OK, so I wasn't going mad. Right place. Right night.

'So who else was there?' Lorraine says, tongue practically hanging out. This should be my cue to call the meeting to order but I'm in no hurry today. I see Juliet shoot me a look.

Roz has already name-dropped Richard Branson and Sting and Trudi. Now she lists two celebrity chefs, an early-morning-TV host and an actress from the biggest show on TV. Lorraine oohs and aahs like the crowd at Wimbledon.

'Please tell me you took pictures,' she drools.

'God, no,' Roz says. 'I wanted them all to feel relaxed, not like they were on show or anything.'

It all sounds so implausible now I know it's not true. I can't believe I used to fall for it myself. She burbles on some more about the food ('Heston did it as a favour!') and the Dominique Ansel cake. She's about to enlighten us about a conversation she had with Nigella in the queue for the Ladies when I remember I'm supposed to be at work here, so I interrupt.

'I guess we should get on. Just in case anyone has to be anywhere else . . .'

Lorraine looks crestfallen. 'I totally want more details later.'

'Oh, me too,' I say with sincerity. 'Now . . .'

Later I shut myself in my office and call Dee.

'Fuck me,' she says once I've filled her in.

'My thoughts exactly.'

I'm interrupted before I can say any more by Glen sticking his head round my door.

'Fancy lunch?'

'Sure,' I say, even though the idea makes me a bit nervous. I've never had lunch with him before.

'One o'clock? I'll get Emma to book that Italian near the station. I'll meet you there because I have a meeting in town with the big boys first.'

'OK. Great.' I assume by the big boys he means the channel. 'I'll see you then.'

I wait for him to leave and then turn my attention back to the phone. 'Gotta go. See you tomorrow.'

*

I'm at the restaurant by five to one. It's raining and I'm half soaked after my walk from the studios, but it's hard not to be cheered by the sight of the fairy lights twinkling in the windows. The whole place looks as if it's been designed for a 'Most Italian-Looking Italian Restaurant' competition. There are empty Chianti bottles hanging from the ceiling, checked tablecloths, dripping candles – unlit at this time of day – and bunches of dried red chillies poking out from behind watercolours of azure skies. Attentive waiters in crisp white shirts hover with giant pepper mills. I love it. But that doesn't make me any less nervous. I tell myself I'm halfway through my probation period, so it makes sense that Glen would want to catch up. It's routine.

I order a bottle of sparkling water just to stop them asking me if I want anything, and then I nibble on a breadstick more for something to do than because I'm hungry.

Glen arrives nearly ten minutes late. I already need the loo because of the amount of water I've drunk.

'Sorry. Trains,' he says as he flicks a red napkin and sits down in one movement. 'Have you been here ages?'

'No. It's fine. Well, since one but . . . you know, it's OK.' Shut up, Holly, I tell myself. Stop wittering.

'Shall we order? I always have the same thing, so I don't even need to look.' He waves one of the waiters over without even checking for an answer. Luckily I've read the menu through from start to finish about eight times. He waits for me to go first and I start to panic about whether ordering a starter is presumptuous or expected. In the end I just go straight for a main course.

'The sea bass, please.'

The waiter smiles as if I've made a fantastic choice. He turns to Glen.

'Burrata followed by the pesto linguine,' he says decisively. I wonder whether to slip in a quick antipasto choice but it seems the moment has gone. The waiter is already off to deliver our order to the kitchen.

Glen pours himself some water. A basket of bread has appeared along with some kind of tomatoey dip and he tears himself off a chunk. I do the same.

'This dip is to die for,' he says. 'But you can only have it if you don't have any meetings in confined spaces for the rest of the day.'

I spoon some on to my bread and taste it. It tastes like heaven, but a heaven chiefly made up of garlic cloves.

'Oh my God, that's amazing,' I say, going straight back for more.

'At least you'll get a seat to yourself on the train home,' he says, chuckling.

So far, so good. It doesn't seem as if he wants to sack me. I wait for him to say something else, to give me a clue why we're here.

'So.' He wipes his mouth with his napkin. I have to stop myself from telling him he has a large breadcrumb in his beard. 'How are you getting on?'

I feel myself relax. I was right. This is just a halfway assessment.

'Good, I think. I . . .'

I stop for a moment while a waiter arrives with his

creamy lump of burrata and drizzles on some balsamic and oil. Glen looks round.

'You not having a starter?'

I shake my head and he digs in, using both his knife and fork to cut precise little pieces.

I pick up where I left off. 'I thought the story conference went well. After the mix-up at the start . . .' I may as well be the one to bring it up. Face it head on.

'Ah, yes, that. So what did happen there?'

I've already decided I'm not going to tell tales. At least not until I have evidence to back them up.

'I honestly have no idea. The document was fine when I read it through on Friday.'

'Very odd,' he says. 'It couldn't have maybe been an early version that Emma printed off by mistake?'

'I would never have written those things,' I say. 'Not at any stage.'

'No. Of course not.' He pushes his plate away, exactly half of the burrata left on it. A waiter appears out of nowhere and whips it away. 'Anyway, yes. We came out with some good stuff, I think.' He strokes his beard and the crumb dislodges.

'We did. Oh, and I have a couple of really great stories from Emma, would you believe? I want to weave them in. I'll get you copies later.'

Emma's stories had proved to be surprisingly good. Not all of them, but a couple. I'd called her in to tell her after I read them.

'Do you honestly think so?' she'd said, blushing from her neck up to her roots.

'We could have done with these at the conference. I'm hopefully going to use these two anyway – the Jono exam-cheating one and the one about Cara getting into debt – and I'll make sure Glen knows they came from you.'

'Oh. You don't have to . . . I mean . . .' If I thought she'd blushed all she could blush I was wrong. She was turning aubergine. I was thinking about calling the medic.

'That's how it works. Credit where credit is due. It's the least I can do because you won't get paid for them.'

'OK. Thank you. Brilliant. Would you like a coffee?'

'And I'll tell him you're interested in the trainee position when it becomes vacant . . .'

She'd handed me two pages of notes on the first drafts I'd asked her to look at – the same ones I gave Lorraine – the day after I gave them to her. They were insightful and clear. Critical but constructive. I'd been impressed. I'd told her so. She'd blushed purple that time too, of course.

'Oh. Well. If you think you should,' she said. 'You don't think he'll mind? That he'll think I'm not happy doing what I'm doing, because I am . . .'

'No. And yes to coffee.'

She exhaled, puffing out her cheeks. 'Thank you.'

'Our Emma?' Glen says now, surprised, so I fill him in on her ambitions.

'Don't tell her I told you, though,' I say. 'She made me

swear. But I'm trying to encourage her to come and have a word.'

'My lips are sealed. Good on her, though. She's wasted where she is.'

I smile. I'm glad he's noticed her potential.

'And Joe seems to have settled in well?' It's a question.

'Yes,' I say. 'Yes he has. He's good news, I think. The writers seem to like him.'

'Excellent.'

There's something coming, I know there is. He's like a cat skirting round the object it really wants to pounce on. I wait.

'So . . . Roz came to see me on Friday . . .'

And there it is.

He pauses while our main courses arrive. My sea bass looks delicious but I'm rapidly losing my appetite.

Glen waits for parmesan to be spooned on to his pasta and then digs in with his fork. He makes 'Mmm-ing' noises as he chews. The waiter watches appreciatively.

'*È buonissimo,*' Glen says once he's swallowed. 'Amazing.' This is obviously a ritual they go through every time. The waiter beams and goes off satisfied. I try to resist the urge to ask him to get on with it, to tell me what Roz said.

'Where was I?' he says eventually after another mouthful and a sip of water. The wait is agony. 'Ah, yes. Roz. She's got this idea in her head that you've got it in for her . . .'

I almost choke even though I haven't even taken a bite yet. 'She's what?'

He holds up his hands. 'I know, I know. But I'm duty bound to take it seriously if someone makes a complaint.'

I take a sip of water. Force myself to swallow it down. 'So what did she say?'

He sighs. 'Something about some script notes going missing from her desk drawer. She thinks you took them.'

'Why would I do that?'

He rolls his eyes. 'I have no idea. I'm just telling you what she said.'

'She's a fantasist, you know that, don't you?' I snap, and then I regret it immediately. Glen raises an eyebrow. 'Sorry. I don't mean that. It's just . . . it's frustrating that she's said that.' It's not lost on me how ironic it is that Roz is actually telling the truth for a rare time in her life.

'Listen, Holly, I have no idea what's going on between the two of you, or why she would feel strongly enough to come and talk to me about it, but whatever it is needs to stop. I need to know that you have the department under control and that everything is going to run smoothly.'

'Of course.' I'm fighting back tears, desperate for him not to notice. One more notch scratched on my unprofessional belt.

'I can't have stupid fallouts between former friends causing ructions. Not to mention that I have enough on my own plate without having to listen to petty personal gripes and feuds. This isn't high school.'

I want to say 'I'm not the one who brought it all to your attention. I've been trying to deal with it without involving you', but, of course, I don't.

'I'll make sure it doesn't happen again,' I say, with no idea how I'm going to achieve that.

'My guess is that she's still upset about the job,' he says, his voice softening. 'It will all calm down. Meanwhile you need to take control and keep everyone focused on the work. I got a bollocking this morning. Our figures are still slipping and they're going to be keeping a very close eye on us over the next few months. I need to be able to rely on you.'

Shit. 'You can,' I say. 'I promise.'

I barely eat any more. I've lost my appetite. Glen changes the subject, asking me about other things, things that are nothing to do with work, and I answer unenthusiastically. I can't get out of there quickly enough. But then we have to walk back to the studios together, blandly making small talk while all the while I want to scream about how unfair this whole thing is.

Back at work I thank him for lunch. I'm worried that I've come across as defensive or abrupt but there's nothing I can do about that now. I stomp through the department barely catching anyone's eye but then, just as I'm shutting the door to my office, I look up and Roz is looking right at me.

She smirks.

21

'Shit. Why didn't you get in there first?'

Dee and I are eating salmon and sharing a bottle of Shloer at my kitchen table. Smokey sits in his basket watching us, hoping, no doubt, that one of us drops a bit of fish on the floor. I fork a bit up and fling it to him to put him out of his misery.

'Because I didn't want to be that person. Because I thought I could handle it. Because I'm not eight years old, running to teacher like a fucking . . . baby.'

'Fair enough,' she says. 'So what now?'

I raise my voice. 'Now it's war. Now she'd better start watching her fucking back . . .'

'Oh, sorry . . . have I interrupted something? Are you OK?' I didn't hear Hattie come in, but now she's standing in the kitchen doorway with her coat still on, looking petrified.

'God, you made me jump,' Dee says.

I smile at Hattie. 'Just letting off steam. Sorry, didn't realize you were back.'

'Only just,' she says.

'Join us if you want,' Dee says. 'We've eaten all the food though, sorry.'

'I'll have a drink with you. I mean, unless you'd rather be on your own . . .'

'No,' I say, although to be honest I rather wish Dee hadn't offered. 'Of course not.'

'I'll just . . .' She indicates her coat and heads to her room, presumably to take it off.

'Sorry,' Dee mouths at me when she's gone. She can clearly see I'm reluctant.

'It's fine,' I say quietly. 'We can talk about it later.'

I find a clean glass while Dee collects our plates and scrapes what's left of the creamy salmon sauce into Smokey's bowl. He licks his lips but doesn't move. Too lazy.

Hattie comes back with an M&S couscous salad still in its container and a fork. It's always a shock to see her out of her thick winter layers because she's so tiny. It's not that she's too thin – she's not. She's just child-sized.

'I thought I'd interrupted a conversation between two mafia dons for a minute there,' she says, laughing. She sits at the table with us, peeling the top off her salad. 'Are you sure you're OK?'

'Really, thanks. Just more work stuff, you know . . .'

'That same woman?'

I nod.

I hope that she picks up my reluctance to go into more detail and it seems she does.

'Sorry, that's rough.'

'How's the world of teeth?' Dee interrupts with a swift change of subject, for which I'm grateful.

'Scintillating,' she says. 'Ask me anything you like about interdental brushes.'

'Don't,' I say. 'Because she will. She's probably heard a conspiracy theory that they give you cancer.'

'We did have someone come into A and E with one stuck between two teeth.'

'You so did not,' I say. 'Who told you that?'

Dee looks affronted. 'One of the EMTs.'

I turn to Hattie, laughing. 'Honestly, I swear they just make stuff up to tell her to see how gullible she is. They must have a bet going.'

'You'd be amazed what goes on down there.'

'Ask her about any implement and she'll tell you a story about someone coming into A and E with one stuck in an orifice. Literally anything.'

'Because it will have happened!'

'Well, obviously I'm going to say toothbrush,' Hattie says, ruffling up her short hair.

'Oh my God, where do I even start?' Dee is in her element. 'What do you want to know, electric or manual . . .'

Thankfully my phone rings. 'It's Ashley – you carry on. You're going to wish you hadn't asked, Hattie.'

I get up and head for the living room, answering as I go. 'Hi, sweetie.'

Any mum will tell you that there's always a moment when your grown-up child rings you when you hold your breath waiting to hear in their voice that they're OK. I wait for her hello. Hear a sob. My heart lurches.

'Ashley. What's happened? Are you OK?' My first thought is the baby.

'It's Ryan. We've split up.'

'Oh, sweetheart.' I sit on the sofa, in for the long haul. 'Tell me . . .'

It all comes out in a rush. 'Things haven't been right for a while. He kept going straight out after work and getting home really late and he stopped coming into the pub when I was working, which he always used to do. He used to like to be there for closing time so we could walk home together, because he hated me having to do it on my own, but he hasn't done that for weeks now . . .'

I try to push the image of my pregnant daughter walking home alone at midnight through the Bristol streets out of my mind. I can just make out the low murmur of Dee and Hattie chatting in the kitchen.

'. . . and I just knew it was because I was pregnant. He can't hack it. He's not ready to be a dad.'

I want to call him every name under the sun but I know that won't help. I'm furious, all my protective maternal instincts rise up like hackles.

'Well, it's a bit late for that, because he's going to be. He needs to grow up. You can't just father a kid and then decide you shouldn't have . . .'

'That's what I said.'

'Maybe he's just having a new-dad panic and he'll be devastated when he comes to his senses,' I say, trying to give him the benefit of the doubt. In actuality I want to kill him. I know that Ashley keeping the baby was as much because it was what he wanted as she did. They'd discussed it endlessly: whether they could give it a good life. Whether they could get their own lives back on track afterwards. Not to mention that Ashley had already given up her dreams and ambitions for this man even before the pregnancy came along.

I manage a few platitudes about people acting before they think, or sometimes it taking a while to come to terms with the enormity of a situation. It sounds like garbage even as I'm saying it and I don't think she buys it for a second.

'You'll be OK,' I say. 'You'll get through it. Has he moved out?'

'Yes.'

'Oh, sweetie. Maybe he just needs some time. He'll come round . . .'

'No, Mum, you don't understand. This is my decision. I told him to go. He's not ready and it's doing my head in. I told him either he stays and fully embraces being a father or we might as well split up now. He hesitated so I knew.'

I'm sideswiped. 'Ashley, you can't bring this baby up on your own. It's hard enough at your age . . .'

She cuts me off. 'Why not? You did.'

I take a deep breath in. 'Yes, and that's why I know how hard it is.'

'But you managed, didn't you? We were OK.'

I think about how hard it was, every single day, making ends meet. How, even though I wouldn't change it for the world, I had cried about the rest of life passing me by. Watching my friends going out at night having fun, not having to explain to every bloke they met that there was someone else in the picture, someone who would always have to come first.

'Come home for a few days.' I just want to take care of her.

'I haven't even got a bedroom any more.'

'You can have mine. I can sleep on the settee. It's fine.'

'I don't know. It'll be weird with Hattie there.'

'She's nice,' I say. 'And to be honest I hardly ever see her.'

She sniffs. 'I'll have to see if I can get the time off work.'

The door opens and Dee pops her head round. 'Everything OK?' she mouths.

I nod. I don't want to worry her. I mouth, 'She's a bit upset,' so she understands why I'm staying on the phone and leaving her and Hattie to it. She pulls a face and makes a gesture like she's holding a phone, which, I guess, means she has to go and she'll call me tomorrow. I blow her a kiss.

By the time I get off the phone the flat is quiet. I can hear faint noises of Hattie moving around in her room so I nip in the bathroom and brush my teeth and then hide myself away in my bedroom. I get in bed with a book, but I can't concentrate. I think about how hard it was being twenty-one and on my own with a baby. How alone I was. I can't bear to think that Ashley is going to suffer the same fate. I assume Ryan will contribute at least. If nothing else I've met his parents and I know that, like me, even though they were shocked, they had come round to the idea and were looking forward to being grandparents. I'm pretty certain they'll make sure he does his bit. If they don't, I will. I've got better at not taking any shit lately.

22

Roz is in my office. I was sitting at my desk, concentrating on reading through some notes, and before I knew it she had come in and shut the door behind her. It's two days since my lunch with Glen and I've avoided her successfully ever since. My mind is full of Ashley and the baby. Real life. I haven't got the time or the energy for Roz's games.

'I need to talk to you,' she says now. Her eyes are red-rimmed as if she's been crying or up all night, or both. I've never seen her look like this. Despite everything my first thought is concern for her.

'Is everything OK?'

'Can we go somewhere? I don't want everyone looking in and seeing me in a state.'

'Um . . . sure. Glen's gone home early; let's head in there.'

I follow her out and down the corridor. Emma looks up at me as I pass and I shrug.

Glen's office has proper walls, not glass, so when I shut the door we're completely on our own. Just us and his wall full of photos from other shows he's worked on. Him gurning matily with various TV stars. Beard in different stages of growth.

I'm about to say something, to ask what the hell is going on, when Roz flops down on to the sofa and puts her head in her hands.

'I'm sorry I've been such a bitch,' she says through tears.

I say nothing. Because I have no idea what to say. I have no idea what's going on.

'I know I've been awful and I did all those mean things and then I went and spoke to Glen about you but I'm having a terrible time, Holly. I don't know what to do.'

I sit on the armchair opposite. I don't feel as if I can say fine, let's just forget about it all then, because the bottom line is she has jeopardized my job. Not to mention that I'm beyond curious to know what's going on.

'Right . . .' I say.

She looks up, tears pouring down her face. In the three years I've known her I've never seen Roz cry. It's so wrong. Like watching a sloth suddenly sprint. It shouldn't be possible.

'Hugh and I split up about three months ago,' she says. That gets my attention.

'What? That's awful, I'm sorry.'

'I've had to move into this shitty little flat in Shepherd's Bush while we try and sell the house because he feels as if he has more right to live there than me. He paid for most of it after all.' She makes quote marks with her hands as she says 'paid for most of it' so I gather this is a sentence Hugh has actually uttered.

I feel as if the rug's been pulled out from under me. In

some ways this explains so much. I'm still confused, though, to say the least.

'But . . . what about the party you just had for him?'

She looks up at me. Manages a watery half-smile. 'That's the party I was planning before this all happened. Those people I was talking about would all have been there. We'd have invited them all, anyway. As it is I have no idea what he did for his birthday because he wouldn't tell me. I don't know if he thought I'd turn up and make a scene or what. I spent the evening at home, crying into a microwave meal for one. I feel like such an idiot, that I told everyone about it as if it had happened. I just couldn't admit the truth; I don't know why. Imagine how smug Juliet would be. And Lorraine knew when his birthday weekend was, and what I'd been planning originally, and you know what she's like, she kept asking me about it . . .'

'I'm sorry . . .' I don't know what else to say.

She looks at the floor. 'I've done some really shitty things to you these past few weeks. All the stupid messages and that meeting that disappeared from your diary. All me. Oh God, and the story conference document . . .'

I realize I've been holding my breath and I let out a long exhalation. 'Why?'

'I don't even know. I think I was just trying to make myself focus on something other than Hugh. Or I was having a breakdown. There's no excuse. I've been an absolute bitch.'

'I shouldn't have retaliated . . .'

'God, no. You should have. I deserved it. But I should

never have gone running straight to Glen. That was unforgiveable. And then when he took you out for lunch on Monday, I knew that was why it was, and I felt good about it. I wanted him to bollock you for it . . . I'm really sorry, Holly.'

'You knew that I blamed Juliet. You told me you were sure it was her.'

'I know. And I'm so sorry. Don't tell her the truth though, will you? I couldn't bear to have her laughing at me behind my back.'

I shake my head. Of course I won't. 'I won't. Why are you telling me all this now?'

'It was that. Monday. Me getting off on the fact that you might be getting told off. Once the initial buzz had worn off I started to feel really shitty. Like I'd taken things to a whole other level and that just wasn't right . . .'

'Did you want my job?' I look straight at her, willing her to look me in the eye, and she does. Then her gaze goes back down to the floor.

'Yes. I applied. And I guess I felt a bit hard done by that I'd been here longer than you but you got it.'

'If that was the criterion then it should just as well have been Juliet's.'

Roz lets out a small laugh. 'Right. I knew I was being ridiculous.'

'It's OK,' I say. 'I mean, it's been shitty, but I understand.'

'I don't really deserve that, so thank you. I'm not sure I'd be so forgiving.'

I sigh. Suddenly everything makes sense. 'I appreciate you coming clean. It can't have been easy.'

She drags a hand through her hair. 'I feel like an absolute bitch. You were my friend . . .'

I wave the comment away. 'Forget about it. Is there someone else? With Hugh, I mean?'

'He won't tell me. I assume so – isn't there always?'

Her throat catches with a sob. I lean over, put a hand on her knee.

'Shit. Do you need to take some time off to sort yourself out? Find yourself somewhere proper to live?'

She shakes her head. 'No, God, thanks, but the last thing I need now is to be flopping around on my own.'

'Well, if you do, just say.'

'I will. Thank you. Listen, don't tell any of the others, will you, not just Juliet? I couldn't bear all the sympathy. Not yet.'

I agree that I won't. I can understand why she feels that way, although I do wonder if it's sympathy or Schadenfreude she's afraid of. 'Of course.'

There's silence for a moment, and then she says, 'Can we be friends again? I'll understand if you say no.'

She looks so pathetic. So desperate for me to say yes. My heart goes out to her. I've never been one to bear a grudge. I can't stand knowing I have bad blood with someone.

'Of course,' I say, relieved that it's all over. 'Of course we can.'

PART TWO

23

Ashley has been home for a week. I'm so grateful to have her here to look after but I'd be lying if I said it wasn't a bit difficult, having a third person in the flat all the time. My back is aching from sleeping on the sofa. I find myself apologizing to Hattie over and over again, that she has to wait longer for the bathroom, or because the kitchen is a mess or a stray packet of cereal has found its way into her one cupboard. Not that she's complained. Not yet.

They seem to be getting on well. I hear them chatting in the kitchen late one night, when I've gone to bed, the living-room door slightly open so that Smokey can come and go between me and Ashley during the night.

'The thing is . . .' Ashley says, 'it felt more like hard work trying to manage his lack of enthusiasm rather than just getting on with things on my own.'

'Exactly,' Hattie says. 'Sometimes it's better to take control.'

'I hope so. Shit.'

'Do you have a relationship with your dad?' I hear Hattie ask, and I hold my breath, waiting for Ashley's answer.

'No. I've never met him,' she says, and leaves it at that.

*

Ashley has only asked me about her dad once in her whole twenty-two-year life. When she was small I waited for the questions, I spent hours trying to compose the perfect answer. Truthful but not too truthful. The fact that I didn't even know his surname could wait until she was older. And then, when they didn't come, I worried that maybe she thought it would upset me if she asked, that she was censoring herself for my sake. Eventually I realized that almost none of her friends at school had two parents. And if they did they were just as likely to have two mums or two dads. I loved that she was growing up understanding that families came in all shapes and sizes, without ever questioning it.

Then, one day when she was about fourteen, already taller than me but blighted with a self-consciousness that made her stoop, we were sitting eating in the kitchen and, out of nowhere she said, 'Have I got a dad?'

I was so surprised I shovelled in a huge mouthful of food to give me time to think. Ashley just sat there, looking at the table, waiting for me to swallow it and answer her.

'Of course,' I said eventually. 'He . . . um . . . he was a boy I was at college with . . . Lawrence. Lol.'

'Have I ever met him?'

I reached across the table and took hold of her hand. 'No. We were very young. Way too young really. He didn't feel ready.'

She nodded as if that made sense. 'Were you in love with him?'

I couldn't lie to her. Not now. 'We didn't know each

other for very long, so no. If you . . . um . . . ever want to try and track him down, though, I could help you . . .'

She shrugged. 'No thanks. I just wondered, that's all.'

'Right,' I said. I waited to see if she had any more questions.

'He's not my dad though, really, is he? Not in the real sense. I mean, he was more like a sperm donor.'

'Ashley!' I said, and then I laughed because I couldn't help myself. And so did she, the pair of us giggling till we had tears in our eyes.

After that I waited for her to ask again, wondering if now she had the bare facts she'd want to know more. But she never did.

I have no idea what she's going to do now. She veers daily between making plans for the baby and thinking about getting rid of it while she still can, between going back to Bristol or staying in London, between returning to her job or returning to college. I know that her work have been phoning, trying to establish when she'll be back, and I imagine there's only so long they'll wait, but when I try to bring up the time pressure on all of her decisions it sends her into a panic. So I'm tiptoeing round the subject and just trying to be there to listen. I remember well enough what it was like to be pregnant so young. That feeling that whatever decisions you made were going to impact the whole of the rest of your life so maybe it was easier not to make any decisions at all. I have to let her come to her own conclusions.

Work, on the other hand, has been much better. For

the first time since my promotion I feel as if I can focus on doing a good job. I go all out to prove to Glen that he was right to have faith in me. Roz is quieter than usual, but we're on good terms and she's getting on with her work. Despite everything I worry about her.

I have just four weeks left of my probation period. I report back to Glen that everything has calmed down, that Roz and I have sorted out our differences – without telling him the details – and he congratulates me for having handled it well. I glow inside like I just got top marks from the teacher.

In the evenings I try to encourage Ashley to talk about the future without making her feel as if I'm cornering her. I tell her that when the baby's born she can come and stay with me until she gets on her feet, even though I haven't even begun to think about the practicalities of how that might work. Hattie, to give her credit, never asks when she might get her peace and quiet back, or if she can have a rent discount because she's having to share the facilities with more people than she signed up for, one of whom seems happy to lie in the bath for a good hour every evening, talking to her friends on the phone. I write myself a mental note to make it up to her somehow.

Ashley, it turns out, is her mother's daughter. When I get home from work on the Friday she announces that she's made a decision. Several decisions, actually. She's having the baby. She's going to move in with her best uni friend Brooke whose flatmate has recently moved out. She's spoken to her work and they're happy to have her back from Sunday, day shifts only. She put her foot down.

No more drunken stag parties or walking home at 1 a.m. I pull her into a tearful hug.

'I'm so proud of you,' I say into her hair.

I breathe a sigh of relief. Everything is going to be OK.

Of course, as soon as you think that you're doomed. It's the equivalent of the teenage girl confidently telling her terrified friends that she's killed the monster in the basement. As soon as she says it out loud you just know he's going to burst through the door with an axe.

Dee, of course, can't leave things alone. Why that woman has never found work as a private detective I'll never know. I haven't seen her all week because I've been coming straight home and cooking healthy balanced meals for my daughter. Sometimes, as a mother, that's all you know how to do. As if eating vegetables for seven days might fix the problems in your offspring's life.

But Dee has been busy.

'Have I got news for you,' she says, wide-eyed, as soon as I let her in on Saturday evening. Ashley left for Bristol this afternoon, both of us teary-eyed. Hattie has gone to her mum's, probably to get away from the drama and hormones. Gavin, so Dee told me when we texted to arrange to meet up, is watching some World Cup warm-up on the big screen at a pub up the road with a couple of his mates.

'What?' I say impatiently. It doesn't even cross my mind that it might be to do with Roz, that's how much progress we've made in the last couple of weeks.

'I need a drink first.' She hands me a bottle of white,

and I put it in the fridge, taking out the cold one I put in there earlier.

'Oh God, Dee. What have you done?' I pour the wine. Put the bottle back. Get it out again. Top up our glasses some more.

Dee flops down at the kitchen table and I join her. 'Don't be cross with me,' she says. Words no one ever wants to hear.

'OK. Spit it out.' I don't know what I'm expecting her to say but it certainly isn't what comes next.

She exhales theatrically. 'Well. I know you sorted everything out with Roz . . .'

I'd called Dee and told her about Roz's apology straight after it happened. 'It explains everything,' I'd said. 'I mean, it doesn't wipe out the things she's done but at least I understand now. I feel bad for her . . .'

Now, though, my heart sinks. 'I did.'

'It just didn't feel quite right . . .'

'Nothing ever does with you,' I snap. 'Why can't you ever accept anything at face value?'

She looks taken aback and I immediately feel bad. 'Sorry,' I say. 'I just thought all this had gone away.'

'I won't tell you if you don't want me to,' she says petulantly.

'No. Go on. I have to know now.'

She carries on, but I can tell I've taken the wind out of her sails a bit. 'So, anyway, something didn't seem right. I mean, I felt bad that Hugh had walked out on her but didn't you think it was odd that she kept on making up all that stuff about the party and the dinners and whatever else she'd been telling you all. And it still didn't really explain why she'd been so horrible to you. Or why she lied about applying for the job in the first place . . .'

I want to tell her to get to the point but at the same time I'm not entirely sure I want to hear what she has to say. Life has been so much easier since Roz and I called a ceasefire.

'And . . .' Dee continues, 'I was telling Gav about it and he agreed. There was something off. Even if Hugh did have a bee in his bonnet about him earning much more than her it still seems unlikely that he'd kick her out and let her move into that shithole when he's the one in the wrong here. Unless he's just an out-and-out bastard, which, of course, it's possible he is. Anyway . . . it was driving me mad trying to work out what was going on. I just didn't want her taking you for a ride, that's all . . .'

'I appreciate that,' I say, feeling guilty about my earlier outburst. 'I do.'

'I'm just going to say this next bit quickly and get it over with. Don't kill me . . .' She looks at me pleadingly. Sweeps her fringe to one side and then smooths it down again.

'Get on with it. Jesus . . .'

'OK. So, Gav said why didn't I check Hugh out. See if there was more to the story. He said why don't you phone up Fitzrovia PR and say you represent someone famous and they need a new press person. You could set up a meeting with him. See if you could get him talking about anything personal.'

'You didn't?'

227

She looks at the table 'I did. This afternoon.'

'No, Dee . . .'

'I asked for Hugh Whitehall. They said that he'd popped out but then they asked me what it was about . . .' She breaks off to pour more wine into her glass.

'Oh my God. Just tell me.'

'I told them I was Eddie Redmayne's manager – I thought I'd better go high-end because most of their clients seem quite knobby – and that he needed new PR and quickly because something had happened. I didn't say what, obviously, because that would have been slandering him and you know how rumours start . . .'

I resist the urge to interrupt and ask her to get to the point. I know how much Dee loves giving a story a full airing. I feel sick.

'And I said that I'd heard Hugh was the best and that he was the only person I wanted to talk to. Anyway . . .' Here she takes a long pause for dramatic effect. '. . . guess what they said?'

'I can't!' I almost shout. 'Tell me.'

'OK. Calm down. They said that I must be mistaken because Hugh doesn't have clients. He works in – get this – the accounts department. He's an accountant.'

I sit there open-mouthed. 'Are you sure?'

'That's exactly what I said. "Are you sure?" And they said of course they were sure and would I like to be put through to someone else, or leave a message so one of the actual PR people could call me back? So I made up a name and number and got off the phone.'

'What the actual fuck?' I can't take it in. All the stories about famous people and fabulous dinners and swanky parties. Are we supposed to believe that the company is so generous – or so fucked up – that it has been sending the accountant to represent them? That David Summers would ask a bloke who does the payroll to rebuild his image after all the rumours swirling around about him threatened to destroy his family-man image?

'Exactly.'

'We must be missing something,' I say.

'Maybe Hugh is related to someone famous and that's how they get the invites. Or he's blackmailing them all. He knows all their secrets through the company and he's been threatening to tell unless they give him and Roz free canapés and champagne.'

I sit back in my chair. Smokey immediately jumps on my lap. 'This is weird.'

'Maybe it's like that Michael J. Fox film where he works in the post room but he's somehow managed to convince potential clients that he's an executive . . .'

I give her a look.

'OK, so maybe it's not like that . . .'

'So she's still lying. It's still all bullshit, it's just different bullshit.'

Dee nods. 'I'm afraid so. I have no idea what it means but she certainly isn't being as honest with you as she claims she is.'

'Does it matter though? I mean, so long as she's stopped trying to stitch me up at work, do I care?'

'How do you really know she's stopped though if you can't believe a word that comes out of her mouth?'

'She can't be making it up. Not all of it. Not for all these years . . .'

She shrugs. 'Stranger things have happened.'

Something occurs to me. 'Do you think Hugh's living a whole big lie too? Pretending to all their friends that he's something he's not?'

She thinks about it for a second. 'Or he has no idea. That would be my guess. The idea of the pair of them going round lying to everyone is just too weird.'

'Do you think he's even left her?' I say. 'Is that a crock of shit as well?'

'Time for a conversation with Hugh, I think,' Dee says with a wicked smile on her face. 'Don't tell me you don't want to find out?'

24

'How can I?' I say, once I've absorbed her statement. 'He might have seen pictures of me. Me and Roz always used to take stupid selfies.'

'Not you. Me. Or, to be more precise, Gav. Hugh'll let his guard down much more with a bloke.'

I twirl my earrings round and round. Realize I'm doing it and force myself to stop. 'No way will Gavin be up for this.'

'He is. Totally.' She sits back and looks at me, eyebrows raised.

'What? The two of you have already decided? He's just going to walk up to him and introduce himself?'

'We haven't worked out the details yet.'

I actually laugh, this is so ridiculous. But then I'm hit with a wave of misery. So this isn't all over. 'To what end though? What's the point?'

Outside there's a crack of thunder. An appropriate sound effect for my mood. Smokey slides off my lap and slinks under the table. 'Aren't you curious?' Dee says.

I shrug. 'I suppose so. I just don't want to get sucked into it all again.'

'You won't. This has nothing to do with anything that's been going on at work.'

'So why bother?'

'Oh my God, Holly. How can you not want to know what's going on? Roz has been telling you stories for three years about how successful Hugh is. I mean, not just in the abstract. All the details. The names of his clients. The dinners. The parties.'

'I still think a lot of it is probably true. I mean, obviously not the clients bit. But he's well connected through family or something. Accountants can earn a lot, can't they? Remember this is the woman who lied about being from a council estate because she was embarrassed about having gone to a posh school.'

She shakes her head. 'It's psychotic.'

'No. It's just a bit sad . . .'

'Either way. I'm not going to sleep till I find out.'

I lean over and fill her glass. 'You're too nosy for your own good.'

'Come on,' she says. 'I could dine out on this story for years.'

'How many clients does Hugh look after?' Lorraine asks innocently. Lorraine is completely besotted by Hugh, I've come to realize, or at least the idea of him. It suits me. It means she brings him up at every available opportunity and I don't have to. I sneak a look at Roz to see if she's OK with having to keep up the pretence that they're still together or if she needs me to step in and change the subject, but she looks completely at ease. We're in the meeting room, waiting for everyone else to arrive.

Roz screws up her face. 'God, I don't know. I want to say about twenty, twenty-five.'

'Wow.' Lorraine takes off her new red cats' eye glasses and cleans them on her (red) jumper. 'What would happen if they all had some big crisis blow up at once? I mean, I know it's unlikely, but it's possible, right?'

'That's why he keeps his list fairly small,' Roz says. 'But he has a whole team of people working for him, so they'd take some of the pressure off.'

I stop myself from saying, 'What, they'd calculate the National Insurance for him? Or would they work out the pension contributions?' Instead I go for a non-judgemental head nod. Given how devastated Roz apparently is by Hugh's leaving she seems to have no problem acting as if all is fine between them in front of Lorraine.

'And I suppose some of them spend half their time in America and have American press people as well, don't they?' Lorraine chips in. She's clearly been paying attention to Roz's shtick.

'Exactly,' Roz says. 'I know what you're saying but I think realistically it would just never happen.'

'Still. It's a lot of responsibility.'

She shrugs. 'That's why they pay him the big bucks.'

Lorraine nods sagely. 'How long did it take him to work his way up to having the kind of clients he has now?'

'Oh God, let's think,' Roz says. I wonder if she already has a whole fake timeline for Hugh's career in her head, or if she's grasping around trying to make sure that whatever she comes up with makes sense.

'He started there, ooh, at least five, six years ago, I think. He'd been at MPP before though. And before that he worked in a bar for a few years because he didn't know what he wanted to do.'

Lorraine nods, lapping up the detail. 'So how did he go from pulling pints to PR? That's quite a change.'

Roz is saved by the arrival of Emma, Juliet, Joe and Glen all at once. 'It was before my time, but I think one of the MPP guys used to drink in there. Something like that. He had to start at the bottom, obviously. Work his way up.'

'Ooh,' Lorraine says, a Pavlovian response to seeing Emma. 'Is there coffee?'

'I'm just about to make some,' Emma says without a hint of irritation.

'Maybe you could help her, Lorraine,' I say with a smile. I almost laugh when I see her affronted expression. I know she wants to protest but she wouldn't dare to in front of the boss. She huffs out in Emma's wake.

I'm coming over tonight. No arguments. Big news! Huuuuuge!! Be there 7.

I text back *OK* and Dee replies within seconds: *Oh my fucking God, you are not going to believe this!!!*

I assume it's something to do with Hugh's job, that Gavin has carried out his mission and found out Hugh isn't even the accountant, he's actually the cleaner or something. I'm curious but, to be honest, I'm feeling so relieved that Roz and I have a detente that I don't really care what

234

she's exaggerated about any more. So long as it doesn't affect me. What does it matter if Hugh is rich because he has a good job or because his daddy has money?

I send back *See you later xx* and leave it at that. I know my lack of curiosity will drive Dee mad, but I also know she wouldn't tell me by text if I pushed her anyway, so I don't feel too bad about it.

She's waiting on the steps when I get home. Dominos box in hand.

'How long have you been here?'

'Five minutes. Open up, the pizza's getting cold.'

'You were early then,' I say defensively. 'Because I'm not late.'

'I didn't say you were.'

I follow her down. 'No Hattie?'

'Doesn't look like it,' she says as I unlock the door. Smokey greets us with an indignant yowl. We head into the kitchen and I fill his bowl and then both Dee and I grab slices of the mushroom and anchovy pizza without even bothering with plates.

'Go on then,' I say, half a slice down. I hadn't realized how hungry I was.

She pulls off a square of kitchen roll. Places it on the kitchen table with the uneaten portion of her slice on top. 'Honestly. This is officially insane now.'

'Hugh is actually a woman?'

She throws me a look. 'So . . .' she says, in her element. 'Gav basically stalked him to a café at lunchtime . . .'

'Did he take a day off for this? I hope he's not going to lose his job because of me.'

'He was off today anyway. Shut up and let me tell you.'

'Carry on. I'll be quiet.'

She takes a theatrical breath in and continues. 'He hung around outside Fitzrovia PR for about an hour with only that picture from Roz's Facebook to go on, but, anyway, eventually Hugh came out, on his own thankfully, and went to this greasy spoon round the corner. Luckily he didn't just go in to get a sandwich to take out, he sat at a table . . .'

She waits for a reaction from me so I just nod encouragingly. Help myself to a second slice of pizza.

'So, Gav goes up to him and says, "Hugh!" as if he knows him. Clearly Hugh doesn't have a clue who he is. So Gav says, "I'm a friend of Roz's. We met at that party." I mean, can you imagine Gavin doing that? I'm very impressed with him.'

'It's nice of him to get involved,' I say, because it is, even if it's unnecessary. I do notice though, that Dee's eyes are shining when she talks about him. Something that hasn't happened for a very long time.

'He's loving it, honestly. It's like he's a different bloke.'

I laugh. 'Maybe he should start a new career as a private detective.'

'Anyway. I'm getting to the good bit. Hugh just says, "Oh, right. Hi," as if he's not really that interested but Gav sits right down opposite him anyway and orders egg and chips. Hugh's trapped there because he's got food coming too. Apparently at one point he says that he's waiting for someone to join him – because they're on a table for two – and Gav just says that's OK, he'll move when they get there. Ha!'

'That is pretty crazy,' I say, because it is, and because I feel as if I should be showing more gratitude for the lengths they've gone to. 'Did they ever show up?'

'Yes, but not for ages. I'll get to that. Gav says he decided he just had to go for it because he realized he didn't have long and Hugh was clearly a bit irritated because he doesn't know him from Adam. So he just says, "How is she?" about Roz, and Hugh says, "I haven't seen her for ages," which, you know, makes sense with everything she's told you . . .'

We both jump and I think I even let out a little scream as Hattie suddenly appears in the doorway.

'I didn't hear you come in,' I say, laughing at my own ridiculous reaction. 'How long have you been here?'

'I just got here,' she says. 'I'm going straight out again. Hi, Dee.'

'Hi. Anywhere nice?'

Hattie screws up her face. 'Yoga. My friend persuaded me. I just came home to get changed.'

'God, rather you than me,' I say. I wait for Dee to offer up a random story about a yoga-related A and E incident, but she's too wrapped up in the story she's telling me to be distracted.

Hattie waves a hand towards her bedroom door. 'Well, I'd better get changed . . .'

'Have fun,' I say.

'See you later.'

Dee opens her mouth as if she's about to launch back into her story, but I flap a hand at her and whisper, 'Wait.' The story has got so mad now that I really don't want to share it with Hattie or anyone else.

Dee takes the opportunity to finish her pizza slice and pull off another one, which she sits on the piece of kitchen roll.

'Do you want a plate?' I say.

'Not unless you want me to use one. I can . . .'

'I don't care either way.'

'OK. Well, this is fine.'

She takes another bite and so do I. We sit there saying nothing until we hear the click of the lock and footsteps on the steps.

'It must be like living with a magician,' she says. 'One minute there's nothing there and then boom! There's a person in the doorway.'

'I have literally never known anyone to be so quiet,' I say. 'Anyway, carry on with what you were telling me.'

'OK, where was I? Oh yes, so Hugh says he hasn't seen her for a while and Gav says, "Oh yes, I heard you'd split up. I'm sorry."'

She looks at me for a reaction, but I don't know what one to give, so I just look back at her blankly.

'This is where it gets really insane. Apparently Hugh looked a bit confused so Gav goes, "Sorry. Maybe she wasn't meant to have told me," and then Hugh says . . .'

She leaves a long pause and I imagine a drum roll. We're clearly coming to the crescendo.

'. . . "I think you must have me mixed up with someone else, mate. Roz and I have never been a couple . . ."'

25

Whatever I was expecting Dee to say it wasn't this.

'What the actual fuck?'

She sits back triumphantly. 'That's exactly what I said.'

I still can't compute what she's telling me. 'Do you think he misunderstood what Gavin was saying?'

'No. Because, obviously, Gav was a bit mind-blown, but he thought he'd better make sure he'd heard what he really heard, so he said, "Have I got you totally mixed up with someone else? Didn't you and Roz Huntingdon" – he remembered her surname, I was so impressed! – "get married in the Caribbean somewhere? About two or three years ago?' and Hugh apparently laughed and said, "Jesus. No. Not me." So Gav said, "You are Hugh Whitehall, aren't you?" just to be sure, and Hugh said yes he was. But by this point he was looking a bit suspicious, like he wondered why Gav was asking all these questions, and then he said, "Where did you say we met again?" and Gav was trying to think of an answer when Hugh's friend turned up and so he thought he'd better cut his losses and get out of there quick. He had to leave his egg and chips behind.'

I'm at a complete loss for what to say. I've been listening to Roz tell stories about her fabulous life with Hugh for three years now. 'Do you think maybe he's the one lying? Like he hates her so much he can't even admit they were ever together?'

Dee shakes her head. 'Gavin said he seemed totally confused. Not like he was hiding something.'

'So all that stuff the other week. Her crying and saying they'd split up . . .'

'Lies,' Dee says. She takes a big bite of pizza. Wipes her mouth with a tissue.

'Unbelievable.'

'I told you it was huge.'

I pull apart the last two slices. Put one on Dee's kitchen-roll nest and take a bite of the other. 'Why though? What's it all about?'

Dee shrugs. 'I think she knew you were on to her. You'd got too close to home and she wanted to throw you off the scent.'

'Well, it worked. Shit, so it wasn't genuine, was it, the apology? Fuck's sake. I still can't trust her.'

She pulls an apologetic face, worries at her fringe. 'I don't think so, no.'

I feel as if the rug's been pulled out from under my feet. How could I have been stupid enough to fall for Roz's bullshit again? I think of her laughing to Lorraine. Telling her how easy it was to fool me again. Stupid Holly who's such a soft touch she falls for a few tears. I think about how worried I was about her. How bad I felt for what I thought she was going through.

I tune back in to what Dee's saying.

'. . . so he was thinking maybe he could go and talk to him again. But be upfront this time . . .'

'What? Sorry . . .'

'Gav,' she says. 'He wants to go and talk to Hugh again. But this time be straight with him. Well, straightish. He says he didn't get the impression they were great friends so he could probably get him to agree not to say anything to her.'

I think about this for a second. I don't need to probe any more into Roz's life. I know she's still lying to me and that's all that matters. I know she's untrustworthy. I know she's gunning for me. Still, the temptation to find out just how extensive her lies are is almost irresistible. Who even is this woman I've been working with for the past three years? Sharing drinks and secrets with?

And I realize that I want to pay her back. I want to hurt her. I want to expose her stupid fake life. I want to make her feel she has no option other than to resign and leave me to get on with my job. I hesitate a moment. And then I say:

'Tell him I think it's a great idea.'

I've made a decision. There's only one person I know who distrusts Roz as much as I now do. She's known her the longest. I can't deal with this on my own. I need a work ally, or at least someone to confide in. Someone who knows Roz. It wouldn't be fair on Emma. She's the assistant, she works for us all equally. Joe is too new to really have any valuable insights. So Juliet it is.

I'm taking a risk. I know I am. In three years we've barely exchanged a friendly word. I lay awake last night worrying about whether I was about to do the right thing. Could I trust her? In the end I decided that she disliked Roz way more than she disliked me. As the saying went: maybe my enemy's enemy could be my friend. Well, not my friend exactly, let's not get carried away. But maybe she'd have as much of a vested interest as I do in bringing Roz down.

Thankfully Roz hasn't yet arrived, so I don't have to face her. Only Juliet and Emma are in the office when I get there, so I make myself a coffee and then I decide to take the bull by the horns.

I sidle over to her desk. She's concentrating on reading, brittle hair hanging down either side of her face like curtains. She doesn't acknowledge me when I approach.

'Could I have a word when you've got a moment?'

She looks up, watery blue eyes wary. 'Of course.'

She gets up and follows me into my office. I shut the door after her.

'Have a seat.'

I'm sure she wants to tell me she doesn't have time for this, she's busy, but I'm basically her boss now, so she knows she couldn't get away with it. I sit down on the sofa and indicate for her to take the armchair. My heart is beating fast. Here goes.

'Listen, Juliet, I know we haven't always got on . . .'

To give her credit she doesn't snort with laughter at that understatement.

'. . . but I need help with something and you're the only person I can think of that I can ask.'

I look up at her. She's looking right at me, expressionless. 'OK.'

'I'm going to tell you something and I'd really appreciate if you would keep it to yourself.'

I have no way of knowing if I can trust her or not, but I'm all out of other options.

'It's about Roz . . .'

I tell her all about the things that have been happening at work. The notes and messages, that it was she who tampered with the story conference documents and Juliet nods along as if none of this is news to her. Then I remind her about Roz and Hugh's wedding photos and the gift we all clubbed together to get them. About Roz's constant boasting about the parties and dinners and Hugh's job and their fabulous house. I even break my self-imposed rule of secret keeping and tell her about Roz confiding in me that they'd broken up.

And then I hit her with the big one. Dee's revelation.

Her first reaction is to laugh nervously as if this might be a trap. And then her cheeks flush even more pink than usual, and she says, 'I don't get it.'

'Neither do I,' I say. 'It's just . . . it's weird.'

'So, everything she's bragged about all these years, it's all made up?'

I nod. 'Seems like it. Oh, and she went to a posh school, not the rough comprehensive she's always on about.' I realize as I say this that, to Juliet, Brighton College is probably not a posh school. It's just a school.

She brays a horsey laugh. 'Ha! All those comments she's made about me.'

'Please don't say anything to her.' I suddenly realize I should have stressed this more. Got her to sign something in blood. Having Juliet go and throw everything I've just told her in Roz's face would not be helpful at this point.

'You're asking me to do you a favour now?' She sits back and crosses one leg over the other.

Shit. This is a mistake. But I know Juliet's not a vindictive person. 'Juliet . . . look, I know we've never got on . . .'

This time she does snort. I swallow. Plough on.

'. . . What I mean is I know I've never been very friendly towards you. And I'm sorry for that.'

'Nothing to do with me. You never exactly gave me a chance,' she says. It's true that I just accepted Roz's word for it that Juliet wasn't someone worth bothering with. Although she never pressed the point it was obvious all the same that my befriending Juliet would have made me an enemy of Roz.

'I know –'

She interrupts. 'Because God forbid you'd risk upsetting Roz by being civil to someone she doesn't get on with.'

'I've always been civil,' I say, and then wish I hadn't. Now is not the time to be defensive. 'Scrub that, you're right. I've always been a cow to you and I can't change that.'

Juliet tuts. 'It's OK, Holly, I'm not asking for an apology. So let's just cut all the crap. Why are you telling me this?'

I sigh. 'Because I don't know who else to tell. That's the truth. She's been trying to lose me my job and I can't expect you to care about that but I need to try and work out a way to get her to stop. Because clearly the whole apology was meaningless. It was just her way of trying to stop me retaliating.' I look up and see that Roz has walked into the main office. I feel as if I've been caught with my hand in the cookie jar. She looks over at me and raises an eyebrow as if to say 'What's she doing in there?' and I pull a face that I hope says 'Wasn't my idea'.

'So I assume her scripts going missing was you retaliating?'

I nod, embarrassed. 'It was stupid. I just felt I had to do something.'

'You know I wanted the job too?' she says.

I nod. 'But, one, you were upfront about it – don't you think it's odd that she didn't tell anybody? And, two, I don't think you're the type of person to hold a grudge when you didn't get it.'

'Lord, you're giving me compliments now. You must be desperate.'

Outside Roz waves as she leaves again, presumably for the kitchen or the Ladies. I know I have to concede defeat. Karma has come back to bite me. There's no way Juliet is going to help. 'Look . . . it was stupid to involve you. I get it. I'll find a way to handle her on my own. But I really would appreciate it if you'd keep it to yourself. Can you at least give me that?'

'Who would I gossip to?' she says, standing up. 'It's not as if I have many friends here.'

*

Later Roz appears at my door. Shuts it behind her. Drapes herself over the armchair. 'What was she doing in here earlier? You looked like you were having a very intense conversation.'

I've prepared for this. 'Oh, she just has a problem with one of her eps. You know what she's like, she wanted to go through every little detail . . .'

Roz yawns. Stretches. She's not interested enough in Juliet to probe. 'Do you fancy a drink? We haven't had a good catch-up for ages.'

No, my brain is screaming. I want to go home to my lovely flat. I want to watch TV with my cat on my lap, eating something unhealthy. Or even share a bottle of wine with my lodger. Anything but this. But I know that the more I keep Roz onside the less she'll suspect I've rumbled her.

'Love to,' I say, smiling and reaching for my jacket.

26

At her suggestion we walk past the nearest pub and on to a smaller, altogether nicer one two streets away. I'm relieved we won't risk bumping into Lucinda and Janet. If I'm going to give up an evening I at least want to know I can use it to pump Roz for more information without having to listen to someone drone on about their toyboy.

There's an empty table in the corner, near an – unlit – fireplace nook, so I nab it while Roz fetches a gin and tonic for me and a glass of red for her. I quickly remind myself what I'm supposed to know – that she and Hugh have split up and she has had to move to a temporary flat; and what I mustn't admit to – that she and Hugh were never together in the first place and so the beautiful mews house never existed, or, if it did, she never lived there, and that Hugh isn't the successful man she says he is. I need to drink slowly so I don't accidentally say something I shouldn't. I decide to play the sympathetic friend and let her do all the talking.

'So, how are you coping?' I say when she puts the drinks down. She rips open a packet of crisps and lays them on the table between us.

'Oh . . . you know . . . shit.'

I help myself to a crisp. 'Have you spoken to him at all?'

'We've emailed about the practicalities. Nothing else.' She takes a long sip of her drink.

'Not to sound mercenary but I've been thinking – you're married, he can't just keep the house and not buy you out. Or not put it on the market so you can split the profit at least.' I watch her carefully as I say this but she seems unruffled. She's a good actress, I'll give her that.

'The thing is he owned it before we got together. It's his.'

'Gosh, did he? But, anyway, I don't think that matters. I think, legally, when you get married you both just co-own everything.' I have no idea whether this is true or not but I doubt she does either.

She hesitates. 'Right. Well, our solicitors will know, I guess.'

'Because that would make a massive difference, wouldn't it? I mean, you'd be left with easily enough money to buy yourself a really nice flat. Unless there's a mortgage to pay back . . .' I remember her slipping into the conversation once how lucky she was that she and Hugh didn't have to worry about anything like that when I mentioned my own repayments. I'd been green with envy.

She clearly remembers too. 'No. He bought it outright. But I don't want any of it. I can look after myself.'

How noble. 'That's crazy, though. At least don't do anything hasty.' I think I've pushed her enough on this subject. I need to move on.

'I won't.'

If someone had really just recently lost their husband of

more than two and a half years, out of the blue, and been chucked out of their beautiful family home, I imagine they might want to talk about it ad nauseam given the chance, but no. Not Roz. She wants to talk about the fact that she's decided Joe is not someone we should be friends with.

'I like him,' I say, because I do. Joe has done nothing wrong except distance himself from Roz and Lorraine because, I assume, he found their bitchiness unappealing.

She scowls at me. 'Haven't you seen the way he sucks up to Glen?'

'Does he? He looks to me like he just gets on with his job.'

'Well, that's because he sucks up to you too.' Four young lads at a table next to us suddenly roar with laughter at something, and one of them slams his glass down emphatically. 'Let's go outside for a bit. I need to smoke.'

Really all I want to do is cut my losses and go home. I don't think Roz is going to offer up any new pieces of the puzzle tonight. But I'm worried it will look too pointed to leave after just one drink, so I agree reluctantly and leave her to go outside and claim a table, while I get the drinks in.

In the small garden out the back it's warm, courtesy of the two patio heaters. The papers have been promising an early heatwave but tonight there's drizzle in the air so we edge under the cover of a large parasol. We're the only people desperate enough to brave the elements.

Roz puffs raspberry-flavour vapour in my direction. 'How's the lodger?'

'Actually really nice,' I say, pulling my jacket tighter round me. 'Quiet. Clean. I hardly know she's there.'

'Exactly what you wanted,' she says.

I nod. 'But I like her too. So that's a bonus.'

'And how's Ashley doing?'

Roz knows about Ashley's pregnancy of course, but not the latest development, her opting to be a single mum. I don't feel comfortable confiding in her any more so I just say, 'Good,' and leave it at that. It must be obvious to her that we haven't regained our easy way of chatting for hours at a time, but I'm at a loss for what to talk about. I can't remember how we used to fill the silences. When I think about it now all I can remember is Roz's bragging and our collective bitching about our co-workers. Was that really all our friendship was based on? I feel embarrassed that that's how I used to spend my time. Looking for weaknesses, giggling in corners, making people feel uncomfortable. Mean girls.

'So, did you notice Juliet's mum jeans today?' Roz says now as if to prove my point. 'I mean, all that money and you end up wearing something that looks as if you bought it in Asda.'

'I don't think she has loads of money.'

She scoffs. 'Like Mummy and Daddy aren't rolling in it.'

I have no reason to believe she actually knows this and, even if she somehow does, Juliet is my age, forty-three; I doubt her parents are giving her cash.

'I have no idea. Maybe she's just not bothered about fashion . . .'

'Clearly.'

'. . . some people aren't, who cares?'

Roz gives me a look. 'Don't tell me you're starting to like her now?'

'No! God.' I don't want her to think I'm no longer her ally. 'I just couldn't give a fuck what she's wearing. I prefer not to think about her at all.'

'Well, there is that,' she says, mollified. 'But, even so, next time she wears those jeans have a look. I swear, George at Asda. She definitely has the hots for Glen, you know.'

I don't believe this for a second. I actually have no idea what Juliet's personal preferences are. Not even whether she's gay or straight, let alone whether she has a significant other at home. It strikes me that this is a bit sad. I've worked with her for three years and I know nothing about her. But assuming she's straight I can't imagine her lusting after Glen and his well-manicured beard. He's just not . . . well, he's just . . . not. It would be like fancying a *Play School* presenter. Just, wrong.

'Do you think? Eew.'

She puffs out another cloud. 'Totally. Have you not seen the way she's always agreeing with everything he says in the meetings?' She sits up straight, sticks her chin out. An impression. 'Yes, Glen. Oh, do you think so, Glen? Would you like me to ride you like I used to ride old Dobbin when I was a girl, Glen?'

I can't help myself; I laugh. 'Grim.'

She exhales. 'I told him that I made a mistake about

you nicking my notes, by the way. I said I found them in the studio room, that I'd forgotten I'd been working on them down there.'

'Oh.' It's a relief, there's no doubt about it. 'Thanks. I appreciate it.'

27

It's the weekly meeting and the ritual of us all having to listen to Roz's tales from the weekend has begun. Except that Juliet and I know that she's making it all up, Joe doesn't want to hear it anyway and Glen is only half listening, reading something on his phone, so that just leaves Lorraine. A loyal fan base of one.

I actually managed to have a nice weekend. Now my mind is made up that I'm going to go all out to bring Roz down I feel calmer than I've felt in weeks. No more angsting. No more trying to see the good in her. Fuck it. I'm anxious to put things in motion, although I have no idea what. So, on Saturday afternoon I texted Dee: *Can you come over later?*

She texted straight back. *Gav's home so promised him a takeaway. You're welcome to join us.*

Usually I would refuse. I didn't want to intrude on one of Dee and Gavin's rare nights in together, but I had to offload on someone and I still don't know Hattie well enough to sound off at her.

I sent her a message back. *Lovely. Be there at 7. I'll bring booze xx.*

It had been a while since I'd spent an evening at theirs, but much longer since Gavin had joined us. If he's not away with work he usually makes himself scarce. Takes the opportunity to see one of his mates, or go to the gym.

We sat in the living room of their Kilburn flat, the middle floor of a three-storey house in a residential road, the two of them squashed on to the small sofa and me in the armchair. Gavin is a big bloke. Not fat, but everything about him is large. He's six foot three for a start. His legs stuck out into the small room, almost reaching to where I was sitting opposite. His arms, thrown out wide across the back of the couch, stretched from one end to the other. I couldn't imagine living with someone who takes up the whole room like that.

Dee and Gavin's flat always smells slightly of candles. Dee loves a candle. I have lain awake at night worrying that she's going to burn the place down after she's had a few drinks. Judging by tonight's delicious aroma I assume the flavour of the night is some kind of citrus.

The room is full of knick-knacks. Not in an old lady kind of way, but eclectic stuff they collected on their travels. A row of wooden toys from Norway, a beaded wall hanging from Turkey, a puppet from Venice. They used to spend months planning the perfect trip, finding hotels that were off the beaten track even in places that were rife with tourists. Earmarking weird and wonderful local sights that were not to be found in the guidebooks. It struck me, sitting there, that they haven't been away for a while. In fact I couldn't remember the last time.

Gavin recounted his run-in with Hugh for my benefit. I wanted to hear it first-hand. His grey eyes were sparkling as he told the story and Dee kept looking from him to me and back again as if to say 'Can you believe it?' I could see how proud she was of the fact that he'd actually pulled it off.

'So, he definitely knew who she was?' I said.

'Yes. I mean, he didn't say "Who?", he just said they'd never been together in the first place.' He reached to the coffee table for his beer. I had come bearing two four-packs.

'Did he seem surprised?'

Gavin thought for a second. 'Now I come to think about it, not particularly.'

'Which says to me that he knows she makes this stuff up . . .' Dee chipped in. 'So this has happened to him before. As if Gav's not the first person to ever make that mistake.'

'And what was he like?' I was curious to know what made the object of Roz's fantasy life so special.

'Oh, your average Adonis. Tanned. Rippling abs under his T-shirt. That type.'

I snorted. 'You looked under his T-shirt?'

Gavin laughed. The whole room boomed. 'Trust me, I could sense they were there.'

'But, as a person,' I said.

He shrugged. 'It was hard to tell because he wasn't happy that I was bothering him. Seemed OK. Posh voice. One of those.'

'So maybe he does live in the nice house,' Dee said.

'Maybe,' I said, taking a swig of my beer. 'At this point I don't even know if the nice house exists.'

'Well, Gavin Fletcher P.I. is going to find out for you.' Dee put a hand on his leg and he covered it with his own. It made me feel warm and fuzzy to see them getting on so well, I'm not going to lie.

I'm paying attention to Roz's showing off now, of course. Nodding and smiling along when she looks at me apologetically, willing me not to expose her secret. Well, the secret she knows I know, that is. The one she told me, which turned out to be just as untrue as all her other bullshit.

She's acting as if she's sharing it all reluctantly, and it strikes me that this is what she always does. So long as she has someone like Lorraine – or me once, although it's hard now to imagine – prodding her for details, she can pretend that she's not showing off, she's just answering the questions she's being asked. It's all in the eye movements, the subtle little shakes of the head and eye rolls that say 'Well, since you asked . . .' It's a masterclass.

Today's stories involve lunch at Sindhu by personal invitation of Atul Kochhar, and Kelly Hoppen popping round to give her and Hugh ideas for the refurb of the mews house that they're planning. Lorraine probes and prods as she's supposed to, practically orgasmic at the splendour of it all.

'Oh, we're just going to freshen it up a bit, you know,' Roz says, eyes cast down like Princess Diana. 'New kitchen, new bathrooms . . .'

'How many bathrooms do you have?' Lorraine pants.

'Only four,' Roz says faux modestly. I look to see if the

257

others are taking this in but no one else is even pretending to listen. 'It's quite a small house.'

'Four. Wow,' Lorraine says, eyes wide.

I have to stop myself from saying 'It must be pretty big
for a mews house, actually, to have four bathrooms. For
any house, to be honest.' Instead I shuffle my documents
loudly and attempt to get the meeting under way.

'Yes,' Juliet says, when I ask for order. 'I have another
meeting at eleven. So could you maybe have this chat
later?'

Roz sneers at her. 'Oh, sorry, your maj. I'd hate for you
to be late for anything crucial. What is it? The Roedean
Old Girls' Association?'

Juliet ignores her. Roz hates to be ignored.

'Oh no, judging by the way you're dressed it must be the
Ladies' Bridge Circle or something glamorous like that.'

Lorraine snorts.

'Enough,' I say. 'Let's get on.'

When I come out of the meeting I have a missed call from
Ashley. She was having her second scan this morning and
it took all my willpower to turn my phone on to silent and
not to check it every thirty seconds. She hasn't left a message, which demands I go into a panic that there might be
some kind of bad news she wants to break to me in person.

I shut my door and hit her number. She answers
immediately.

'Girl!' she shouts before I can even say hello.

'Oh my God! And it – she's – all OK?'

'Perfect. You should have seen her . . .'

I get a lump in my throat. I hate the thought of her going to the hospital alone, having no one to celebrate with. Or at least, no one who's as invested as she is.

'I wish I could have come with you.'

'I'm sending you a picture.'

I put the phone on speaker and then I stare at it, waiting for Ashley's message to pop up.

'There. You should get it any second.'

Just as she finishes saying that there's a beep. I tap on the message, open the photo. It's a scan; what can I say? A grey blob floating on a grey background. But it's just about the most beautiful thing I've ever seen.

'That's my granddaughter!' A tear edges out of my right eye and splatters on the screen.

'I know. Isn't she gorgeous?' I can hear that she's crying too.

'She is,' I say. I wipe the phone clean, stare at the picture in silence, sharing the moment with my daughter.

About an hour later, when Roz is in a meeting with one of the writers, Juliet taps on my open door. I haven't spoken to her since we had our conversation about Roz, apart from work essentials, so I'm surprised to see her there.

'Hi,' I say, looking up. Despite everything I find myself noticing her shapeless jeans, slightly too short for her low court-shoe heels.

'OK,' she says. 'Watching that performance has made my mind up. I'll help you.'

'Really?' I glance past her at the general office to check no one is listening in, but it's hard to tell. 'Shut the door.'

She talks in a stage whisper. I have to strain to hear but, at the same time, I'm worried it's too loud. 'No. We shouldn't talk about it here. Are you free to pop round to mine for a bit after work? It's only up the road.'

I can't really imagine anything I'd rather do less. I think about suggesting the pub but I know there's a chance we'll bump into someone from work. Lucinda or Janet. Or even Roz herself. How would we ever explain that one away? And I have to admit, I'm curious to see where she lives.

'OK. It'll have to be quick though.'

'Of course,' she says stiffly. 'I'm not asking you on a date.'

She gives me the address and directions because, naturally, we don't want to be seen walking there together. 'I'll leave first and then you follow five minutes later,' she says. We exchange phone numbers in case of any hold-ups.

As soon as she leaves I text Dee: *Going to Juliet's after work. If you don't hear from me by half seven send help.* I get a smiley face in response almost immediately.

By half past five I'm watching Juliet, willing her to make a move, but knowing she'll never leave this early. At exactly six o'clock she straightens up the papers on her desk and reaches for her jacket. Roz and Lorraine are both sitting at their desks, as is Emma who is starting to pack up for the day too. I keep my head down, listen for

Juliet's 'Bye' to Emma and then force myself to stay put. I'm hoping that Roz and Lorraine will leave before me, but when I get up they're still sitting there.

'Drink?' Roz says as I pass.

I pull a face that hopefully implies regret. 'Can't, sorry. I've got to meet someone. I'm late already.' I keep moving so there's no chance she suggests walking out together. 'See you tomorrow.'

Juliet's house is only five minutes' walk away and, thankfully, in the opposite direction to the Tube station where both Roz and Lorraine will be headed later. It's a street of neat two-storey terraces, yellow brick with bay windows in the front. Tiny front gardens, some lavished with love, some nothing more than a place to put the bins. A couple have been paved over to make parking spaces. Number twenty-six has a wooden fence and a small tree in a round bed with tulips round the bottom. The front door is painted in a tasteful dark red with the number of the house and the letter box in brass. The bay window has white sheer half blinds across the bottom panes. I like it. It's small but it's somewhere I'd aspire to live.

I ring the bell. Juliet answers almost before I take my hand away.

'Nice house,' I say, by way of greeting. She looks at me suspiciously as if I might be being sarcastic.

'Come on in.'

I follow her into the small hallway, through a door on the left into the living room. The pale wooden floors are covered by a patterned rug. There's a small sofa in off-white, a blue armchair and a low dark coffee table. The walls are a warm grey-green. There's no real individual style, but it's homely.

'Oh, do you want a cup of tea or something?' she says, turning to head out of the room again.

I don't really want to prolong this any longer than I have to. 'No, I'm fine.' I sit on the armchair in the bay. Juliet takes the sofa.

'OK, so what do you propose?' she asks.

'I have no idea,' I say, realizing as I say it how true this is. 'I just know I don't want her to get away with it any more. And you've known her even longer than me so . . . the truth is I can't do it on my own and I know you dislike her as much as I now do . . .'

She smiles. 'Well, there is that.'

'I need to find something concrete on her. I mean, it might be enough if I can prove half the stuff that comes out of her mouth is fake, but since she's been working there and doing a good job for five years are they really going to care?'

'It's a start,' she says.

I jump as I hear the front door bang. Juliet doesn't flinch. 'That'll just be Jake.'

OK, so Juliet must have a partner. Or a lodger. Or a cleaner called Jake. I don't like to ask. But then a tall, gangly teenage boy fills the doorway.

'Hi, Mum,' he says and then he spots me. 'Oh, hello. Sorry, I didn't see you . . .'

I cover my confusion with a smile. 'Hi. I'm Holly.' I'm not sure whether to hold out a hand for him to shake or whether that feels too weirdly formal. I'm gobsmacked that Juliet has a child. An almost adult giant child.

'Jake,' he says with impeccable manners. 'I'll leave you to it.'

'There's cold pizza in the fridge, but I'll make dinner in a bit.'

'Splendid,' he says. He has his mum's straw-coloured hair but it's cut in a choppy style with a fringe that flops into his eyes. 'Nice to meet you, Holly.'

'You too,' I say. He strides off and the room immediately feels twice as big. I'm lost for words.

'Sixteen,' Juliet says. 'He grows about a foot a night.'

'I didn't . . .' I start to say. Can I honestly admit that I've worked side by side with her for three years and I had no idea she had a son?

'You know how people can be about mums at work. You should've seen how Roz was about Sally,' she says. Sally was an editor before I arrived. Roz has often talked scathingly about the way she always put her children before her job. 'I picked up pretty quickly that she'd use it against me if she knew I had a child so I kept it quiet. People know, obviously. I told them when I applied for the job. I just made a decision never to talk about him in the department. It's not like it's a big secret.'

'I . . .' I don't know what to say. 'She was always OK with me.'

Juliet sighs. 'Because Ashley was already, what . . . eighteen, nineteen, when you started? Jake was only eleven, and I knew there'd be days when I'd have to be late because of him, or take a last-minute day off because he'd forgotten to tell me it was sports day. It just made it easier if I invented other excuses for those things.'

'I had no idea. Sorry.'

'You don't know anything about me, Holly. Because you've never asked.'

She's right, of course. Roz has always made sure Juliet is the department pariah. And I went along with it. Happy to have a common enemy. No one ever really bothers to make an effort with her any more. 'Sorry,' I say. I mean it.

'I'm not asking for an apology. It is what it is. Anyway, I'll need to get on with cooking in a minute so . . .'

'Of course.' I try to focus on Roz but I'm still trying to take in that Juliet is a mother. 'And Jake's dad, is he . . .?'

'Not in the picture,' she says brusquely. So she's a single mum. Like me. With all the extra stress and worry that that brings. I have so many questions I want to ask her, but I can tell she's effectively shut down that conversation.

'Right.'

We sit there for a moment in silence. I can hear Jake moving around in another room. I decide I need to get us back on topic.

'I just feel as if the more I can unearth about all the lies she's told the more likely it is I'll find something that I can use against her.' I realize how that makes me sound. 'I'm not a vindictive person . . .'

'Save it,' she says, not unkindly. 'After what she's been doing to you I don't think you have to make excuses for trying to find a way to make her stop, however drastic.'

'You've known her longer than me. Maybe you can think of something she's said that we could use.'

'What? Something more than making up a husband and fabulous celebrity-filled life? Is there more, do you think?'

My mouth is dry. I wish I'd said yes to a cup of tea or even a glass of water. 'There must be. That stuff will embarrass her when everyone finds out but it won't get her sacked.'

'If you could prove it was her that tampered with the story conference documents, I suppose . . .'

'I can't, though. And even if I could she'd just claim it was a practical joke.' I talk her through all the things I think Roz has done – all of which I've already told her, but I feel as though I need to keep reminding both her and myself that I'm not going mad, that there really has been a sustained campaign against me. She listens politely. Although her eyebrows do shoot up when I fill her in on Gavin's plan to confront Hugh.

'Sounds a bit risky,' she says. 'What if he goes straight to Roz and asks her what the hell she's up to? I would.'

'I suppose he might want to confront her once he hears all the things she's been saying about him for years. Gav thinks he can persuade him not to, though. He got the impression that Hugh knows exactly what she's like.'

'Just from the way he reacted when your friend said her name?'

When she puts it like that it does seem a bit flimsy. 'I guess so. Is this a really stupid thing to do?'

'Probably,' she says. 'But it doesn't sound as if you've got much else. Maybe try and work out what would be the worst that could happen if he did tell her and take it from there.'

'I just feel as if I want to make something happen. Be the proactive one for once instead of waiting around to see what she'll do to me next.'

Juliet nods. 'It's understandable. I'd be lying if I said I hadn't fantasized myself about bursting her bubble from time to time.'

'Any ideas gratefully received.'

'There'll be something. If I can think of anything I'll let you know. Meanwhile I'll look forward to hearing how your friend Gavin gets on.'

I feel as if I'm being dismissed and, to be honest, I can't wait to get out of there. This is a bad idea, I don't know what I'm doing here. I'm putting my trust in a woman who has nothing but dislike for me. Understandably.

'OK. Well . . .' I'm about to get up and leave when the door opens and Jake reappears bearing a small tray with two mugs of tea and a bowl of sugar. Juliet smiles at him and her face is transformed. I know that look; I recognize it from myself. Pride that your child has done something good without being asked.

'I was making myself one,' he says, his face reddening. 'I took a chance on milk but I wasn't sure about sugar . . .'

I want to say no, that I'm just leaving, but I also don't want to be rude to him. I'm sure that Juliet wants me to leave as much as I want to go, though. In the end, not wanting to be dismissive of a sixteen-year-old who's made an effort, I take the mug he hands me.

'Thanks. That's really kind of you.'

I wave away the offer of sugar. He places the other mug in front of Juliet.

'Homework . . .' he says, pointing up to, I assume, his bedroom.

'I'll call you for dinner,' Juliet says as he retreats.

'I don't have to stay and drink this if you need to get on,' I say, giving her a get-out clause.

'It's fine,' she says with a dismissive wave of her hand. 'I've got ten minutes before I need to do anything.'

Now I really don't know what to talk about. I'm scared to ask her anything about her life in case she gets defensive, or thinks I'm looking for something to take the piss out of, so I just sip my scalding tea, burning my throat as it goes down.

'So I gather Ashley's father isn't around either,' she says suddenly. I jump and almost spill my tea.

'Um. No. Never has been. Didn't want to know. We were kids practically . . .'

She nods. 'Jake's father and I got divorced when Jake was three. He has two children with his new wife. I say new wife – they were married a year after we split up. She was his secretary.'

'Oh,' I say. 'I'm sorry.'

She brays a laugh. 'What a cliché. Anyway, he's always paid his child support, so that's something.'

I feel I can risk a personal question. 'But he doesn't see Jake?'

She shakes her head. 'He did for a while but – not that

I'm excusing him in the slightest – Alexandra made it very difficult. And then she had two boys of her own so . . . Jake decided when he was about ten that he'd be better off saying he didn't want to see him at all. All the let-downs, you know.'

'Poor kid.' I've just learned more about Juliet's life in five minutes than I have in the past three years. 'At least Ashley never had any expectations, I suppose.'

She nods.

'She's pregnant, by the way. Ashley. And she's just split up with her boyfriend.' I don't know why I've just shared this. Not that it's a secret but Juliet is not someone I would ever have imagined telling.

She raises her eyebrows. 'That's tough.'

'Yep.' I drain the last of my tea. Put the mug on the coffee table. Juliet takes that as her cue.

'Well, I'd better get dinner.' We both stand. It's awkward. I feel as though there's been a bit of a thaw, but you can't erase three years of animosity in half an hour.

'Thanks for hearing me out. Say bye to Jake.'

'I will,' she says as I leave, none the wiser about whether she really has any intention of trying to help me or not. 'See you tomorrow.'

28

Dee and Gavin's plan basically consists of him turning up at Fitzrovia PR and asking to see Hugh. That's all they've got. It's hardly *Ocean's Eleven* but who am I to criticize? I've got nothing.

Dee has decided to take the day off and go with him, although only as far as the front door and then she'll wait in the café round the corner. If Hugh agrees to step out for a coffee with Gavin they will sit at a different table and she'll pretend to read a book while earwigging. If there's no other table free she will offer them hers saying she is just leaving, and then lurk about in nearby Fitzroy Square until Gavin gives her the all-clear.

The pair of them are like a couple of children who've overdone it on the tartrazine when we meet up to talk about it in the bar at the end of my road.

'How are you going to persuade him to see you in the first place?'

'I'm going to be honest,' Gavin says, fingers scrabbling round in a packet of dry roasted peanuts. 'How will he be able to resist when I tell him Roz has been claiming to be married to him for the last few years? I'll tell him I thought he ought to know. Man to man, like.'

'Clearly she only spins this story at work,' Dee says. This

had never occurred to me. Obviously Roz couldn't be telling her friends and family the same set of lies because they would know immediately that it wasn't true. 'So he probably has no idea. That's what we figure, anyway.'

A lightbulb goes off in my head. 'That's why she does the whole thing about not putting anything personal on Facebook.'

'Exactly. Why would Mrs Oversharer Show-Off not be boasting to her whole circle of acquaintances every chance she got? Because they'd know it was bollocks.'

'What are you going to do if he's not in the office? If he's on holiday, or he's off sick? You'll have taken the day off for nothing.'

'Go shopping,' Dee says with a big smile. 'Or to the British Museum or the cinema. Who cares?'

'OK, so let's assume he decides to hear you out. What then?'

Gavin rifles round in his jacket pocket and produces a scrappy bit of paper. 'We came up with a list of questions.'

'We sat up till two o'clock this morning writing these,' Dee says proudly, snatching the paper out of his hand. She hands it to me. 'What do you think?'

I can't concentrate at work the next day, thinking about what's happening and the many ways it might backfire. Dee and Gavin's plan is to turn up at Fitzrovia PR close to lunchtime – not too close that Hugh might have already gone somewhere to eat, but close enough so that he can't make the excuse that he can't leave the office. Of course,

I pointed out that he could have a lunch date or back-to-back meetings, but they didn't really care. The whole thing has turned into a big adventure for the two of them. It has a significance way beyond the actual task.

Of course I stayed awake half the night picturing Hugh, righteously angry on Roz's behalf, calling her up straightaway to tell her I've set two weirdos on him to investigate her. Her going straight to HR to put in a formal complaint about me. Glen having to break it to me that I haven't passed my probation. Is it a sackable offence to enlist two middle-aged idiots to pry into a colleague's personal life? I almost texted Dee this morning to call the whole thing off. Nothing they found out from Hugh about Roz would help me defeat her anyway. Surely.

In the end I decided to throw caution to the wind. Curiosity about the extent of Roz's lies has won out. I'm both appalled and fascinated that I have no idea who she really is. Maybe it's to do with the fact that I make up stories for a living, but I need to know what the ending is.

She's all smiles this morning. No idea about what's happening a few miles down the road in Fitzrovia. No idea how much I know about her already. She's covering the studio and I can see her and Lorraine both gathering up their stuff to head down there, in the guise of Lorraine shadowing her as part of her training, but really, I have no doubt, so that they can sit there and gossip all day, and Roz can show off to a captive audience – but I have other ideas. Emma called me earlier to say she was staying home with a cold. Someone needs to answer the phones.

'Lorraine,' I call as I see them getting ready to leave. She stops in her tracks. 'You need to cover for Emma today, I'm afraid.'

She grimaces. Looks at Roz as if hoping she'll step in and save her. 'Why?'

'She's had to stay at home.' I smile apologetically, as if I hate to have to ask her.

'God, don't tell me,' Roz pipes up. 'She's sick. Again.'

In so far as I can remember Emma has taken maybe four impromptu days off because of illness in the three years I've worked here.

'It's hardly a regular occurrence,' I say.

'I don't see how it's my job,' Lorraine says, emboldened by Roz's attitude.

I almost laugh. 'Whose job do you think it is, just out of interest? Mine? Juliet's? Joe's? Or shall I see if Glen's free?'

Lorraine rolls her eyes. 'Don't be stupid.'

'It's a genuine question. Someone needs to cover for Emma today and if you think it's beneath you then who else would you suggest?'

She dumps her bag on her desk. 'That's not what I was saying. I just meant no one has ever told me I'd be expected to cover for Emma if she decided to have an unscheduled day off, that's all.'

'I think decided is the wrong word.'

'I'm not a secretary,' Lorraine says imperiously.

'No,' I say, adopting a sterner tone. Everything else aside, her attitude is appalling. 'You're not an anything yet. You're a trainee.'

'Ha! That told you,' Roz shrieks and I'm reminded of how we used to delight in moments like these. Something we could dissect over lunch, making each other cry with laughter as we relived the moment. I feel a sudden pang of sadness for the loss of my friend.

Lorraine seems to realize that she's lost the war. She grabs her bag again, huffs over to Emma's desk and slumps down.

'I don't even know how to put calls through,' she says sulkily.

'Well, then now's the time to learn,' I say, smiling. 'If all else fails, take messages.'

As Roz goes off, waving in Lorraine's direction, I accidentally catch Juliet's eye. She raises her eyebrows, but I can see she's suppressing a smile.

I've told Dee not to call me at work once their mission is over, because I wouldn't be able to concentrate on anything for checking my phone every five seconds. But now I'm regretting that I didn't at least ask her to text me to let me know they'd got through it unscathed. And I'm still looking at my messages on average every four minutes, just in case. I've timed myself. So I might as well not have bothered.

Once it's a respectable time for me to leave for the day I'm out of the door without even stopping to say goodbye to anyone. I told Dee I would be round at theirs by quarter to seven and I have no intention of getting there a second later. Lorraine, who could now run a masterclass in accidentally cutting off numerous phone calls, sees me leaving and immediately grabs for her own bag. I experience a tiny jolt of happiness that she's had a shitty day.

Thankfully Dee is home. I can tell by the look on her face when she opens the door that there's news that she's dying to tell me. I also know that she'll want to eke out every little detail of the story before she gets to anything of substance, so I give myself a silent talking to: be patient. Let her have her moment.

'Just tell me the worst bit now,' I blurt out as we hug. I've never been one to listen to my own advice.

'There's no worst bit. It's all fine,' she says as I follow her in. Today's candle is either basil or cat pee, it's hard to tell. My eyes start watering.

'That's not a good one,' I say, wafting my hand in front of my face.

'I know! I blew it out as soon as I smelt what it was like but it's lingering.' She pours me a glass of wine without asking while I open the window. Gavin, I know, has already left to drive to Manchester, ready for an appointment first thing. She opens the oven and puts in a suspiciously home-made-looking moussaka.

'When did you have time to make that?' I can't remember the last time I made anything other than a bowl of pasta from scratch. Probably Christmas.

'This afternoon.' She wipes down the surfaces. 'We were back here by four.'

I sit at the kitchen table. Gulp my ice-cold wine. 'OK. Tell me.'

She sits across from me. Inhales a long slow breath like she's preparing to swim a length underwater. 'So . . .'

After five minutes she's still only got as far as them getting on the Tube, having agonized for way too long about what Gavin should wear (they settled on a pair of chinos and a long-sleeved T-shirt). I almost have to physically restrain myself from asking her to get on with the story. Ordinarily I love the random details that Dee provides ('We bumped into the downstairs neighbour on our way out and she told us that the woman next door shagged a bloke who delivers for Ocado. She says she's never seen anyone order so much food. And, of course, it's never him, because they're different every time') but this evening I'm too anxious to even take half of it in. I file this one away in my 'ask later' bank, though, because it sounds like a good one.

I tune back in. Dee and Gavin have arrived at the café round the corner from Fitzrovia PR. There are several empty tables. Dee settles herself at one in the window, orders a coffee and tells the waitress she'll probably order some lunch but not for a while. The waitress has a cool tattoo of a snake going all the way up her forearm. Gavin goes off on his mission.

'So . . .' She leans forward, elbows on the table. 'He went into reception and said could they call Hugh White-hall and tell him that Gavin Sanders was downstairs to see him. He was hoping that Hugh might just come down to see who it was but, of course, he didn't, he asked the receptionist who the hell Gavin Sanders was. So Gav said tell him I met him in the café the other day. Tell him I need to have a conversation with him about Roz Huntingdon if he can spare me a few minutes. Anyway, thankfully, Hugh bought it. Next thing Gav knew the lift was opening and there he was –'

I interrupt. 'Did he seem pissed off?'

'A bit, apparently. He came over and said, "What's she done now? I'm a bit busy." Not in an angry way but a bit wary, Gav said. I mean, why wouldn't he be? Someone he doesn't know from Adam, who's already accosted him over his egg and chips, turns up at his work and demands to speak to him . . .'

'No way would I have gone to reception,' I chip in. 'I might have sent Emma though.'

'Well, big shot Hugh probably doesn't have an assistant. So Gav says, "I know this sounds a bit odd, and I'm really sorry to bother you at work, but a friend of mine works with Roz and she's discovered that she's completely fabricated her whole personal life and a lot of it involves you. I thought that you should know. And that maybe you could help my friend understand what's going on."'

She pauses to get up and peer into the oven at the moussaka. It's like a drama cutting to a commercial break just as it gets to the juicy bit. It's actually unbearable sitting there watching her faff around.

I can't help myself. 'And . . .'

She slams the oven door shut. 'Hang on.' I watch as she fannies about with the timer. 'Couple more minutes.'

'So,' I say impatiently. 'Did they go to the café?'

Dee sits down again. 'Where was I? Yes, so, Gav asks Hugh if he wants to grab a coffee and Hugh says OK.'

There was a table free next to where Dee was sitting apparently, so Gavin steered Hugh there. Dee kept her eyes down on her menu, not acknowledging them, listening in. She tells me (in detail) what they all ordered – a pot of English breakfast tea and a salted chocolate brownie for her ('Unreal!'), an Americano for Gavin with hot milk on the side, and a flat white for Hugh. Clearly they'd been chatting on the walk from the offices, because Gavin was part way through telling Hugh that apparently he'd been married to Roz for nearly three years and they lived in a Holland Park mews.

'She's told everyone you're a bigshot PR with loads of celebrity clients,' Gavin was saying as they sat down. He told Hugh some of the stories Roz had shared about their fabulous social life.

'What was Hugh saying to all this?'

'Gobsmacked, apparently. I mean, who wouldn't be? So, Gav says to him, "How do you know Roz, if you don't mind me asking?"'

At this point Dee's ears had pricked up, obviously. She wanted to be sure to remember everything Hugh said so that she could pass it all on to me. Unfortunately that was also the moment some woman asked if she could sit at the empty seat at Dee's table – it was getting close to lunchtime and the place had filled up – and then proceeded to try and engage her in chit-chat. Dee, who had been staring at her phone as a cover for her mission, had to shut her up by saying she was revising for the theory part of her driving test that afternoon and she really needed to concentrate.

'And then she said she could test me if I wanted!'

I sip my wine. 'Well, that was nice of her. Not many people would do that.'

Dee laughs. 'Yes, I suppose it was. But I just wanted her to be quiet so I may have snapped at her to leave me alone.'

'Ha! That's the last time she ever offers to do a kind deed. You have literally ruined that woman.'

She waves her hand dismissively. 'Collateral damage.'

'So, what, then you just sat there glaring at each other?'

'Basically. At least, she glared at me while I looked at my phone. It was a bit uncomfortable, in all honesty.'

The upshot was that Dee had missed half of Hugh's response, but Gavin filled in the details later.

Roz and Hugh met about seven years ago when they worked in the same bar. She was trying to get a break in TV, reading scripts as a freelance for as many companies as she could on the side to try and get a foot in the door. He had a business degree but he'd decided he wanted to be an actor, although in reality, by this point, he was someone who worked in a bar. They hit it off immediately – same sense of humour, same crazy side, same drive – and they quickly became best friends. But then . . .'

I let out a yelp as the timer pings. 'Jesus Christ. Did you somehow set that up so it would go off just as you got to a juicy bit?'

She looks at me, deadpan. 'Of course.'

'Please dish up and talk at the same time, I can't bear the suspense.'

Thankfully she does, spooning steaming hot moussaka on to plates and producing a salad from the fridge. 'So he said after a while things got a bit weird. They got drunk at a party and Roz started telling him she fancied him and she wanted them to be more than friends, but he didn't feel that way at all, she was his mate, his wing woman, so he batted her away gently. He put it down to the drink and the next day he just pretended it hadn't happened, and so did she, so he thought, hopefully, she didn't even remember . . .'

I heap salad on to my plate. Tuck into the moussaka. 'God, this is delicious. Sorry, go on . . .'

'But then it happened again. And again. Only the third time they hadn't even been drinking, so he realized she actually meant it. He broke it to her gently that he wasn't interested but she wouldn't take no for an answer. He said it got really awkward after that because whenever they were on their own together she would start on about it again. It got so that he just couldn't enjoy spending time with her any more. At least not one on one. So they drifted apart a bit and then she got the job on *Churchill Road*, which made life a bit easier.'

'So they've never had any kind of romantic involvement?'

Dee sticks her fork into her moussaka and leaves it standing there. 'Never. He said that every now and then she would turn up pissed on his doorstep late at night and

279

try again to persuade him they should. They still hung out with the same people though.'

'I wonder how soon after she started on *Churchill Road* she told people he was her boyfriend,' I say through a mouthful. I do at least put my hand in front of my mouth. I'm not a complete animal. 'I'll ask Juliet if she remembers.'

'Well, obviously he had no idea about any of that. Gavin asked him about the Holland Park mews and he said that's his mum and dad's house. He took Roz there once to meet them when they were still getting on. They loved her, and she loved them. She kept saying she wished her mum was like his.'

I push my plate away to stop me eating any more, although I'm tempted to pile the rest of the moussaka on there and scoff that too. 'That was fabulous. How did he end up being the accountant if he was trying to be an actor?'

'He said something about realizing he was never going to make it as an actor so he went on an accounting course. He ended up at Fitzrovia PR and he liked it there so he stayed. He has nothing to do with the clients, though. Gav reeled off all the names he could remember Roz had dropped and he'd never met any of them.'

I twist one of my earrings round and round. See Dee watching me and stop. 'Does he look like a Greek god?'

Dee raises an eyebrow. 'He does. Drop dead gorgeous. Obviously a good few years older than that picture she has on Facebook. He says he hasn't even seen her in at least three or four years. He was a bit freaked out by the whole thing, to be honest.'

'I don't blame him.' I notice Dee has finished eating too so I grab both our plates and carry them over to the sink. 'Did Gav ask him about her background? The posh school stuff?'

She nods. 'He didn't really know anything about that. He said he knew she was from Brighton but not much else.'

'Nothing else? Nothing I can use against her?' I can't help feeling a bit disappointed.

'No, sorry. Oh,' she says, reaching for the wine bottle. 'But I forgot the best bit. He's married to a woman called Annabel and they have one-year-old twins.'

'Whoa! Do you think Roz knows?'

Dee shrugs. 'God knows. Maybe she wouldn't care. Like he said, they haven't even seen each other for years; it's not as if she's stalking him. I think she just turned bits of him into the perfect partner for her fantasy life.'

29

When I get home from Dee's I bump into Hattie coming out of the living room. I'm so surprised I don't say anything other than 'Oh, hello'.

'Hi,' she says with a big smile. 'Sorry, I was looking for Smokey. I've been in for ages and I haven't seen him so I thought you might have accidentally shut him in there . . .'

It's possible. I've done it before, because he likes to cram himself in between the armchair and the wall, and there's no way of knowing he's there without checking. 'Right. Had I?'

'I can't see him. He's probably under one of the beds.'

I probably should say something, remind her that the living room is out of bounds but, on the other hand, if I really had shut my cat in there away from his food and water, wouldn't I want her to look for him? So I keep quiet.

'How was your day?' she says. I think she realizes I'm a bit pissed off with her. I feel bad, so I go overboard with a big smile, which is probably even more frightening.

'Great, thanks. Yours?'

'Yeah, good. Actually, I'm just on my way out. I should . . .' She indicates her room, and I take it to mean she needs to get ready.

'Sure. Have fun,' I say.

'Oh.' She turns back just as I'm about to walk off. 'Sorry I haven't paid this month's rent in yet. I completely forgot. Can you believe it's been that long since I moved in?'

I hadn't even noticed. Some landlady I am. 'No problem,' I say. 'Do it when you can.'

I head into the kitchen. Smokey hops down from one of the chairs to greet me. Stretches sleepily. 'He's here,' I shout.

She sticks her head round the door. 'Oh, right. Maybe he just came in.'

Once she's left I go into the living room. I can't help but look round to see if she's left her mark. A dent in a sofa cushion or a ring on the coffee table where she's placed a glass of wine. I don't want to have to start worrying that she's taken to invading my private space when I'm not there. I'm relieved to see there's no evidence. Even so, I resolve to put a lock on the door. I'll just have to make sure I really don't shut Smokey in there by mistake when I go out.

Roz is in the studio again, and Emma is back so Lorraine is with her, which gives me a chance to talk to Juliet without too much scrutiny. I ask her to bring a set of scripts to my office, just for Joe and Emma's benefit, and then we proceed to talk about anything but. She's rocking the mum jeans and low court shoes again today, with some kind of silk scarf arrangement round her neck. I automatically bank the details to share with Roz before I remember that's not me any more.

'Do you remember when she first started mentioning Hugh?' I ask when I've filled her in. Like me she gasped when she heard the bit about Hugh being married to someone else and having twins. I don't know why out of the whole story that feels like the most shocking part.

She thinks for a moment. 'No. She was always an appalling show-off. I do know that when she announced they were getting married it didn't feel like a surprise, so she must have been talking about him for a while by then. And there was at least a year of regaling us all with the preparations.'

I remember that part. When I arrived the wedding planning was in full swing. Juliet and Roz have been here the longest of all of us. Since the beginning. Then Emma and then, I realize, me. 'So probably most of the time she's been here then?'

She nods. 'I would say so.'

'Was she vile to you from the beginning?'

She considers for a moment, as if she's trying to make sure she gives as honest an answer as possible. 'The show was only twice a week at the beginning, and there were only the two of us editors. I don't know if it was insecurity or what, but I think she wanted to create some kind of rivalry between us. I was all gung ho, thinking we were all in it together. It was exciting. But it became pretty obvious right away that her way of making herself look good was to try and make me look bad. That's a long way of saying yes. From the beginning.'

'I'm sorry,' I say, as if it was my fault, but what I'm really saying sorry for is the fact that I joined Roz's team so unquestioningly.

'Did they find out anything else?' she says. 'Anything useful?'

I let out a sigh. 'Nothing.'

She hooks a piece of hair behind an ear. 'How long now till your probation is up?'

'Two and a bit weeks.'

She stands. 'She seems to be behaving now. She's probably given up.'

I don't think so. Roz is acting like we're friends. Like everything is OK. But I don't believe it. We know too much about each other. 'I doubt it. I think she's keeping me onside until she can hit me with something big. People like her don't give up that easily.'

I feel as if someone has handed me a ticking time bomb, with no instructions on how to defuse it. I have two weeks to learn which wire is which. And I have to make sure I cut the correct one.

30

'Of course, if she's really that crazy she could still try and get you sacked even after your title is made official,' Dee says helpfully. We're walking to Golders Hill Park. Dee has lured me there with the promise of the tiny outdoor zoo with its donkeys and lemurs. The attraction for her clearly being the seven-thousand-odd steps it'll take us to get there and back. It's a beautiful day. The promised heatwave has suddenly arrived fully formed. It's just a shame I forgot to take any Piriton because I'm punctuating my walking with sneezing.

'Thanks. That makes me feel a whole lot better.'

She looks at me defiantly. 'What? I'm just stating a fact.'

She's right of course. In a way. 'Once I have a proper contract it gets much more complicated though. There would have to be warnings and hearings. She'd really have to prove I'd done something irredeemable.'

'I suppose.'

'I'm sure she'll look for another job if I survive my probation. There's no way she'll want to stay and work under me.'

Dee laughs. 'She'll probably ask you for a reference.'

'Good luck with that,' I say, sidestepping an old lady hunched over a walking frame.

We stomp on along the path at the edge of the heath,

me puffing as it climbs uphill. 'She's on holiday next week, so that's something.'

Dee looks at me. She's not even breaking a sweat. 'That's fantastic. That's fifty per cent of her opportunity gone. Where's she supposed to be going?'

'I heard her telling Lorraine she and Hugh were off to Positano but it's anyone's guess. Maybe she really is going there but on her own, or with a friend.'

We emerge from the path back on to the pavement. 'Do you think she has friends?' Dee says.

I consider this for a moment. Outgoing, show-off Roz. The life and soul of the party. 'Yes. She must have. She's out practically every night.'

Dee raises her eyebrows at me. At least, I think she does. Her fringe has got so long it's hard to tell.

'What?' I say.

'We could check them out. Me and Gav.'

'No, Dee. There's no point. Nothing we find out about her personal life is going to help get rid of her. I just have to hope I get through my trial period and she resigns. It's two weeks. One if you count her holiday.'

Dee looks unconvinced. 'It seems crazy not to try everything when you know she's still gunning for you.'

I shrug. 'The only thing that would help at this point would be if I could prove it was her doing all those things to me all along. And we both know that's not going to happen.'

'Even more reason to explore every avenue.'

We turn into the gates of the park. 'Let's get a coffee,' I

say, spotting the little café. I've never been here before and now I wonder why. It's a beautiful ordered oasis set against the wildness of the heath and, despite the warm day, it's quiet. A few people with dogs on leads, a couple with their two children. There are more squirrels than humans, it seems.

Dee knows me well enough that she picks up immediately that I've exhausted the topic of Roz. I can't allow her to occupy my mind all the time or I won't be able to do my job properly and then she'll win by default. I'm grateful for the change of subject.

'How's Ashley getting on?'

'Not great. She's struggling, I think. Panicking about whether she's doing the right thing, and how she's going to manage.' I remember that feeling well. Veering from excitement about the baby to absolute terror that I'd ruined my life. I remember watching a young mum struggle with a screaming baby and a heavy basket of shopping in the queue at Sainsbury's when I was pregnant, and all the other waiting customers tutting and glaring at her. I let her go ahead of me and she was so tearfully grateful it terrified me. Was this what I'd signed up for?

'Can't you persuade her to move home?'

I've thought about it. Telling Hattie she would have to move out when her six months was up. Having my daughter safe under my roof where I could take care of her. But I remember the pressure my mum put on me when I was in Ashley's situation. How feeling as if I was disappointing her just added to my worries. 'She said she doesn't want to. I don't want to push it. You know what she's like, she's always been independent.'

'I wonder who she gets that from,' Dee says, giving me a one-armed hug. We order two skinny lattes from the young girl behind the counter.

'It's not the life I wanted for her.' As soon as I say it I realize it's a stupid thing to say. Ashley's life is Ashley's life. She has to work out for herself what she wants.

'Would you go back and change things in your own if you could?'

I don't even need to think about the answer. 'Of course not.'

'Well, there you go then.'

I suddenly realize how insensitive I'm being. All Dee's wanted for the past God knows how many years is to get pregnant and she's finally had to accept that that's never going to happen.

'You're right. Of course you're right.'

'She'll be OK,' she says, picking up her coffee and then putting it down again quickly. 'Ouch.' She finds two cardboard sleeves and places the cups in them, hands me mine. 'It must be scary for her, that's all. To suddenly decide she's doing it on her own.'

'Ryan has sent her one text. *Let me know if there's anything I'm supposed to be doing.* Dick.'

'We should feel sorry for him. He'll wake up one day and realize he has a teenage child he barely knows and he's fucked up royally.'

'Let's hope so,' I say.

*

Work without Roz is a joy. I'm not looking over my shoulder all the time watching out for what she might do next. I don't feel as if I'm being scrutinized. My every move analysed. My failings noted. The department seems lighter, all the tension gone. Even Lorraine makes an effort with the rest of us, although I see she draws the line at Juliet.

'Where did Roz go in the end? I forgot to ask her,' I say to her at the start of the department meeting. I'm interested to hear what Roz told her, whether she's spun her the 'me and Hugh have split up' sob story yet.

'The Amalfi coast. One of Hugh's clients has a villa down there. He's lent it to them.'

'Dare we ask who?' Glen looks up from his phone.

'Oh,' Lorraine says, looking caught out. 'I'm not sure. I didn't ask.'

I find that hard to believe. Lorraine asks Roz questions with the zeal of a quiz show host. It's as if she's studying her as her specialist subject on *Mastermind*.

When the meeting wraps up Lorraine shadows me towards my office. 'It's David Summers's villa,' she hisses in my ear. 'I didn't think I was allowed to say.'

'Oh God, no, well done,' I say, trying not to laugh. I wonder what David Summers would think if he knew he had such a starring role in Roz's fantasies, but I'm guessing he has more important things on his mind at the moment.

For the first time since I was promoted I can throw myself into work without any distractions. I'm sharper. I have more ideas. This is what it could be like if she left, I find myself thinking. Joe, who has kept his head down and got on with the job but in an increasingly isolated fashion, re-emerges from his shell and is back to being the funny, confident young man he seemed to be when he first started. Even Emma seems different. Less nervous. More self-assured. What's fascinating is that the change is almost instant, too. As if just knowing Roz wasn't going to walk through the door casting her critical eye over every-one, looking for flaws and weaknesses to make fun of at any moment, was enough.

'Peaceful, isn't it?' Juliet says when we pass in the corridor.

'Lovely,' I reply with a smile.

By lunchtime I'm feeling relaxed. Positive. Roz won't be back until Monday. My probation period officially ends on the Friday of next week. Five days. What's the worst that can happen?

OK, so maybe the worst that can happen is that Glen calls me in to tell me that Patricia has been to see him to complain about the email I sent her.

I didn't send her an email.

31

'When was it sent?'

I don't know if it confuses him that this is the first thing I say. He frowns slightly.

'I didn't ask her. She came up here in a fury so I assume she'd only just received it. Holly, what is going on?'

'I need to know when it was sent. Not when she got it. When it was sent.'

'You don't want to explain yourself first?' Glen has adopted his steely look. Gone is the slightly vague, benevolent ageing smoothie. I realize I need to take a step back.

'I didn't email her. Obviously. I don't even know what it says . . .'

He consults a piece of paper. I assume a copy of the email. The time and date it was sent must be on there and I have to resist grabbing it out of his hand.

'"Patricia,"' Glen reads. '"I absolutely loved that black dress you wore to the Soap Awards. It made you look two stone lighter and, dare I say it, almost feminine. You must let me know where you bought it. Might it have been in the tent section of a camping shop?"'

I snort. I can't help it. It's so ludicrous it's almost funny. Except that it isn't. Does he really think I would send something like that? It has Roz written all over it. But Roz is in Italy. 'I'm sorry for laughing,' I say when he remains stony-faced. 'But you honestly can't think that came from me. Could I look at it, please? It might have the date and time on there.'

I hold my hand out but he keeps hold of the paper, looking at the top right hand corner. 'Today at eleven-oh-three.'

'OK. Well, I don't know who did it but someone must have gone on to my computer.' I try to think where I was at three minutes past eleven. I mean, I was in my office all morning but could I have been in the loo or making a coffee? It's possible. I've done both things. But it feels as if it would have been very risky for someone to have gone in there knowing I was only out of the way for a few minutes. The logical suspect is Lorraine. I imagine she'd do pretty much anything Roz asked her to do. But there's no way she could get away with sitting at my desk and using my computer in front of the others. Not to mention the fact that she couldn't know my password. Only Emma knows my password now.

Could it be her? Sweet helpful Emma? I dismiss the thought the second it enters my head. Imagine thinking that Paddington Bear had stabbed your grandmother. And laughed while he was doing it. It's about as likely as that.

Glen breaks my thought process. 'Obviously Patricia is spitting blood. And who can blame her?'

'Well, the first thing she needs to know is that it didn't come from me.' I have to remember what's important here. Fight fires.

'Are you really trying to tell me someone went on to your computer and sent this pretending it came from you? What, as a joke?'

'No. I mean, yes, but I don't think it was a joke. I've had . . . There's no point me even telling you because I can't prove any of it. But this isn't the first time it's happened. That email you got from me that I said I meant to send to someone else . . . I didn't send it at all. And what happened at the story conference . . .'

Glen sighs. 'Is this Roz we're talking about? I know there's been something going on between the two of you.'

'Yes. But if you ask her about it she'll just deny it. And, like I say, I have no proof.'

'And it clearly wasn't her who emailed Patricia this morning . . .' There's a cynical note to his voice that makes me think he doesn't believe any of it. That I might be the liar in all this. This is why I didn't want to say anything to anyone until I could prove it. It all sounds so far-fetched. 'I told you before you needed to sort out whatever your problem with Roz is. This is getting ridiculous now.'

'I know. She did come and tell you that the thing about me hiding her script notes was all a big mix-up though, didn't she?'

'No. She didn't. And to be honest I have much more pressing things to be worrying about than your playground squabble.'

So she was lying about that too. All this time I was thinking that at least we'd wiped the slate clean and all I had to watch out for was a new assault from her, Glen has still been under the impression that I'm the one in the wrong. I want to explain myself. Beg him to believe me over her. But I can tell that now is not the moment.

'Will you speak to Patricia or should I?'

'I think you should do it. It's you she's angry with. But for God's sake don't make the situation worse. I don't want her thinking we're all amateurs.'

I bite my tongue. The last thing I want to do is speak to her, but I know I have no choice. I need to put this right. I know that a lot of the cast don't like Glen — or, at least, they don't like the direction he's taking the show in. The last thing I want is to be responsible for a mutiny, however indirectly.

'Of course. I'll go down now.'

I stop in on the room where the editors watch the monitor and communicate with the studio to see Juliet and fill her in — not to mention ask her advice about what I can possibly say to Patricia that won't have her campaigning for me to be fired or just flooring me with one punch — but Fay, the producer of this week's eps, is in there with her, chatting, so I just check if Patricia is on a break between scenes and leave it at that.

I'm terrified to knock on her door, let alone speak to her. I decide to track down Chris the runner to find out if she's left any specific instructions not to be disturbed. I find him puffing along a corridor with two Starbucks coffees in his hand. There isn't a Starbucks in walking distance so I have no idea where he's been to get them.

'I have to drop these off,' he says as soon as he sees that I'm going to approach him. I want to ask where he got the coffees from, and who has insisted that the local café won't do, but I decide to save that for later. 'They're going cold.'

'I have to speak to Patricia,' I say, following him. 'Is it OK to knock?'

'God. I mean, no. But if it's urgent . . . She's not napping or anything. I think she was going to watch something on iPlayer.'

'It is urgent. Don't let anyone disturb us for a bit, OK?'

He nods with a cursory 'Fine' and rushes off. I stop outside Patricia's door trying to summon up courage. This is ridiculous, I tell myself. You've done nothing wrong.

I force myself to knock. For a blissful second I think that maybe she's not there. She's in make-up or one of the other actors' dressing rooms. But then the door is flung open and she's right in front of me.

'You!'

Imagine a cartoon bull, up on its back legs, smoke coming out of its nostrils, furious that someone is waving a red flag at it.

'Could I come in for a second?'

She doesn't answer, just stands back from the open door to let me in. I've never actually been into her dressing room before. She's inhabited it for five years so it's packed to the brim with home comforts. Photos and throws and jars and pots of both cosmetics and her favourite snacks. A kettle and a tiny fridge. There's a sofa but also an armchair on which sits a huge knitting bag.

There's a pile of CDs and an old CD player. It smells a bit fusty, like the windows haven't been opened in a long time.

She doesn't offer me a seat but I feel as if I need to sit down before I keel over so I plonk myself in the armchair. I've decided that despite her harsh exterior Patricia must have a heart in there somewhere – doesn't everyone? – so I am going to appeal to her softer side.

'I . . . I . . .' I stutter. I just need to get it out. She has placed herself on the sofa, facing me, and looks as though she might quite like to kill me. I clear my throat. Twist my gold hoops round. Here goes. 'I understand you got an email that supposedly came from me. It didn't. Well, that is, it came from my account but I absolutely, 100 per cent, didn't send it. I would never say anything like that. I didn't even see the dress you wore to the Soap Awards . . .' Stop, Holly, I tell myself. Slow down.

'I don't want to tell tales but something strange has been happening. Someone has been doing things in my name to try and make me look bad . . .'

Shit. I can feel tears forming. I don't want to show her weakness. She already thinks I'm flaky after the Post-it note incident. This would confirm that I'm not someone to be taken seriously. She'd go in for the kill. I can't look at her so I stare at a stain on the carpet. Will myself not to cry.

As usual I ignore myself. A big heavy tear plops on to my cheek. I bat it away but then there's another and another and my nose starts running in sympathy. I don't even have anything to stop the flow of bodily fluids. I think about using my sleeve I'm that desperate, but then a tissue wafts in front of my face.

I look up as I take it. Patricia is staring at me, stricken. 'Oh, my poor dear girl, what on earth is going on?'

I'm so taken aback I don't know what to do so I just cry some more and blow my nose and wipe my tears. She hands me about five more tissues.

'Take your time,' she says.

I don't know if it's the adrenalin or the relief but I can't stop crying. 'You have to believe me,' I say through a miasma of snot and tears. 'I would never do something like that. I'm going to lose my job . . .'

'Don't be silly.' She leans over and puts a hand on my knee. The gesture absolutely floors me. 'Of course you won't. Who is it then? Who's doing this to you?'

'I can't,' I gulp. 'I mean, I know but I can't prove it.'

'Someone here? On the show?'

I nod.

'It's not that Roz girl, is it? I've never liked her. None of us do. Way too full of herself.'

For a second I think I've misheard. Roz, Ms Popular, disliked by the cast. Well, if Patricia's to be believed.

'I really can't . . .' I say, but I look her right in the eye as I say it. I see the moment she gets what I'm not saying.

'No. No. Of course you can't. But, whoever it is, why do you think they're doing it?'

I know I shouldn't say any more. Glen has made it clear he doesn't want the cast to think the ship is being steered by a bunch of incompetents. But it's so tempting.

'Because they want my job . . .' There. I've said it. I can't take it back. Maybe she'll believe me. Maybe I'll have people in my corner.

'Oh, for God's sake,' she says. 'She would never get it anyway. Surely Juliet would have if it wasn't you?'

I've never really thought the cast took any notice of what was going on in our department. Beyond complaining every now and then if they didn't like a storyline. But why wouldn't they? They're reliant on us to do our job well so they can do theirs. It has an impact on them.

'Not that I've said it's her,' I say, suddenly nervous. For all I know Patricia might be the world's biggest gossip and she can't wait to go and spread this around until it gets back to Glen that I've been bad-mouthing Roz to the cast.

'No,' she says. 'Don't worry. I'm not about to call her out on it.'

'I appreciate you being so nice to me about this,' I say and I almost start bawling again. 'You didn't have to be.'

'Trust me, I know an actress when I see one,' she says. 'And I know you're not one.'

She rustles round in a cupboard. Produces a half-empty bottle of whisky and two glasses. Pours two fingers in each. 'Here you are.'

I know I should say no. I'm hopeless with spirits. But I don't want to ruin our bonding moment. I'm embarrassed that I've made an idiot of myself but if it's going to stop her calling for me to be publicly hung, drawn and quartered then it's been worth it.

'Thank you.' She knocks hers back in one, so I do the same. Cough. Recover. Cough again.

'That'll start rumours on the set,' she says with a cackle. 'Patricia's a drunk.'

'I'll defend you,' I say with a laugh, the glow hitting me. 'Medicinal.'

'OK. What do you want me to say to Paul Holly-wood?'

I have to think for a moment. Realize she means Glen. 'Um . . . I don't know really. Maybe just that you're satisfied it wasn't me? I mean, if you are . . .'

'I am. I'll tell him I'm happy that it was some kind of practical joke someone played on you and that I don't want to take it any further.'

'Don't say I told you it was Roz . . . I mean, if you don't mind . . . He thinks we'll all look really unprofessional if people know . . .'

She taps my knee again, her hand so heavy with the weight of her big gold rings that I imagine this is what it must feel like to be pawed by a bear. 'Leave it with me. Now, clean your face up a bit; you don't want her to see you looking like shit.'

'She's not here. She's on holiday this week,' I say, and then I wish I hadn't.

Patricia frowns. 'Then how did she . . .?'

'I have no idea. I know the other things were her because she admitted it to me but this . . .'

Why would I expect Patricia to believe me now? I can hardly even believe it myself.

'She must have roped someone else in to help her,' I say unconvincingly.

'Well, let me know when you find out who that is.' Patricia hands me a wet wipe and I dab under my eyes to remove any streaked mascara. I curse myself for saying too much.

The thing is, I'm clueless. I have no idea how someone could have accessed my computer at eleven this morning. Can you send an email on a timer? Could Roz have composed her missive last week and set it to send today? Maybe. It sounds feasible. Except that she has no idea what my password is now and I've made sure neither she nor Lorraine are ever around when I enter it. The only person who knows it is Emma.

'Have you got a second?' I say as I walk past Emma's desk on the way back in. I put my head round Glen's door first to let him know things had been smoothed over with Patricia. I almost laughed when I saw him and thought of her comment. OK, so he's Paul Hollywood with a full beard and not a goatee, but yes, he's Paul Hollywood. I managed to control myself though. If I laughed I would probably cry and I didn't think that would help.

'Good,' was all he said, and then he went back to work so I left it at that.

Emma follows me into my office and I close the door behind her. She looks nervous, as if she can pick up that I'm not happy. I indicate for her to sit in the armchair and she does. I look at her in her baggy cardigan, knee-length skirt and trainers, with her shapeless Velma bob, and I just can't imagine her doing anything so mean, so calculated.

I walk round to the other side of the desk and sit down. 'OK, I'm just going to come out with it. Did you tell anyone my new password?'

She opens her eyes wide. 'No. Of course not. Has it happened again?'

I ignore her question. 'And if anyone saw you put in your password and went on to your computer could they get into my email that way?' Emma is the only person who has access to my email other than me.

'Yes, but they'd still have to know your password too, because I don't have it saved. Just in case.'

'So could someone have seen you log into mine? Seen the password you put in?'

'Theoretically yes. But I don't think I've even looked at it since you changed it. I only really do it if you're on holiday or off sick. In fact I'm sure I haven't.'

I exhale loudly. 'Is it possible to send a timed email? So, for example, someone could have gone on to my computer last week and set something to send this week?'

'No. I mean, yes, that can be done but not on our system. So, no.'

'Were you at your desk all morning?'

'Well, apart from making tea, and you were in here when I did that. Oh, and I went to the Ladies but, again, you were here. Since you asked me to keep an eye on things I try to make sure I only leave if you're at your desk.'

I believe her. She's conscientious to a fault. 'And you

didn't see anyone come in here? When I wasn't here? Lorraine?'

'Lorraine?' she says, incredulous. 'Do you think it's her? I mean, I know she's a bit of a bitch but I don't think she's clever enough to even think of it, let alone do it.'

'Just indulge me,' I say.

'No. I didn't see anyone come in. If I had I would have asked them what they were looking for.'

I lean back in my chair. I'm stumped.

'Change your password again,' Emma says. 'Don't even tell me what it is. If you ever need me to check your email you can tell me then.'

'Good idea,' I say. 'Not that I don't trust you. At all. I just need to narrow down the field.'

'It's fine. I understand.' She talks me through how to do it again and then she makes a point of turning away when I enter my new details. Unless she has eyes in the back of her head or the ability to decipher text from the sound of the keys she has no way of knowing what I'm typing.

'Let me know if there's anything else I can do. Any-thing,' she says. 'I feel terrible that this is happening to you.'

'Thanks. I really don't think it's you. Don't worry.'

I know how awful it feels to be blamed for something you haven't done.

32

When I get home from work Hattie is doing something in the kitchen. I can't really face being sociable so I grab a glass of wine and tell her I have some work I need to do. I wake up my desktop. Open my work email. I want to check that there's nothing there that shouldn't be, whether there are any tell-tale clues. A box pops up, telling me that my stored password is invalid. I enter the new one, the one that only I know and I tell it yes when it asks me if I want that password to be saved. I know I'll forget it at some point.

Of course there's nothing to see. Whoever sent the email deleted it as soon as it was sent. I take my wine over to the sofa. Flop down. Stare at the ceiling. She's started the endgame but she's changed the rules. I don't even know who or what I'm fighting against now. All I can do is wait to see what happens next.

Another day, another email. This time I get a call from HR. Thank God she – Karen – phones me and not Glen. She thought it was a bit odd, she says. She wondered if I meant to send it.

I've only met Karen once. She was on the interview panel when I got my promotion. I liked her. She was good cop to a man called Alan's bad cop. She obviously thought I deserved the job over Roz.

'I don't even know what it says,' I say. 'I haven't sent you an email.'

There's a pause and then an 'Oh'. I know I have to explain myself quickly or she'll think I'm being crazily defensive. Or just crazy.

'What I mean is that someone keeps messing around on my computer. Sending people things that are meant to be from me and then deleting them so I don't even know about them until the recipient asks me what the hell I'm on about. I'm really sorry. I didn't think they'd start sending them to people outside the show. I can only apologize.'

'No. Gosh, how awful for you. Do you know who it is? I mean it would be a disciplinary offence . . .'

'I'm trying to find some proof. Could you let me know what it said? The email. I might as well know the lengths she – they – are willing to go to.'

'I'll forward it on to you. Let me know if I can help in any way, Holly.'

'Thanks. And I'm really sorry again that you got dragged into this. I appreciate you calling me.'

I wait anxiously for the ping that will let me know I've got mail. I've been lucky so far that the people affected have taken it so well. At least in so far as I know. Maybe there's something sitting in someone's inbox at this moment that will spark World War Three. The Head of Continuing Series, the channel Controller. Someone I've never met, who won't be so ready to believe my defence.

I see Karen's name pop up at the same moment I hear the sound. I'm almost too scared to open the message.

I force myself to do it.

'Here you go,' it says.

Ten twenty-three a.m.

And then underneath:

Dear Karen,

I hope you're well. As you know my probation period for the position of script executive is almost at an end. I'm sure you're aware of the stresses and responsibilities of the job and I'm hoping you'll agree with me that once my appointment is confirmed (as I assume it will be!) it would be only fair for us to have a full and frank discussion about my pay level, and whether it could be improved.

Yours sincerely . . .

I stare at it in horror for a full thirty seconds. Then I bang out a response:

Thanks, Karen. Just for the record I hope you know that I'm extremely happy with what I'm being paid and if I'm fortunate enough for my post to be made permanent (which I'm by no means taking for granted) I have absolutely no expectation for it to be increased and would not even consider requesting it. I really appreciate you coming to me with this, and not Glen, as I'm sure you realize this is a very delicate situation. I'll do my best to ensure nothing like this ever happens again.

And then I get up and close my office door. I don't want to have to deal with anyone.

I text Dee to see if she wants to come over, but she's covering a late shift. I don't feel like being alone. I feel completely at a loss, under siege. I actually thought about sending an email to everyone in my contacts saying that they should ignore any communications from me that seem out of character or just a bit odd, but who knows who she'll target next, and I don't want to start a whole rumour mill going unless I have to.

As luck would have it Hattie arrives home at the exact same moment I do. She's clutching a Waitrose carrier bag, swaddled in a baggy jumper even though it's so warm I'm sweating in my cap-sleeved shirt.

'Hey,' she says with a big smile. 'Good timing.'

I already have my key out, so I let us in. 'How was work?'

'Good,' she says, heading for her room. 'I finished early because my last client cancelled.'

'Lovely.' I shrug out of my jacket. Hang it up. 'Do you fancy a drink?'

'Definitely.' She indicates the carrier bag. 'Let me just put this lot in my fridge. I have wine in here too.'

'I'll open one. White?'

She nods yes and I go into the kitchen and find a bottle in the fridge. I'm so relieved to have company, and someone who knows at least part of the story. I don't often feel as if I just want to wallow in my own misery but tonight I definitely do. I want sympathy. I want someone to tell me it's all going to be OK.

'You look knackered,' she says as she comes back in. She puts the bottle she's brought with her into the fridge, accepts the glass I offer her. 'Rough day?'

'You could say that.' I move an old newspaper off one of the chairs and sit down. Smokey appears out of nowhere and jumps up, kneading his claws into my lap.

Hattie sits opposite me, pulls her too-long sleeves over her fingers so only her blue-painted nails are showing. 'Not still the same thing?'

'It's got so much worse,' I say and out of nowhere a fat tear runs down my cheek. Followed by about twenty of its friends.

Hattie reaches over the table and puts her hand on top of mine. 'Oh God, you poor thing. Do you want to talk about it?'

'I wouldn't know where to start.'

'I'm pretty up to speed. Dee told me most of it when you were on the phone to Ashley the other week . . .'

I should be pissed off with Dee, but actually I'm relieved that Hattie already has a pretty good idea what I'm going through. I fill her in on the last couple of days.

'Wait, so she confessed everything to you, begged for your forgiveness and then she carried on doing it?'

'Apparently,' I say. 'Although now, like I said, she's on holiday and it's still happening. She's still getting into my email somehow.'

Hattie exhales exaggeratedly, and a wisp of hair stands up off her forehead. 'Or this is someone else entirely.'

'That's too crazy.' I ruffle Smokey's ears one time too many and he makes a half-hearted attempt to bite me. 'That would be like a really bad film where there are two serial killers targeting the same town at once.'

She shrugs. 'It could happen.'

'God,' I say, putting my face in my hands. 'I really must have done something wrong in a past life.'

She laughs. 'OK, it probably couldn't happen. So she must have someone doing her dirty work for her while she's away.'

I shake my head. 'There's only one person who even likes her at this point and she's too stupid. And how is she getting into my office without anyone seeing her? The walls are glass.'

'I know,' Hattie says, slamming her hand down on the table. I jump. 'Magic.'

I start laughing and so does she. 'Or . . . no . . . it's a ghost,' she snorts and I'm helpless. It feels so good to be able to find the situation funny that I can't stop. Smokey yowls in protest at finding the comfy lap he had settled on vibrating, and jumps down, landing on the floor with a thud.

'It's not even funny,' she says, and for some reason that makes me laugh even more. The pair of us guffaw like we're at the greatest comedy club in the world. Every time I think I'm about to stop I start again and then so does she. I know it's a reaction to the tension I've been bottling up all these weeks but that doesn't mean I have any power to control it.

Eventually we both run out of steam. I have tears streaming down my face but I feel better than I have in days. As if a valve has been opened and the pressure finally released.

'Oh God, I needed that,' I say, wiping my eyes.

Hattie leans across the table again and pats my hand with her own again. 'It'll all be OK. You just have to hang in there.'

By Wednesday afternoon I allow myself to breathe a sigh of relief. Nothing has happened. The day is almost over. Maybe the assault is paused until she returns next Monday. One last hurrah before it's too late. All guns blazing.

It's almost half past five when I hear a tell-tale ping. My stomach lurches as it has every time I've received an email in the past few days. It's from Tommy, the show's undisputed heart-throb. Forty years old, a twinkle in his roving eye. Well, the character Jimmy's roving eye. In real life Tommy is always doing magazine spreads with 'the missus' and their five daughters whose ages range from about twenty down to four. He's been in *Churchill Road* since day one and he's always the unofficial spokesperson for the cast when they've got a mass grievance. He's also known for getting drunk at award shows and lairy with journalists or anyone else who gets in his way. He scares me a bit, if I'm being honest.

His email is titled 'WTF?'

I swallow a wave of nausea. Clamp my hand over my

mouth as if that might help. I open up the email, force myself to scan down past his response – although I do catch the words 'who the fuck do you think you are' as I go – and read what I am supposed to have written.

Tommy,

I know I shouldn't send this but I can't keep quiet any longer. I really like you. And by like you I mean I basically want to rip your clothes off. I'm pretty sure you feel the same because I've seen the way you look at me. I know you're married but no way do I believe you only have eyes for your wife, especially after all those kids. Anyway, I just wanted you to know that I'm here if you're interested. Could we meet up for dinner or even a drink to 'discuss'? Xx

P.S. Obviously this is just between me and you!

I start to shake. I feel sick, humiliated, embarrassed. I scroll back up to face the worst. There's no greeting, nothing to soften his reply.

Where the hell do you get off sending me an email like this? I barely even know who you are, let alone fancy you. And who the fuck do you think you are having a dig at my wife?? I'm sure you wouldn't like the boss to hear about this?

Shit. I dash out a quick reply, hoping I can get to him before he takes it further.

I didn't send that email. Please believe me. I would never say anything that unprofessional, or be mean about your family.

Someone is sending out emails pretending to be me (ask Patricia).
Please don't speak to Glen before I can fully explain myself.

There's no time to say any more. For all I know he's
already on his way up to Glen's office. I glance at the TV
on the wall outside and there doesn't seem to be any sign
of him on screen. He must be on a break. It's almost surreal to look out and see Juliet, Lorraine and Emma just
getting on with their work. Unaware of the tsunami that's
just hit me. Unaware that I'm drowning.

I double-check the address my email was sent from but
of course it's the correct one because he's just hit reply and
his response has reached me. Dee had a theory when I
spoke to her last that maybe Roz had created a new email
address that was one subtle key stroke different to mine.
Something the recipient would never notice. Sadly, this
proves that theory wrong.

I check my sent box: nothing.

I know I should try and head Tommy off before he gets
to Glen but I'm not sure I can face either of them. Either
Tommy got my email in time or not. Either – if he did –
he's decided to give me the benefit of the doubt, or not. I
could forewarn Glen that there might be trouble on the
horizon but that'd just remind him that I'm the cause of it.

I grab up my bag and my jacket. Juliet looks up as I
walk past but I just keep moving.

'I'm going home,' I mutter to Emma as I pass. I don't
wait for a reply.

In the corridor I keep my head down as I walk past

312

Glen's office. The door is closed, signifying that he has someone in with him. I can't even bring myself to think about what might be being said.

I'm sitting on the station platform in a daze when I get a text. Dee.

Come straight to mine after work, it says. *Don't go home first x*.

I don't want to. I want to shut myself away and not see anyone. I want to hide.

Why? I answer. And then I add, *I'm knackered*.

My phone beeps again. *Just do it*.

'Oh, thank God,' Dee says when she opens the front door.

'What? What's going on?'

'Don't kill me.'

'Oh, for fuck's sake, Dee. I'm exhausted, I'm fed up, I'm probably unemployed. I just want to go home and veg out.'

She grabs me by the arm and drags me inside. I follow her up the stairs. 'We might have found the key . . .'

'What key? Why are you being so cryptic?' Today's candle smell is something churchy. It's so comforting it makes me want to cry. It reminds me of when I was little and being dragged reluctantly to mass by my mum on a Sunday. Sitting there bored out of my mind, not really understanding anything anyone was saying. She leads me through to the living room. A bottle of red and two glasses sit on the coffee table. 'Where's Gavin?'

'Birmingham.' She unscrews the cap and pours two glasses. 'I'm not being cryptic. Gav found something out.

It might be your way to prove that Roz is trying to stitch you up.'

My heart starts to race. I'd all but given up. 'Tell me.'

We sit at either end of the sofa.

'OK. I'm going to try and get to the point really quickly . . .'

'Good.'

She practically inhales half her glass of wine. 'So, Gav and Hugh exchanged numbers, just in case Hugh remembered anything significant. And you know how I was wondering if Roz had any friends and who they are? Well, Gav decided to call him and ask if he remembered anyone. Just out of curiosity.'

I have no idea where this is going. I just sit there and wait for her to carry on.

'He could only really remember one. She used to come into the bar most nights to hang out with Roz while she was working . . .'

'And?'

'Her name was Hattie.'

PART THREE

33

'No, Dee. I mean, I know you love a conspiracy, but there are literally thousands of people called Hattie in the world. Hundreds of thousands, probably.' I can't believe that this is what she's dragged me over here for. The dramatic instruction that I not go home. All the talk of finding the key.

'He said he remembers she worked at a dentist's.'

OK, maybe that is a bit odd. 'Even so . . .'

Dee fixes me with a stare. 'Can you access your work email from home?'

'Shit. Yes.'

'And is your password stored?'

I think back to bumping into Hattie leaving my living room. 'Fuck.'

'Exactly.'

'But, what? You think she just happened to end up renting my spare room and then Roz saw an opportunity? That seems a bit far-fetched.'

Dee rolls her eyes. 'I may be gullible but even I don't believe in coincidences like that. Who apart from me knew all the qualities you wanted in a lodger? Roz. And then Hattie breezes in and basically lists all those things about herself – quiet, away most weekends, never uses the kitchen. No wonder she seemed too good to be true.'

'You think Roz set her up to rent the room?'

She nods. 'Although God knows what was in it for her.'

I sit there trying to get my head around it. Something occurs to me. 'Did you tell her everything we'd found out about Roz that night Ashley phoned to say she'd broken up with Ryan?'

'Probably. I remember filling her in on some of it because I was struggling to find stuff to talk about without you there.'

'It was right after that that Roz spun me that line about her and Hugh having split up. About her having had to move into that awful flat in Shepherd's Bush and the fact that his birthday party didn't happen. Maybe even the next day. She knew I was on to her. What she told me explained away everything I thought she'd lied about.'

'Hattie reported straight back! Everything I told her.' She suddenly looks crestfallen. 'I made things worse.'

'Don't be stupid. You weren't to know. I didn't ask you not to tell her.'

We're interrupted when Gavin FaceTimes from his mum's.

'Did you tell her?' he says as soon as Dee answers. 'Hi, Holly.'

Dee swivels the phone round so he can see me and I wave. 'I did.'

'Mental, isn't it?' he says. 'I wish I'd met her now.'

'Absolutely mental,' I say. 'I can't get my head around it at all.'

'We need to think of a plan,' Dee chips in. 'Now we know how she's doing it we can get her. I know it.'

'Act completely normally with this Hattie, Holly,' Gavin says. 'Don't give her any clue that you're on to her.'

'I won't. You don't think she's a psycho, do you?'

'Saddo more like,' Dee says, and that makes me feel better.

I don't really want to go home later. It feels as if my sanctuary has been invaded by a hostile force. It's no longer my safe space. There's a light on in Hattie's room as I creep down the front steps. I go straight into the bathroom without even taking my jacket off, brush my teeth, and then gather up a disgruntled Smokey – I can see that Hattie's fed him. How odd. She's helping try to destroy my life while simultaneously worrying about my cat's welfare – and shut us both in the bedroom.

I know she would never try to access my computer while I'm at home, so I toy with the idea of not going into work tomorrow, but I know the Tommy situation needs dealing with. Damn, I should have checked my work email before I came to bed to see if he'd responded to my begging message. I know I won't sleep now unless I know, so I get up again and tiptoe into the living room and fire up my computer. Nothing. I wonder if she's read his earlier angry missive. Phoned up Roz wherever she is so they could have a good laugh about it. About me.

A wave of absolute anger hits me. How fucking dare they? I'm tempted to change my password again. Say no when my computer asks me if I want to store it. But Dee, Gavin and I talked for a long time about how we would never catch her in the act if we did that. They persuaded me I had to risk another humiliation for the greater good. Of course, that could mean I've lost my job before I can prove myself innocent. But it's a risk I have to take.

Tomorrow morning I am at least going to go in late, giving her no chance to send anything before she leaves for work – although she seems to have had some time off this week already judging by the times the emails have been sent so, who knows, maybe she's taken holiday to correspond with Roz's. But, assuming she goes in, once she heads out the door I will text Dee who, luckily, is on a late shift. She'll hotfoot it round here via the Argos in Swiss Cottage and I'll leave her here installing a nanny cam hidden on a bookshelf and pointing right at my desktop. Even if Hattie is only pretending to go to work to fool me she won't dare go into my living room when she returns home if she can hear that someone is in there. If she sees Dee then so what? She'll just think I've asked her to come round for some reason. Dee will have thought up the perfect excuse.

And then if Hattie sits at my desk, accesses my email, we'll have her.

I barely sleep at all, unsurprisingly. I'm so furious with Hattie that the thought of her sleeping peacefully across the hall incenses me. I realize that I'm going to have to give her notice. The thought of having to deal with her head on gives me chills. And then I remember that she still hasn't paid me her second month's rent, that it's now weeks late. I assume once Roz's campaign is all over she'll just do a moonlight flit. I'll have her deposit but she'll have been living rent free for weeks. As angry as that makes me I realize it's actually preferable to us having to live side by side, pretending everything is OK while I wait for her to leave.

I allow myself to lie in for a bit, sending Emma a text from my bed that says I'll be in an hour or so late. I know I have to face Hattie this morning – only for the pretence that I'm going to be home all morning in the hope that she then goes off to work, or at least pretends to. The last time I saw her she held my hand across the table and told me everything was going to be OK. We solidified what I thought was a new friendship. I breathe in slowly and then out again. I have to act as if everything is still good between us.

I go into the kitchen, feed Smokey and then bang around making myself breakfast. I want her to hear that I'm still here and wonder why. It works. After a few minutes she's at the kitchen door, PJs on, eyes wide.

'I thought I heard you. Are you not going into work today?'

I give her a big smile. 'I decided to take the morning off. I'm going in at lunchtime.'

'Lucky you,' she says, yawning. 'Can you do that? Just take a morning off?'

'Not really,' I say. I pour some water into my mug, wave a teabag at her as if to ask if she wants one. She nods. 'But what's the worst that can happen?'

'Good for you.' She waits while I make the tea. 'Are you feeling any better?'

'Shit,' I say. 'But the rate it's going it will all be over by the end of next week. I'll be looking for another job.'

She takes the mug from me. 'Poor you.'

It sounds completely genuine. She looks just like she always looks. I hate her.

'Well, I'd better get ready. Thanks for the tea.'

'No problem,' I say with a smile. 'I'm going back to bed for a bit.'

About half an hour later I hear the front door bang. I creep out into the hall and just catch sight of her heels on the top step. I have no idea whether she's really gone to work or just to hide out for a few hours to convince me that's what she's done. I text Dee: *Get round here now.*

I use the time while I wait for her to get ready for work myself. By quarter to ten she's on the doorstep, Argos bag in hand.

'I owe you,' I say. 'And I don't just mean for the nanny cam.'

We agree where the best place to put it will be, hidden behind a small wooden box that I keep pens in, on the bookshelf. If you looked for it you'd see it, but Hattie has no reason to suspect anything has changed. I hug Dee and leave her to it. I don't want to be later to work than I have to be. Another black mark against my name.

The first person I see when I enter the building is Glen. My heart leaps into my mouth and then sinks down to my heels. I brazen it out, smile at him.

'Morning,' he says. It doesn't seem as if he's been dealing with another complaint about me. I smile and say hello.

In the office I go straight over to Emma. 'Is Tommy Fletcher in?' I say after a cursory hello. I make sure Lorraine can't hear what I'm asking. Just in case. Keep my voice low. I wait while Emma checks the schedule.

'No,' she whispers, picking up my tone.

'Was he in yesterday?'

Another few clicks. 'No. Not since Monday. Do you need to speak to him?'

'No, it's OK. It can wait. When's he back?'

She turns back to her computer. 'His call is eleven.'

'Thanks.'

I accept her offer of a coffee. So, Tommy must have received my email while he was on a day off. Hopefully he's decided that he needs to see Glen in person to make his complaint. I need to get to him before he does.

It's almost impossible to concentrate on anything. I just wait for a message from Dee to tell me mission accomplished. I've already downloaded the app so that I can watch the cameras. We've agreed on a user name and a password we'll use once it's set up. I know how to switch on the alert function so that my phone tells me if it's registered any movement in the room. I'm ready.

Just after half past ten she texts me: *All systems go. Try it now.*

I open the app, enter my details and there's my living room. With Dee in it, gurning up at the camera.

Brilliant, I text back. *Now get out of there.*

And then I wait.

*

Thankfully I have no meetings scheduled. I'm pretty sure nothing will happen this morning because Hattie won't risk going home again until lunchtime. She wouldn't want to bump into me and give away that she hadn't gone into work after all.

I can't just sit there waiting for Tommy to turn up, so I call Juliet in, asking if I can speak to her for a moment. Lorraine looks up from her work, but I keep my voice neutral and businesslike. When she closes the door behind her I pick up a script from my desk and wave it at her for Lorraine's benefit. She takes it from me and sits with it open on her lap.

I tell her about Tommy, and about Hattie. She listens with a suitable expression of shock and horror. I'm just about to mention the webcam when my phone bursts to life with a noise I've never heard before.

'Hold on,' I say, heart pounding. The screen tells me the webcam has detected movement. I log in and there's the room again but I can't see anyone in there. Not in the sliver I can see any way. I look up and Juliet is looking at me quizzically.

'I'll explain in a minute.'

I keep watching. Maybe she just pushed open the door to see if anyone was in. It seems a bit early for her to risk it. I told her I was going in at lunchtime. If it was me I'd wait till at least one, half past.

It's like watching an empty film set. A film of my life but without me in it.

'I could come back . . .' Juliet says. I'd forgotten she was there.

'Webcam,' is all I manage to say.

'Of your house?'

I nod. Don't take my eyes off the phone. There's a blur on the screen and I jump. Smokey leaps up on to my desk, sits down and raises one leg in the air for a wash.

'Oh, for God's sake.' I laugh out of nerves. 'It's the fucking cat.'

I dismiss the picture, my heart still pounding. 'That's what I was about to tell you. We've put a webcam in my living room pointing at my desk. If Hattie uses my computer we'll have the exact time it recorded logged on there too.'

'Clever,' Juliet says. 'And then you'll just have to prove she was doing it on Roz's behalf and she's not just a crazy person.'

My phone makes its strange new noise again and both Juliet and I flinch. Smokey is up and pacing the desk. He jumps off, hopefully heading for somewhere more comfy to sleep. 'I should have told Dee to shut him out of there,' I say. Under different circumstances I can't imagine anything I'd like more than to watch what my cat gets up to when I'm not around.

'Yes,' I say, going back to her point. 'I can get proof that they're friends. It might be enough to convince Glen. I mean, it's not like we're going to court here.'

'Hopefully. If you need me to watch your phone let me know.'

'Will do.' I look at the time. 'I have to go and face Tommy.'

'Do you want me to come with you?' She looks concerned.

'Why? Do you think he's going to hit me?'

Juliet laughs. It may be the first time I've ever seen her laugh. It changes her face completely. 'Of course not. Just as moral support.'

'Oh. Thanks. No, I think I'll be OK.'

'You will.'

'Then my plan is just to sit here all afternoon till I see something. With my sent box up on the screen so hopefully I'll see who she's writing to before she deletes it. That way I might be able to do some damage limitation before they see it.'

'Well, I'm there if you need a loo break.' She gets up. Undoes the arms of the cardigan that's sitting across her shoulders, and does them up again.

'Thanks.'

I make my way over to the studio, feeling sick. I know that there's a possibility Tommy will go straight from the car park to Glen's office so I hover outside the doors from where I can keep an eye on both places. He's notoriously always late so I'm pretty sure I can't have missed him. I pace up and down anxiously, eyes flicking between the main gate and the two buildings.

Eventually a car pulls in. It looks like there's a driver and someone sitting in the back. Tommy is currently on a driving ban after being caught doing 120 on the A40, so has to use a car service to get to and from the studio. My heart starts pounding in my ears. I haven't even worked out what I'm going to say to him. Shit, I should have made a plan.

The car pulls up in front of me and the rear door opens.

I've almost started stammering out a half-plea, half-apology (what am I apologizing for? I've done nothing wrong) when Robbie aka Jono climbs out of the back of the car. Of course. He may have once worked in a garage but he's still too young to drive himself. I breathe out, plaster a smile on my face.

'Morning.'

'All right,' he says, and then he looks nervous as if he suddenly remembers who I am. 'What are you doing out here?'

'Waiting for someone,' I say as casually as I can. I will him to go inside before Tommy arrives. 'You OK?'

'Good,' he says. He looks even younger when he's anxious. I can tell he's dying to ask me how the story conference went. It's against all the rules but I can't help wanting to put him out of his misery.

'If anyone asks, I didn't tell you this but you have a couple of good stories coming up,' I say, importing as much meaning as I can into the words without saying anything specific.

His face breaks into a grin. 'Really? Like what?'

'Oh no, that's all you're getting. Don't tell anyone I said anything.'

'No way,' he says. He gives me a spontaneous hug. It's so sweet and I'm in such a state of nervous anticipation that I feel tears prickle behind my eyelids. Thankfully he lopes off up the steps before he notices and I wipe my face with the heel of my hand, turning it up to the sun to help dry any tell-tale signs.

When I open my eyes again there's another car coming

through the main gate. I force myself to breathe in and out slowly, in an attempt to calm myself down. It draws up right in front of me and Tommy clambers out of the back seat.

'Thanks, mate.'

I stand there waiting for him to clock me. Wait for the assault.

'Morning, darlin'.'

For a second I think everything is OK; he's taken pity on me. And then I realize that he has absolutely no idea who I am. He's heading into the building. I need to say something quickly.

'Tommy, it's Holly. From the script department . . .'

He stops dead. Looks back. Scans me up and down.

'Well, if I'd known that's what you look like . . .'

Jesus. I decide to ignore that comment.

'Look, I really need you to believe it wasn't me who sent that email. I would never be that disrespectful . . .'

I don't add 'and I wouldn't fancy you if you were the last man alive', but I'm thinking it.

'I got your reply,' he says. 'You said all that.'

'I know. But I wanted to ask you not to speak to Glen. Things have been happening – actually someone's been trying to get me sacked by sending stuff out that's supposed to be from me . . . I just need a few days and then I'll be able to prove it's them. If I can't, well, you can go and see him then.'

'So you don't fancy me?' he says, and I can't tell if it's a test or a challenge. I have no idea what the right answer is.

'Only joking.' He laughs. 'Your face!'

I smile nervously.

328

He strokes the stubble on his chin. It makes a scratching sound. 'Lucky for you I've had time to calm down. I can keep it to myself for a while longer.'

'Thank you. Thanks. I really appreciate it. Honestly.' I tell myself to stop burbling.

He leans in towards me. I can smell last night's booze under minty toothpaste. 'Let me know if you fancy that drink.'

It's not threatening. I think he thinks he's being charming. So much for the missus and the five kids.

'I've got enough problems in my life,' I say, chuckling as if I just made a joke.

Thankfully he takes it on the chin.

'No worries, mate. You sort yourself out.'

'I will. And thanks again.'

I try to concentrate on work but really I just read the same page over and over again. Every now and then Juliet looks over and raises her eyebrows and I shake my head.

At ten to two my phone chimes. I fumble as I hit the notification to go on to the app. Refresh my computer screen and double-check that my sent box is open. I look up at the main office. Juliet is there alone. It's a beautiful day and I assume the others have decided to get some fresh air. I beckon her in urgently.

There on the screen is my lodger. Hattie. She looks around the room as if making sure there really is no one there. I check that the footage is recording.

'Is it her?' Juliet sits opposite me, on the other side of

329

my desk, and I lay the phone down between us. We can go into work mode if any of the others come back but for now this is more urgent.

'Yep.'

'Gosh,' she says. The understatement of the year.

As we watch, Hattie sits in front of my computer. Clicks the screen on. She consults a piece of paper. Types rapidly.

'Do you think Roz has written out what she wants her to say?' Juliet asks.

I stare at my computer screen. 'Probably.'

And suddenly there it is. In my sent box. An email to Glen entitled 'Tommy Fletcher'. I go to click on it but it's already been deleted.

'Shit. Glen,' I say. 'Keep watching.' I rush out of my office and down the corridor to Glen's. His door is open but there's no one in there. I head on down to the general office where, thankfully, his secretary Danielle is at her desk.

'Someone just sent a stupid joke email from me to Glen. Can you delete it before he sees it?' I gabble.

'Sorry, what?'

I repeat it, trying to slow down. 'It's a practical joke,' I add unconvincingly. 'But it's really not funny.'

Luckily Danielle and I have always got on. She's not one of those Rottweiler assistants you come across sometimes.

She looks at her screen. 'This one?'

I peer round. 'Yes. I don't even want to see what it says. Oh, wait . . .' It suddenly occurs to me that I need the evidence. 'I need to print it off. And this sounds insane, but could you take a photo of the screen and text it to me. Just showing the date and time the email arrived. And that it came from me. I don't have my phone . . .'

She looks a bit confused. 'It's on the email, look.' She hits print.

'Yes, it is. Of course. Forget about that bit. I owe you one.' I take a deep breath.

'No problem,' she says, smiling, and hits delete.

Back in my office Juliet is still sitting waiting. 'She left the room as soon as it had been sent,' she says when she sees me. 'Nothing since.'

I hand her the printout of the email. 'I can't even look.'

She scans it. 'More of the same. Forget about it.'

'I need to make sure I save that clip from the webcam.' Juliet hands me my phone and I tick the box next to the most recent activity. Then I text it to myself, and to Dee for good measure.

'Now what?' she says.

'Now we have to prove the link between her and Roz.'

34

It's only a few minutes later. I'm feeling a huge sense of relief that not only did we catch her in the act, but we stopped the email in its tracks. One very toxic train derailed before it reached its destination. Everyone is back from lunch, but the office is quiet. Juliet is at her desk, reading. Lorraine is scribbling notes. Emma mutters quietly into the phone.

There's a tinny noise and my mobile lights up. *Activation alert!* flashes on the screen. I jab at the message and the app opens. It'll just be Smokey. It's bound to be Smokey. I keep telling myself this even as the image of my living room appears and there she is again. Hattie. I look over at Juliet. I need someone else to witness this with me. But there's no way I can get her attention without making it obvious.

I bring up my email and open the sent items, flicking my eyes between that and my phone. In my living room Hattie wanders past the camera, then back again, then settles herself at the desk. She looks at the back of her hand as if reading something on there. Clicks the computer back on. Types something in. Sits back. Reads it. Hits another key. I stare at my sent items, terrified to blink in case I miss the name of the recipient before she deletes it.

I hold my breath.

A name flashes up and then is gone almost before I can register it. Malcolm Gardener. The Head of Continuing Series at the channel. Glen's boss. The *capo dei capi*.

I've only met Malcolm once when he did a set visit a couple of years ago. I remember him as a humourless man in his fifties. One of those people who seems to be grey all over. Hair, skin, clothes. A face you forget the second it's not in front of you. I know he's much more important than me. I know he's the person who has been giving Glen a hard time about the ratings. I know he could have me fired in a heartbeat.

I have no idea who his assistant is so I just dial the main switchboard and ask. An officious-sounding woman answers when I'm put through.

'Malcolm Gardener's office.'

I stutter through my request for her to delete the email after printing it off and putting a copy in the internal mail for me so I have a record of the time and date it was sent. She sounds a bit bemused, and who can blame her?

'I don't wish to be rude, but I have no idea who you are so I'm not sure I can delete an email meant for Malcolm just because you ask me to.'

'But it was sent from my account,' I say. I'm trying to keep half an eye on the screen of my mobile. Hattie is still at my desk.

'But you see my dilemma,' Mrs Jobsworth says. 'I only have your word for that. I could be talking to anyone.'

For fuck's sake.

'I know,' she says. 'Why don't you send me another email now from the same account asking me to delete the previous email?'

I'm about to say yes when I realize I can't. Hattie will see it. She'll know the game is up.

'That won't work,' I say. 'It's hard to explain, but I don't want the person who sent it to know I'm on to them.'

She sighs. 'I'm not sure Malcolm would be happy about being part of your little joke.'

'It's not my little joke. It's not a joke at all. Someone is trying to make me look bad by sending random things out in my name.'

'Oh,' she says. When she speaks again her voice is softer. 'I tell you what. I'll look up your number on the database and then call you on that number. If you answer I'm happy to believe it's you.'

I don't quite follow but it sounds as if she's trying to help so I say OK. I put the phone down and wait. Thirty seconds later it rings and I snatch it up. 'Holly Cooper,' I say breathlessly.

'Holly, hello. It's Malcolm Gardener's office –'

'Yes. Hi. So, are we OK? You'll print it then delete it?'

'Yes. I'll put it in the internal mail right –'

'Thank you,' I say, cutting her off. I don't have time for niceties.

I realize that I've been so distracted I haven't been watching the screen. I look at my mobile first. Hattie is getting up from the desk. I flick my glance back to my computer, to the sent box.

Just in time to see a name disappear from the top before I can read who it was . . .

I send Juliet a text. *Shit. She's just sent 2 more. I missed the second one.*

I see her look at her phone as it vibrates. Shoot a concerned look up at me. I catch her eye briefly.

'Go and work from home,' she says five minutes later when she sticks her head round my office door. I look out at the main office. Lorraine is gone from her desk so I assume she's in the Ladies. 'That way she won't have a chance to send any more.'

'I'm scared I'll miss something on the way.'

'Would you be comfortable giving me your email password?' She looks me right in the eye. I don't even need to think about it.

'Yes. Of course. I'll text it to you and I'll let you know when I get there.'

I grab up a handful of scripts, knowing I have no intention of looking at any of them. The webcam is showing me an empty room. Or, at least, there's no sign of Hattie in the section I can see. Now is as good a time as any to make the break.

'I'm going to work at home this afternoon,' I say to Emma on my way out, as if it's the most normal thing in the world. To be fair we all do it from time to time, and no one bats an eyelid. 'I'm totally on the end of the phone and email, though.'

'OK,' she says, barely looking up. 'See you tomorrow if I don't speak to you.'

I text Juliet my password from the Ladies on the way out, along with *Don't email me anything you wouldn't want Roz to know about.*

On the way to the station I get a reply. *Of course. Don't worry.*

She's in the kitchen, filling the kettle, when I let myself into the flat. There's no doubt she looks shocked to see me. She recovers quickly, though. Flashes me a mega-watt smile.

'Hi! Are you OK? You're not sick, are you?'

I raise my stuffed bag as proof. 'Too noisy in the office. I thought I'd come home and get these read. Didn't you go to work in the end?'

'Tea?' she says as if I haven't just asked her that question. She's dressed in black leggings and an oversize white T-shirt that drowns her tiny frame. A slogan on the front says 'Grill Power' with a retro drawing of a couple having a barbeque. 'This is really bad but I just fancied the afternoon off. I claimed a migraine.'

I remind myself to act normally. Don't give anything away. 'Good for you. And yes to tea, please.'

'I won't disturb you,' she says, getting out another mug. I pluck a teabag from the box and drop it in. 'In fact I was thinking about going for a walk after I've drunk this.'

'You should; it's a lovely day. I'll just shut myself in the living room anyway. I'll be fine.'

'Do you have to read all those?' she asks, peering at my bag.

'I thought I might as well bring enough to keep me occupied tomorrow too.' This is a lie. I need to go into work tomorrow. I can't let my job slide. But if she thinks I'm definitely going to be at home then there'll be no reason for her not to go to work herself. What would be the point of taking another day off if I'm going to be guarding the computer all day?

'Ah, the old sneaky long weekend,' she says, sloshing milk into my tea.

'Exactly,' I say, smiling. I'll still need to watch the webcam all day just in case but I'm pretty confident I've put her off.

My journey home was uneventful, by the way. My reception is good on the Overground so I was able to keep an eye on my living room. I knew that Juliet would be glued to my sent box. I sent her a text as I approached my front door. *Home in 2.* She sent back *All OK* before I'd even reached the steps.

The minute I'm on my own I check my email. I know there's an unexploded hand grenade out there, I just don't know where. Until whoever Hattie sent her last missive to reacts I won't have any idea who they are. For all I know they've already put the wheels in motion to put in a formal complaint about me or worse.

I hear Hattie's door click shut. I settle down in the armchair, an unopened script on my lap, like a pioneer woman with a shotgun.

35

I get up and walk to the desk to check my email approximately every five seconds. Dee would be proud of me for getting my steps in. Nothing. In the end I decide I can't just sit here waiting for the bomb to go off. I send Juliet a text: *Can you call me when you're on your own?*

Three minutes later my phone rings. 'I'm in the car park,' she says breathlessly. 'Everything OK?'

'No. I mean, yes, nothing's changed. I just can't stand not knowing where that last email went. I need to do something to lessen the impact.'

'Then do the mail-out.'

Juliet and I decided earlier that if the waiting got too much I should think about sending out a company-wide message now – well, company-wide except for our department. Roz and Lorraine for obvious reasons, Joe and Emma because I want to be sure they won't say anything in front of Lorraine when the message pops up. Oh, and Glen, because he already thinks I'm an idiot – in an effort to flush out the recipient and stop the problem in its tracks. I need to protect myself and if, in doing so, I draw attention to what's been going on I'll just have to suck it up.

'OK. That's what I think too.'

We bat the wording back and forth and then, when I'm satisfied, I sit down at the computer. We decide to keep it short and to the point:

'If anyone in the company has received an email from me that seemed unusual in any way please contact me ASAP. I believe someone may have gained access to my password and sent some rather bizarre messages but, hopefully, the problem is now dealt with.'

Then I hit the button to bring up the addresses of everyone at the channel, painstakingly trawl through to remove Roz's, Lorraine's, Joe's, Emma's and Glen's names from the list. I double-check again, take a deep breath and press send.

Then I sit and watch my inbox like a cat watching a mouse hole, only taking my eyes off it to go to the kitchen or the loo. There are a few 'Oh, poor you, I didn't receive anything though' type replies, and a curt note from IT asking if they should be worried about a security breach. I ignore the former for now, and send IT a quick message back saying there's nothing to worry about.

I wait, expecting that at any minute I'll receive something from the Controller's PA saying she'd wondered why I'd emailed him earlier to tell him I'd like to re-enact the Human Caterpillar with me, him and the bloke who cleans the toilets, or from the Head of Drama's assistant saying he'd thought it was odd that I'd felt the need to let her know I felt sorry for her husband because she's such an uptight bitch, but there's still nothing. Either whoever was the target hasn't seen my latest email, or they have but they've decided to ignore it. Because whatever was sent to them in my name in the first place incensed them so much. That's assuming whatever Hattie sent was to someone within the company, because if losing me my job is Roz's aim I can't see what she'd have to gain from winding up anyone else.

By half past six when I hear Hattie let herself in I'm practically a nervous wreck. I can't face seeing her. I'm not a good enough actress. Thankfully I get a text from Dee saying she's coming round, bringing pizza because she knows I'll be cowering behind the closed living-room door all evening. I text back: *Brilliant. Bring booze.*

I hear her coming down the steps and I run to open the door before she rings the bell. I can hear the low sounds of Netflix coming from Hattie's room. I beckon Dee in frantically.

'Act normal,' she hisses. And then she greets me loudly, giving me a hug. 'I'll just get some plates and glasses,' she booms.

'Why are you shouting?' I mouth. She rolls her eyes. Nods at me as if to say 'Say something then'.

'I'm just in the middle of something. Bring it all in here,' I say, in what I hope is a clear but natural tone. Dee gives me a thumbs up.

I take the wine and the pizza box from her and retreat into the living room.

'What was all that about?' I say when she appears with a tray bearing everything else we need. It strikes me that as it's my flat, and she's brought all the food and drink, I probably should have been the one to do the work while she relaxed, but it's too late now. I shut the door behind her.

'You don't want her thinking you're on to her.'

'I can't even look at her.' I pour two glasses of wine and we both dive into the pizza. 'Thanks for this.'

'I was hardly going to leave you hiding in here on your own.'

'I daren't leave the computer. I mean, I can't imagine she'd risk it again while I'm home but even so, I might have to sleep in here . . .'

'Can't you change the password again now? And don't save it this time.' Dee pushes Smokey's nose away from her plate.

'I suppose so. But then, what if she does try? She'll know.'

'She won't know we know it's her. It would seem pretty odd if you didn't change it again after all those emails going out this week, wouldn't it?'

I think for a second. 'Yes, but for all she knows I have done. I've just saved it on my home computer as usual.'

Dee sips. 'True.'

I tell her about the group email I sent. 'So maybe even if she does do anything else it doesn't matter at this point. I just wish I knew what that last one was. Why they haven't responded . . .'

My phone rings. Both of us leap out of our chairs as if we've been electrocuted. The pizza slice that was on a plate on my lap lands on the floor right next to where Smokey – who was on Dee's – also lands, so that's fortuitous. For him. I grab the phone, laughing about how on edge the pair of us are. It's as if we've seen the finish line, we just need to work out how to get across it. I look at the screen.

'It's Juliet.'

'Answer it. I'll go to the kitchen and make sure Hattie can't listen in. Talk quietly.'

'Hi,' I say.

'Have you got a sec?' Juliet sounds agitated.

'Yes. What? What's happened?' I keep my voice as low as I can.

'All good. Just . . . listen, I hope you don't mind, but I gave Jake your email password. He's totally trustworthy, I guarantee it. But, you know, he's a teenage boy and sometimes they know how to do things that we might not . . .'

I wait but she's leaving a long dramatic pause for me to respond to. 'No, it's fine, but what are you trying to tell me?'

'Apparently there's this thing where, even if you think you've deleted the things you've deleted from the sent box from the deleted items folder . . .'

I'm lost already. Never have I heard the word deleted so many times in one sentence.

'. . . there's a way to still recover them within a certain time period. I don't really understand. But, anyway, Jake has. He's found the email that you missed.'

'Oh my God!' I say way too loudly. 'Who was it to? I've been having kittens because no one's told me they've received anything.'

'It was to Roz,' she says.

36

The email that I have apparently sent to Roz is an incoherent diatribe telling her that I will make sure her
working life is hell, that I've planted false rumours about
her carrying out a hate campaign against me, that it's my
mission to make her look as bad as I can. Juliet takes a
photo of it and texts it to me so that I can show Dee.

Clearly Roz's masterplan is that she returns from her
week's holiday on Monday to find this upsetting, not to
mention offensive, message has arrived while she was
sunning herself in Italy. The shock! The horror! She'll
take it straight to Glen or to HR or to anyone she thinks
will listen. There will be an outcry and I will be hauled
over the coals. They will all be sorry to say it but they
don't see how they can possibly make my job permanent
now. If I'm not sacked I'll almost certainly be so demoral-
ized and humiliated that I'll leave. Job done.

She has no way of knowing, of course, that I've gone
part way to covering my tracks by letting everyone – HR
included – know that rogue emails are being sent in my name.
Or that I have evidence that Hattie was using my computer at
the time it was sent. It's not enough though. I need people to
know that Roz is guilty, not just that I'm innocent.

Dee reads the email open-mouthed. She saw Hattie in

the kitchen, she tells me. She claimed I had a headache and that's why we were being anti-social.

'We had a nice chat, actually. Which is beyond weird when you think that she wrote this.'

'So what do we do now?' I'm feeling despondent again.

'Change your password like you were going to.'

'I will. I'll let Juliet know though, in case Jake needs to look at anything else.' I go and sit back at the computer.

Dee fills my glass and puts it down next to me. 'She's got a sixteen-year-old kid and you had no idea?'

'None.' I send Juliet a quick text to tell her what I'm doing. Click through to find the option to create a new password, like Emma showed me to.

This time I say no when asked if I want my computer to save it. I change it to FuckYouRoz101, something I'm unlikely to forget.

'Don't kill me.'

Juliet is at my office door. It's lunchtime and there's no one else around. Why do people keep saying this to me?

'Do you know my friend Dee?'

She looks at me confused. 'What? No. I have to tell you something.'

'Come in and shut the door. What?'

She grabs a script from a pile on my desk, a reflex action so that it will look as if we're talking about work if anyone comes in.

It all comes out in one long sentence. 'So Jake and I were trying to think what else we could do, and I thought, maybe, if you could delete that email from Roz's computer then she would come back on Monday all guns blazing, but what would she have to attack you with? Only, of course, none of us know Roz's password now, so it would be impossible . . .'

She gives me a meaningful look, only what its meaning is I have no idea. 'And . . .?'

'There's a thing you can do . . . you set up a page, and send them an email from a fake address that looks as if it might be from the channel. So, it's the same email address but just with one of the l's changed to a figure one, something like that.'

'Are you talking about phishing?'

She gulps audibly. 'Something like that. Anyway, he did it. Don't tell anyone, obviously. He sent her an email pretending to be from tech support saying she had to verify her details because there had been a security breach, with a link to the page he made . . .'

'Jake might be a genius,' I say.

Juliet flushes red. 'He is very clever. He just googled how to do it. He said it wasn't that hard. Anyway, on the page it just asked her to confirm her password and that was it. And she has. She's done it.'

I try to take this in for a second. 'Fucking hell, Juliet.'

'I know.'

I twiddle my earrings. 'So then what?'

'Nothing. I didn't want him to get in any deeper. But we have her password. We can access her email without her knowing.'

'And it won't get traced back to Jake?' I would hate for him to get into some awful kind of trouble because of me.

She shakes her head. 'No. Well, it could be if there was some kind of big investigation. I mean, you can't truly hide anything. But we both know that won't happen. She would come off far worse than you. We decided, on balance, it was worth the risk.'

'Wow. Thank you.'

'No problem,' she says, her pink face turning red. She digs in her pocket for a piece of paper, hands it over. 'Here it is.'

I look at it. Just a random sequence of numbers, letters and punctuation. 'God, she really didn't want anyone to guess it.'

'Indeed,' Juliet says.

Now I have a weapon I have no idea what the best way is to use it. I have the chance to strike one killer blow, or to do nothing. It's all in my hands.

'Do you think I should?' I say.

Juliet shrugs. 'That's up to you. I would, I think. But think about it carefully. Don't do anything rash.'

'Say thanks to Jake for me. I really appreciate it.'

She smiles. 'He enjoyed himself. I told him not to get any ideas. This is a one-off.'

'Oh God, I've helped turn that lovely boy into a cyber-criminal.' I laugh, and I'm gratified to see that she does too.

'Next week's going to be interesting,' she says after a moment.

'Shit,' is all I can manage.

37

I'm spending the evening at Dee and Gavin's, trying to make a plan. Even though Hattie has almost certainly gone away for the weekend I didn't want to risk her gliding in unheard and listening in on our conversation.

'Do you think she's even got a sick mum?' Gavin passes the tarka dhal container to where I'm sitting on the floor on the other side of the coffee table.

'Oh God, don't. She wouldn't make that up, surely?'

He shrugs. 'Roz would have told her that you wanted a tenant who went away every weekend.'

'Of course!' Dee says.

I look between them, fork in hand. 'So where the fuck does she go?'

'Shepherd's Bush would be my guess,' Gavin says. 'I mean, I doubt she's paying for herself to stay anywhere else. Not when this whole thing seems like some weird favour for a friend.'

Dee stands up abruptly. 'Let's go down there now.'

'What? No!' I throw a cushion at her. The corner lands in the sauce on her abandoned plate. 'Oh, sorry. Besides, we've all been drinking.'

She sits back down. 'Tomorrow, then.'

'Maybe. I don't know. Let's work out what we're going to do with Roz's email first.'

I have a very small window of opportunity. I need to delete the email Roz sent from me to her from her inbox. But if I do it too soon she might notice. She might remember getting the random message from the IT department asking her to confirm her password, put two and two together. If she does nothing else she might change it again while she tries to work out what's gone wrong. So we've decided that the middle of the night on Sunday would be the best time.

And I need to decide what to do with the evidence I have. I only have one chance. I need to end this.

We stay up way too late trying to work out the best plan of action. Stupidly I log into Roz's email on Dee's laptop and lose myself in a series of bitchy back and forths between Roz and Lorraine.

'Stop looking,' Dee says after I've read out a couple to her.

'Listen to this one. "God, she's so up herself now. Anyone would think she got this job on merit and not just because she flirts with Glen." When the fuck have I ever flirted with Glen? Glen?'

'You know what she's like. You've told me yourself the way she talks about people.'

'But . . .' I stammer. 'Glen?'

Dee takes the laptop out of my hands. 'This is why you should never listen at closed doors.'

'I'm going to kill her.'

'Yes. Yes, you are. So let's just concentrate on how.'

'OK.'

Gavin comes back in with three cold cans. 'She thinks I only got the job because I flirted with Glen,' I wail.

He looks confused, and who could blame him.

'She doesn't,' Dee says. 'She just has to find a way to justify it to herself other than you were a better candidate than her.'

In the end we turn in without deciding anything. I bed down on their sofa because it's easier than trying to get home but, even with the windows open, it's too hot to sleep. After the shortest spring in history a sweltering summer seems to have arrived with a vengeance. Some time around 2 a.m. and five cans of lager down each we made a plan to stake out Roz's flat over the weekend, in the hope of catching sight of Hattie. In the bright light of morning I realize that Gavin is the only one of us neither of them would recognize so he's going to have to go it alone.

Dee, however, has other ideas. She brings me in a mug of tea at what I think is three minutes after I drop off, but turns out to be ten o'clock. She perches on the arm of the sofa, by my feet, her long dark hair held up in a knot on top of her head and yesterday's mascara shading the underneath of her eyes.

'Did you sleep OK?' She yawns as she says it, so I do too.

'Not really.'

'Me neither. Gav's making tea.'

'Shall we go shopping and leave him to do the stake-out?' I say hopefully.

'No way. We're a team.'

She's smiling. 'You seem much happier,' I say.

'We are. I am.'

I rub her leg with my foot. 'I'm glad.'

Dee makes a picnic fit for a family of six on a day out at the seaside, and Gavin hotfoots it to the shop round the corner for soft drinks, which he puts in a giant cooler. There's a flask of coffee and one of tea (made by me) and a bag of 'snacks' just in case we get hungry between bites of sandwiches. I stop myself from asking how long they think we're going to be there, and whether we should take sleeping bags.

'What are we going to do when we need the loo?' I say.

'Don't think about it,' Dee says. 'Half the time it's psychological anyway. And if you get desperate you can walk over to Westfield.'

'We should have got some of those Shewee things,' Gavin says in all seriousness.

Dee nods. 'Or I could have nicked a few of those cardboard bedpans from work.'

I stare at them. 'Oh my God. The pair of you have officially gone insane.'

We park as far away from number five as we can, but still with a clear view of the front door. Dee and Gavin are in the front: she with all her hair pushed up into a woolly hat, despite the fact it's eighty degrees outside, and big sunglasses. I'm in the back in a long blonde wig that Ashley wore in a school play once and that Dee remembered was in her stuff when we cleared out her room. We had stopped by mine on the way so I could feed Smokey, and also to check that Hattie wasn't at home, thus making the whole trip pointless. Dee is all for breaking out the sandwiches immediately, despite the fact we only had breakfast an hour ago.

'We should save them,' I say. 'What if we get stranded and they're all we have left? Those, and the contents of all the food shops in Westfield and the many restaurants and cafés in the local area.'

She turns round and pulls a face at me. 'You'll be grateful when it's 3 a.m. and you're starving.'

I look at my phone. It's five past eleven in the morning. 'Oh God,' I say. 'Kill me.'

There's something about being in a confined space with people for hours at a time that turns it into a kind of confessional. Once we've gossiped idly about people we know, and played a few stupid word games, we somehow get on to the subject of their IVF failures. I've never spoken to Gavin about their desire for – and inability to have – kids before. I think I assumed he just didn't care as much as Dee did, that he was going along with it to keep her happy, but then once it was no longer an option he was fine with that too. I think it was easy for me to blame him for giving up so finally. I think I misjudged him.

'I've wanted to be a dad ever since we first met,' he says, the atmosphere in the car sticky and still. He reaches out a hand and squeezes hers. 'That's the whole point, isn't it? Being a family.'

I don't know what to say. It breaks my heart that they've been having this struggle for years when I – and now Ashley – just got pregnant without thinking about, or even wanting, it.

'There are other –' I start to say, but he cuts me off.

'It's not the same though, is it?'

'It's OK,' Dee says. 'It's fine.'

At half past three there's a flurry of excitement as the front door to number five opens. Gavin grabs his camera and zooms in on the steps. We all hold our breath. An unkempt-looking couple saunter out, presumably from one of the other flats.

'No,' I say, to let Gavin know neither of them are Hattie. We let out a collective sigh.

Fifteen minutes later I can't take it any longer. 'I need to stretch my legs.'

'Go on then,' Dee says.

'Won't be long.' I jam my wig down over my ears and keep my head down as I get out. The last thing I need is to bump into Hattie on the street. I walk away from number five as quickly as I can and head along the main road towards Westfield. I know that I'm raining on Dee's and Gavin's parade a bit by not really entering into the spirit of things. They're giving up their entire weekend for me, after all. I at least need to look as if I'm having fun, even though this might as well be life or death for me. I find the Ladies eventually and then I stop off at Starbucks on the way back and get us all lattes and brownies. As I turn back into Roz's road I stop dead as I see her blonde, pink-tipped head walking up the steps of number five. I assumed that she would be arriving back from her holiday – if indeed she's been on holiday – today or tomorrow, but she has no suitcase, no, so far as I can tell, suntan. I hang back, pretending to look at my phone, my head bent over it so she wouldn't be able to see my face if she looked round. I peer up from under the heavy fringe without lifting my head. Once she's safely inside I make a bolt for the car, fling the back door open and throw myself in.

'Shit. Did you get that?'

Dee and Gavin beam at me from the front seats. He waves the camera at me and I can see Roz clearly on the digital display.

'Of course,' Gavin says.

'Oh, I brought treats.' I hand them the coffees and cakes. My heart is pounding from the excitement of my near miss. 'What happened? Did she just appear?'

'From round that corner,' Dee says, pointing up ahead, past the house.

'Oh my God! If I'd been a minute earlier she might have seen me.' The hand holding my latte is shaking.

'I told you it'd be fun.' Dee smiles.

The afternoon passes agonizingly slowly. There's only so much you can talk about with even your closest friends.

And then at ten to six the front door to number five opens again and there they are. Roz and Hattie. Coming down the steps together.

'It's them!' Dee and I say simultaneously. Gavin goes into overdrive with the camera and I take a couple with my phone in case he fucks up somehow, but we're so far away that I'd have trouble convincing even myself who was in the picture.

'Shit, they're coming this way,' Dee says. She bends her head down over her phone. I throw myself on to the floor behind the front seats. I'm not taking any chances.

'I just need to get a couple with their faces in,' Gavin says. His camera has a very fancy zoom that could pick out a flea on a cat from half a mile away.

'Be careful,' I mutter into my wig, which has slipped down over my face.

'They're still miles away,' he says confidently. 'There. Done.'

I hear a rustle as he grabs up a newspaper and places it over the camera on his lap, his agreed disguise.

'Don't look at them,' Dee hisses.

'I'm not,' he says. 'I'm looking at the paper.'

'How far away are they?' I say. I daren't put my head up to look.

'Hundred metres,' Gavin says. I try to imagine how far a hundred metres is. Picture Usain Bolt steaming along. He'd be passing the car . . . now. I hold my breath.

'Ninety,' Gavin says.

He counts down as they get closer. Obviously his spatial

awareness isn't what it should be, because after 'Ten' there's an interminable gap and then finally I hear the clip-clop of Roz's heels on the other side of the road. They're talking, but I can't make out what they're saying. I can feel the tension in the car, all of us scared to move a muscle. The chatter fades. Gavin looks up into the rear-view mirror.

'They've gone.'

He checks the photos. Shows them to Dee.

'Perfect,' she says. 'We've got her.'

I don't get up from my hiding place on the floor until I can feel the smoothness of the Westway under the wheels.

38

By late Saturday night we've compiled a document that tells a story. The printouts of the emails, with the times and dates that they were sent highlighted. Stills from the webcam footage – with the times and dates clearly visible on the screen – showing Hattie at my computer. The pictures of Roz and Hattie together. It's enough.

I don't want to create a big fuss. Dee was all for me causing a shitstorm, disgracing Roz in front of anyone who'd listen but, to be honest, I don't want to draw any more attention to myself than I have to. I want to try and retain what dignity I have left. God knows what my reputation at the channel is like now. At best it's as someone who attracts drama. Someone who is so hated by her peers that one of them is plotting her downfall. I'm going to wait outside Glen's office on Monday morning and grab him as soon as he comes in. I'm going to show him all the evidence, calmly and rationally. And then I'm going to leave it up to him.

I'm at my post by five to eight. Glen doesn't usually come in till at least nine o'clock but I'm not taking any chances. I couldn't sleep last night anyway. Hattie arrived back at about seven, surprising me in the kitchen, and I could barely look her in the eye. I managed to ask how her weekend had been and she talked about her mum as if everything was normal. It was surreal to say the least.

By ten past eight I've drunk the coffee I brought in with me and I'm severely tempted to go and make myself another, but I daren't take the chance. I need to get to Glen before I have to go down to the studio for the rest of the day. Before Roz can get in and tell her side of the story. I decided last night not to delete from her account the email I supposedly sent her. Not just because Roz might realize and come up with a Plan B, but because I thought it would help my case if Glen saw her in action for himself, how convincing she could be even when he would know for a fact that what she was telling him was a lie. It's my trump card.

I lean against the wall and idly scroll through Instagram on my phone. The place is deserted. People will already be arriving at the studio, and in hair and make-up, but up here on our little corridor it's silent.

I hear a noise. I look round but there's no one there. And then I realize that it's coming from Glen's office. Someone's in there. When I first arrived I tapped lightly on his door, just in case, not expecting a response. Now I feel like an idiot because he's clearly come in early and I've been waiting out here for fifteen minutes like a loser. Maybe I knocked too softly, or he was doing something that meant he didn't hear. Cleaning out his ears with a cotton bud, or wearing headphones. Actually, the latter is quite likely. Glen is often plugged into music on his journey to work. I've seen him on the train before, ear buds in, eyes closed. I pick up my bag and go to knock again.

'Shh!'

I hear it. As clear as anything. I freeze, hand raised. Press my ear to the door. There's a rustling and then a murmur of voices. Glen's not in there alone. Even though it feels a bit odd that I've been here all this time and not heard any talking I assume that he must have come in early for a meeting. I'm not sure if I can interrupt but, on the other hand, I need to let him know that I have to speak to him ASAP. I'm about to rap on the door again when I hear another sound from inside the room. An unmistakeable sound. A groan. Or rather . . . a moan. I step away from the door as if I've had an electric shock.

What the . . .? Maybe Mrs Glen likes to come to work with her husband sometimes and they play boss and secretary in his office? I hear a louder moan, look around as if to check it can't be coming from anywhere else. Our corridor will still be empty for at least another fifteen, twenty minutes. Obviously there's no way I can interrupt Glen now, and there's also no way I want him to find me standing here when they eventually come out. I still need to see him, though, so I slip into the print room opposite and keep watch through a crack in the door.

The noise is so loud now that if anyone else did arrive there'd be no mistaking it. I imagine they must know they're safe this early on. That if they heard my knock they would have assumed it was the cleaners and just waited until they thought the coast was clear before they carried on. Maybe that's part of the excitement? Imminent discovery.

Despite everything, it's funny. Dee would love this, I think, and I turn my phone on to video to record the noise so I can play it to her later. The crescendo reaches its peak and then stops abruptly. I freeze. What now?

I wait for what seems like an age, hear the occasional scrabble of movement. I check the time. It's twenty-five to nine. Still long enough for me to present my evidence. I hear the key turn in the lock. I flatten my back against the wall but I still keep watching through the little gap. The door opens inwards. I hold my breath. This would not be a good look if Glen were to see me now. It wouldn't help in my attempt to prove that I'm someone he can trust.

I see a flash of colour as a pair of long legs in orange skinny trousers and red heels step out. I almost gasp out loud, or maybe I do. Instinctively I hold my still recording phone up to the gap. Roz, now with a glowing light tan that wasn't there on Saturday, turns to face the person behind her. Maybe it's not Glen. Maybe she's having a thing with someone – Joe or Jeremy the producer – and they thought it would be funny to get it on in the boss's office. A hand snakes round and grabs her backside. She laughs, leans in for a quick kiss. Then a face peers round the door. Looking up and down the corridor, checking they haven't been seen. A face with a well-manicured beard. Glen.

My hand is shaking but I manage to keep filming. He says something that I can't make out and she murmurs a reply, pats him playfully on the arm and practically skips along the corridor towards our department. He watches her go for a second, a small smile on his face. And then he shuts the door.

Fuck. I can't process this at all. Glen and Roz? She despises him, and definitely not in an 'I hate him so much I actually really fancy him' kind of way. She laughs at him, how ridiculous he is with his overgroomed look and his trying-too-hard-to-be-hip clothes. How long has this been going on? When did it start?

The only thing I know for certain is that there's no point going to speak to him now. He's no longer an unbiased judge. Whatever I say to him about Roz now he'll hear through a filter of her appreciative groans. I need to get out of there, down to the studio before either of them sees me. I'm about to make a break for it when I hear her heels clopping down the corridor towards me. I wait, breath held, eyes closed as if that might help. She walks past and into the Ladies along the corridor. I grab my bag and practically run to the staircase and out into the car park.

I'm fucked.

39

Once I'm safely tucked away in the room by the studio I call Dee, but she's at work and doesn't answer. I leave her an incoherent message telling her what's happened. Then I sit there, staring off into space.

I've been in there all of thirty seconds when there's a tap at the door and it's being opened before I can even say anything. The last thing I need now is a conversation with a member of the cast about why they think their character wouldn't order the fish and chips in the school canteen or whether they really would say 'sofa' and not 'settee'. I try to plaster a professional look on my face.

Patricia peers round the door. 'I just saw you come in. I was wondering how it's going.'

I sigh. 'Pretty badly.' So much for being professional.

'Oh no, what now? Can I sit down? I'm not needed for another twenty minutes.' She plonks herself on the other chair, looks at me concerned.

I'm past caring. I know I shouldn't tell anyone what I've just witnessed but what have I got to lose? Well, my job on Friday probably, but I don't think there's anything I can do about that now.

'I just . . . you mustn't tell anyone what I'm about to tell you . . .'

She leans forward in the chair, all ears. 'My lips are sealed.'

I tell her the brief version. How I'd compiled all the evidence against Roz, about how I was waiting outside Glen's office out of hours so as not to miss him.

Patricia's eyes are wide. She knows something juicy is coming.

I pick up my phone. 'And then this happened . . .' I turn the sound right up and play the video. 'It's a bit all over the place . . .'

We sit there in silence, both staring at the shaky film of the outside of Glen's door. You can hear my breathing over the top, which doesn't help. But then, there it is, as clear as day, a loud groan. I look at Patricia to see if she caught it and her mouth has dropped open, so I assume she has. I wait to let her hear a couple more and then I fast forward to the moment they were about to reveal themselves.

She looks at me questioningly. 'Keep watching,' I say. She glues her eyes to the screen. When she spots that it's Roz coming out, followed by the man himself, she makes a noise that sounds like a cross between a gasp and a snort. The film ends.

'Well . . .'

'So you can see why I'm done for. There's no point me complaining to him about her now.'

'Go over his head,' she says as if it's the most obvious thing ever.

'To who though? I don't have a relationship with any of those people. I'll just look like a crazy woman who's trying to cause trouble.'

She takes the phone out of my hand and I think she's going to watch the video again, but she just presses a few keys.

'What are you doing?' I say nervously.

'I just sent it to myself, that's all.'

Oh God. 'Oh. No . . . I mean . . .'

'They have no idea you filmed this, am I right?' I nod warily. 'And neither of them have seen you this morning?'

'No. But . . . what are you going to do with it?'

She gives me a big shark-like smile, pats me with her bear paw. 'I have no idea yet, but we'll think of something. Don't you worry.'

I sit there feeling sick. Patricia stands. 'Right. I need to get to make-up.'

I want to say 'Please don't do anything to make the situation worse' but I realize it couldn't really get any worse, so I keep quiet. May as well go out with a bang.

I sit there on eggshells all morning. I can't concentrate, can't think straight. I don't pass a single note through to the director because I'm only half aware of what's being said. They could all be calling each other by the wrong names for all I care.

At lunchtime I can't face going up to the office so I call Emma and ask if she'd mind picking me up a sandwich when she gets her own, and bringing it to me here. I know that Juliet will be waiting for news, wanting to know about my triumphant audience with Glen this morning. I dash her off a quick text: *Didn't speak to Glen. Have news. Not good.*

363

Fifteen minutes later there's a tap on the door and Juliet appears brandishing my lunch.

'I intercepted Emma,' she says, handing it over. 'I don't think she was very happy.'

She sits down and I fill her in on the whole story while I eat, right up to Patricia sending herself the video.

'I thought Roz couldn't stand him,' she says when I show it to her.

'She can't. This has nothing to do with attraction.'

'And he's married. My God, what a mess.'

'How's she been this morning?' I put down the sandwich. I've got no appetite.

'Showing off to Lorraine about all the amazing places she went to. The usual.'

The phone on the coffee table rings. I grab it up. 'Hi, Holly here.'

'Holly, do you think you could come up for a word?' It's Glen. My stomach flips.

'Now?'

'If you don't mind,' he says. He doesn't sound happy.

'Of course. Two minutes,' I say, putting the phone down. I turn to Juliet. 'Glen wants to see me.'

'She will have shown him the email. The one you supposedly sent.'

In all the drama of the morning I'd forgotten that Roz still had this weapon to use against me.

'Well, it doesn't matter now. She's won.'

'Don't go down without a fight,' she says.

'I won't.' I pick up my bag with all the evidence against

364

Roz in. I can't really summon up the energy to defend myself, but I know Juliet's right. For my own self-esteem I need to know that I tried.

We walk over to the office building together. I still have half an hour before filming starts up again. Juliet gives my arm a squeeze as she leaves me at Glen's door. I knock.

'Come in.'

I close my eyes, force myself to push the door open. Glen is sitting behind his desk. He smiles, but it doesn't reach his eyes.

'Have a seat. How are you?'

'Good,' I stammer. 'I've been better.'

'Some things have come to light that I have to take very seriously,' he says.

'If this is about an email I supposedly sent to Roz while she was away I have proof that she sent it to herself. Or at least that she got her friend to do it.'

A tiny frown flits across his face. I dig into my bag, pull out the cardboard file with the emails and photos in. I lean across and put it on his desk. He ignores it.

'I don't want to hear any more excuses, Holly. Roz is very upset. I'm afraid I have to take this up with HR.'

I steel myself. Force the words out. 'Me too. If you won't hear me out then I have copies of all of this to give to them.'

'Very well,' he says. 'If that's how you want to play it, but Roz has been with the show for a long time – I don't think you want to get into your word against hers . . .'

There's a movement on the TV screen mounted on the wall beside his desk. I check my phone quickly; it's still too early for them to be back after lunch. Sometimes they turn the cameras on though, to test the positions for the next shot.

'I'd like it noted that I want to make a formal complaint against her too. I can put it in writing to HR if you would rather.'

Something flickers on the screen again. I try to stay focused. I need him to listen to what I'm saying.

'I mean, if you want me to tell them you discouraged me from trying to stand up for myself . . .' I have no idea where that came from. I've shocked even myself. I almost take it back, apologize if I phrased it badly, say that wasn't what I meant. But somehow I stand my ground. I have nothing left to lose.

He glares at me. Actually glares. 'Of course not.'

I try to hold his gaze, but then the feed from the studio catches my eye again. A piece of white paper is moving in to fill the screen. Glen seems to notice it at the same moment. He frowns. There are words on the paper.

'Sound up at 1.50 p.m. everybody!!'

Suddenly I know exactly what is going on. I'm glad I'm sitting down because if I wasn't I'd probably pass out.

'It must be someone's birthday,' I say, trying to inject my voice with a confidence I don't feel. It's not unheard of for the cast and crew to sing 'Happy Birthday' to someone from the studio with the cameras running. I remember they did it for Catherine, Glen's predecessor.

'We'll talk more,' Glen says, looking back at me. 'But I want you to know I'm very disappointed.'

I look him straight in the eye. 'So am I.'

I don't want to be anywhere near the studio at ten to two, and I also can't quite resist seeing Roz's reaction if she's back from lunch, if she's watching. So, despite the fact I don't really want to come face to face with her, I wander down towards the department. It's a full house, everyone at their desks, eating their lunches and working (Juliet, Joe and Emma) or chatting (Roz and Lorraine).

'What do you think this is?' Emma says as soon as she sees me, and I could kiss her. She waves the remote at the TV screen.

'No idea. Birthday?'

Roz looks up at the sound of my voice. I offer her a fake smile. 'Good holiday?'

'Fabulous,' she says with an exaggerated stretch of her arms above her head.

I keep moving towards my office. As I pass Juliet I give her a look that I hope says 'Watch the TV!' but I imagine just gives the impression I'm about to throw up. She must get something from it though, because she calls across to Emma, 'Turn it up, it's nearly ten to.'

Roz rolls her eyes. 'It'll just be some cringy self-indulgent backslapping by the cast.'

Emma ups the volume anyway. The sheet of paper slides out and is replaced by another. It reads '8 a.m. this morning. SOUND UP!!!' The screen goes black and then there's my shaky video. Patricia must have got one of the crew to help her because it fills the whole screen, it's not just a shot of her phone.

'What the . . .?' Joe says. Emma raises the volume some more and there it is, the first, unmistakeable moan.

'Shh!' Juliet commands. We all stand there, glued to the screen as the camera picks up the nameplate on Glen's door. Everyone lets out a collective half-laugh, half-gasp. Except for Roz. I sneak her a look and she's rigid, her hand resting on a pile of scripts to hold herself steady.

The picture on the screen wobbles about, and it's almost unwatchable, but the soundtrack is unambiguous. I wonder if Glen's watching. If he's calling down to the gallery to insist they stop the video, and Patricia's in there making sure no one answers the phone. Most of the crew will only just be wandering back from lunch, but there are TVs showing the feed from the studio in all the departments, in the actors' green room, in reception, in random offices all around the building.

Everyone is transfixed. Lorraine looks as if all her Christmasses have come at once. I wonder if, when she looks over at Roz, eyes wide, she picks up that something is not quite right.

'That's it, I think,' Roz says, her voice shaking slightly. 'Turn it off.'

Lorraine looks at her as if she's gone insane. 'Don't you want to know who it is?'

Roz doesn't get a chance to answer because everyone gasps again when there's a rustling and they realize that the occupants of the room might be about to walk out into view. I can hear my breathing clearly on the screen, and I wonder if there's any way any of them could work out it's me.

As the door handle rattles it feels as if the whole of our building takes a breath in, holds it. I can hardly look. The door opens. And then an orange-clad leg with a bright red sandal on the end steps out. The picture becomes more steady – I was pressing the phone up against the door frame to try to stop the shaking – and there's no mistaking who the person is exiting the room.

The real-life Roz, the one standing a few feet from me, snatches up her bag and walks out of the room without saying anything. Lorraine watches her go, opens and shuts her mouth, like a fish needing air, but then turns back to the screen when she hears Emma's 'Eww' as Glen playfully grabs Roz's behind. And then he looks out. There's no doubting it's him. The picture cuts out.

I look around the room. Juliet is smiling. Emma, Lorraine and Joe are frozen to the spot, tongues lolling.

'Well,' I say, finally able to breathe. 'That was interesting.'

And then it's as if the silence breaks and I can hear chatter and laughter from all over the building.

40

Immediately after the video finishes playing I head back down to the studio. Juliet winks at me as I leave, and I know she won't give away my secret to anyone. Glen's door is closed, and I have no way of knowing whether he is aware of what has just been broadcast round the building or not. I rush past, anxious not to bump into him. I can hear people gossiping about Glen and Roz in every room I pass.

In the studio block I head straight for Patricia's dressing room and, ignoring Chris the runner's pleas, knock on her door. She must know it's me because she opens it without complaint. She puts her finger to her lips and ushers me inside. Once the door is closed she raises her eyebrows at me as if to say 'Well?' and I fling my arms round her, give her a kiss on the cheek.

'Thank you,' I say.

'I don't know what you're talking about,' she says, but she's beaming.

'How did you . . .?'

'One of the camera boys owed me a favour,' she whispers. 'Not that it was me.'

'Of course it wasn't, but thank you anyway.'

'Accepted,' she says, digging around in her cupboard for the whisky bottle. 'Hopefully that'll stop them in their tracks. They'll know that no one in HR will believe her now.'

'Let's hope so.' I accept a finger of liquid. Clink my glass against hers. 'Fuck knows what's going to happen next.'

Glen's office door remains closed all afternoon. None of us has any idea whether he is even still in there or not. The atmosphere in the office is charged. We're all slightly giggly, slightly hysterical but also nervous. Unsure how this is going to play out. Only Lorraine looks stricken. Left out at sea without her life raft. I play innocent in front of her, Emma and Joe, but later, in the office kitchen, Juliet and I hug and jump up and down like two over-excited schoolgirls.

Once I call Dee and tell her what's happened, and she's finished shrieking, she insists that she meet me on my way home so we can go back and confront Hattie together. I have no intention of giving her notice on the room. She owes me rent, she can leave as soon as she can organize transport. She's lucky I'm not intending to take things any further.

Dee is hovering on the corner of my road as I walk up from the station.

'Any sign of her?' I say. I feel anxious. I hate confrontation.

She shakes her head. 'I've only been here two minutes though.'

'Let's get it over with.' The excitement of the day has dissipated. I've won a victory but I have no idea whether the war is over.

The first things I see when I open the front door are Hattie's keys on the mat, where she must have posted them through the letterbox.

I bend down to pick them up. 'Shit, she's gone already.'

I look in her room. There's still a mess of bits and pieces – hairgrips, an open box of cereal, a single sock – but her little fridge, her microwave, her bedcovers, her cases have disappeared. I look around the flat for a note. Nothing.

I find a bin bag under the sink in the kitchen and we start clearing up.

'You should change the locks,' Dee says. 'I read a story the other day about someone who got all their stuff nicked five years after their tenant had moved out, because they'd never changed the locks.'

'No you didn't,' I say, not unkindly.

She smiles. 'OK, so in this case I didn't. But I could have.'

'I will. I feel cheated, not being able to ask her what the hell she was doing.'

'Who says you can't?' Dee says. She puts the bin bag beside the front door, heads into the kitchen and pulls a bottle of wine from the fridge. 'But for now, let's celebrate.'

Roz doesn't show up for work the next day. The rest of us try to carry on as if nothing has happened, and I'm thankful I'm on studio duty so I can keep out of Glen's way. Juliet comes down to visit me and tells me that Lorraine is sitting looking at Roz's empty desk like a devoted dog watching the front door for hours after its mistress leaves for work. Glen, she says, seems to be trying to bluff it out, although he did pull her aside and ask her to fill him in on what people were saying.

'What did you tell him?' I sip the coffee that she brought me.

She leans back in her chair. 'I said, "What do you think they're saying? Just be thankful no one can accuse you of giving Roz any preferential treatment, because that would look really unprofessional right now."'

'You didn't!'

'I certainly did. I nearly added "Maybe you should be more worried about your wife than your job" but I thought that was getting too personal.'

'You're a legend,' I say, and I mean it.

'There's no way he's going to take her complaint to HR now. And if he does you just add the video to the rest of the evidence you have.'

I think for a second. 'Was it a one-off, do you suppose? I mean, no way is she really interested in him.'

'I imagine so. A last-ditch attempt to make sure he would be on her side.'

'Grim.'

She pulls a disgusted face. 'Doesn't bear thinking about.'

She offers to cover the last hour of the studio for me, because Dee and I have a date – lurking about in a smart Marylebone street at ten to six. We haven't really thought through what we're going to say once Hattie emerges from her practice, but it's the only way I could come up with to confront her without having to go to the Shepherd's Bush flat and risk seeing Roz. We lean against the iron railings and wait for her to leave work. I'm a bit worried she might turn round and go straight back inside, slamming the door in our faces, but it's the only option we have.

At about two minutes past six the door opens and she comes down the steps with another woman. She clocks us and it seems as if she's just going to ignore us and keep walking. Not on my watch.

'Hi, Hattie,' I say, stepping out in front of them.

'I'm in a hurry,' she says, pulling her sleeves down over her hands.

'Really?' I say, raising what I hope is an ominous eyebrow. I'm sure she won't want me to make a scene here, in front of her colleague.

She hesitates before turning to the other woman. 'I'll see you tomorrow,' she says with a smile. 'Have a good evening.'

We all stand there for a second and then she looks right at me. 'What do you think you're doing here, coming to my work? I know I owe you rent but you have my deposit.'

'You really think that's what this is about?' I say. 'Money?'

'What else?'

Dee snorts. We've agreed that I'll do the talking but I know she can't help herself. 'Why did you move out so suddenly?'

'Because I wasn't happy there.' She looks at me. 'You never told me your daughter would be staying in the flat sometimes.'

374

'Once since you've been there. And if that was all it was, wouldn't you just have raised it with me?' I say.

'We know everything,' Dee says. 'About Roz, about the emails . . .'

Hattie turns white. 'I don't know what you're on about. Who's Roz?'

'Drop the stupid act.' I'm angry now. All I want is for her to tell me the truth. 'There's a webcam in my living room . . .'

'What? You can't film people without their permission,' she snaps. She sounds panicked.

'I'm pretty sure you'll find I can if they're somewhere they're not meant to be. You're lucky I haven't been to the police. I still might.' I'm guessing the police would be less than interested if I did; I mean, what's the crime? But I'm banking on her being too scared to think it through.

She puts a hand out to steady herself on the railings. 'It was just a few emails.'

'How did you even end up living in my flat in the first place?'

She sighs. 'Roz asked me to do it as a favour. I really did have to move out of my place because my landlady was selling so she said maybe I should live at yours for a bit, while I looked for somewhere else, you know . . .'

'And she told you exactly what to say at the interview so there was a pretty good chance Holly would pick you?' Dee says.

Hattie sits down on the steps of the building next door to the dental practice. She looks as if she's given up. 'Yes.'

'Why, though?' I say.

'I don't know. It felt like a bit of a laugh and she was having such a shit time . . .'

'And she wanted my job?'

Hattie nods. She runs her hand through her short hair. 'You don't understand. Work is all she's got.'

I think about all the lies Roz has told me, about her fabulous adventures. I have no idea what her life actually is.

'Why is it so bad?' I sit down on the step next to her. Dee towers over the two of us.

Hattie looks at me as if she's unsure what to say, but then I think she decides she has nothing to lose. 'I don't have a sick mum, but I guess you've worked that out already . . .'

I nod. 'You just said that so I'd like the fact I'd have the flat to myself at weekends if you moved in.'

'Yes. But the reason we thought of it is because Roz does . . .'

I look at Dee. I don't know whether to believe this or not, but I can't see what Hattie would have to gain from lying at this point. 'Since when?'

'She's been ill for years, but it's got worse recently. She needs to go into full-time care really, but she just refuses to. It's not fair on Roz, I don't think.'

I'm so confused. 'I had no idea. So she's the one who has to go down to stay with her in Eastbourne at weekends?'

Hattie looks at the ground as if she's deciding how much detail she should tell us. 'Um . . . no. Her mum lives with her. In the flat.'

'In Shepherd's Bush?' I think about the scruffy building,

the curtains coming away from the rails. 'No way. Her parents are well off. They must be. She went to that posh school.'

'She did. And then her dad died when she was at uni and it turned out he owed loads of money and he hadn't made any provision . . . and then her mum got sick. She couldn't afford to pay for carers full time so Roz insisted she moved in with her. That was about six years ago, and she's still there. You know when the two of you go to the pub after work? That's about the extent of her social life. Do you know how hard it is to hang on to your friends when you have to say no to everything all the time?'

'I don't understand . . .' I say. Understatement of the year. Even though I knew Roz's anecdotes were all fabrications I assumed she had friends. A life. She's funny, smart, gorgeous. How could she not? 'She has you, you're her friend . . .'

Hattie looks at me. Shrugs. 'I'm her cousin.'

I stare at her elfin face. I can see it, a vague likeness around the eyes. Not enough that I could ever have guessed, but it's there.

'Why would she never have told anyone what was going on?' Dee says impatiently. 'It makes no sense.'

'She didn't talk about it to anyone except me really. I remember her telling me she'd never told anyone at work because she didn't want you feeling sorry for her. She didn't want to be "the one who cares for her sick mum". She just wanted to get on with her job and be able to forget about what was happening at home.'

I put my head in my hands. I'd been intending to tell Hattie about Roz's fake life, to expose her as a pathetic liar. Fantasist even. But the wind has been taken out of my sails.

'Think about it,' Hattie says, looking at me. 'You've got a lovely flat, a daughter, you can do whatever you want, whenever you want. And now you have the job . . .'

'And she thought that wasn't fair?' I think I'm beginning to understand.

Hattie shrugs. 'I don't think it was as calculated as that. I think she just wanted one area of her life that was a success. Something that was hers —'

Dee interrupts. 'It still doesn't excuse anything she's done. Anything either of you have done.'

'I know. You don't have to tell me that,' Hattie says, looking at the ground. 'I'm sorry. I really am. I actually loved living at your place, Holly. I didn't mean it about moving out because of Ashley . . .'

Dee waves an arm at me. 'You nearly lost her her job.'

'It's OK, Dee,' I say. Because it is. It might not have been, but it is.

'Why did you move out so quickly if you didn't know we were on to you?' Dee says, determined to leave no detail unchecked.

Hattie looks up at her. 'Roz sent me a text saying something had happened at work and I should just get out, because it had all gone to shit. I would have been gone at the end of this week otherwise, anyway.'

I swallow. 'Once my probation was up. Once my job had been taken away from me.'

'Yes,' she says in a voice so small I can hardly hear her.

We leave her sitting there. There's nothing else to be said.

'Roz is like some kind of weird guru,' Dee says as we walk off. 'It's like she can hypnotize people into doing whatever she wants.'

'I can't take it in,' I say. 'How could I not have known she was dealing with all that?'

I'm reeling from what Hattie told me. I think of Roz the peacock, all dressed up with nowhere to go. Spending her evenings and weekends looking after her mother. Watching life go on without her. It makes me feel like crying.

41

Roz doesn't come back to work the following day. Or the day after. No one wants to call her to find out what's going on, including Lorraine who flops around as if she's had the stuffing knocked out of her. She does go through Roz's list of episodes though, completely unbidden, and makes a list of what's due to be done and by when. I tell her I'm grateful and I mean it. The department meeting is scheduled for Wednesday. It's in Glen's diary, but he doesn't show up. I carry on as if everything is normal, and everyone plays along. No one brings up what's happened. It's as if we've all signed a confidentiality agreement.

The atmosphere is still charged though. Glen hardly leaves his office so it feels as if we're on a rudderless ship but cruise control takes over and everything gets done somehow. And then on Thursday two things happen. I get an email from HR telling me that Roz Huntingdon has handed in her notice and opted to take unpaid leave for the duration. She will not be coming back. As relieved as I am I can't help feeling a pang of worry about how she'll make ends meet.

And Glen calls me into his office.

I actually feel sick as I walk along the corridor. There's

no way he can know that it was me who filmed him and Roz together but I'm worried my face will give it away. I knock on his door.

'Come in.'

Glen is sitting behind his desk looking not quite as well groomed as usual.

'Take a seat.' He gives me a slightly desperate smile. I imagine he thinks we're all laughing at him behind his back – and I'm sure some people are – but all most of us want is for everything to go back to normal.

I sit, nervously.

'So, good news,' he says, cutting straight to the chase. My anxiety lifts a little. I swallow and it makes a noise like a frog, my mouth is so dry. 'I've been talking to HR and I can confirm that your position is being made permanent.'

Despite everything, a huge grin spreads over my face. I've done it. 'Thank you.'

Glen smiles back and this time it seems genuine. 'Congratulations. You deserve it.'

I want to ask if he now knows I was innocent of all Roz's charges. I don't want to think there's a doubt hanging over me. But somehow I think he does.

Back in the script department I give them the good news, and I also let them know that Roz won't be returning.

'It's her own decision,' I say.

Juliet, Joe and Emma all suddenly look visibly younger.

As if a heavy weight has been lifted. Ding dong, the witch is dead. They cheer and grab me in a group hug, and I feel a bit overwhelmed. Only Lorraine looks lost. I reach out an arm and pull her into the group.

'It'll be OK,' I whisper in her ear.

42

Six weeks later

I hear a pop and then a cheer. We're toasting again. There's Prosecco being passed around and Glen is about to make a speech.

I look around my department. Juliet is blushing red, uncomfortable with all the attention. Joe holds his glass high, Emma clinks glasses with her fizzy water and even Lorraine – back now to her old way of dressing, no more clashing colours, no more red glasses and pink lipstick – joins in with the congratulations. I wonder, as I've done a few times lately, how well I really know these people. I spend all day with them – our department is a happy place now – but do I actually know who they really are?

So much has changed, I hardly know where to start. Once Roz announced she wasn't coming back we had two vacant script editor positions to fill – mine and hers. I decided to give Lorraine a chance. Without Roz around she had been forced to mix more with the rest of us, to lose the cynical sneer she'd hidden behind, and she's actually turned out to be a hard worker, an asset. She has the talent. I think she'll do well.

We all leaned on Emma to interview for the other

slot, and she found out last week that she's got it. She's a different person – although I still have to keep stopping her from offering to make everyone tea all the time – a confident, more comfortable version of her old sweet self. She has a presence that she didn't have before. She and Lorraine are becoming good friends – who'd have thought it? – and helping each other navigate their new responsibilities.

But the reason for our celebrations today is a much bigger deal. Glen has decided to move on. Whether it was entirely his decision or he was helped out of the door I'm not sure. He doesn't seem to have anything else lined up; he says he needs some time off, a chance to regroup.

'I think we might go travelling for a while,' he said when he told me. The announcement had not yet been made, and he asked me to keep the news to myself. I was desperate to ask him whether he'd kept in touch with Roz, but I knew it was none of my business.

In the end he told me without me having to ask.

'I owe you an apology,' he said. We were sitting in his office at the end of the day. 'I should have taken your comments about Roz more seriously.'

I didn't know what to say. I was happy he'd reached this conclusion but there was no doubt he'd let me down. 'It's all in the past now,' was all I could come up with.

He cleared his throat. 'I . . . um . . . it only happened the once . . .'

'You don't need to tell me . . .' I said, feeling uncomfortable. I didn't know where to look so I studied a stain on the coffee table. I was curious to know but I really didn't want the details.

He wasn't finished though. 'I realized straight away that she was just trying to make sure I'd be on her side. I should never have . . . I'm ashamed of myself for being such a cliché fool, if you really want to know. Anyway, I want to spend some time with my family. Put it all behind me.'

'Good for you,' I said. I meant it. He wasn't a bad man. I couldn't imagine he'd ever get himself in that position again. He was just swept away by the force of her spotlight. As was Lorraine. As was I.

That afternoon I got an email from Karen in HR. Top Secret. Fay had been appointed as Glen's successor. Which meant there would be a producer position becoming vacant and she would strongly suggest I applied for it if I was interested.

I wrote back to say that I was very flattered to be considered but that I wanted to give my current position a fair crack. I wanted to enjoy it and to try to do the best job I could. I'd barely had the chance to think straight since I'd been promoted. There would be another opportunity in the future.

I asked her if Juliet knew. If maybe she should mention it to her. She'd be fabulous, I said. She had years more TV experience than me, and the cast loved her.

So, to cut a long story short, that's what we're celebrating today. Juliet's promotion. She beat off all the external candidates easily, according to Glen. I'm thrilled for her. She's become my friend, my ally. I owe her a lot.

And now there will be a whole other round of interviews – to replace her, to find a new trainee, a new assistant. The department is in chaos but it's thriving. Everyone is pitching in. It's like the spirit of the Blitz with less bombing. And it's just what the show needs. I'm excited about the future.

43

Dee is waiting for me on a bench at the top of Parliament Hill. At her feet is a – well, I don't know what he is – part lurcher, part hyena, part warthog by the looks of him. This is Rufus. Dee and Gavin's new addition, rescued from the streets of Romania. Baby substitute? Yes. Heartbreakingly adorable canine? Definitely.

He wags his tail half-heartedly a couple of times when he sees me. He's still nervous with people he doesn't know so well, still wary. But he has fallen for Dee and Gavin like they're the saviours he's been waiting for all his life. Which I suppose they are. When they go to work, the neighbours tell them, he howls like a dysfunctional wolf. She's worried they might have to move. Or give up work to stay home with him and starve to death.

I reach down and gently pat his head. He flattens his ears and goes rigid.

Dee stands up and gives me a hug.

'How's he doing?'

'Getting there,' she says, looking down at him proudly. 'It's going to take a while.'

We sit looking out over London, Rufus at our feet. He sighs contentedly.

'Ashley's moving home,' I say.

Dee's head whips round to face me. 'Oh my God, that's fantastic. It is, isn't it?'

I nod, unable to keep the smile from my face. 'It is.'

I told Ashley the whole story of everything that had gone on at work as soon as I heard my job was secure. It felt wrong to keep it from her. She was about to have a baby and I needed to start thinking of her as an adult.

'Shit, Mum, why didn't you tell me?'

'I didn't want to worry you,' I said. I was in my kitchen, blissfully enjoying knowing the flat was my own again. I knew I was going to have to put another advert in though. I needed a lodger or I couldn't help Ashley pay her way.

'Well, that's just stupid,' she said indignantly. 'All I do is worry you. The least you could do is reciprocate.'

I laughed. 'It's all sorted itself out now anyway.'

'You should be proud of yourself,' she said. 'I know that goes against every facet of your personality.'

'Do you know what, I am. I've decided to become an insufferable show-off.'

'Go for it.'

There was a silence for a second.

'Mum,' she said in that way that always makes me instantly anxious.

'Yes?'

'I've been thinking. It's crazy for you to have to rent out a room just to help me pay the rent. I mean, you have an empty room. I can't afford to pay to live anywhere any more . . .'

I actually felt my heart skip a beat. 'What are you saying?'

'Can I move back? I mean, it's nice at Brooke's and she's pretty cool about the idea of having a baby about the place, but, I don't know, it seems a bit mad . . .'

I want to say 'Yes. Of course. Come now' but I need to know she's asking for the right reasons.

'What about all your friends? And your job?'

'I'm due to finish work in a few weeks anyway. And it's not like they're going to hold my position open for me. I'm a part-time barmaid. And most of my friends have moved away. There's only Brooke really. Plus I still have friends in London, you know.'

'And what about Ryan?'

She huffed. 'What about him? Do you know I haven't even heard from him? And if he ever decides he wants to see the baby it wouldn't be as if we were on the other side of the world.'

'I don't want you doing this because you're worried about me,' I said. 'I'm fine. I can cope with another lodger. I just need to make sure I find one who isn't friends with anyone I work with.'

There was a silence for a second.

'I need you, Mum. I don't want to do this on my own.'

I blinked back tears. 'Then yes, of course you can.'

'I can babysit,' Dee says now. 'I can be Auntie Dee and spoil her rotten.'

'Be careful what you wish for. Is he good with kids, do you know?' I nod down at a now sleeping Rufus.

'I have no idea.'

As if on cue a couple with a toddler walk past. The toddler coos at the dog. Dee and I sit coiled for action, ready to spring if she gets too close. Dee holds tight to Rufus's lead.

'We're not sure how he is with kids,' she says to the parents, who are following their daughter over to say hello. 'We only just got him.'

The mother smiles and goes to take the little girl's hand to lead her away, just as Rufus opens his eyes and sees her there. He leaps up, tail swinging backwards and forwards like a rudder. He practically bounces on the spot he's so happy.

'He seems OK,' the mother says. The dad goes to scruffle his head and he cowers a bit but then he walks over to the little girl and puts his head on her shoulder. She laughs and pats his ears. His tail is practically a blur.

'Well, look at that,' Dee says. 'He's a natural.'

44

Ashley arrives with a huge bump and a car full of all her worldy goods. We unload it slowly, stopping between each trip for a sit down or a cup of tea on the patio. It's ninety degrees out and has been for what seems like weeks. The country is in party mode. For once you can plan an event outside and know that the weather will be fine. The whole capital smells of barbeque.

'Have you heard from Ryan yet?' I say, pouring what's left of my tea into a pot of geraniums out the back. I'm trying to conserve water like a good citizen.

She shakes her head. 'His mum called me though, so I gave her your address. They'll probably come and meet the baby when she's born, even if he doesn't.'

'And how do you feel about that?' I move the umbrella to give her more shade.

'Them coming?'

'Him not coming.'

'Oh.' She thinks about it for a second. 'All right actually. I did OK without a dad, didn't I?'

I want to say 'If he does decide he wants to have a relationship with the baby, don't stand in his way though', but I don't want to lecture her the minute she's arrived. She'll work it out.

She looks at the table. 'Do you think . . . Should I try and find him, tell him he's going to be a granddad?'

'Lol?' Should she? It's not as if he's been beating a path to her door to try to be a father. 'Only you can decide that, sweetheart. I'll help you if you like, but you have to be prepared that you might not get the outcome you want . . .'

'He could have found me easily enough, couldn't he? I mean, you still have the same surname . . .'

'Yes.' I don't want to influence her either way, but I owe it to her to be honest.

'So I guess he decided not to.'

I squeeze her hand. 'You can always change your mind.'

'Maybe,' she says. 'One day.'

I leave her pottering around in her old room. We still have half a carful to unload but both of us need a break. I could do with a lie-down, to be honest. But I have something I need to do.

I open up my work email on my phone. I noticed this morning that I had a new message, and I have to decide what to do about it. It's from the producer of a long-running hospital show that films up in Manchester. It's been on for years – longer than us – one hour a week for about ten weeks of the year. It's a bit of an old dinosaur to be honest, but it still pulls in an audience.

I read it through again.

Hi Holly,

Apologies for contacting you out of the blue. We're in the process of hiring a new script editor, and I interviewed Roz Huntingdon this week, and really liked her. But she hasn't put anyone from *Churchill Road* down as a reference, which seems a bit odd given she's been there for the last five years, so I just wanted to check if she's someone you would recommend.

I'm around all weekend. My mobile's at the bottom of this email if you have the chance to call me. We're hoping to make a decision on Monday, because we're up against it. You know how it is!

Thanks so much in advance,
Kerry

I have no idea what to do. I could ignore it altogether, but that would look bad. Who knows where Kerry might end up one of these days? A head of drama. A controller. I might find myself applying to her for a job somewhere and she'll think 'that's that cow who ignored my email'.

I could tell the truth. But that would, without a doubt, result in Roz not getting the job. And then what? She'd apply for something else, somewhere else, and I'd be asked to give a reference there too. I could pretty much make sure she never works in this industry again. But would I sleep at night knowing she was struggling, knowing how much she loves what she does, knowing work is her respite?

Or I could lie. Praise her to the hilt and hope it never comes back to bite me. But what if she hasn't learned her lesson? What if she makes someone else's life a misery?

Even as I dial Kerry's number I have no idea what I'm going to say. She answers on the second ring.

'Kerry Walker.'

'Hi, Kerry. It's Holly Cooper.'

'Holly! Thanks for calling me back. How's your weekend?'

'Good, thanks,' I say, not keen to get sidetracked into a social conversation with someone I don't even know.

'So, Roz Huntingdon. It's our current editor's last week this week, and you know what it's like, you need someone like yesterday . . .'

'How many do you have?'

'Editors? Just the one and a junior. It's his first job, and he only joined us this series so, even though he's great, he's not ready to take over the whole shebang . . .'

I think for a second. Maybe if Roz were the only editor she might not feel the need to compete, or at least she'd have no one to compete with. And she would need an ally, and one who wasn't a threat, so she might take the junior under her wing.

Kerry is still talking. 'I thought it was a bit odd that she didn't put down any references from *Churchill Road*, that's all. Is there something I should know?'

I can't be completely untruthful. It wouldn't be fair. And this industry is incestuous, so anyone from *Churchill Road* might know someone from *Stratford General* and spread the gossip. But I honestly think this might be a good fit for Roz.

'No. I mean, she left very suddenly – for personal reasons, entirely her choice, but she got herself in a mess with someone on the show and I think she thought it would be better to make the break . . .'

'By "mess" you mean . . .?'

I hesitate. 'I don't think it's my place to give the details. It was nothing bad, just messy and a bit unfortunate. Nothing to do with her work. Her work is great.'

'And she's a nice person?'

What can I say? 'We didn't really get on the last few months, I have to be honest. But the writers rated her. And so did lots of other people.'

'She wasn't happy you got promoted over her?' Like I said, news travels fast in this industry.

'Something like that. But she'll do a good job.'

'So, if you were me, and I promise I won't hold you to this, would you take her on?'

'I think I would. Sometimes you just have to take what she says to you with a pinch of salt, that's all. Just . . . generally . . .'

'Forewarned is forearmed,' Kerry says. 'I really appreciate your honesty. I think I'm going to go for it. There's no one else around so . . .'

I'm glad. That Roz has a new job. That I haven't had to completely perjure myself. That she'll be moving away to Manchester. I wonder briefly what that means for her mum. I assume she'll move with her. Maybe Roz'll be able to afford a bigger place. Maybe carers will be less expensive. Maybe it'll make life easier.

Either way I'm happy I don't have to think about her any more. I realize I've been holding on to a residual worry about what would happen to her, how she would cope. I hate what she became but there's no getting away from the fact that for the best part of three years she was my friend.

Now she's just somebody that I used to know.

45

Today's candle is something figgy apparently, although it's hard to tell. We're sitting in the living room with the windows wide open, partly because the summer heat is unbearable otherwise, but also because Rufus ate some broccoli earlier and the results are toxic. He's been with Dee and Gavin over a month now, and he's started to relax around me a little, but he's still got his defences up, and he's jammed between my two old friends on the sofa that was barely big enough for the two of them in the first place.

The pair of them are beaming, proud dog parents. I've noticed how affectionate they've been with each other recently, how playful. It's as if the whole Roz thing reminded them of who they were – who they used to be before disappointment got in the way. It makes me so happy to see them like this. It almost makes the whole thing worth it.

A couple of weeks ago I decided to have a dinner for the people who had supported me when I needed it. A thank you. Alongside those two were Juliet and Jake, Emma, and Patricia and her partner Howard, a tiny delicate-looking man. Dee whispered to me in the kitchen that Patricia and Howard looked as if they'd been made from the material needed to make two people, but Patricia had got first dibs, and then every time I looked at them together I started to laugh.

It was a random collection of people. We ate on our laps because my table isn't big enough, and we all drank too much except Jake who, I'm sure, wished he could, and we laughed about God knows what till three in the morning. Patricia told us scurrilous stories about the rest of the cast, and Howard tried to stop her but then he started telling us even worse things that she'd told him over the years. We all made a pact never to divulge them to the rest of the world. It was honestly one of the best nights I've ever had.

The most bizarre outcome was that Dee and Juliet hit it off incredibly well. I have no idea why. Somehow they found a wealth of stuff they have in common – mostly a sense of justice and straight talking, I think.

'Tell us a story about something that happened this week,' Juliet had said. I'd told her about Dee's job at the hospital. She's looked like a different person since she got promoted. Still rocking the mum jeans but confident, glowing. Maybe it's her new responsibility or maybe it's just that she can feel free to be herself at work now, without worrying that someone is looking for reasons to take the piss.

'Oh,' Dee said, 'let me think. Oh yes, someone came into A and E with a fork stuck in their eardrum . . .'

'It didn't happen,' I said, turning to Juliet. 'I mean, think about it, it would have to be a stupidly narrow fork or one with one long prong to fit.'

'You can get really skinny ones,' Juliet said. 'Those things they use for getting cockles out of their shells.'

'Oh my God, you're as bad as she is.'

Dee told me the next day that I was an idiot for never having given her a chance, and I agreed.

Tonight the three of us are toasting the fact that Gavin has a new job – we always seem to be toasting something at the moment. Isn't that how life should be? Always looking for any small success, both yours and your friends', to celebrate? He's grown increasingly fed up with selling pharmaceuticals, bored of having to spend so much time away from home. He wants a challenge but he also wants to be able to spend more time with his wife. After a lot of soul-searching he hit on what he wanted to do. Before selling, before he got in a rut of good wages and better prospects, he had trained as a teacher. I'm talking years ago. Twenty probably. And now he has a job starting in September. OK, so it's in a failing school where none of the teachers seem to stay more than a year and so they were happy to take on someone with the training but no experience at all. OK, so he's shit scared and the pay is terrible and he can't remember anything he ever learned. But still he can't wait to be Mr Sanders, Chemistry teacher: years seven to nine.

'You've both got new jobs,' Dee says at one point. 'Everyone's got a new job except for me.'

'Do you even want a new job?' I say.

'God, no. I love it where I am.'

'What are you on about then?' I turn to Gavin. 'What's the chemical symbol for antimony?'

He looks startled. It's my favourite new game to ask him questions like this out of nowhere to test him on his forgotten chemistry knowledge. I have no idea of any of the answers myself, by the way, but I like to watch him sweat.

'Um . . . S something. Shit. Dee, google it.'

She fiddles around with her phone. 'Sb. So you were half right.'

'Half right's no good. Oh God, they're all going to know more than me.'

'Juliet told you Jake'd be happy to give you some coaching,' I say. 'She says he could do with the money and he's very discreet.'

Gavin puts his head in his hands. 'Oh my God, what have I done?' he says, but he's laughing.

'So,' Dee says when we're all half-cut, having finished our takeaway and two bottles of wine. She reaches a hand across the dog to set it on top of Gavin's. 'We have more news.'

I know it can't be anything bad but I'm suddenly nervous. There's been far too much change lately for my liking.

Gavin gives her a 'go ahead' smile and Dee takes a deep breath. 'We've made a decision. Actually we've done more than that, we've had an interview and everything.'

She looks at me triumphantly as if I'm supposed to know what she's on about.

'What? Tell me.'

'It might come to nothing. Or we might end up getting rejected or being too old by the time it all gets processed . . .'

'Fucking hell, Dee. Just tell me what you're on about.'

Gavin gives Dee's hand a squeeze. Smiles at her with a smile so loving it almost breaks my heart.

'We're going to try for adoption,' she says. 'The woman we saw said she was sure we'd be suitable but, you never know. Oh God, are you OK?'

Gavin whips his head round to me. Tears are pouring down my face. They've just appeared out of nowhere. Nought to sixty. 'Yes. I'm just . . . I'm so happy for you,' I wail.

'It really might not ever come to anything,' Gavin says gently. 'I mean, there are so many hurdles you have to get through.'

'I'm just so happy you're trying, that you both want to try,' I sob. 'Whatever the outcome.'

'We're being philosophical about it,' Dee says, and then I worry that she feels she has to reassure me, as though, if it doesn't work out, I'm the one who's going to fall apart. 'We know it's probably a long shot.'

'That's good.' Suddenly I'm worried that Dee will have to deal with another crushing disappointment.

'Hopefully it'll happen,' Gavin says. 'But if it doesn't we'll be OK. Really we will. We have Rufus.'

'He'd love it!' I say. 'He loves kids, remember, Dee.'

She strokes his beard and he looks at her with his soppy brown eyes. 'He does.'

'Oh my God,' I say with a sudden realization. 'If you adopt then you'll be a mum but I'll be a granny.'

Ashley is meeting up with Clare's son Charlie this evening, rekindling their friendship. I'd be lying if I wasn't harbouring a tiny hope that they might end up more than just friends. That he might have a hankering to help bring up a baby regardless of who the father is. I'd phoned Clare when I heard and we'd spent half an hour planning what to wear to the wedding again, just like we did when they were fifteen.

'That's the only reason I want to do it.' Dee laughs. 'So I can rub that in your face.'

'I love you,' I say, realizing I'm drunker than I thought. 'Both of you. I don't know what I'd have done without you these past few months.'

'Oh God,' Dee says. 'She's going to make a speech. Quick, fill my glass up.'

Gavin leans over to pour us all another drink. I put my hand over my glass, to say I don't want one.

'I'm not. That's it. That's all I've got to say.' I look at my phone. 'Shit, it's late, I should make a move before I pass out in your living room.'

'Feel free,' Dee says. 'You might have to share the sofa with Rufus though.'

'I've had worse,' I say, but I pick up my mobile to ring a cab.

Back home Ashley is sitting up in the kitchen eating ice cream from the tub. Smokey sits on the table gazing at both her and the ice cream adoringly.

'What time do you call this?' she says, getting up and giving me a hug. Or trying to. It's like being attacked by a space hopper. Her arms only just reach ahead of her bump.

'Did you have fun?' I say, flopping down at the table. I pick up the spoon she's discarded and dig in.

'It was nice,' she says. 'All that catching up. It's weird that he's been here all the time I've been away so he knows all the gossip on everyone. I'm going to meet up with a few of them next week.'

'It's nice you still have friends here.'

She shrugs. 'We'll see. People go a bit funny when you're pregnant. Like they just assume you won't be fun any more so why bother?'

'Well, fuck 'em then.'

'Mum,' she says, eyes wide, as if she's never heard the word before. Which she hasn't coming out of my mouth, I suppose.

'What?' I say, laughing. 'You're a fellow mum-to-be. I have to treat you like an adult.'

She takes back the spoon. Scrapes it round the tub. 'In that case shall we talk openly and frankly about our sex lives?'

'Jesus, no. Besides, I don't have one.'

'You should. I might make you go on Tinder.'

'OK. You win. I'm the adult, you're still my little girl and let's never speak of this again.'

She reaches her hand across the table. 'I'm glad I'm here, Mum.'

'Me too.'

'You are OK about the baby living here, aren't you? I'm not expecting you to have to look after her for me or anything.'

'I can't wait,' I say. And I mean it. Even though I can't imagine trying to juggle the broken nights with work. I'll manage somehow.

She stands up, stretches. 'I'm going to bed.' She leans down and gives me a hug, and this time the bump hits me in the face.

'You need a licence for that. It's out of control.'

Ashley straightens up and clutches her stomach. 'She's kicking.'

She takes my hand and puts it on her tummy. I wait, and there it is, the tiniest of movements. I gasp.

'Did you feel it?'

'Yes! Oh my goodness. Hello, little thing.'

'Thing meet Granny.'

'Oh God,' I say, 'maybe I'm not ready for this after all.'

She pats me on the head. 'See you in the morning.'

I sit there and watch her go off towards her room, Smokey following closely behind.

''Night.'

She lifts one hand and waves. I turn on the kettle to make myself a camomile tea, sit back down to wait for it to boil.

My phone beeps. It's late to get a text so I assume it's Dee. Checking I got home OK. I pick it up, see the name Roz and my heart starts thumping. I force myself to open the message.

I got the job. Thank you.

I hesitate for a moment, unsure what to do. I have no desire to get into a conversation with her. Ever again.

I feel good, I realize. Content with my life exactly as it is. I have a job I love, the best friends I could ever want, my daughter is healthy and doing well, and I'm about to be a grandmother. I think about Roz. Wonder if she can ever feel like this. If anything will ever live up to the fantasy world she created for herself. If she can ever be truly happy.

Despite everything I hope she can.

I send her a text back. *I'm glad.* And then I turn off my phone.

Acknowledgements

Huge thanks to my tireless and amazing editor, Maxine Hitchcock, for all of her help with this book. Also to Louise Moore and everyone else at Michael Joseph (this means you Claire Bush, Gaby Young, Jenny Platt, Matilda McDonald, as well as countless others), Jonny Gellar and all at Curtis Brown, and Charlotte Edwards for her research.

Also by
Jane Fallon . . .

'Brilliant, original, edgy and compulsively readable' *Daily Mail*

🐦 JaneFallon

🄵 JaneFallonOfficial

Also by

Jane Fallon . . .

'A deliciously devious plot'
Daily Express

Also by
Jane Fallon . . .

'A deliciously edgy read full of
double-dealings and divided loyalties'
Good Housekeeping

🐦 JaneFallon

📘 JaneFallonOfficial